TRAVELING EUROPE WITH SAMANTHA BROWN

TLC 互動英語

珊曼莎教你 用英語

暢遊歐洲

珊曼莎教你 用英語暢遊歐洲

發 行 人　鄭俊琪

總 編 輯　王琳詔

責任編輯　邱姵嘉

中文編輯　廖慧雯

英文編輯　Jeff Curran

英文錄音　Mike Tennant、Mandy Roveda、Stephanie Buckley、Joseph Schier

封面設計　蕭暉璋

美術編輯　蕭暉璋、鄭恩如

技術總監　李志純

程式設計　李志純、郭曉琪

光碟製作　簡貝瑜

介面設計　陳淑珍

點讀製作　李明爵、高荔龍

影片處理　黃文英

出版發行　希伯崙股份有限公司

　　　　　105 台北市松山區八德路三段 32 號 12 樓

　　　　　劃撥：1939-5400

　　　　　電話：(02)2578-7838

　　　　　傳真：(02)2578-5800

　　　　　電子郵件：service@liveabc.com

法律顧問　朋博法律事務所

印　　刷　禹利電子分色有限公司

出版日期　102 年 12 月　初版一刷

國家圖書館出版品預行編目資料

TLC 互動英語：珊曼莎教你用英語暢遊歐洲
王琳詔總編輯．
——初版．——臺北市：希伯崙公司，民 102.12
面；　公分
ISBN 978-986-5776-23-7（平裝附光碟片）

1. 英語 2. 旅遊 3. 會話
805.188　　　　　　　　　　102023822

TRAVELING EUROPE WITH SAMANTHA BROWN

TLC 互動英語
珊曼莎教你 用英語
暢遊歐洲

英語數位學習第一品牌

UNIT 1
英國 牛津 & 史特拉福

DENMARK
Copenhagen

UNIT 2
丹麥 哥本哈根

UNIT 4
瑞士 日內瓦

UNIT 3
法國 里昂

UNIT 5
義大利 威尼斯

UNITED

IRELAND

KINGDOM
Leeds
Liverpool
Birmingham
Stratford
Oxford
London ★

NETH

BEL.

GERMANY

CZECH

Lille

LUX.
Strasbourg

★ Paris

Nantes

LIECH.

AUS

Zurich
Bern
Geneva
SWITZ.

FRANCE

Lyon

Milan
Venice

Bordeaux

Turin

Genoa

SAN
MARINO

CRO

Florence

Toulouse

Andorra
la Vella

ANDORRA

ITALY

★ Rome

UGAL

SPAIN

BALEARIC
ISLANDS

UNIT 6
希臘 聖托里尼

CONTENTS

UNIT 1 英國 牛津 & 史特拉福
OXFORD&STRATFORD, ENGLAND

UNIT 2 丹麥 哥本哈根
COPENHAGEN, DENMARK

UNIT 3 法國 里昂
LYON, FRANCE

跟著珊曼莎
一起暢遊歐洲

　　古人說：「讀萬卷書不如行萬里路」，觀光旅遊成為增廣見聞的最佳途徑。隨著網際網路的發達，旅遊資訊更是隨手可得，只要事前做點功課，就可以背起行囊，說走就走。旅遊能夠打破國界的藩籬及狹窄的視野，讓你做個有世界觀的人。到歐洲旅遊一直以來是許多人（也是小編和小編隔壁的小編）心目中的聖地，您也許礙於時間或預算考量（小編謎之音：或老闆不給假）而無法前往朝聖？這裡有個好方法，藉由本書可以幫助我們一邊體驗歐洲各國的浪漫風情及歷史文化、增廣見聞，又可一邊學英文。

　　這次與TLC旅遊生活頻道合作的節目是《暢遊歐洲第二季》（Passport to Europe with Samantha Brown Season 2），此節目曾獲艾美獎（Emmy Award）「最佳生活導演獎」（Outstanding Lifestyle Directing），主持人珊曼莎・布朗（Samantha Brown）主持風格自然、詼諧有趣，在節目中帶領觀眾遊覽歐洲各大城市和小鎮，與當地居民互動，探訪熱門地標、美食、介紹當地歷史由來，以及挖掘隱藏版美食及當地的黃金景點，是愛旅遊的您一定不能錯過的旅遊知性節目。

　　歐洲國家不管是白天或夜晚，都充滿了絢爛的魅力。本書編輯群特地挑選出六個國家共六個單元，每個單元再依主題細分成三至五課，您可以利用這本書跟著珊曼莎一起暢遊英國、丹麥、法國、瑞士、義大利、希臘，無論您是

否造訪過這些國家，您都可以利用本書好好品味歐洲，並且學習實用的旅遊生活對話。

　　我們將節目原汁原味呈現在文字書本上，在每一課當中，除了珊曼莎精彩的旅遊介紹及對話之外，還挑選出文中的單字、片語、慣用語、文法句型等，提供相關用法說明和例句，即該課的「學習重點」和「單字」。另外，每一課也針對珊曼莎提到的景點、人文歷史、美食等，提供詳細的「背景知識」介紹，從背景知識中，更能夠幫助您快速融入珊曼莎的節目、了解歐洲的各國民俗風情。「旅遊小幫手」則是編輯群們幫您整理出珊曼莎在該課當中去過的景點資訊，還有編輯群推薦的旅遊景點資訊，方便您迅速查詢該景點的資訊，因此本書還可當作旅遊手冊喔！

　　由於本書作為英語學習書，我們特地將影片中口誤的用字作修正，而此課文朗讀則是以無贅字、正確的英文說法錄製，讓您在學習的同時，也能說出一口流利正確的英文。

[例如：They were making caves because they were ~~more safe~~ [safer], because pumice is a kind of very flexible cement.]

　　除了利用書中的重點內容來學習之外，您可利用書上的互動光碟來搭配學習。使用互動光碟觀看本節目影片，這裡沒有廣告，您可以反覆收看，快轉或倒退，隨心所欲的想要看哪個國家，就看哪個國家，若是覺得對話速度太快，也可以選擇朗讀，聽聽老師怎麼唸。另外，本書支援發音點讀筆，您亦可利用點讀筆反覆聆聽以熟悉老外口音，練習聽讀輕鬆又方便。

　　把每一頁都當作一個藝術品來經營，這是所有編輯群們對此本書的用心。與其說這是一本英語學習書，不如說是一本帶您完成夢想的旅遊工具書。期待您，讀完這本書後就像是走遍六個國家一樣，學習滿載而歸！

扉頁

本書是由 TLC 旅遊生活頻道《暢遊歐洲第二季》的節目中精選出六個國家集結而成。本書依照六個國家分成六個單元,每一個單元再依照旅遊主題分小章節。讀者可從「精彩內容預告」初步掌握節目的內容。

一分鐘速寫

精彩內容預告

國家簡介

單元名稱與主題

影片原音 & 課文朗讀

內文上方均有影片原音與課文朗讀的 MP3 軌數,讀者可以依據喜好聆聽節目影片原音,也可聆聽由專業美籍老師朗讀的聲音。

學習重點

將節目內容中的口語用法、片語或是特殊俚語,在這裡向讀者解釋該如何使用。課文中也有一些重要的文法觀念,也會特別提出來讓讀者了解這些句型結構。

單字學習

課文中的關鍵字會以粗體標註,並有編號,編排在右頁或課文下方,方便立即學習。

內文

本書內容完全根據節目影片,依照主持人的自述和與友人的對話編輯而成,基本上左頁是原文內容及中文翻譯,右頁是單字、學習重點或背景知識。

自述

主要是珊曼莎在介紹各個景點的內容,以段落方式來呈現。

對話

課文上方會先列出此為珊曼莎與友人受訪對象的談話。並以每個人名字的第一個字母代替。例如,珊曼莎 Samantha Brown, Hostess 就是以 S 來表示。

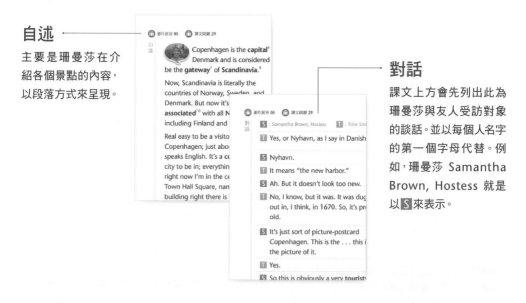

背景知識

課文中提到的人名、景點食材,或當地特殊的背景文化,會在這裡提供補充資訊,讓學英文不只是學會日常會話,還能深入了解各國的文化及風俗習慣,像是丹麥熱狗介紹、義大利的紅酒分級制度和品酒時會用的詞彙等等。

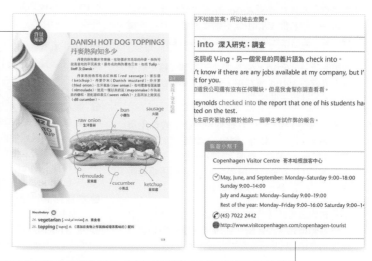

旅遊小幫手

每一課珊曼莎去過的景點或是飯店,或是編輯們推薦的景點,會在這邊提供景點相關資訊:像是票價、開放時間、連絡電話及網址,供有興趣的讀者查詢。

系統建議需求

【硬體】

- 處理器 1GHz 以上
- 記憶體 1GB 以上
- 全彩顯示卡 1024*768 dpi（16K 色以上）
- 硬碟需求空間 200 MB
- 16 倍速光碟機以上
- 音效卡、喇叭及麥克風（內建或外接）

【軟體】

- Microsoft XP、Win 7、Win 8 繁體中文版系統
- Microsoft Windows Media Player 9
- Adobe Flash Player 10

光碟安裝程序！

步驟一 進入中文視窗。

步驟二 將光碟片放進光碟機。

步驟三 本產品備有 Auto Run 執行功能，如果您的電腦支援 Auto Run 光碟程式自動執行規格，則將自動顯現【TLC 互動英語珊曼莎教你用英語暢遊歐洲】之安裝畫面。

如果您的電腦已安裝過本公司產品，如【CNN 互動英語雜誌】或【Live 互動英語雜誌】，您可以直接點選「快速安裝」圖示，進行快速安裝；否則，請點選「安裝」圖示，進行安裝。

如果您電腦無法支援 Auto Run 光碟程式自動執行規格，請打開 Windows 檔案總管，點選光碟機代號，並執行光碟根目錄的 autorun.exe 程式。

如果執行 autorun.exe 尚無法安裝本光碟，請進入本光碟的 setup 資料夾，並執行 setup.exe 檔案，即可進行安裝程式。

如果您想要移除【TLC 互動英語珊曼莎教你用英語暢遊歐洲】，請點選「開始」，選擇「設定」，選擇「控制台」，選擇「新增／移除程式」，並於清單中點選「TLC 互動英語珊曼莎教你用英語暢遊歐洲」，並執行「新增／移除」功能即可。

當語音辨識系統或錄音功能失去作用，請檢查音效卡驅動程式是否正常，並確認硬碟空間是否足夠且 WINDOWS 錄音程式可以作用。

麥克風設定請參照光碟主畫面中的「操作及語音辨識說明」。

執行光碟時，若遇見某些單元無法播出聲音，請安裝以下這支解碼器：

K-Lite Codec 2.82f 解碼器下載、安裝教學：

http://www.liveabc.com/liveabc_cd/install_klcodec.asp

在 Win 7 / Win 8 系統中安裝互動光碟，如出現【無法安裝語音辨識】訊息：

請依照以下步驟操作：

❶ 進入控制台
  Ⓐ 進入「程式和功能」
  Ⓑ 解除安裝或變更程式。
  Ⓒ 移除本書互動光碟軟體。
  Ⓓ 移除「Microsoft Speech Recognition Engine 4.0 (English)」
❷ 開啟檔案管理員，讀取本光碟，進入資料夾「setup」下
❸ 按滑鼠右鍵點選「MSCSRL.EXE（語音辨識程式）」，點選「以系統管理員身分執行（A）」來進行安裝
❹ 重新執行本互動光碟之安裝步驟

主畫面

進入主畫面就會看到歐洲地圖上標示出本書的六個國家單元名稱,點選想學習的單元就可以進入課程內容。

影片學習

觀看完整節目,跟著珊曼莎學英文。讀者可以依據自己的喜好選擇顯示中文字幕、英文字幕,或是都出現,或都不出現。也可以隨時暫停影片切換到文字學習的模式。

文字學習

在文字學習的模式裡,點選課文的任何一句都會有老師清楚的朗讀,點選藍字部分則會出現用法和例句。點選左方的「單字解說」,則會出現本課重要單字音標、詞性及中譯。

貼心提醒

請使用 DVD 光碟機在電腦上安裝本程式學習,並用電腦抓取光碟內的 MP3 檔案來使用。直接放在 MP3 播放器裡是無法播放的。光碟當中無法出現特殊字,如法文的 é 或是希臘文的 í,只能以英文 e 或是 i 顯示。另外,光碟因為完整呈現原文的關係,也不會出現刪除號。

點讀筆介紹

功能說明

準備利用點讀筆學習前，請先將互動光碟裡的檔案安裝至點讀筆中，再點選封面上 LIVE PEN 點讀筆 圖示，即可進入本書的內容學習。

【如何安裝點讀筆檔案】

1. 將互動光碟放置於電腦中，從「我的電腦」點選光碟機，按右鍵以「檔案總管」開啟光碟資料。

2. 找到光碟中「點讀筆」資料夾中的檔案（*.ecm），解壓縮到點讀筆的「BOOK」資料夾裡，即完成安裝。

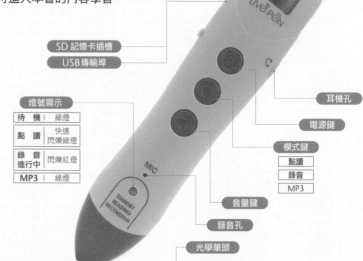

SD 記憶卡插槽
USB 傳輸埠

燈號顯示

待 機	綠燈
點 讀	快速閃爍綠燈
錄 音進行中	閃爍紅燈
MP3	綠燈

耳機孔
電源鍵

模式鍵

| 點讀 |
| 錄音 |
| MP3 |

音量鍵
錄音孔
光學筆頭

錄音卡

RECORD & PLAY

停止錄音鍵
錄音垃圾桶
增加音量
降低音量

錄音鍵
暫停鍵
上一首鍵
下一首鍵
播放鍵
停止鍵

1. 使用錄音功能，請搭配左方**錄音卡**使用
2. 點 [RECORD & PLAY]，啟動錄音模式 (Recording Mode)
3. 點 聽到 Start Recording，開始錄音
4. 點 聽到 Stop Recording，停止錄音
5. 刪除最近一次的錄音內容，請點
6. 錄音檔案存放記憶卡之位置：
   \recording\meeting\ 資料夾

LIVE PEN

音樂卡

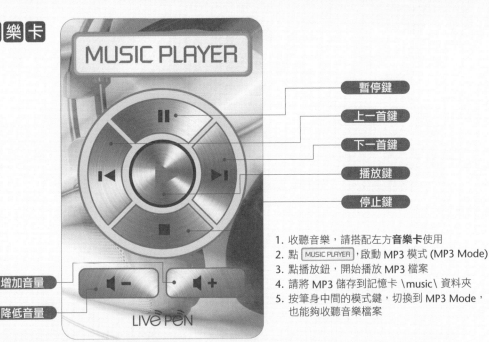

MUSIC PLAYER

- 暫停鍵
- 上一首鍵
- 下一首鍵
- 播放鍵
- 停止鍵
- 增加音量
- 降低音量

LIVE PEN

1. 收聽音樂，請搭配左方**音樂卡**使用
2. 點 MUSIC PLAYER，啟動 MP3 模式 (MP3 Mode)
3. 點播放鈕，開始播放 MP3 檔案
4. 請將 MP3 儲存到記憶卡 \music\ 資料夾
5. 按筆身中間的模式鍵，切換到 MP3 Mode，
   也能夠收聽音樂檔案

本書用法

將點讀筆點在「學習重點」或「*Vocabulary*」後方的 🔊 圖示，就能
聽到一整段由專業美籍老師朗讀的聲音。

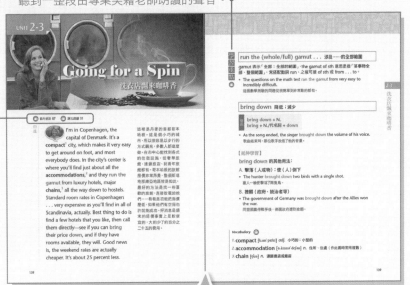

將點讀筆點在影
片原音前方的 🔊
圖示，就能聽到
一整段影片中主
持人說話的影片
原音。

點在課文朗讀前
方 🔊 圖示，就
能聽到一整段由
專業美籍老師朗
讀的聲音。

點選各別句子、片語、例句、單字上，就能聽
見各別句子（影片原音）以及片語等的朗讀。

英國

ENGLAND IN ONE MINUTE

　　英國這個西歐島國的正式名稱為 The United Kingdom of Great Britain and Northern Ireland（大不列顛及北愛爾蘭聯合王國），簡稱 United Kingdom（聯合王國）或 Britain（不列顛），國土包括大不列顛島上的英格蘭（England）、蘇格蘭（Scotland）和威爾斯（Wales），以及愛爾蘭島東北部的北愛爾蘭（Northern Ireland）和其他附屬島嶼。而中文所說的「英國」則由英格蘭而來。

　　這次我們將隨著珊曼莎一起到英文文學大師莎士比亞（Shakespeare）的出生地埃文河畔史特拉福（Stratford-upon-Avon），一探莎翁故居的小鎮風情，以及拜訪英語世界中最古老的大學——牛津大學（University of Oxford），這裡也是著名童話故事《愛麗絲夢遊仙境》（Alice's Adventures in Wonderland）的創作靈感來源。

首都：倫敦
CAPITAL: LONDON

官方語言：英語
OFFICIAL LANGUAGE: ENGLISH

貨幣：英鎊（£）
CURRENCY: POUND STERLING (GBP)

人口：63,181,775（2011 年統計）
POPULATION: 63,181,775 (2011)

📞
國際電話區碼：+44
CALLING CODE: +44

UNIT 1

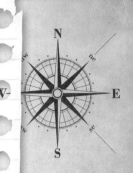

1-1 造訪莎士比亞

珊曼莎參觀了著名的莎翁景點，及帶你重溫莎劇的皇家莎士比亞戲院，令人驚喜的是，她發現了一個不能說的祕密。

1-2 有誰需要莎士比亞

史特拉福四周都是都鐸式（Tudor-style）建築，這裡有非常受歡迎的莎士比亞飯店。在史特拉福劇院開幕時，到處是人山人海。然後到了七點左右，大家全都聚到髒鴨酒吧（The Dirty Duck）。什麼是「最後的招待」（Last Orders）？讓珊曼莎驚呼「誰還需要莎士比亞啊？」

1-3 乘哈利魔梯到愛麗絲兔子洞

牛津大學的「基督教堂書院」是《愛麗絲夢遊仙境》靈感來源地，珊曼莎意外得知，愛麗絲其實是真實存在的人，同時，故事中的場景靈感全都咫尺可得。而紅遍全球哈利波特電影中的「霍格華茲」場景設計也是源自於此。

1-4 在牛津，划過鏡中奇遇

路易斯・卡羅（Lewis Carroll）筆下不只愛麗絲生長在牛津，就連故事的場景、人物都與這裡的人事物有關，趕快跟著珊曼莎一探究竟，與牛津大學學生一起划船，享受這裡獨有的午後時光。

Visiting Shakespeare

造訪莎士比亞

 影片原音 01　 課文朗讀 25

自述

This is Stratford-upon-Avon, one of the busiest destinations for visitors in all of England and the hometown of a **playwright**[1] of some **renown**.[2] Stratford-upon-Avon can be very busy, especially in the summertime. But, I found the best place; this is called the Great Garden of New Place. And no one really knows about it, or at least I don't see many people here. [It's] Sort of hidden from the street, and you'll love knowing that this was actually Shakespeare's land. He wrote his three last plays here in Stratford, so who knows, maybe he was sitting right where I'm sitting, under this tree, being **inspired**.[3] So I thought I'd bring out my little **journal**[4] myself and see what inspires me.

這裡是埃文河畔史特拉福（簡稱史特拉福），是全英國最熱鬧的觀光景點，也是某位小有名氣劇作家的故鄉。史特拉福的人潮洶湧，尤其是在夏季。但我發現了一個最棒的地方，叫做新地花園。沒有人真正知道這個地方，至少我在這裡看到的人並不多，可説是隱密在巷弄之間，更讓你興奮的是，這裡其實是莎士比亞的地產。他就是在史特拉福完成他最後三齣的劇作。誰知道呢？或許他當初就是坐在我現在坐的這棵樹下獲得靈感的。所以我也把自己的記事本拿出來了，看看我會得到什麼樣的靈感。

SHAKESPEARE
莎士比亞

背景知識

莎士比亞（William Shakespeare,1564–1616）是文藝復興時期的英國詩人暨劇作家，被公認為英國文學史上最偉大的作家。他一生共創作一百五十多首十四行詩（sonnets）、劇作包括悲劇、喜劇與歷史劇。作品中精練生動的辭彙、鮮明的角色刻畫以及豐富的情節與多線結構，其深度與廣度數百年來無人能及。莎翁作品直指人性，語言優雅而富創意，因此常被後人改編演出，其經典劇作如下：

四大喜劇	四大悲劇
A Midsummer Night's Dream 仲夏夜之夢	*Hamlet* 哈姆雷特
Much Ado about Nothing* 無事生非	*Othello* 奧賽羅
Twelfth Night 第十二夜	*Macbeth* 馬克白
As You Like It 皆大歡喜	*King Lear* 李爾王

* 四大喜劇中較受爭議的是這部 *Much Ado about Nothing*《無事生非》，因為也有人將 *The Merchant of Venice*《威尼斯商人》或 *The Taming of a Shrew*《馴悍記》列入四大喜劇。

Vocabulary

1. **playwright** [ˋpleˏraɪt] *n.* 劇作家

2. **renown** [rɪˋnaʊn] *n.* 名望；聲望
   （N. of renown 表示「著名的……」）

3. **inspire** [ɪnˋspaɪr] *v.* 啟發；
   給……靈感

4. **journal** [ˋdʒɝnl] *n.* 日誌；日報

旅遊小幫手

New Place 新地花園

莎士比亞長眠之處。

💲 Shakespeare Birthplace Pass:
   Adult: GBP 14.95
   Child: GBP 9.00
   Family: GBP 38.50

🌐 www.shakespeare.org.uk

自述

We are in Stratford-upon-Avon. Avon is **Celtic**[5] for river. Stratford is a town that is, you guessed it, upon it. Now this spot has always been a main crossing point of the rivers. For 3,000 years people have used it as a **thoroughfare**[6] to get to London and just points beyond, so naturally a **bustling**[7] marketplace started here for trade.

About 51,000 residents here in Stratford-upon-Avon, yet it receives over three million visitors a year. And really for one main reason: to see the birth home, the wife's home, and the final **resting place**[8] of one, William Shakespeare. And I know you never understood one word the guy wrote. Why would you want to see any of his homes? Well, actually, let me ask you this: Have you ever used the phrases, **"one fell swoop,"** or **"too much of a good thing," "it was all Greek to me"**? Well you, my friend, have been quoting Shakespeare. Yes, you have. And I believe you'll find that you relate to him more than you know. Let me show you.

我們現在在埃文河畔史特拉福，Avon就是凱爾特語中「河流」之意。你猜對了，史特拉福就是一座位在河上的城鎮。這個地方一直以來都是各河流主要的交匯點。三千年來人們一直把它當作通往倫敦那一邊的幹道，所以自然而然地，熙來攘往的交易市集就在這裡形成了。

史特拉福這裡約有五萬一千名居民，但每年的遊客人數卻超過三百萬人。而主因只有一個，就是為了參觀莎士比亞的出生地、他妻子的家鄉和他長眠的地方。我知道他寫的東西你根本一點也看不懂。為什麼還要來參觀他的家園呢？讓我來問大家一下，大家是否曾經用過這些詞彙，譬如說「一下子」、或者是「過猶不及」、「這事我一竅不通」。是的，我的朋友，你們一直都在引用莎士比亞的話。沒錯，你的確用過。而且我相信你跟他的關係比你所知道的還深。讓我證明給你看！

造訪莎士比亞

學習重點

one fell swoop 一下子；一舉

fell 當形容詞時，指「殘忍的；兇惡的」，例如 a fell disease 表示「凶猛、致命的疾病」。in/at one fell swoop 是指動作極為迅速，表示「一下子；一舉」的意思。此說法出自莎士比亞名劇 *Macbeth*《馬克白》。

- He lost all his wealth all at one fell swoop.
  他一下子失去了所有的財產。

too much of a good thing 過猶不及

用來指有些事物原本是好的，但一旦超過反而會造成反效果，即「好事過頭就變成壞事」的意思。此說法來自莎士比亞的 *As You Like It*《皆大歡喜》。

- Cable TV is great, but be careful not to get too much of a good thing.
  有線電視是不錯，但小心別沉迷過了頭。

it was all Greek to me 我完全不懂；我一竅不通

Greek 是「希臘語；希臘人」，用來表示「難以理解、聽不懂的事」。此說法出自於莎士比亞的一齣悲劇 *Julius Caesar*《凱撒大帝》中。

- I don't understand physics. It's all Greek to me!
  我不懂物理學，我對物理一竅不通！

Vocabulary

5. **Celtic** [ˋkɛltɪk] *n.* 凱爾特語

6. **thoroughfare** [ˋθɝoˏfɛr] *n.* 通衢大道；幹道

7. **bustling** [ˋbʌsəlɪŋ] *adj.* 繁忙的；喧鬧的

8. **resting place** [ˋrɛstɪŋ] [ples] *n.* 駐足休息之處
   （final/last resting place 是指「長眠之處」）

CONTEMPORARY USAGE OF SHAKESPEARE

你又再引用莎士比亞了

To be, or not to be, that is the question.
生存還是死亡——那是一個值得思考的問題。

to be 在此是指「生存；活下去」，not to be 則指「毀滅；自我了斷」，此句最常用來指做與不做之間那種進退維谷的內心掙扎。而劇中獨白的原文與中文翻譯節錄如下：

> To be, or not to be, that is the question:
> Whether 'tis nobler in the mind to suffer
> The slings and arrows of outrageous fortune,
> Or to take arms against a sea of troubles,
> And, by opposing, end them.
>
> ——Hamlet, Act III, Scene I

> 生存還是毀滅——那是一個值得思考的問題：
> 默默忍受坎坷殘酷的命運，
> 或是挺身對抗人世無涯的苦難，
> 在奮鬥中結束一切，
> 這兩種行為，那一種是比較勇敢的？

莎士比亞的劇中有許多名言字詞至今仍常被引用，常見的例子有：

名言字詞	出處	
eyesore 礙眼的東西或建築物	The Taming of the Shrew 《馴悍記》	
not budge an inch 寸步不讓；毫不改變看法或決定	The Taming of the Shrew 《馴悍記》	
high time 正是時候；恰當的時機	The Comedy of Errors 《錯中錯》	
cold comfort 於事無補、起不了作用的安慰	King John 《約翰王》	The Taming of the Shrew 《馴悍記》
play fast and loose 滑頭；玩弄；對……反覆無常	King John 《約翰王》	
laughingstock 笑柄	The Merry Wives of Windsor 《溫莎的風流娘兒們》	
salad days 少不更事的時期；年紀輕、涉世未深時	Antony and Cleopatra 《埃及豔后》	
foul play 謀殺、暴行；犯規動作	Hamlet 《哈姆雷特》 Pericles, Prince of Tyre 《泰爾親王佩力克爾斯》	The Tempest 《暴風雨》
the game is up 一切都完了（對犯罪事跡敗露者而言）	Cymbeline 《辛白林》	
vanish into thin air 消失地無影無蹤	Othello 《奧賽羅》	The Tempest 《暴風雨》
tongue-tied 結結巴巴的；說不出話來的	Shakespeare's Sonnets: "Sonnet 85" 《十四行詩》	

自述

So William Shakespeare was born here in 1564. What really surprises me about this man is that, well, here we have this **master**[9] of English literature and yet his **upbringing**[10] was what we consider quite **middle class.**[11] And in fact he never went to college—didn't go to Cambridge or Oxford. So William Shakespeare was just a small-town boy who made good.

One of the biggest complaints I've heard about Shakespeare is that he, quote, doesn't speak our language. But a trip to his wife's family home tells us that we take more from his **era**[12] than we think. It's Anne Hathaway's **cottage.**[13] John Coulton is the guide who is showing me the cottage.

威廉莎士比亞於一五六四年在這裡誕生，這個人讓我驚訝的是他是一位英國文學大師，而他的成長背景就我們認為是非常中產階級。事實上，他從未上過大學，沒有讀過劍橋或牛津，所以莎士比亞只是一位表現優異的鄉下小孩。

我最常聽到人們對莎士比亞的批評是：他根本不會說我們的語言。但參觀過他妻子的老家後，就會發現他那個年代對我們的影響超過我們的想像。這就是安妮哈瑟維的小屋。約翰·柯爾頓是帶我參觀小屋的導遊。

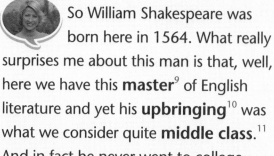

ANNE HATHAWAY
安妮哈瑟維

Anne Hathaway 的個性以及她與莎士比亞的關係一直以來都是歷史學家和作家們的研究主題。

　她在二十六歲的時候跟當時才十八歲的莎士比亞倉促結婚了。當時 Anne 已經懷有身孕，婚後六個月，長女 Susanna 出生，兩年後，她又生了龍鳳雙胞胎 Hamnet 和 Judith。

　十八歲的莎士比亞從人夫變成人父，似乎可從他的作品中一窺究竟他當時的心境。例如莎士比亞花了一大篇篇幅描述茱麗葉如何心急如焚，也許就來自當年先有後婚的 Anne Hathaway。

Anne Hathaway's Cottage
安妮·哈瑟維的小屋

$ Adult: GBP 9.00
  Child: GBP 5.00
  Family: GBP 22.50

☎ (44) 01789 204016

🌐 www.shakespeare.org.uk

圖片來源：Wikipedia / JschneiderWiki

學習重點

quote　原話是……

quote 作動詞用時表示「引用、引述」，名詞則是「引言、引語」。在交談中，若要原文轉述別人的話時，則可加上 quote，再帶出所引述的話語。

- You can quote me on that.
  你可以引用我的話。

- When I asked Jill why she separated from her husband, she said, quote, "It's none of your business!"
  當我問吉兒她與她丈夫分開的原因，她回答：「這不關你的事」。

Vocabulary

9. **master** [ˈmæstɚ] *n.* 大師；高手

10. **upbringing** [ˈʌpˌbrɪŋɪŋ] *n.* 家庭教養

11. **middle class** [ˈmɪdl] [klæs] *n.* 中產階級

12. **era** [ˈɪrə] *n.* 時代；年代

13. **cottage** [ˈkɑtɪdʒ] *n.* 小屋；村舍

對
話

S : *Samantha Brown, Hostess*　　　**J** : *John Coulton, Guide*

S It's **amazing**[14] how . . . how much we take from this period.

這個時期對我們的影響真是驚人。

J Yes.

沒錯！

S I mean, you walk into a home like this and you think, "Well this is so very different from what we **are used to.**"

我指的是，當你走進像這樣的房子，你會覺得它跟我們所熟悉的事物相差很多。

J Yes. **And yet** there are lots of things that we actually carry over into the twenty-first century.

沒錯，然而其實這裡有很多東西一直沿用至二十一世紀。

S Like a **wooden**[15] dinner plate, on which you'd be served a **square meal.**[16] Like a kitchen floor that would be covered with **threshings**[17] of **rushes**[18] and the **threshold**[19] that would keep them in the kitchen. And upstairs . . .

Oh. It's a beautiful bed.

像是木製的餐盤，用這盤子來招待你一頓豐盛的佳餚，廚房的地板鋪上了層層的燈心草，而這門檻可以讓它們置於廚房內。至於樓上……

好漂亮的床啊！

學習重點

be used to 習慣於……

be used to 為「習慣於……」的意思，用於表示現在仍持續的一種習慣或狀態，而 get used to 指「逐漸適應於、習慣於……」，強調養成此習慣的過程。要注意 to 在此是介系詞，後面必須接名詞或是 V-ing。

用法 **be/get used to N./V-ing**

- I still haven't gotten used to driving in Taipei's traffic.
  我到現在還無法適應在台北的車陣中開車。

- She gradually got used to the cold weather in Iceland.
  她逐漸習慣了冰島寒冷的天氣。

and yet . . . （雖然……）然而……

yet 在此作連接詞用，乍看之下 and yet 為兩個並用的連接詞，不過這是一個特殊用法，加上 and 可緩和語氣，帶有「（雖然……）然而……」的意思。此外，and . . . 是承接前面的句子而來，在書寫中，需避免用連接詞 and 或 but 等來起始句子。

- The man is blind and deaf, and yet he is able to get around on his own.
  那個人既盲且聾，然而他能夠自己到處走。

Vocabulary

14. **amazing** [əˋmezɪŋ] *adj.* 令人驚訝的；驚人的

15. **wooden** [ˋwʊdn̩] *adj.* 木製的；木質的

16. **square meal** [skwɛr] [mil] *n.* 豐盛、飽足的一餐飯

17. **threshing** [ˋθrɛʃɪŋ] *n.* 脫粒；打穀（文中 threshings of rushes 是指將經過處理的燈心草堆疊在地板上）

18. **rush** [rʌʃ] *n.* 燈心草；藺草（可以用來編織草蓆、籃子或是用作材料）

19. **threshold** [ˋθrɛʃͺhold] *n.* 門檻

27

對話

S : Samantha Brown, Hostess　　**J** : John Coulton, Guide

J We forget that in the past, beds had such a huge importance. They could cost as much as a small house.

我們忘記了，在過去，床具有極大的重要性。它的價值跟一間小屋差不多。

S Oh, really?

真的？

J Yes!

沒錯！

S So it was [a] **luxury**[20] to have a bed at all.

所以擁有床其實是一項奢侈品。

J Absolutely. It's like somebody buying that wonderful luxury Porsche car that you **accidentally**[21] leave on the drive, so your neighbors can see. When they would come into your **parlor**[22] and actually see your bed, they could **adjust**[23] and, "Oh, they're doing very nicely, **thank you**." And . . .

的確如此！就像有人買了一輛奢華的保時捷，無意間留在車道上，所以，你的鄰居還真的會看到。而當鄰居進入客廳看到你的床，他們可能會改變看法地對你表示讚嘆。

S And I read somewhere that our term "raining cats and dogs". . .

我曾在某處讀到有關「傾盆大雨」這個詞的由來。

學習重點 🎧

thank you「謝謝你」?

大家都知道 thank you 是用來向別人道謝,可是有時候,有些人在句尾加上 thank you 並不是要向對方道謝。這種用法在英式英語中比美語中常見,通常說話者認為對方的看法或見解有誤,甚至有點冒犯人時,就會在句子之後加上 thank you。

文中導遊 John Coulton 表達的訊息是:鄰居進到屋內後發現你家裡有極具價值的床,而對你的看法改觀,因此在稱讚主人一番(they're doing very nicely)之後加上 thank you。附帶一提,這裡的 they 是泛指家裡擁有床的主人們。

* A: Do you know how to install this software?
  你知道怎麼安裝這個軟體嗎?

  B: I'm a high-level software engineer at Google, thank you!
  我可是谷歌高階的軟體工程師。

* A: Steve is a terrible cook.
  史帝夫是很差的廚師。

  B: He is a top chef at a famous hotel in Paris, thank you!
  他可是巴黎一家著名飯店的首席廚師。

rain cats and dogs 下傾盆大雨

俚語 rain cats and dogs 常用現在進行式,用來表示雨下得很大,與 rain heavily、pourdown rain 意思相同。

* It's raining cats and dogs. Let's go inside!
  下起傾盆大雨了。我們進去吧!

Vocabulary 🧳

20. **luxury** [ˋlʌkʃəri] *n., adj.* 奢侈品(作可數用)、奢華(為不可數);奢華的

21. **accidentally** [͵æksəˋdɛntḷi] *adv.* 偶然地;無意間地

22. **parlor** [ˋpɑrlɚ] *n.* 客廳;起居室

23. **adjust** [əˋdʒʌst] *v.* 改變(行為或觀點);調整(文中是指鄰居看到內觀後而改變原先的看法)

對話

S : Samantha Brown, Hostess　　J : John Coulton, Guide

J Yes, **thatch**[24] roofs are wonderful homes, for mice, for birds, bird's nests. If the roof **leaked**,[25] things would often fall down. So, in fact, that's, indeed it could be, you know, "raining cats and dogs."

沒錯，茅屋的屋頂很適合成為老鼠和鳥類的家。如果屋頂有裂縫，上面的東西就會掉下來。所以事實上，屋頂上的貓狗真的也會像雨水一樣掉下來。

S So that **canopy**[26]. . .

所以那個頂篷……

J This is the expression that we come from. It would protect that because . . .

這就是這個用法的典故，而頂篷有保護作用，因為……

S From a cat falling down on your **lap**.[27]

可以防止貓掉到你腿上。

J . . . it would actually **seal off** the **dust**[28] and the **vermin**[29] and the **debris**[30] that might fall on the **occupants**[31] inside.

事實上可以將灰塵、害蟲或瓦片隔離在外，而不會掉到屋內住戶身上。

學習重點

seal off　封閉；隔離

seal 當動詞指「密封」。過去分詞 sealed 作形容詞，用來指「密封的」。

- You will need to seal the bag so that the food stays fresh.
  你需要密封那個袋子，才能保持食物新鮮。

- I do not know what is inside the sealed box.
  我不知道那個密封盒裡裝了什麼。

另外，seal 當名詞還可用來指「印章；玉璽」

- The king's seal was lost in the war.
  國王的印信在戰爭中遺失了。

Vocabulary

24. **thatch** [θætʃ] *n.* （蓋屋頂的）茅草、稻草；茅草屋頂(= thatch roof)

25. **leak** [lik] *v.* 滲漏

26. **canopy** [ˋkænəpi] *n.* 頂篷；天篷

27. **lap** [læp] *n.* 膝部

28. **dust** [dʌst] *n.* 灰塵

29. **vermin** [ˋvɜmən] *n.* 害蟲

30. **debris** [dəˋbri] *n.* 瓦礫；殘骸碎片（複數同形，唸作 [dəˋbriz]，英語發音為 [dɛˋbri(z)]）

31. **occupant** [ˋɑkjəpənt] *n.* （房屋等的）居住者、住戶

自述

You can't come to Stratford-upon-Avon without visiting the Royal Shakespeare Theatre. The company here has been performing Willy's works for over 125 years. So **basically**,[32] if these guys can't help you understand and enjoy Shakespeare, nobody can.

The world-renowned Royal Shakespeare Company has its home base in Stratford-upon-Avon. There are two beautiful theaters located on this river. The famous RSC Theatre and the newer **playhouse**,[33] the Swan. Naturally the actors get **the lion's share of the glory**.[34] But these plays couldn't **come to life** without a **well-tuned**[35] **army**[36] of artists and technicians behind the scenes. There are guided tours for visitors. And I'm being treated to a special visit inside the costume **workshop**.[37]

來到史特拉福，一定不能錯過皇家莎士比亞劇院。這裡的劇團演出威廉的作品已經超過一百二十五年了。所以基本上如果連他們都沒辦法幫你瞭解並欣賞莎士比亞創作的話，那真的愛莫能助了。

舉世知名的皇家莎士比亞劇團在史特拉福有自己的總部。在這條河流上，一共有兩座美麗的劇院，分別是著名的皇家莎士比亞劇院和較新的天鵝劇院。演員的演出機會自然多又多，但精彩的戲劇表演少不了一群合作無間的演員和幕後的技師。這裡有為旅客準備的導覽服務。而我備受禮遇能有機會參觀戲服工作坊。

The Royal Shakespeare Theatre　皇家莎士比亞劇院

圖片來源：Wikipedia / David Dixon

造訪莎士比亞

the lion's share of . . . 最大的一份

字面意思指「獅子的那份」，用來引申為「最大的一份；最好的一份」。用法出自於「伊索寓言」(Aesop's Fables)，有隻獅子和其他動物一起獵取食物，後來捕到一隻鹿，在商量食物分配時，獅子提議牠要分得整隻鹿，其他動物只能任森林之王拿走，不敢吭聲。於是 lion's share 就引申為「最大的部份」，常用 the lion's share of sth 來表示。

- He inherited the lion's share of his father's money.
  他繼承了父親絕大多數的遺產。

come to life 活躍起來；變得生動

come to life 的主詞為事物，可用來表示「變得有趣、栩栩如生」，也可用來指一個地方或場合「變得熱鬧起來、充滿活力」。

- The painter makes the farm scene come to life on the canvas.
  這位畫家把農場景象栩栩如生地呈現在畫布上。
- After Willis turned up the music, the party really came to life.
  在威利斯把音樂調大聲後，派對確實變得熱鬧起來。

Vocabulary

32. **basically** [ˋbesɪkəlɪ] *adv.* 基本上

33. **playhouse** [ˋpleˏhaʊs] *n.* 劇場；劇院

34. **glory** [ˋglorɪ] *n.* 榮耀

35. **well-tuned** [ˋwɛlˋtjund] *adj.* 和諧的（引申指合作無間以致於表現出色）

36. **army** [ˋɑrmɪ] *n.* 大群；大批（an army of 之後接複數可數名詞）

37. **workshop** [ˋwɜkˏʃɑp] *n.* 工作坊；研習班

對話

S : Samantha Brown, Hostess　　**F** : Female in Black, Costume Artist

S What are you doing? Is this **dyeing**[38] or is this just making dirty?	妳在做什麼？這是在染色或只是把它弄髒？
F This is just making dirty.	我只是要把它弄髒。
S And it's to give the look of it's been **worn**[39] for a while.	讓它看起來像穿了一陣子的樣子。
F Yeah, he's been camping for about four weeks, living **rough**[40] in the forest, so he's going to be quite **grubby**[41] by the time they're finished.	沒錯，他已經露營大約四星期，在森林餐風露宿地，所以最後他應該會變得很邋遢。
S What other tools do you use?	妳還會用到什麼工具？
F Becky's using a cheese **grater**[42] at the moment. And she's **balding**[43] the **velvet**[44] on that jacket.	貝琪正在使用乳酪磨碎器，她要把外套上的絲絨磨掉。
S You use a cheese grater?	妳用乳酪磨碎器？
F Yeah, it's like painting in 3-D really. So you kind of . . . you think about the character and what they've been through, and then you just kind of work on the costume.	沒錯，就像是在畫立體畫一樣。你先想像一下這個角色，還有他們遇到什麼事，之後只要專注於服裝製作上。
S It's a . . . it was a beautiful shirt.	它原本是一件漂亮的襯衫。

34

SKILLS USED IN A COSTUME WORKSHOP
戲服製作技術

戲服製作包含了各種層面的技術，主要如下：

tailoring
裁縫技術

printing
印刷技術

corsetry
緊身衣（女性胸衣）裁縫技術

leatherwork
皮革製作

dyeing
染色技術

jewelry making
珠寶首飾製作

millinery
女帽製作

beading
串珠飾物製作

mask making
面具製作

Vocabulary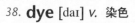

38. **dye** [daɪ] *v.* 染色

39. **worn** [wɔrn] *adj.* 破舊的；損壞的

40. **rough** [rʌf] *adv.* 餐風露宿地；無家可歸地（常搭配動詞 live 或 sleep）

41. **grubby** [ˋgrʌbi] *adj.* 骯髒的；邋遢的

42. **grater** [ˋgretə] *n.* 磨碎器

43. **bald** [bɔld] *v.* 使磨平；磨光

44. **velvet** [ˋvɛlvət] *n.* 天鵝絨；絲絨

對話

S : Samantha Brown, Hostess　　　**F** : Female in Black, Costume Artist

F We have, look, **cowpat**[45] as well, which is in the same show. We got . . .	我們還，妳看，同一齣戲，我們還使用了牛派。
S What's cowpat?	牛派是什麼？
F It's cow **poo**.[46]	是牛糞。
S It's cow poo?	牛糞？
F Yeah.	沒錯。
S This is?	真的？
F So what we have to do . . . obviously we have to make **pretend**[47] cow poo because the actors would probably **revolt**.[48]	我們必須要做的是，顯然要做出假的牛糞，因為演員可能會覺得噁心。
S So this is **fake**[49] cow poo?	所以，這是假的牛糞？
F Yes.	是假的。
S Can I open it?	我可以打開嗎？
F Yeah, do have a look.	可以，請看。
S Oh my gosh, that's awful.	天啊，真是噁心！
F It's a secret recipe. We can't tell you what's in it.	這是秘方。我們不能透露放了什麼。
S Is it, really? It's your . . . it's your own, though? Oh, that's lovely. I . . . I smell a **tinge**[50] of **nutmeg**.[51]	真的嗎？不過這是你們的自己研發的？喔，好香。我聞到了些許肉豆蔻的香味。
F Oh right.	沒錯。

smell 聞出……

smell 除了如文中表示「聞出」的意思之外，最常見的用法是作為連綴動詞。常見的連綴動詞有：smell（聞起來）、taste（嚐起來）、look（看起來）、sound（聽起來）、feel（感覺起來）。用法如下：

用法 S. + 連綴動詞 + Adj. / like + N.

• Those candles smelled terrible, so we threw them away.
那些蠟燭很不好聞，所以我們把它全丟了。

• Sonya's cookies taste great, and they're very cute, too.
桑雅的餅乾嚐起來很棒，而且也非常可愛。

• The cup felt like glass, but it didn't break easily.
這杯子感覺起來像玻璃，但是它不容易破。

Vocabulary

45. **cowpat** [ˋkaʊˌpæt] *n.* 牛糞（= cow pie）

46. **poo** [pu] *n.* 糞；便便（為兒語）

47. **pretend** [prɪˋtɛnd] *adj.* 假裝的；假扮的

48. **revolt** [rɪˋvolt] *v.* 令人作嘔

49. **fake** [fek] *adj.* 假的；偽造的

50. **tinge** [ˋtɪndʒ] *n.* 些許、微量（色彩、特質、感情）

51. **nutmeg** [ˋnʌtˌmɛg] *n.* 肉豆蔻（多用作調味品）

自述

So, this is what a theater looked like back in Shakespeare's time. It is amazing how close the audience is—kind of **intimidating**[52] as well. Everyone from wealthy **aristocrats**[53] to poor **commoners**[54] would come to, as they would say, hear a play. They wouldn't come to see it; they were here to hear it.

Another thing that's going to surprise you is that Shakespeare never **intended**[55] his plays to be read. He wrote them to be performed and enjoyed. It's his **version**[56] of popular entertainment, very much like how we enjoy movies today. So, you'd come to Stratford-upon-Avon when you want to see how Shakespeare lived. You come to the theater when you want to see how Shakespeare lives.

所以，這就是莎士比亞時代劇院的模樣了。這非常棒，跟觀眾的距離竟然如此地近，感覺還挺嚇人的。無論是富裕的貴族或窮困的平民，就如他們所說的，都可以來這裡聽一齣劇。他們不是來看戲，而是來聽戲的。

另一件令人驚訝的事是莎士比亞從來沒想過他的作品是要供人閱讀的。他寫作的目的是要供人演出和欣賞。這是他對大眾娛樂的定義，就跟今天看電影很像。如果你想認識莎士比亞的生活，一定要來史特拉福看看。如果你想了解莎士比亞的存在，就要來這座劇院看看了。

造訪莎士比亞

旅遊小幫手

Royal Shakespeare Theatre　皇家莎士比亞劇院

費用包含幕後導覽。

$ Adult: GBP 7.50
Child: GBP 3.00
Disabled: GBP 3.00
Group Rate (up to 20): GBP 135.00

☎ (44) 844-800-1110

🌐 www.rsc.org.uk

Vocabulary

52. **intimidate** [ɪn`tɪmə͵det] *v.* 恐嚇；威脅（現在分詞 intimidating 表示「駭人的；令人膽怯的」）

53. **aristocrat** [ə`rɪstə͵kræt] *n.* 貴族

54. **commoner** [`kɑmənə] *n.* 平民

55. **intend** [ɪn`tɛnd] *v.* 打算；預留（作為某種用途）

56. **version** [`vɝʒən] *n.* （有別於他人的）說法；描述（用法為 sb's version of . . .）

Who Needs Shakespeare?

有誰需要莎士比亞

🎬 影片原音 02　　📖 課文朗讀 26

自述

 Stratford-upon-Avon is one of England's most popular destinations. Most people coming here are just visiting for the day. So there aren't a lot of hotels here. What you will find are small **hotels, inns, and . . . and B&Bs**. Now, I'm staying at one of the largest hotels here, and I think you'll **recognize**[1] the name. We've seen his home, we've seen his wife's home, we have seen the theater he inspired; yes, I am staying at the Shakespeare.

埃文河畔史特拉福是英國最受歡迎的渡假去處。多數到此地的遊客僅僅是一日遊,所以這裡的飯店並不多。但這裡還是有很多小旅館、旅店及民宿。現在我要住的飯店是這裡最大的飯店之一,我想這個名字你應該會認得。我們去過他的家、看過他妻子的家、還看過受他啟迪的劇院。沒錯,我要入住的飯店就叫做「莎士比亞」。

Vocabulary

1. **recognize** [ˈrɛkɪɡˌnaɪz] *v.* 認出

HOTELS, INNS, AND B&BS
飯店、旅店以及民宿

有誰需要莎士比亞

來看看旅行時，除了 hotel 之外，還有什麼其他住宿選擇。

旅館種類

B&B (bed and breakfast)
民宿

youth hostel
青年旅舍

guesthouse
招待所；賓館

inn
客棧；旅店

motel
汽車旅館

apartment hotel
短期出租公寓

vacation rental
渡假別墅

resort
渡假村

旅遊小幫手

Mercure Stratford-upon-Avon Shakespeare Hotel
埃文河畔史特拉福莎士比亞美居酒店

屬四星級飯店。

$ Double or Twin:　　　　　from GBP 59.00

Privilege Double or Twin: from GBP 79.00

Junior Suite:　　　　　　 from GBP 89.00

☎ (44) 2477 092802

🌐 http://www.mercure.com/gb/hotel-6630-mercure-stratford-upon-avon-shakespeare-hotel/index.shtml

圖片來源：Fickr / brianac37

41

自述

This is one of the most popular hotels here in this town. One, because of its location; I mean, we're really in the center of it all. And also its style and **atmosphere**.[2] I mean, just look around. It's hard to **resist**[3] not staying in one of the **original**[4] buildings of this town, this Tudor-style **architecture**.[5] Parts of this building **date back to** 1637.

So this is my room, and it's small, but it just **oozes**[6] character, doesn't it? I love having this **exposed**[7] **timber frame**[8] and these tall, **exaggerated**[9] **head-boards**.[10] It's all old and **English-y**, but it's not like **dank**[11] or **musty**,[12] because sometimes I look at rooms like this on TV and it's like, "Oh, does it smell?" But it doesn't. It's very nice and fresh. Love it.

這是這座城鎮最受歡迎的旅館之一，其中一個原因就是位置，它位於整個鎮的中心，還有就是它的風格和氣氛。看看四周，這座城鎮最原始的建築——都鐸式建築，真的會讓人無法抗拒地想來住。這棟建築有部份可追溯至一六三七年。

這就是我的房間，不大，但別具特色，對吧？我好喜歡這裡寬大外露的木製窗架，和超高的床頭板。具有古色古香的英國風情，但又沒有一點濕氣或霉味。因為有時在電視上看到這種房間的介紹時，就會懷疑會不會有異味，但一點味道也沒有。這裡舒適，空氣又清新，我很喜歡。

都鐸式建築（Tudor-Style Architecture）是指英國都鐸王朝（1485–1603）時期開始興建的房子。以厚重的橡木作為主架構，屋頂尖而斜，橡木之間則以木條、灰泥、磚石填充牆面，並用黑色木條隔出幾何形狀的小窗格，而呈現出各種不同的面貌。此外高而窄、向外推出的窗戶，和煙囪頂端常見的裝飾都是都鐸式建築的特色。

有誰需要莎士比亞

學習重點

date back to 追溯到；從……至今

date 作動詞指「寫上日期；確定年代」。而片語 date back to 指「始於；追溯到」，表示某事物發生或建造的時間。

- This building dates back to the late nineteenth century.
  這座建築建於十九世紀末。

English-y 像英國的；具有英國特色的

形容詞字尾 -y 表示「像……一樣的；具有某種特質的；充滿……的」之意。其他例子包括：

home + y = homey 像家一樣（舒適）的；自然樸實的

salt + y = salty 鹹的

thirst + y = thirsty 口渴的

wind + y = windy 風大的

Vocabulary

2. **atmosphere** [ˈætməˌsfɪr] *n.* 氛圍；氣氛

3. **resist** [rɪˈzɪst] *v.* 抵抗、抗拒

4. **original** [əˈrɪdʒənl] *adj.* 起初的；原始的

5. **architecture** [ˈɑrkəˌtɛktʃə] *n.* 建築

6. **ooze** [uz] *v.* 突顯、洋溢（特性或特點）

7. **exposed** [ɪkˈspozd] *adj.* 裸露的；未受到保護或遮蔽的

8. **timber frame** [ˈtɪmbə] [frem] *n. phr.* 木框

9. **exaggerate** [ɪɡˈzædʒəˌret] *v.* 誇大；誇張

10. **headboard** [ˈhɛdˌbord] *n.* 床頭板

11. **dank** [dæŋk] *adj.* 陰冷潮濕的

12. **musty** [ˈmʌsti] *adj.* 有霉味的；發霉的

對話

S : *Samantha Brown, Hostess*　　**F** : *Female with Long Hair*

S "Last orders" is the British term for the final drinks of the day. And I had an early **pint**[13] with Stratford **residents**[14] Katie and Nicola. They gave me the **lowdown**[15] on this very **tourist-heavy** town.

「最後的點餐」是英式用語，指的是一天結束前所點的飲料。而我跟當地的居民凱蒂和妮可拉正提前飲用一杯啤酒。她們告訴我這座極受遊客歡迎城鎮的真實情況。

F What you do find in Stratford is that when the theaters open . . . I mean, they . . . you got sort of . . . I think it's about two and a half thousand seats, so you can find that you can be **heaving**[16] with people. And then it'll come around seven o'clock— they're gone. Everyone's gone.

史特拉福的特色是，當劇院開幕時，可容納約兩千五百個座位，所以你會發現到處都擠滿了人。然後到了七點左右，你會發現所有人都不見了。每個人都不見了。

S So is that when you know to go out to the pubs?

所以大家都到酒吧去了？

F Yeah.

沒錯！

S So, you know what? Let's go.

那還等什麼？走吧！

F It's time to go. Everyone's gone.

是時候了，大家都去了。

學習重點

tourist-heavy　遊客眾多的；遊客聚集的

tourist 指「觀光客」，heavy 當形容詞，指「大量的；充滿……的」，如 be heavy with 就指「充滿……的」。文中的 tourist-heavy 則為複合形容詞表示「到處都是遊客的；遊客聚集的」。

- The movie's plot was heavy with allegorical meaning.
  這部電影的故事情節充滿了寓意。

圖片來源：Flickr / Martin Pettitt

旅遊小幫手

The Dirty Duck　髒鴨酒吧

提供各種含酒精飲料及其他飲料，如茶或咖啡；亦提供餐點，如牛排、海鮮、漢堡及甜點等。套餐費用如下：

One Course（一道主菜）：GBP 5.95

Two Courses（一道主菜及開胃菜或甜點）：GBP 7.95

Three Courses（含開胃菜、一道主菜及甜點）：GBP 9.95

☎ (44) 01789 297312

Vocabulary

13. **pint** [paɪnt] *n.*　一品脫啤酒；（容量單位）品脫

14. **resident** [ˋrɛzədənt] *n.*　居民

15. **lowdown** [ˋlo͵daʊn] *n.*　實情；內幕

16. **heave** [hiv] *v.*　擠滿人；人頭攢動

對話

S : Samantha Brown, Hostess　　F1 : Female with Long Hair

F2 : Female with Short Hair

S And this pub, The Dirty Duck, **is specifically**[17] known as **sort of**[18] an actors' **hangout**.[19]	這間髒鴨酒吧尤其可以說是因為演員常去這裡而為人所知。
F1 Yeah, yeah, I mean if you go inside, you'll see ~~there's~~ [there are] sort of signed pictures of the actors that have been at the theaters over the years—all over the walls.	沒錯，如果妳進到店裡，會看見餐廳的牆壁上掛滿了多年來在劇院演出的許多演員的簽名照。
F2 The **interior**[20] probably hasn't changed for many years. I think everybody in Stratford really loves the interior and wouldn't like it to change. And it's very **typically**[21] English.	裡面的裝潢多年來或許都不曾改過。我想史特拉福的居民都很喜歡裡面的裝潢，而不會想改變它。那是很典型的英式風格。
S And what do you find special about Stratford?	你認為史特拉福有何獨特之處？
F1 The main thing is, we're absolutely **spoiled for** restaurants here, because of the visitors. You have a . . . a **vast**[22] **selection**,[23] yeah.	主要是因為遊客的關係，我們這裡有多樣化的餐廳可供選擇。妳的選擇有很多。
S You can have Indian food and . . .	這裡有印度料理還有……

學習重點

be known as 以（身分、名稱）為人所知；被稱為

後面需接身分，而要說明被什麼人熟知時，會用 to sb。

- Sigmund Freud is known as the father of psychology.
  西格蒙・佛洛伊德被稱為心理學之父。

- The Greek god Zeus was known to the Romans as Jupiter.
  希臘的宙斯神就是羅馬人所知的邱比特。

be spoiled/spoilt for . . . 有很多的⋯⋯

spoil 作動詞表示「寵壞；溺愛」的意思，過去分詞為 spoiled 或 spoilt。sb be spoiled/spoilt for 為比喻用法，以某人被寵壞來形容東西非常多，如：be spoiled for choice 即指「可供選擇的東西非常多」。

- These days, customers are spoiled for choice when buying a new cell phone.
  近來，消費者購買新手機時有許多的選擇。

Vocabulary

17. **specifically** [spɪˋsɪfɪklɪ] *adv.* 特別地；尤其地

18. **sort of** [sɔrt] [əv] *adv.* 有點；有幾分；可說是

19. **hangout** [ˋhæŋˏaut] *n.* （一群人）常去的地方；聚集處

20. **interior** [ɪnˋtɪrɪəˋ] *n., adj.* 內部（的）

21. **typically** [ˋtɪpɪklɪ] *adv.* 典型地；有代表性地

22. **vast** [væst] *adj.* 廣大的；巨大的

23. **selection** [səˋlɛkʃən] *n.* 可供選擇的物品

對
話

S : *Samantha Brown, Hostess*　　F1 : *Female with Long Hair*

F2 : *Female with Short Hair*

F2 Thai restaurants, Chinese, **as well as** English, French. So, it's . . . it's really wonderful for eating out. So a typical night out would be coming for a drink at a pub like The Dirty Duck and then going to one of the many wonderful restaurants that we've got here in Stratford.

泰國餐廳、中式料理,還有英國菜和法國菜。所以這裡真的很適合外食。最典型的夜間活動就是先來像髒鴨酒吧的酒吧喝一杯,然後再去一家這裡最棒的餐廳。

And then **hurrying**[24] your desserts in time for last orders, and sending out somebody to the pub first of all before eleven o'clock to buy as many beers as possible for . . . for you to drink in **literally** fifteen minutes **flat**,[25] before . . . before the pub closes and you're thrown out.

然後要點最後一杯酒的話就得趕緊吃完甜點,然後在十一點之前先派一個人去買盡可能多的啤酒,在酒吧打烊被趕出去前十五分鐘將酒快速地喝光。

S A runner. Go, go!

好像在比賽,加油,加油!

F1 And basically everyone just **staggers**[26] home and then goes to sleep and then wakes up the next day and it all starts again.

然後基本上每個人都會搖搖晃晃地回家,倒頭就睡,隔天醒來後同樣模式又重來一次。

S Well, I can't think of a better reason to come to Stratford-upon-Avon. Who . . . who needs Shakespeare?

我想不出來到史特拉福,還有其他更吸引人的理由了。誰還需要莎士比亞啊?

學習重點

as well as　和；以及；而且

as well as 前後連接的詞性須一致，連接兩個主詞時強調前面的事物，因此句中動詞需配合第一個主詞。

- I saw a lion as well as some zebras during my trip to Africa.
  我在非洲之旅中看到一隻獅子和一些斑馬。（a lion 和 some zebras 皆名詞）

- The dinner was healthy as well as tasty.
  這頓晚餐健康且美味。（healthy 和 tasty 皆形容詞）

- You can sail on the lake as well as swim in it.
  你可以在這座湖上划船及在水裡游泳。（sail 和 swim 皆動詞）

- This house as well as many others on the street needs to be painted.
  這間房子和這條街上很多其他的房子都需要粉刷。（配合 this house，用單數動詞）

literally　照字面意思地

literally 當副詞用，文中表示「照字面意思地」；也可用於加強語氣，表示「簡直」的意思。

- Gus took the boss's order to "drop everything" literally and dropped all of the files on the floor.
  老闆叫葛斯「放下手邊的東西」，葛斯便依老闆說的，把所有檔案都放到地上。

- The mountain scenery in Nepal is literally breathtaking.
  尼泊爾的山色簡直令人屏息。

Vocabulary

24. **hurry** [ˋhɝɪ] *v.* 迅速（做某事）；匆忙

25. **flat** [flæt] *adv.* 在明確的時間內（用來指速度非常快）

26. **stagger** [ˋstægɚ] *v.* 蹣跚前進、搖晃地走

49

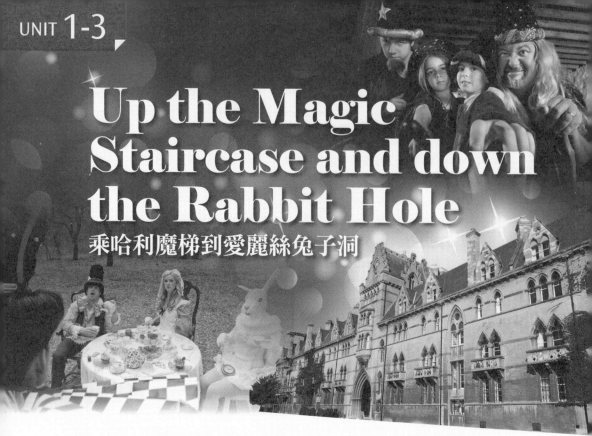

Up the Magic Staircase and down the Rabbit Hole

乘哈利魔梯到愛麗絲兔子洞

 影片原音 03   課文朗讀 27

自述

We are now traveling to the English city of Oxford. It's located to the northwest of London, about an hour's drive. It's home to the oldest English-speaking university in the world. An **epicenter**[1] of learning for more than nine hundred years. David Womersley, who I met on my visit to Salzburg, is an Oxford **graduate**,[2] the perfect choice for a guide.

現在我們要前往英國的牛津市,它位於倫敦的西北方,約一小時車程。它有全世界歷史最悠久的英語系大學,九百年來都是一座學術中心。我到訪薩爾茲堡時所認識的大衛·沃姆斯里是一位牛津的畢業生,是擔任此次導遊的最佳人選。

學習重點

be home to N. （某地）擁有……；是……的所在地

此片語字面意思為「是……的家園」，可譯為「（某地）擁有……；是……的所在地」，可用來強調說話者認為某事物屬於此地，或用來指某人居住或出生的房子、城鎮或國家，home 在此作不可數名詞用。

- This restaurant is home to the best chocolate cake in the city.
  這家餐廳擁有全城最棒的巧克力蛋糕。

- Taipei used to be home to the tallest building in the world.
  台北曾經是世界第一高樓的所在地。

- Tainan is home to many well-known baseball players.
  台南是許多棒球名人的故鄉。

【延伸學習】

be the home of N. （某地）是……的發源地、棲息地

home 在此作單數可數名詞用。

- This park is the home of many pigeons.
  這座公園是許多鴿子的棲息地。

Oxford 牛津的由來

　　Oxford 位於泰悟士河（River Thames）和查威爾河（River Cherwell）的交會處，由於當時水深很淺，牛車可涉水而過，因此 Oxford 就是由 Ox（牛）+ ford（淺灘；涉水而過）而來。而中文中的「津」有「渡口；交通要道」的意思，故 Oxford 就譯成了「牛津」。

Vocabulary

1. **epicenter** [ˈɛpɪ͵sɛntə] n. 中心

2. **graduate** [ˈɡrædʒəwət] n. 畢業生

對話

S : *Samantha Brown, Hostess*　　D : *David Womersley, Oxford Graduate*

| D | I think people sometimes **assume**[3] that there's going to be a campus **of sorts**[4] here. | 一般人有時會以為這裡算是牛津大學的校園。 |

| S | Sure. | 是啊！ |

| D | The Oxford University campus. | 牛津大學的校園。 |

| S | Right. | 沒錯！ |

| D | But, we have, I believe, ~~it's~~ thirty-nine **colleges**[5] that are just **scattered**[6] through the city basically. So the university is everywhere here. But, each college ~~it's~~ [is] sort of like a little world. For example, I lived in college. I ate in formal **hall**[7] in college. I ate sandwiches from the **buttery** in college. Could have gone to **chapel**[8] if I wanted to. Every college has a chapel. But **crucially**[9] . . . | 但基本上牛津一共有三十九個學院，分散在城市各區，所以到處都是牛津大學。每個學院有點像是一個小世界。譬如說我住在學院裡面，我到學院裡的餐廳用餐，也會到學院裡的速食餐廳買三明治，有需要的話也可以上教堂。每座學院都有教堂，但最重要的是…… |

| S | Yes. | 是什麼？ |

| D | . . . every college also has a bar. | 每個學院都有自己的酒吧。 |

| S | Are you kidding me? | 你在跟我開玩笑嗎？ |

| D | No, no. | 沒有。 |

學習重點

buttery 輕食咖啡店；速食餐廳

buttery 當名詞，專指英國牛津、劍橋等大學裡的露天咖啡座、販賣輕食的咖啡店、或專門為師生供應點心飲品的餐廳。另外，buttery 也可用來指「儲藏食物及酒的地方」。

【延伸學習】

下面列出英式英語與美式英語的不同說法：

	英式英語	美式英語
輕食咖啡店	buttery	snack bar、café
膳宿雜費帳單	battel	college account
學院院長	warden、principal	dean

旅遊小幫手

University of Oxford 牛津大學

沒有提供導覽，但有開放觀光客參觀，不過部分學院需付門票才能入內參觀。各學院收費方式，可至下列網址查詢：

🌐 http://www.ox.ac.uk/

📞 (44) 01865 270000

Vocabulary

3. **assume** [əˋsum] *v.* 以為；認為

4. **of sorts** [əv] [sɔrts] *phr.* 勉強稱得上……；算是（亦可用 N. + of a sort 表示）

5. **college** [ˋkɑlɪdʒ] *n.* （英國）學院；（美國）大學

6. **scatter** [ˋskætə] *v.* 使分散；散落在各處

7. **hall** [hɔl] *n.* （開會、用餐或演出）的建築物或廳堂

8. **chapel** [ˋtʃæpəl] *n.* （學校、醫院等的）小教堂

9. **crucially** [ˋkruʃəli] *adv.* 重要地是

對話

S : *Samantha Brown, Hostess*　　**D** : *David Womersley, Oxford Graduate*

S You had your own bar?

你們有自己的酒吧？

D Every college. I spent most of my nonworking hours, of course, there.

每座學院都有。我的課餘時間大多是在那裡度過。

S That's why Oxford students are so much smarter.

這就是牛津的學生比別人聰明的原因了。

D You think?

是嗎？

S I think so.

沒錯。

D It's all written all over my face, isn't it?

看我就知道了，對不對？

S One of the largest and most **esteemed**[10] colleges at the university is Christ Church. It has produced **no less than** thirteen British **prime ministers**.[11] It was here that David gave me a little more **insight**[12] into student life.

牛津大學裡規模最大也最備受尊崇的就是基督教堂書院了。這裡培養出至少十三位英國首相。在這裡，大衛讓我更深入瞭解學生的生活。

學習重點

no less than 多達；不少於

no less than 之後接數量，表示「多達……」，用於指數量之多而感到驚訝的意思。

 用法 **no less than** + 數量 + 名詞

- There are no less than five shopping malls in the financial district.
  這個金融區裡的購物中心多達五間。

旅遊小幫手

Christ Church 基督教堂書院

這是牛津最大的學院，也是童話故事愛麗絲夢遊仙境的起源地，以及哈利波特電影場景靈感來源。

$ （票價資訊有效期間：2013.09.01–2013.12.31）：
Adult: GBP 7.00   Family: GBP 14.00
Child (5–17 years): GBP 5.50
Student (with Student Card): GBP 5.50
Children under 5 years old are admitted free of charge.

因為開放時間經常更動，提醒要進入參觀前，可事先上網查詢。

🌐 www.chch.ox.ac.uk

Vocabulary

10. **esteem** [ɪ`stim] *v.* 尊敬；敬重

11. **prime minister** [praɪm] [`mɪnəstə] *n.* 首相；總理

12. **insight** [`ɪn͵saɪt] *n.* 深入了解；洞悉

對
話

S : *Samantha Brown, Hostess*　　**D** : *David Womersley, Oxford Graduate*

D This is the main **quad**,[13] Tom Quad, here at Christ Church. It's named after the tower. London has Ben, Big Ben. We have Tom, the name of the bell.	這是基督教堂書院最主要的方庭－湯姆方庭。以湯姆塔的名稱命名。倫敦有大本鐘；我們有湯姆鐘。
S I see.	原來如此。
D But the doors here . . . this is **essentially**[14] the student **dorms**[15] that you're looking at.	妳現在看到的這些門，基本上是學生宿舍。
S Oh, OK.	噢，好的。
D Professors have their rooms there.	教授在那裡也有自己的房間。
S Right.	是。
D And here, right in the corner, do you see those two windows right by the **drainpipe**[16] there?	就在角落那裡，你看到排水管旁那兩扇窗戶嗎？
S Uh-huh.	嗯。
D That is where Charles Dodgson had his rooms. And that was where he wrote *Alice in Wonderland* there.	那正是查爾斯・道吉森住過的房間，他就是在那裡撰寫出《愛麗絲夢遊仙境》的。

TOM QUAD 湯姆方庭 & GREAT TOM 湯姆鐘

湯姆方庭（Tom Quad）是牛津大學基督教堂書院的一個方庭，也是牛津大學最大的一個方庭，264×261 英尺，名稱是取自湯姆塔（Tom Tower）上的湯姆鐘（Great Tom；亦稱作 Old Tom）。湯姆鐘重六噸多，從第二次世界大戰開始，每到了晚上九點五分，鐘就會敲 101 下，這 101 下代表最初學院人員數目。大鐘敲時，鐘聲清澈嘹亮，遠播數英里。在湯姆方庭的中心，有一個噴水池，池裡有一個羅馬神話裡的水星（Mercury）雕像。在過去的傳統中，運動型學生（hearties）會將藝術型學生（aesthetes）拋進此池。如今，此池僅供參觀，若進入池裡，會被罰款。

BIG BEN 大本鐘

大本鐘（Big Ben）亦稱作大笨鐘，是倫敦西敏宮（Palace of Westminster）北端鐘樓的大報時鐘的暱稱，也常指該鐘所在的鐘樓。鐘樓坐落在英國倫敦泰晤士河畔，是倫敦的標誌之一。高 320 英尺（約合 97.5 公尺）、重 13.5 噸，是英國最大的鐘，世界第三高鐘樓。二〇一二年英國政府宣布為慶祝伊莉莎白二世登基六十周年，將大本鐘所在的鐘樓正式改名為伊莉莎白塔（Elizabeth Tower）。

Vocabulary 📖

13. **quad** [kwɑd] *n.* （大學裡）方庭；四方院（= quadrangle）

14. **essentially** [ɪˋsɛntʃəlɪ] *adv.* 基本上、大體上；根本上

15. **dorm** [dɔrm] *n.* 宿舍（= dormitory [ˋdɔrməˏtɔrɪ]）

16. **drainpipe** [ˋdrenˏpaɪp] *n.* 排水管；雨水管

對話

S : *Samantha Brown, Hostess*　　**D** : *David Womersley, Oxford Graduate*

S	Charles Dodgson?	查爾斯・道吉森？
D	Lewis Carroll. That was his . . . his pen name.	路易斯・卡羅是他的筆名。
S	Oh, I didn't know he had a pen name.	我不知道他用筆名。
D	Yeah, yeah.	沒錯。
S	Oh, OK.	好的。
D	So you know it was all real, of course, you know, Alice was the daughter of the **dean**[17] here. There was the door in the garden.	所以這個故事有它的真實性，愛麗絲是這裡院長的女兒，花園裡也確實有這麼一扇門。
S	Wait Alice . . .	等一下，愛麗絲……
D	The rabbit hole.	兔子洞。
S	Alice was real?	愛麗絲是真有其人？
D	Yeah. Oh yeah.	沒錯。是的。
S	Alice was a real girl?	真有愛麗絲的存在？
D	Of course; she was the daughter of the dean.	沒錯，她就是院長的女兒。

Vocabulary

17. **dean** [din] *n.* 大學的學院院長

58

背景知識

LEWIS CARROLL, 1832–1898
愛麗絲夢遊仙境作者：路易斯・卡羅

路易斯・卡羅（Lewis Carroll）本名查爾斯・路威治・道吉森（Charles Lutwidge Dodgson），英國作家，同時也是著名的數學家與攝影師。卡羅早期著作多為短詩與趣味短篇小說，之後他帶著朋友的小女兒划船同遊泰晤士河（River Thames），順便編了一則冒險故事。小女孩聽得興趣盎然，希望卡羅寫下這則故事，《愛麗絲夢遊仙境》（Alice's Adventures in Wonderland）就此誕生，於一八六五年發表。

《愛麗絲夢遊仙境》裡怪字連篇，許多情節荒誕不經，但其實都是卡羅刻意安排的文字遊戲，例如 I see what I eat 與 I eat what I see，只有動詞順序不同，但句意完全不一樣，讓人一邊閱讀妙趣橫生的故事，一邊訓練邏輯思考，因此本書吸引了各個年齡層的讀者，獲得廣大迴響，出版後立即銷售一空。

圖片來源：Wikipedia

路易斯・卡羅重要年表

1851 年	進入牛津大學（University of Oxford）的基督教堂書院（Christ Church College）就讀，之後取得數學講師職位
1865 年	出版《愛麗絲夢遊仙境》（Alice's Adventures in Wonderland）
1871 年	出版《愛麗絲鏡中奇遇記》（Through the Looking-Glass），銷售成績更甚前作

對話

S : *Samantha Brown, Hostess*　　**D** : *David Womersley, Oxford Graduate*

S Living in Oxford?	住在牛津大學裡？
D Yes, **absolutely**.[18] The **enchanting**[19] garden that she couldn't go into.	沒錯。因為她不能進入那座迷人的花園。
S So he wrote about Alice here at Christ Church.	所以他寫了有關愛麗絲在基督教堂書院裡的事。
D Absolutely.	沒錯。
S So essentially Christ Church is Wonderland.	所以基本上基督教堂書院就是仙境？
D Yeah, I suppose you could say that.	沒錯，我想妳可以這麼說。
S That's pretty amazing.	真是令人驚訝！
D Let me show you some more.	我帶妳去看更多東西。

Vocabulary 🔊

18. **absolutely** [ˈæbsəˌlutlɪ] *adv.* （用於強調）
確實地；完全地

19. **enchanting** [ɪnˈtʃæntɪŋ] *adj.* 迷人的

A POEM WITH A HIDDEN ALICE
藏頭詩裡藏著愛麗絲

　　路易斯‧卡羅寫過一首詩，在這首詩裡，將每一句的第一個英文字母拿出來，便可以拼成愛麗絲‧里德（**Alice Pleasance Liddell**），你發現了嗎？

A boat, beneath a sunny sky	晴空下的小船
Lingering onward dreamily	如夢似幻地漂啊漂
In an evening of July	在七月的夜裡
Children three that nestle near,	三個孩子靠在身旁
Eager eye and willing ear,	眼神充滿期待，豎直了耳朵
Pleased a simple tale to hear.	等著要聽故事
Long has (had) paled that sunny sky,	那時的晴空已是多年前的往事
Echoes fade and memories die;	只剩模糊的迴聲與記憶
Autumn frosts have slain July,	秋霜終結了七月的夏日
Still she haunts me, phantomwise,	但是我一直記著她
Alice moving under skies	愛麗絲在天邊翱翔
Never seen by waking eyes.	沒有人看得見
Children yet, the tale to hear,	孩子們等著聽故事
Eager eye and willing ear,	眼神充滿期待，豎直了耳朵
Lovingly shall nestle near.	靠在身旁，模樣惹人憐愛
In a Wonderland they lie,	她們躺在仙境裡
Dreaming as the days go by,	在夢中一天一天過去
Dreaming as the summers die:	在夢中夏天漸漸結束
Ever drifting down the stream	就順著河水而去
Lingering in the golden gleam	只留下金色的斜陽
Life, what is it but a dream?	人生不就是一場夢？

對
話

S : *Samantha Brown, Hostess*   **T** : *Tony Fox, the Head Custodian*

S I'll admit, I was still sort of **skeptical**[20] about this "Alice is real" idea. So David called in an **expert**.[21]	我承認，我對愛麗絲是否真有其人還是有些懷疑，所以大衛找來了一位專家。
T Now we're coming into a very **private**[22] garden.	現在我們要進入一座非常隱密的花園。
S This is Tony Fox, the Head Custodian. His job **used to** be referred to as "**bulldog**,"[23] because they would **police**[24] the students. Now they are here to make sure that visitors **know their way around**.	他是東尼‧福斯，這裡的守衛長，過去是稱作「惡犬」，因為他們的職責是管理監督學生。現在他們的任務是讓遊客熟悉這裡的一切。
T This is the **forbidden**[25] garden in the *Alice in Wonderland* stories.	這就是《愛麗絲夢遊仙境》故事裡那座禁止進入的花園。
S This one right here is.	就是這一座。
T Yes.	沒錯！
S Oh, it's wonderful.	真是太棒了。
T Yes. If you look to your left, there's a little green door . . .	沒錯！如果妳往左邊看，那裡有一扇小綠門。
S Uh-hum.	嗯嗯。
T . . . and that was where you all see a picture of Alice looking through a **keyhole**.[26]	在故事中愛麗絲就是從那扇門的鑰匙孔看出去的。

學習重點 📖

乘哈利魔梯到愛麗絲兔子洞

used to　過去常常做⋯⋯

used to 用來表示過去的習慣或經驗，而現在已戒除。要注意的是 used to 中的 to 是不定詞，後面需要接動詞原形。

- George used to work in our office.
  喬治以前在我們的辦公室上班。

- I used to live in Tainan, but I moved to Taipei two years ago.
  我以前住台南，但在兩年前搬到了台北。

know one's way around　對⋯⋯完全熟悉、通曉

此動詞片語之後通常接地方或事情，如某個主題、系統、工作等，表示「對⋯⋯非常熟悉；擅長使用或操作⋯⋯」。

- Mike is new to the city, so he doesn't know his way around yet.
  麥克剛到這個城市，所以他對這裡還不是很熟悉。

Vocabulary 📖

20. **skeptical** [ˈskɛptɪkəl] *adj.* 懷疑的

21. **expert** [ˈɛkspɚt] *n.* 專家

22. **private** [ˈpraɪvɪt] *adj.* 私人的

23. **bulldog** [ˈbʊlˌdɔg] *n.* 鬥牛犬

24. **police** [pəˈlis] *v.* 維持治安；管理監督、守衛

25. **forbidden** [fɚˈbɪdn̩] *adj.* 禁止進入的、謝絕參觀的；禁止的

26. **keyhole** [ˈkiˌhol] *n.* 鑰匙孔

對話

S : *Samantha Brown, Hostess*　　**T** : *Tony Fox, the Head Custodian*

D : *David Womersley, Oxford Graduate*

S	And that's the door.	就是那扇門。
T	That is the door. Yes. Now, the **horse chestnut**²⁷ tree is where the Cheshire Cat used to sit all day smiling.	沒錯，就是那扇門。那棵七葉樹就是柴郡貓以前整天坐在那裡微笑的地方。
S	Was there a real cat?	那隻貓也是真的嗎？
T	Yes, there was.	沒錯，是真的。
S	Wow.	哇！
T	Yes, it was Alice's cat.	那是愛麗絲的貓咪。
S	*Alice in Wonderland* isn't the only work of **fiction**²⁸ which was inspired by Christ Church.	《愛麗絲夢遊仙境》並不是唯一一靈感來自基督教堂書院的小說。
D	So this is the main entrance to the hall here at Christ Church. I **mentioned**²⁹ to you that every college has got a hall. A **canteen**³⁰ essentially. But, you perhaps maybe recognize it more from the entrance scene from *Harry Potter*. Do you remember that they all come up here?	這裡就是基督教堂書院餐廳的主要入口。我說過每個學校學院都有自己的餐廳，基本上是供應食物和飲料的商店。但這裡或許是會讓你想起《哈利波特》裡進場的那一幕。你記得嗎？他們全走上這裡……
S	Oh. Oh right.	喔，對。
D	They're met by the professor.	他們在上頭這裡遇到了教授。
S	McGonagall.	麥教授。

卡羅的仙境—「瘋狂」才是唯一的秩序

摘錄自第六章 PIG AND PEPPER

乘哈利魔梯到愛麗絲兔子洞

"But I don't want to go among mad people," Alice remarked.

"Oh, you can't help that," said the Cat: "we're all mad here. I'm mad. You're mad."

"How do you know I'm mad?" said Alice.

"You must be," said the Cat, "or you wouldn't have come here."

愛麗絲在仙境中遇到了柴郡貓（Cheshire Cat），牠對愛麗絲說：這裡每個人都是瘋子，可見愛麗絲也是瘋子。不同的環境有不同的體制，在仙境裡，「瘋狂」便是唯一的秩序，每個人都必須接受仙境的遊戲規則才能生存。

* 文中的 mad 音近 made，其實是作者運用的文字遊戲，可見在這個仙境裡，一切都是虛構的（made），愛麗絲這個角色也是虛構的。

Vocabulary

27. **horse chestnut** [hɔrs] [ˈtʃɛsˏnʌt] *n.* 七葉樹

28. **fiction** [ˈfɪkʃən] *n.* 小說

29. **mention** [ˈmɛnʃən] *v.* 說到；提及

30. **canteen** [kænˋtin] *n.* （工廠、學校等供應食物和飲料的）食堂、商店

對
話

S : *Samantha Brown, Hostess*　　**D** : *David Womersley, Oxford Graduate*

D McGonagall here at the top.	麥教授在上頭。
S Right. First day of school at Hogwarts.	對。他們在霍格華茲的第一天。
D First day of school, and they're let in here.	開學的第一天,他們就進去那裡。
S Oh wow.	哇!
D Come through here.	跟我來吧!
S The **staircase**[31] then leads to the great hall at Hogwarts. Now, the movie wasn't filmed here, but this **cavernous**[32] room was used as its main inspiration. This has caused the average age of a visitor to Christ Church to drop from **roughly**[33] forty-five to about eleven.	這座樓梯通往霍格華茲的大廳。這大廳並非是電影真正的拍攝地,但卻是電影場景的主要靈感來源,導致來到基督教堂書院的遊客,平均年齡從四十五歲掉到十一歲。
D Odd[34] to think that it's students that eat in here.	想像學生在這裡用餐真是奇特。
S It really . . . this . . . this is your dining hall.	這真的是你們的餐廳。
D Yeah, and **as a rule** you try to seat yourself gentleman lady gentleman lady.	沒錯,而且規定要男女交錯而坐。
S Oh, how **social**.[35]	可以聯誼一下。

學習重點

Odd to think that it's students that eat in here.
想像學生在這裡用餐真是奇特。

本句前面省略了 It is，it 是虛主詞來代替真正的主詞 to think that it's . . . in here。此外，主詞中還用到了分裂句：

> 用法 **it is/was + 強調部分 + that + 剩餘部分**

分裂句又稱為強調句，用來強調敘述句中的主詞、受詞、時間副詞或地方副詞等。本句強調主詞 students，其原句可平鋪直述寫為：Odd to think that students eat in here。

- The actor got his first film role in New York City over ten years ago.
  這名男演員十多年前在紐約得到他的第一個電影角色。
  ↳ It was <u>the actor</u> that/who got his first film role in New York City over ten years ago.（強調主詞）
  ↳ It was <u>his first film role</u> that the actor got in New York City over ten years ago.（強調受詞）

as a rule 通常；一般來說

as a rule 為副詞片語，表示「通常；一般而言」。

- As a rule, I don't drive over the speed limit.
  我通車開車不會超速。

Vocabulary

31. **staircase** [ˋstɛrˌkes] *n.* （大樓內的）樓梯

32. **cavernous** [ˋkævənəs] *adj.* 寬敞的；大的

33. **roughly** [ˋrʌflɪ] *adv.* 大約；粗略地

34. **odd** [ɑd] *adj.* 奇特的；奇怪的

35. **social** [ˋsoʃəl] *adj.* 社交的；交際的

對話

S : *Samantha Brown, Hostess*　　**D** : *David Womersley, Oxford Graduate*

D Just for, yeah, for the conversation of the whole thing.

就只是方便大家聊天。

S Very nice.

這樣很好。

D Rather than the **clump**[36] of guys.

不是一群男生聚在一起。

S Right, right.

沒錯。

D You would be served by **livery**[37] waiters.

這裡的服務生還會穿制服。

S Really?

真的？

D Yeah, the menu was always very, very good indeed. Very un-student food.

沒錯，一直以來菜單也都非常棒，一點也不像是學生的餐點。

S You had a menu. So you're presented a menu.

你們還有菜單，所以會按照菜單點菜囉。

D Yeah, you would eat things like, depending on what night of the week it was, **pheasant**[38] or wild **boar**.[39] Very un-student type food, actually.

沒錯，視當天是星期幾而定。有時候會吃野雞肉或野豬肉，真的不像是學生的餐點。

S No chicken-fried steak.

沒有炸雞排？

D No, no, no, no, no.

沒有，沒有。

S That's what I lived on in college.

那是我在大學時常吃的。

D Absolutely not.

沒有這種東西。

S You're **missing out on** a lot.

你錯過了很多東西。

學習重點

miss out on N./V-ing　錯過（機會）

miss out (on N./V-ing) 表示「錯失……」的意思，受詞通常為機會或對自己有利的事情。

- Alice arrived late, so she missed out on meeting the famous writer.
  愛麗絲晚到，所以她錯過與那個知名作家碰面的機會。

- Don't miss out on that store's big sale!
  不要錯過那家店的大特價！

【延伸學習】

miss out　遺漏；未將……包括在內

在英式英語中，miss out 亦可表示「遺漏」，與 omit 意思相同。

- Your presentation was interesting, but you missed out some important details.
  你的簡報很有趣，但遺漏了一些重要的細節。

Vocabulary

36. **clump** [klʌmp] *n.*（人）群、組；（電線、頭髮等）團

37. **livery** [ˈlɪvəri] *n.*（侍者、侍從的）制服

38. **pheasant** [ˈfɛznt] *n.* 野雞（肉）；雉（肉）

39. **boar** [bɔr] *n.* 野豬

對
話

S : *Samantha Brown, Hostess*　　**D** : *David Womersley, Oxford Graduate*

D And what is interesting about Christ Church is they're probably the largest wine **importer**[40] in the UK.

基督教堂書院有趣的是它大概是英國最大的酒類進口商。

S A **bunch of** nineteen-year-olds are drinking some nice Châteauneuf-du-Pape, are they? That just seems strange. I mean really, did you really **deserve**[41] that?

一群十九歲的小伙子竟然喝上等的法國名酒？真是太奇怪了！你們真的應該得到那種待遇嗎？

D Well, I don't know whether we deserved it or not, but they have a **superb**[42] wine list, and we always used to get it **subsidized**,[43] of course, for students. So you could eat great food in here. And you . . . I think you really do feel a part of the history in here.

我不知道是否應得，但它們有很棒的酒單，而且學生以前可享有很多津貼，所以你可以在這裡享受美食，同時也可以感受到這裡的歷史悠久。

S Oh, absolutely.

沒錯！

D Really wonderful. And do you remember the rabbit hole, the **bolt-hole**?[44]

真的很棒！妳還記得那個兔子洞嗎？兔子逃脫用的穴路？

S Uh huh. I'm late, I'm late.

我遲到了，我來不及了。

乘哈利魔梯到愛麗絲兔子洞

學習重點

a bunch of 一群；一堆

bunch 通常是用來形容一些性質相同的東西，a bunch of 通常後面接可數名詞。像是 a bunch of grapes（一串葡萄）、a bunch of flowers（一束花）。也可用來指人，表示「一群、一夥」，a bunch of friends（一群朋友）。

- A bunch of friends came to visit.
  一群朋友來看我。

以下列舉一些其他單位詞用法：

▶ a pile of books 一疊書

▶ a flock of birds 一群鳥

▶ a gang of laborers 一組工人

▶ a school of fish 一群魚

▶ a jar of jam 一瓶果醬

▶ a can of soda 一瓶汽水

▶ a package of crackers 一包薄脆餅乾

Vocabulary

40. **importer** [ɪmˋpɔrtɚ] *n.* 進口商

41. **deserve** [dɪˋzɝv] *v.* 應得；值得

42. **superb** [suˋpɝb] *adj.* 超棒的；極佳的

43. **subsidize** [ˋsʌbsəˏdaɪz] *v.* 資助；發津貼

44. **bolt-hole** [ˋboltˏhol] *n.* 躲避藏身處

對話

S : *Samantha Brown, hostess*　　**D** : *David Womersley, Oxford Graduate*

D That's right. That's right. Just here in the corner, that's the door the Dean and the **fellows**[45] would enter through.	沒錯！就在那個角落，那是院長和教職員專用的門。
S The rabbit was Alice's father in real life, the Dean.	原來在真實世界中兔子就是愛麗絲的院長父親。
D That's right, yeah.	沒錯！
S Oh that's wonderful.	真棒！
D Do you want to go down it?	妳想下去看看嗎？
S Yeah.	好啊！
D Come on, then.	那走吧！
S Oh, this is great.	哇！好棒！
D It's all the way down.	一直往下走。
S Curiouser and curiouser.	好棒，越來越古怪了。
D Curiouser and curiouser.	越來越古怪了。

Vocabulary

45. **fellow** [ˋfɛlo] *n.* 同事；夥伴

PHRASES FROM WONDERLAND
兔子洞與柴郡貓

在童話故事《愛麗絲夢遊仙境》中有些說法至今仍常被引用，列舉如下：

rabbit hole　進入奇特的情況或混亂的狀態

rabbit hole 原指兔子洞，引申為進入一奇特、難理解的情境或狀態當中，down the rabbit hole 表示「通往未知的探險旅程」。

- You're not making any sense, Sandy. You need to climb back out of the rabbit hole.
  珊蒂，妳說的一點都不合理。妳必須清醒點。

- Watching that bizarre movie was like taking a trip down the rabbit hole.
  看那部古怪的電影就像是進行一趟未知的旅程。

grin like a Cheshire Cat　咧嘴傻笑

grin可當動詞或名詞，意思是「露齒笑」。Cheshire Cat 是愛麗絲故事中的那隻露齒嘻笑的柴郡貓。後來此說法便用來表示「咧嘴傻笑；無緣無故傻笑」的意思。

- When he heard that he was getting promoted, Timothy started grinning like a Cheshire Cat.
  當提摩西聽見升職的消息時，便一直傻笑著。

- He had a grin like a Cheshire Cat when he came to work today, so he must have had a great night.
  他今天進公司的時候一直傻笑，昨晚一定是有什麼好事發生了。

《愛麗絲夢遊仙境》剛出版時評價不佳，卻因天馬行空的故事情節而漸漸受歡迎，成為極具影響力的童話故事。許多電影或戲劇作品也取材自此。最著名的有：愛麗絲夢遊仙境（迪士尼動畫）以及魔境夢遊（提姆波頓導演之電影作品），兩部發行的年份相差了六十年，但仍為人們一看再看的好作品。

Punting through the Looking-Glass
在牛津，划過鏡中奇遇

🎧 影片原音 04 　　🎧 課文朗讀 28

自述

 I'm in Oxford, England, the city of dreaming **spires**.¹ This is a city, yes, but a very **manageable** and **walkable** one. If you're driving here, you do not want to drive in and find parking in the city center. You want to **take advantage of** their **park-and-ride**² system. Park outside the city, and take public transportation in. The transportation is **frequent**,³ and there's no **hassle**.⁴

And because we are in **merry**⁵ old England, you do want to remember that they do drive on the opposite side of the road as us. So when you're walking and you want to cross the street, look both ways before you cross, because if you just **dart**⁶ out, you will be hit by a car or a bus.

我置身於英國號稱夢幻尖塔之城的牛津。沒錯，這是一個非常易於駕馭和適合步行的城市。如果你開車的話，你不會想要開進市中心找停車位的。你會想利用這裡的停車轉乘系統，把車停在市區外，然後搭大眾交通工具進市區，往返班次頻繁便利，一點也不麻煩。

因為我們現處可愛傳統的英格蘭（編注：merry old England是昔日對英國或其傳統的稱呼），在這裡開車的方向跟我們相反。所以當你過馬路時，記得兩邊都要觀看，因為如果你隨便衝出去，很可能會被汽車或公車撞上。

學習重點 🛄

-able 可以……的；能……的；值得……的

-able 作字尾時表示「可以……的；能……的」，接在動詞之後構成形容詞。其他 able 作字尾的字有：

forget + able = forgettable 容易遺忘的

walk + able = walkable 適合走路的

manage + able = manageable 容易掌控或處理的

question + able = questionable 可疑的；不可靠的

knowledge + able = knowledgeable 博學的

take advantage of 利用

名詞 advantage 指「優勢；有利條件」。後面接的受詞不同而有不同意思。受詞為人時，指「占某人便宜；利用某人」；受詞為物時，指「善用某事物；趁某機會」。

- Sometimes Chuck feels like his friends take advantage of him.
  有時候查克覺得他朋友占他便宜。

- I took advantage of my days off work and went on a camping trip.
  我趁我工作休假時去露了一趟營。

Vocabulary 🛄

1. **spire** [spaɪr] *n.* （建築物如教堂頂端的）尖塔；尖頂

2. **park-and-ride** [ˋpɑrkəndˋraɪd] *n.* 停泊及轉乘（即指可供停放車輛再轉乘其他交通工具）

3. **frequent** [ˋfrikwənt] *adj.* 頻繁的

4. **hassle** [ˋhæsl̩] *n.* 困難；麻煩

5. **merry** [ˋmɛri] *adj.* 歡樂的；愉快的

6. **dart** [dɑrt] *v.* 狂奔；猛衝

在牛津，划過鏡中奇遇

自述

 I'm still trying to get my head around that fact that Alice in *Alice in Wonderland* was a real girl and that the book is based on stories of what she saw right here at Oxford. In real life, Alice visited **regularly**[7] a shop to buy her **sweets**.[8] And that shop is still here.

It's now called Alice's Shop, a **tiny**[9] wonderland-like store selling all things Alice. Now, this shop is actually in *Through the Looking-Glass*. Let me show you; maybe you'll recognize the **illustration**.[10] Find it here. Yeah, here it is. See, there's Alice buying her **barley**[11] sweets from a sheep, and that's because the old woman at the time who worked here, her voice sounded like a sheep. So Lewis Carroll **turned her into that animal**.

我仍努力要去了解《愛麗絲夢遊仙境》的主角真有其人,而故事的靈感正是來自她在牛津的所見所聞。在真實的世界中,愛麗絲常常光顧一間糖果店。而這間糖果店至今還存在著。

這間店叫做愛麗絲之店。這間像仙境一樣的小商店,販售各種跟愛麗絲相關的商品。這間店曾出現在《鏡中奇遇》的故事中。讓我翻給大家看看,或許你會認得這張插圖就是在這裡,找到了,沒錯就是這裡,瞧,故事中的愛麗絲向一隻羊買了一些麥芽糖,那是因為當時在這裡工作的婦人,聲音很像綿羊。所以路易斯・卡羅把她變成了一隻綿羊。

旅遊小幫手　　　　　　　　　　　　　　　圖片來源：Wikipedia / Andrew Roberts

Alice's Shop　愛麗絲之店

《鏡中奇遇》故事中,愛麗絲購買糖果的那間店。

🕐 Monday–Sunday: 10:30 a.m.–5:00 p.m.
　　July and August: 9:30 a.m.–6:30 p.m.

📞 (44) 01865 723793

🌐 http://www.aliceinwonderlandshop.co.uk

學習重點

get one's head round　瞭解；明白

get one's head around sth 指「能夠理解、明白（某事）」，否定 can't get one's head around sth 則表示「一頭霧水」。

- I still can't get my head around this difficult math problem.
  我還是不瞭解這道困難的數學題。

turn . . . into . . . 將……變成……

用法一 **turn sb/sth into . . .**　　將某人或某事物變成……

- Jillian turned her apartment into a shelter for stray animals.
  Jillian 把她的公寓變成了流浪動物之家。

用法二 **sb/sth turn into . . .**　　某人事物變成……

- The ugly duckling turned into a beautiful swan.
  那隻醜小鴨變成了美麗的天鵝。

Vocabulary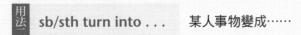

7. **regularly** [ˋrɛgjələli] *adv.* 經常地

8. **sweet** [swit] *n.* 糖果（作此義為英式英語，多用複數形，美語用candy）；甜食

9. **tiny** [ˋtaɪni] *adj.* 很小的

10. **illustration** [ˌɪləsˋtreʃən] *n.* 插圖

11. **barley** [ˋbɑrli] *n.* 大麥

自述

Also, the shop **constantly**[12] **flooded**,[13] so there is Alice **rowing**[14] about in a boat. The illustrations for me, what made this book so special, one John Tenniel. And Lewis Carroll actually wanted to do his own illustrations, but they weren't that good, so he got this man to do it, and they were **exceptional**.[15] But he did give . . . Lewis Carroll did give special instructions to the **publisher**.[16] And one of them was that Alice's neck was to grow **specifically**[17] five and one eighth inches. Also, with the Cheshire Cat (remember his big grin?), well, that . . . the grin was to be a full ten lines of the page, so a very **exact**[18] man— **obviously**[19] a **mathematician**.[20]

還有因為那間店常常淹水，所以愛麗絲才會划船。這本書因插畫變得很特別，是出自約翰·田尼爾之手。原本路易斯·卡羅想親自畫插畫，但效果不佳，所以就請了這個人來畫，結果非常出色。但路易斯·卡羅確實有特別吩咐出版商。其中一點就是愛麗絲的脖子長度必須為五又八分之一吋。還有那隻柴郡貓（記得它那露齒的笑容吧？）關於嘴巴的寬度必須佔據十行的空間，他是一個要求精準的人，顯然就是一個數學家。

SMILING AND LAUGHTER
笑聲哈哈音量表

文中提到的 Cheshire Cat 總是咧嘴而笑（grin），而英文中用來表示「笑」的說法有好幾種，依笑聲大小圖示如下：

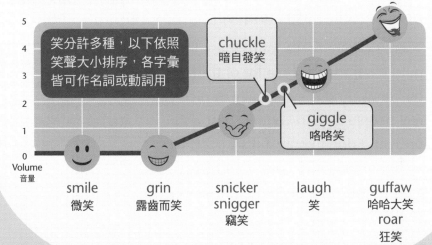

笑分許多種，以下依照笑聲大小排序，各字彙皆可作名詞或動詞用

| | | chuckle 暗自發笑 | | |
| | | | giggle 咯咯笑 | |

Volume 音量

| smile 微笑 | grin 露齒而笑 | snicker snigger 竊笑 | laugh 笑 | guffaw 哈哈大笑 roar 狂笑 |

Vocabulary

12. **constantly** [ˋkɑnstəntli] *adv.* 經常地

13. **flood** [flʌd] *v.* 淹沒

14. **row** [ro] *v.* 划船

15. **exceptional** [ɪkˋsɛpʃən!] *adj.* 優秀的；出色的

16. **publisher** [ˋpʌblɪʃɚ] *n.* 出版社（或機構）；出版商

17. **specifically** [spɪˋsɪfɪkḷi] *adv.* 確切地；準確地

18. **exact** [ɪgˋzækt] *adj.* 精準的；精確的

19. **obviously** [ˋɑbvɪəsli] *adv.* 顯然地

20. **mathematician** [͵mæθməˋtɪʃən] *n.* 數學家

自
述

While walking in Oxford, you want to look up because the view is absolutely **grotesque**.[21]

在牛津散步時，你要往上觀看，因為上面的景觀非常奇特。

~~There's~~ [There are] a lot of these little guys here; they're on a lot of the buildings. And they actually **depict**[22] real people here in Oxford, past and present. I don't know if it's a . . . if it's an honor or not to have your face as a grotesque on a building, but who knows.

在建築物上面可以看到很多小人雕像。它們其實是牛津從古至今的代表人物。我不知道把自己的臉當做建築物上怪異的裝飾是不是一項榮耀，但誰知道呢？

Now, also while in Oxford it is said that you have to visit a pub. Really, that's like everywhere in England, so let's go.

也有人說，來到牛津就一定要走一趟酒吧。的確，就像到訪英國的其他城市一樣，那我們走吧。

Vocabulary

21. **grotesque** [gro`tɛsk] *adj.* 怪誕的；古怪的   *n.* 奇形怪狀的人；醜陋的怪人

22. **depict** [dɪ`pɪkt] *v.* 描述；描寫

牛津景點再發現 ~~
THE BRIDGE OF SIGHS 嘆息橋

牛津赫特福德橋（Hertford Bridge），亦是牛津著名的嘆息橋（The Bridge of Sighs）。牛津嘆息橋與義大利威尼斯的里亞托橋（The Rialto Bridge）外表看起來很相似。

● 義大利威尼斯里亞托橋

牛津嘆息橋此名稱來源有此一說：過去學生過橋時，想到要去參加考試，就邊走邊嘆息，嘆息橋因而得名。因為獨特的設計和名稱，這座橋也成為了牛津著名景點之一。

不只在英國，其他國家如：義大利、瑞典、德國、秘魯也都有「嘆息橋」，美國更是有五座「嘆息橋」。英國除了牛津之外，劍橋大學裡也有一座嘆息橋。不同的是牛津大學的嘆息橋是在陸地上，而劍橋大學的則是在河上。

劍橋大學嘆息橋

義大利嘆息橋

位於義大利威尼斯聖馬可廣場（St. Mark's Square）附近，是在一六〇二年由石灰岩打造的密閉式拱橋。該橋連接法院和監獄，過去囚犯在入監或行刑前必經此處，透過小小的窗戶可看見威尼斯最後一眼，因而發出嘆息。十九世紀英國浪漫主義詩人拜倫勛爵（Lord Byron）寫了一首關於嘆息橋的詩，此橋因此出名。根據傳說，如果情侶在日落時乘船行經橋下之際接吻的話，他們的愛情就會長長久久。

對話

S : *Samantha Brown, Hostess*　　**A** : *Alex Luscomb, Oxford Student*

S The pub I'm visiting, The Bear, has been **in operation**[23] since the eleventh century. And I'm meeting a student here who's **considerably**[24] younger than that. His name is Alex Luscomb.

我來的這間熊酒吧,從十一世紀起就開始營業了。我在這裡遇見了一位學生,他的年紀肯定沒那麼大,他叫做艾力克斯‧路斯康。

So this is the oldest pub here in Oxford?

所以,這裡是牛津最古老的酒吧。

A Yep.

沒錯。

S 1242.

一二四二年就開始了。

A Yeah, older than the eldest college, which was built in 1249.

比建於一二四九年、最古老的學院還要久遠。

S And this one has a lot of ties.

這裡有很多領帶。

A Yes.

沒錯。

S It seems to **distinguish**[25] it from the rest of the pubs here in Oxford.

這項傳統似乎是使它有別於牛津的其他酒吧。

A Oh, yeah. It was a tradition started that when the graduates finally finished their last exam at the university, the pub here would take that tie and **attach**[26] it to the wall. Sort of as a **reminder**[27] of the history here.

喔,沒錯。這是開創的傳統,當大學畢業生考完最後的考試後,這間酒吧就會拿走學生的領帶掛在牆上,多少有種記載著歷史的意味。

暢談英國飲酒文化
BUYING ROUNDS

　　在英國，酒扮演很重要的角色，到處都有酒吧，甚至連英國大學裡亦廣設酒吧。多數酒吧沒有服務員，客人必須自己去吧台買酒。英國人都會空腹喝酒，和台灣喝酒時要邊吃東西的習慣很不同。另外，在英國有一種「買酒文化」（buying rounds），幾個人一起喝酒時，會輪流買酒請客，我先買一輪請你，你再買一輪請我，晚到的人也要買一輪請大家喝，即使你不喝酒，或是你只喝一點點酒，皆要加入買酒分享的行列。通常，當對方杯子裏的酒剩下四分之一時，就是提出買酒的最佳時機。最特別的是英國酒吧十一點就停止賣酒，而在接近十一點時，酒保經常會通知酒客最後一次點酒（last orders）的時間，因此到晚上十一點，大家都喝醉了。然而對英國人來說，每天下班到酒吧喝酒，是最快樂、輕鬆的時光。

Vocabulary

23. **in operation** [ɪn] [ˌɑpəˋreʃən] *phr.* 營運；運作、運轉

24. **considerably** [kənˋsɪdərəbli] *adv.* 非常多地

25. **distinguish** [dɪˋstɪŋgwɪʃ] *v.* 區別；使有別於……

26. **attach** [əˋtætʃ] *v.* 附上；貼上

27. **reminder** [rɪˋmaɪndə] *n.* 使人回憶起某事的事物

對話

S : *Samantha Brown, Hostess*　　**A** : *Alex Luscomb, Oxford Student*

S I've seen that they're sort of cut off, aren't they? They weren't taken off; they've just kind of snapped behind them and . . . with the scissors.	我曾看過有被剪斷的領帶，對不對？那些領帶並不是被取下的，而是用剪刀從背後強行剪斷的。
A I think that was probably from when the students had had enough to drink, that they wouldn't notice that their tie was missing; they woke up after been snapped off.	我想那可能是因為學生們喝多了，所以當他們醒來，完全沒發現到領帶被剪斷不見了。
S Now, if you are in a pub in Oxford, is there sort of, I don't know, **pressure**²⁸ to have very **philosophical**²⁹ conversations?	現在，如果你在牛津的酒吧，不知道是不是會有壓力要談些很哲學的內容之類的？
A No.	不會。
S Do we have to **debate**³⁰ or can we just like **celebrity**³¹ **gossip**?³²	那會要辯論一番或者是會聊一些名人八卦嗎？

Vocabulary

28. **pressure** [ˈprɛʃə] *n.* 壓力
29. **philosophical** [ˌfɪləˈsɑfɪkəl] *adj.* 哲學的
30. **debate** [dɪˈbet] *v.* 辯論
31. **celebrity** [səˈlɛbrəti] *n.* 名人；明星
32. **gossip** [ˈgɑsəp] *n.* 流言蜚語；八卦、閒話

back 非酒精類的飲料

- I would like a shot of whiskey with a Coke back.

  我想要點一杯威士忌加一杯可樂。

straight 不加任何冰塊或其他飲料的酒

- I would like a bourbon straight, please.

  我想要一杯不加冰塊的美國威士忌酒，謝謝。

double 雙份的調酒或酒精濃度

- I would like a whiskey double, please.

  我想要一杯雙份的威士忌酒，謝謝。

on the rocks （酒）加冰塊

- Could I have a double whiskey on the rocks, please?

  麻煩給我兩份威士忌加冰塊？

neat 純的、不稀釋的（酒）

- Could I have that 15-year-old Scotch neat, please?

  麻煩給我那個十五年份純的蘇格蘭威士忌？

對話

S : Samantha Brown, Hostess　　**A** : Alex Luscomb, Oxford Student

A You can do whatever you want. I mean, you can sit in the pub and then just have a nice conversation; it's what it's for, it's a meeting place. It's a place where people get together and they have a drink and they can sit on their own and read a book. Quite often if you come into a pub in Oxford, you'll see a student sitting there with a pint in one hand and a book in the other, sitting down, enjoying their reading.

妳想做什麼都行。我的意思是，妳可以坐在酒吧裡，盡情跟人聊天，把它當作是一個聚會的場所。就是一個大家聚在一起喝東西、或獨自坐在那裡看書的地方。在牛津可以常常看到學生一手拿書，另一手拿著啤酒，坐在那在享受閱讀。

S Yeah, I **gathered**[33] that. It is always a very relaxing and enjoyable place to be. So **on that note**, why don't we . . . why don't we eat? I'm **starving**.[34]

沒錯，我想也是。這一直都是一個令人輕鬆愉快的地方。那我們現在趕緊吃東西吧，我好餓。

A Sounds good to me.

好啊。

S A long **established**[35] way to spend a lazy afternoon in Oxford is to enjoy a slow, **languid**[36] ride on a punt. A punt is a **shallow**,[37] long boat **propelled**[38] by a long **pole**.[39] Alex and David joined me on my punt ride accompanied by their friend Jane. So this is all we do then, just drink and **sit back and relax**.

想在牛津慵懶地度過下午時光，有一個廣受採用的方法，就是坐平底船享受緩慢慵懶的乘船之旅。平底船是一種長形的淺舟，利用長竿撐船前進。艾力克斯和大衛陪我一起坐平底船，同行的還有他們的朋友珍。所以在船上只需要好好的享用飲料、放鬆地享受旅程即可。

學習重點

on that note 關於；說到

on that note 是個轉折詞，用來強調或讓對方注意到剛提到的話題，意思類似於「關於、說到……」，並沒有其他的意思。

- And on that note, I need to get up early in the morning, so I am going to bed now.
  說到這，我早上得早起，所以現在要去睡了。

sit back and relax 放輕鬆

sit back 通常用來指某事發生時，不介入、一派放輕鬆的樣子。常會在之後接 and . . . 來表示，常見的用法有：

▶ sit back and relax 放輕鬆

▶ sit back and enjoy the ride 放輕鬆好好享受

▶ sit back and wait 坐著等

- The dentist told the patient to sit back and relax.
  那名牙醫要病人坐著、放輕鬆就好。

- You just sit back and enjoy the ride.
  妳只要放輕鬆好好享受就好了。

Vocabulary

33. **gather** [ˈgæðɚ] v. 理解；認為；猜想

34. **starve** [stɑrv] v. 挨餓

35. **established** [ɪˈstæblɪʃt] adj. 已被接受的；已被認可的

36. **languid** [ˈlæŋgwəd] adj. 懶洋洋的；無精打采

37. **shallow** [ˈʃælo] adj. 淺的

38. **propel** [prəˈpɛl] v. 推動；推進（常用被動語態）

39. **pole** [pol] n. 竹竿；篙

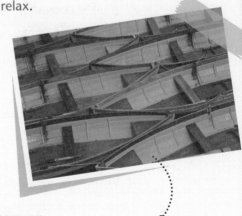

用篙撐行的平底長船

對話

S : Samantha Brown, Hostess　　**A** : Alex Luscomb, Oxford Student

D : David Womersley, Oxford Graduate

A Yup.	沒錯。
D Just taking your time. No rush. Where are you going? You know the . . . the reason why you do this whole sport is . . .	慢慢來，不用急。妳要去哪裡？你知道你從事這項運動的原因就是……
S Oh, it's a sport, is it?	喔，這算是運動的一種嗎？
D It is a sport. I tell you, it's very . . . it's quite tiring if you are the **punter**.[40]	當然算是。我告訴你，當船夫是件挺累人的事情。
S And it is a . . . is it a . . . it seems like a very romantic thing, **company**[41] **excluded**.[42] David, have you . . . have you taken many women out punting?	如果不是一大堆人一起坐的話，這似乎是很浪漫的事情。大衛，你有帶很多女生出來坐平底船嗎？
D Yeah, I have taken a number out. I mean when I was a student here, it was very much . . . not just women. You'd go as a whole **gang**,[43] and you'd totally **overload** these things with three back here and five of you in the middle, and you'd just **inevitably**[44] go with some beers, say, or **champagne**.[45]	有，曾經帶不少人過。學生時代曾經跟很多人一起坐過平底船，不只是女生，有時候是跟一群朋友出遊，完全超出這艘船的負荷了，三個在後面這裡，五個在中間，以及一定還會來點啤酒或香檳。

學習重點

> **overload** 使負荷過重；使超載

字首 over- 表示「過度；超過」的意思，常見的字如下：

over + **load** = **overload** 超過負荷；超載

over + **weight** = **overweight** 超重的

over + **fish** = **overfish** 過度捕撈

over + **react** = **overreact** 過度反應

over + **time** = **overtime** 超時工作；加班

over + **heat** = **overheat** 過熱

- Be realistic; don't overload yourself.
  認清現實、別超出負荷。

牛津大學奧里爾學院女子
八人划船競賽照片

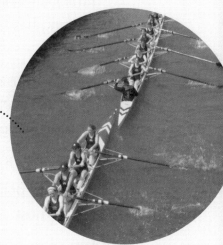

圖片來源：Wikipedia / Tri6ky

Vocabulary

40. **punter** [`pʌntə] *n.* 撐平底船的人；船夫
    （punt [pʌnt] 可作動詞，表示「用篙撐平底船」）

41. **company** [`kʌmpəni] *n.* 一群人；同伴

42. **exclude** [ɪks`klud] *v.* 將……排除在外；不包括……

43. **gang** [gæŋ] *n.* （口）一群朋友

44. **inevitably** [ɪ`nɛvətəbli] *adv.* 無可避免地；必然地

45. **champagne** [ʃæm`pen] *n.* 香檳酒

對話

S : *Samantha Brown, Hostess*　　**A** : *Alex Luscomb, Oxford Student*

D : *David Womersley, Oxford Graduate*　　**J** : *Jane, Oxford Student*

S	And, Alex, you were saying that you fall into the river a lot actually.	艾力克斯，你是說你其實常常掉進河裡。
A	Yes.	沒錯。
S	It's actually quite **common**.	這是常有的事。
A	Yeah, well it's not very deep, so falling in is **no real big thing**. But I think anybody who has been punting has fallen in at least once or twice.	其實水並不深，所以掉下去沒什麼大不了。我想每個坐過平底船的人至少都會有一兩次落船的經驗吧。
D	Yeah, because it's just if you **place**[46] the pole wrongly, you can just find yourself being . . .	沒錯，因為只要竿子的位置放錯，你的身體就會……
S	Being **dragged**[47] by it.	被拉下去。
D	. . . being pulled off the boat by the pole almost.	竿子快要把船打翻。
S	Jane, have you fallen in?	珍，妳有掉下去過嗎？
J	I've fallen and I've jumped.	我掉過還有跳下去。
S	And jumped?	妳跳下去？
J	Yes.	沒錯。

學習重點

---

common　常見的；普遍的

用法　it's common (for sb) to V.

此句型表示（某人）做某事是很常見、稀鬆平常的。

- It's common to see **pigeons** in the streets of New York.
  在紐約街頭看到鴿子是稀鬆平常的事。

- It's common for kids to feel **nervous** on the first day of school.
  開學第一天對孩子們來說感到緊張是常有的事。

---

no real big thing　沒什麼大不了

從字面上即可了解是指「這不是什麼大事；這件事情沒什麼大不了」的意思。相同用法有 no big deal，其中 big deal 是指「特別重要的事物；了不起的人事物」，常用於否定句。no big deal 就是指「沒什麼大不了」。

- Terry thanked me for giving her a ride home from work, but it was no real big thing; I was going to drive in that direction anyway.
  泰芮謝謝我載她回家，但是對我來說只是順路，沒有什麼大不了的。

- I hope you can come to my party, but it's no big deal if you can't make it.
  我希望你能來參加我的派對，不過如果不能來也沒關係。

Vocabulary

46. **place** [ples] *v.* 放置

47. **drag** [dræg] *v.* 拉；扯；拖

對話

S : *Samantha Brown, Hostess*　　A : *Alex Luscomb, Oxford Student*
J : *Jane, Oxford Student*

A And my sister on several occasions managed to leave the pole directly behind her and **ended up** standing straight upright in the river, **clinging**[48] on the pole as we sailed off **gently**[49] down the river. She was not best pleased.	我妹妹好幾次設法要將長竿放在身後，但最後卻變成直立在水中，只好緊抓著長竿順流而下。她當時不是非常開心。
S Is there any sort of **friction**[50] between Oxford students and Oxford **civilians**?[51]	牛津的學生跟牛津的市民有沒有什麼摩擦？
J Not so much now, but there used to be a lot.	現在不多了，但以前常發生。
S There was?	以前會？
J Yes.	沒錯。
S Even in . . . you . . . you lived here?	即使……你……你家住這裡？
J Yes.	沒錯。
S Have grown up here?	在這裡土生土長？
J Yes. When I was a teenager, there was . . . there was a sided atmosphere.	是的。在我十幾歲的時候，兩方充滿著壁壘分明的氣氛。

學習重點

end up 最後；結果

end up 表示「最後以……作為結束、結局」，後面可接 N.、V-ing、p.p. 或介系詞片語。

- Hans started out poor but ended up a millionaire.
  漢斯出身貧窮但最後成為百萬富翁。

- We were supposed to go to the movies, but we ended up staying at home because of the rain.
  我們本來要去看電影的，但最後因為下雨而待在家裡。

- After hiking for miles, we ended up lost in the middle of a forest.
  我們徒步走了幾英里後，結果在一座森林中迷路了。

- I have no idea how my wallet ended up in the closet.
  我不知道我的皮夾最後怎麼會在衣櫥裡。

Vocabulary

48. **cling** [klɪŋ] *v.* 緊抓住；緊握

49. **gently** [ˋdʒɛntlɪ] *adv.* 和緩地；徐緩輕柔地

50. **friction** [ˋfrɪkʃən] *n.* 摩擦、衝突；摩擦力

51. **civilian** [səˋvɪljən] *n.* 平民；老百姓

對話

S : *Samantha Brown, Hostess*　　　**D** : *David Womersley, Oxford Graduate*
J : *Jane, Oxford Student*

D **Historically,**[52] it used to be, you came to Oxford if you were very wealthy. Your **name** would get you in. From a very **privileged**[53] background. But . . . but it's not like that anymore. I think the university very specifically tries to say we take our **intake**[54] from every ~~strata~~ [**stratum**][55] of society. With or without money. With private education, without private education. I think as Jane says, it's . . . it's calming down a lot now. I think.

Has anybody mentioned to Sam about the first-timer's **ritual?**[56]

在歷史上，如果你是有錢人，就可以進牛津念書。有權有勢有強硬的後台也可以。但此時非彼時。我想現在牛津大學試著要廣招社會各階層的人。不論貧富，不論是否讀過私校，我想就像珍說的，現在摩擦平息許多了。

有人跟珊曼莎提過我們的新生入學儀式嗎？

J You have a change of clothes, right?

妳有帶衣服來換，對吧？

D Come on, Brown, you know you're ready; you've been looking for this all day.

來吧，珊曼莎，我知道其實妳早有準備，期待此刻已久。

S I'm not going in, Womersley, I'm not going in.

沃姆斯里，我才不要下水。我才不要。

學習重點

name　名聲；聲譽

名詞 name 可以指「名聲；名人」。在文中 name 表示「有權勢的名人」，your name would get you in 則是指「你的權勢可讓你進入牛津就讀」。

【延伸學習】

make a name for oneself　出名；成名

- The reporter made a name for himself when he broke the major story.
  那位記者報導這則大新聞之後便聲名大噪。

make one's name　成名

- That actor made his name by acting silly onstage.
  那名演員以在舞台上的搞笑演出成名。

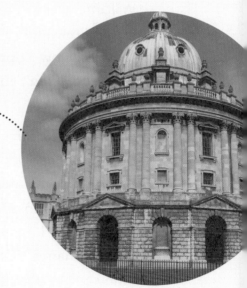

瑞得克里夫圖書館（Radcliffe Camera）為博德利圖書館（Bodleian Library）的分館，圓頂加上古典風格的義式建築，成為牛津的重要地標。

Vocabulary

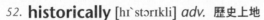

52. **historically** [hɪˋstɔrɪklɪ] *adv.*　歷史上地

53. **privileged** [ˋprɪvlɪdʒd] *adj.*　享有特權的；享受特殊待遇的

54. **intake** [ˋɪnˏtek] *n.*　（某組織或地方）新招收、納入者

55. **stratum** [ˋstrætəm] *n.*　社會階層（複數形為 strata [ˋstrætə]）

56. **ritual** [ˋrɪtʃuəl] *n.*　儀式；典禮

自述

Oxford and Stratford-upon-Avon are two lovely English destinations. And I realize that there exists between them this whole theme of the English language. And I know this is sort of a strange travel **concept**,[57] but I really felt like I was revisiting it by being in Oxford, **arguably**[58] the epicenter of the English language, and, of course, Stratford-upon-Avon, whose very own William Shakespeare **heightened** and . . . and **relished**[59] in it. And I just thought, wow, I don't use my own language. I don't enjoy it as much as I should.

Now I use the same phrases over and over again, and when I send e-mails, I type, "How are you? I'm smiley face icon period." So after visiting these destinations, I think I'm going to work hard to change that. You know, it's funny because most of the time you travel to discover things that you never had, but then there are the other times when you discover the things that you yourself have let slip away.

牛津和史特拉福是兩個迷人的英國城市。我發現到它們的共同點就是以英國語言為主題。我知道這是有點奇特的旅行概念，但我真的覺得自己好像重遊舊地一樣地參觀了可說是英語重心的牛津，還有因為莎士比亞而更出名的史特拉福。當我遊歷其中，我想如果不用自己的語言，我就無法盡情享受這趟旅程。

現今，我寄電子郵件一直重複著相同的用詞，我會打上你好嗎？加上了我，再加上一個笑臉，句號結尾（I ^_^.）。在我參觀過這兩個地方之後，我想我應該更努力改變這個習慣。有趣的是我們常常到處旅遊去發掘一些從所未見的事物，但有時候你發掘到的竟然是你自己讓它溜走的東西。

學習重點

> **-en 使……**

-en 接在形容詞或名詞後面，變成動詞。文中 heighten 是由名詞 height（高度）加上 -en 而來，表示「使提高、增強」的意思，其他例子如下：

dark + **en** = **darken**（使）變暗

sweet + **en** = **sweeten**（使）變甜

light + **en** = **lighten**（使）變輕

- Doctors say that smoking can heighten the risk of heart disease.
  醫生說吸菸會提高心臟病的風險。

- I darkened the room by closing the curtains.
  我拉上窗簾使房間變暗。

- Please pass the sugar so that I can sweeten my tea.
  請給我糖，我要喝甜一點的茶。

- I can help lighten your load if you give me one of your bags to carry.
  如果你將一個包包給我拿就可以幫你減輕重擔。

在牛津，划過鏡中奇遇

Vocabulary

57. **concept** [ˈkɑnsɛpt] *n.* 概念；觀念

58. **arguably** [ˈɑrgjuəbli] *adv.* 可說是；堪稱是

59. **relish** [ˈrɛlɪʃ] *v.* 享受；品味、欣賞

丹麥

DENMARK IN ONE MINUTE

丹麥全名為「丹麥王國」(The Kingdom of Denmark)，是一個北歐國家，國土包括法羅群島（Faroe Islands）和格陵蘭（Greenland）兩個自治區，由於相近的歷史、文化及語言，而與挪威（Norway）和瑞典（Sweden）合稱為斯堪地那維亞國家（Scandinavia）。

提到丹麥，就會想到丹麥麵包和安徒生童話。安徒生的童話故事舉世聞名，其中耳熟能詳的包括：《拇指姑娘》(*Thumbelina*)、《小美人魚》(*The Little Mermaid*)等。而首都哥本哈根則是最受歡迎的綠色城市，單車、花園、童話，在在讓世人對這裡心儀不已。在這單元，珊曼莎將帶我們去哥本哈根看這裡居民的生活與浪漫，我們也去瞧瞧吧！

DENMARK
Copenhagen★

首都：哥本哈根
CAPITAL: COPENHAGEN

官方語言：丹麥語
OFFICIAL LANGUAGE: DANISH

貨幣：丹麥克朗（**kr**）
CURRENCY: DANISH KRONE (DKK)

人口：5,602,536（2013 年統計）
POPULATION: 5,602,536 (2013)

國際電話區碼：+45
CALLING CODE: +45

UNIT 2

Wonderful Copenhagen

美哉！哥本哈根

影片原音 05　　課文朗讀 29

自述

Today we are in Copenhagen, Denmark, named one of the top ten dream cities in the world. It was here that this city's most famous resident, Hans Christian Andersen, wrote *The Little Mermaid, Princess and the Pea, The Emperor's New Clothes*. So this must be some sort of **fairy-tale**[1] place, right? Or is it? I mean, looking down on it with its tiny **canals**[2] and **crammed**[3] colored homes, it certainly appears to be. But what if we got closer? What would we find? A charming city perfect for **tourism**[4] or something more urban, more real? And what of the **Danes**[5] themselves? Do they keep to themselves or are they excited to share their city? Well, only one way to find out.

我們今天來到丹麥的哥本哈根，這地方號稱是世上十大夢幻城市之一。在這城市最有名的居民莫過於漢斯・克里斯欽・安徒生，他就是寫下《小美人魚》、《豌豆公主》和《國王的新衣》的作者，所以這裡應該算是童話般的地方吧？或是，俯瞰這些小運河和充滿繽紛色彩的房屋，丹麥確實似乎如童話般一樣。但如果我們靠近點看，會發現什麼呢？是適合觀光的迷人城市，還是較貼近真實的都市風情？丹麥人自己又是覺得如何呢？他們是只將城市點滴留給自己，還是樂於與他人分享呢？這，只有一個方法能得到解答。

背景知識

HANS CHRISTIAN ANDERSEN
漢斯・克里斯欽・安徒生

漢斯・克里斯欽・安徒生（Hans Christian Andersen, 1805–1875）為丹麥的作家及詩人，以其童話故事聞名於世，被視為現代童話之父，也讓丹麥享有「童話王國」的美譽，為丹麥的觀光業注入源源不絕的活力。安徒生也因此成為丹麥人傲視世界的瑰寶。

安徒生最有名的童話故事我們大多至少讀過或聽過，除了影片中提到的故事外，其他像是 *The Ugly Duckling*《醜小鴨》、*Tin Toy*《小錫兵》、*Thumbelina*《拇指姑娘》、*The Little Match Girl*《賣火柴的小女孩》等都是大家耳熟能詳的故事。

據說安徒生是國王克里斯欽七世（King Christian VII）的私生子。當時王公貴族常將私生子交由信賴的僕人養育，因此安徒生童年生活過得很艱苦。雖然這個說法很難獲得證明，但他後來從童年經驗中瞭解到，在貧困中力爭上游亦是一種高貴。安徒生的童話經常探討苦難、疏離感和死亡等主題，這些也是他個人生命的一部分，或許，他的一生正是最了不起的童話。

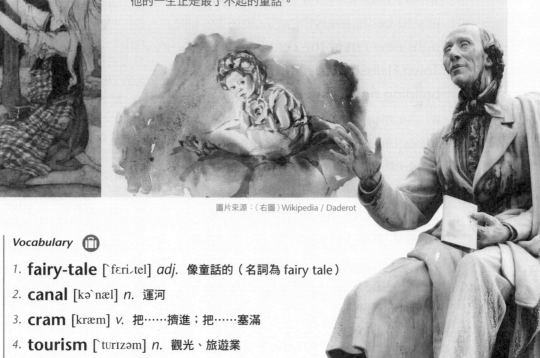

圖片來源：（右圖）Wikipedia / Daderot

Vocabulary 📖

1. **fairy-tale** [ˈfɛrɪˌtel] *adj.* 像童話的（名詞為 fairy tale）
2. **canal** [kəˈnæl] *n.* 運河
3. **cram** [kræm] *v.* 把……擠進；把……塞滿
4. **tourism** [ˈtʊrɪzəm] *n.* 觀光、旅遊業
5. **Dane** [den] *n.* 丹麥人

自述

Copenhagen is the **capital**[6] of Denmark and is considered to be the **gateway**[7] of **Scandinavia**.[8]

Now, Scandinavia is literally the countries of Norway, Sweden, and Denmark. But now it's a **term**[9] **associated**[10] with all **Nordic**[11] countries, including Finland and Iceland.

Real easy to be a visitor here in Copenhagen; just about everyone speaks English. It's a **cozy**,[12] charming city to be in; everything's close by. Like, right now I'm in the center of it all, Town Hall Square, named because that building right there is Town Hall. And all the museums, **attractions**,[13] and shopping you want to do are **either** right off the Square **or** just a short walk from it. Now, it's not the . . . the prettiest place in Copenhagen, but what it lacks in beauty it . . . it more than **makes up for** in purpose. Now, ~~there's~~ [there are] still a few things I need to pick up—**get my bearings**—so why don't you follow me to the . . . the tourism office.

哥本哈根是丹麥的首都，同時也是通往斯堪地那維亞的重要門戶。

斯堪地那維亞就是挪威、瑞典和丹麥三國。但現在儼然成了北歐國家的代名詞，包括芬蘭和冰島。

在哥本哈根對觀光非常輕鬆，這裡幾乎每個人都會說英語。這是個舒適迷人的城市，一切都近在咫尺。譬如說：現在我正在市中心，市政廳廣場就是以市政廳這棟建築命名的。所有你想去的博物館、觀光勝地和購物場所，不是在廣場四周就是在不遠處。這裡並不是哥本哈根最漂亮的地方，但它的用途足以彌補它的美中不足。現在我還得先去找一些旅遊資訊——弄清楚方位再看接下來要做什麼，你們何不跟著我一起去旅客中心逛逛。

either . . . or . . . 不是……就是……

either A or B 連接兩個主詞時，動詞單複數須與較靠近的主詞即 B 一致。

• Either my elder sisters or <u>my younger brother</u> <u>was</u> responsible for making a mess in the kitchen.
不是我的姊姊們就是我弟弟要為廚房一團亂負責。

make up for 彌補；補足

• The basketball player makes up for his slow speed with his very accurate shooting.
這名籃球員以精準的射籃彌補他速度上的不足。

get one's bearings 清楚所在方位

名詞 bearing 指「（羅盤上的）方位」，作此義時常用複數。get one's bearings 表示「弄清楚所在方位」，常用來比喻「熟悉新環境」。

• Today is my first day of work, so it will take me a while to get my bearings.
今天是我第一天上班，所以我需要一下子來熟悉環境。

Vocabulary

6. **capital** [ˋkæpət!] n. 首都

7. **gateway** [ˋgetˌwe] n. 通道；門戶

8. **Scandinavia** [ˌskændəˋnevɪə] n. 斯堪地那維亞
（包括挪威、瑞典、丹麥，有時亦包括芬蘭和冰島）

9. **term** [tɜm] n. 術語；用語

10. **associate** [əˋsoʃɪˌet] v. 聯想

11. **Nordic** [ˋnɔrdɪk] n. 北歐人

12. **cozy** [ˋkozɪ] adj. 溫暖舒適的

13. **attraction** [əˋtrækʃən] n. 吸引人的地方或事物

自述

The tourism center, called Wonderful Copenhagen, is a block from Town Hall Square.

OK, so the first thing you want to do is pick up a good map, and this is actually one of the most user-friendly tourist offices I've ever been in. However you want your information, it's here. If you want to read it, it's in front of you. If you want to talk to someone personally about it, you can get your information that way. Also, just **look it up** on the Web. This is nice. Just a **category**[14] screen. From nightlife to supermarkets. And here's a category that I **rarely**[15] see, local's tips. Let's click onto that. Let's see what that is. That's great. So these are all locals here that are giving you advice of what you should do in their city while you're here. And this Fleming, he's from Nørrebro. "You should spend a full day in Nørrebro, one of the most exciting neighborhoods in Copenhagen." Well, how about that. Let's **look into** that.

名為「美好的哥本哈根」的旅客中心，距離市政廳廣場只有一個街區。

首先我們要先找一份好的地圖，這真的是我去過的旅客中心當中，最便利的一個了。不論你要什麼樣的資訊，這裡都有。你可以閱讀眼前張貼的資訊，也可以親自詢問服務人員。同時也能上網查閱。真的很棒。這是目錄頁，項目從夜生活到超市都有。有一項是我很少看到的：當地旅遊小秘訣。點選看看吧，看看會是什麼。太棒了，這些全都是當地人建議遊客在這裡該做些什麼。這位是來自諾布羅的富蘭明。他寫著：「你應該花一整天拜訪諾布羅，那是哥本哈根最刺激的地區之一。」這主意如何，讓我仔細瞧瞧。

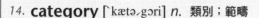

look up 查閱；查詢

- Let's look up the movie times on the Internet.
  我們上網查詢電影場次吧。

- Claire didn't know the answer, so she looked it up.
  克萊兒不知道答案，所以她去查閱。

look into 深入研究；調查

之後接名詞或 V-ing。另一個常見的同義片語為 check into。

- I don't know if there are any jobs available at my company, but I'll look into it for you.
  我不知道我公司還有沒有任何職缺，但是我會幫你調查看看。

- Mr. Reynolds checked into the report that one of his students had cheated on the test.
  雷諾先生研究著這份關於他的一個學生考試作弊的報告。

旅遊小幫手

Copenhagen Visitor Centre 哥本哈根旅客中心

May, June, and September: Monday–Saturday 9:00–18:00
Sunday 9:00–14:00

July and August: Monday–Sunday 9:00–19:00

Rest of the year: Monday–Friday 9:00–16:00 Saturday 9:00–14:00

(45) 7022 2442

http://www.visitcopenhagen.com/copenhagen-tourist

Vocabulary

14. **category** [ˋkætə͵gɔri] *n.* 類別；範疇

15. **rarely** [ˋrɛrli] *adv.* 很少；難得

自述

So, English is spoken widely here. Menus are all going to be in English as well. However, signs and names are in Danish, of course. Danish is the type of language that the words themselves give you absolutely no **clue**[16] **as to** how to pronounce them. It's almost impossible. Luckily, the . . . the transportation system here is really easily **laid out**.[17] So, I'm going to go to Nyhavn to meet a friend, and it looks like I take bus number 29. It's over there.

There is a subway, but buses seem to be the most convenient way to **get around**. The ride to Nyhavn takes about ten minutes. I should get there just in time to meet my guide, Trine Steffensen. So, this is Nyhavn?

英語在這裡廣泛地被使用。菜單也都是用英文寫的。然而招牌和店名,當然還是丹麥文。丹麥文是屬於那種無法讓你照著字來發音的語言,所以根本不可能直接唸出來。幸好這裡的運輸系統設計得簡單明瞭。我要去新港和一位朋友見面,看來我得搭乘二十九路巴士,就在那裡。

這裡有地下鐵,但巴士似乎才是最方便的交通工具。從這裡到新港大約花十分鐘。我應該能準時到達那裡和我的導遊翠娜·史蒂芬森碰面。這裡就是新港?

as to 關於；至於

as to 表示「關於」，意思同 about，多用於句中。as to 用於句首時用來承接前面所提的內容而引出其他話題，可用 as for 代替。

- The actress had a hard time deciding as to which gown she would wear to the awards ceremony.
  那位女星很難下決定要穿哪件晚禮服參加頒獎典禮。

- Three possible building sites have been chosen. However, as to/for where the new offices will be built, it is still being considered by the president of the company.
  已選定三個可能的興建地點。然而，關於新辦公室要蓋在哪裡，董事長還在考慮當中。

get around 到……四處旅遊、到處走走

片語動詞 get around 在此指「四處遊歷」，可作及物或不及物動詞用。

- The new MRT system makes it easy to get around the city.
  新的捷運系統使之能在城裡來去自如。

- A bicycle is more than just a way to get around. It's also a great way to get some exercise.
  單車不僅可以四處遊歷，也是很好的運動方式。

【延伸學習】

get around to + N./sth 抽空去做某事

- I didn't get around to cleaning my bedroom today, but I'll do it tomorrow.
  我今天抽不出時間打掃臥房，但我明天會做。

Vocabulary

16. **clue** [klu] *n.* 線索；提示

17. **lay out** [le] [aut] *v.* 規劃；設計（場地或建築）

對
話

S : *Samantha Brown, Hostess*　　**T** : *Trine Steffensen, Guide*

T Yes, or Nyhavn, as I say in Danish.	是的。丹麥語發音是唸成紐罕。
S Nyhavn.	紐罕。
T It means "the new harbor."	其實就是指「新的港口」。
S Ah. But it doesn't look too new.	但看起來並不是太新。
T No, I know, but it was. It was dug out in, I think, in 1670. So, it's pretty old.	我知道,但當時是新的。這是在一六七〇年時鑿建而成。所以,現在當然相當古老了。
S It's just sort of picture-postcard Copenhagen. This is the . . . this is the picture of it.	這裡的風景,就跟哥本哈根的明信片一樣。這裡就是明信片上的風景。
T Yes.	沒錯。
S So this is obviously a very **touristy**[18] area. Everyone's enjoying drinks and salads, and kids are having ice cream.	所以,很顯然地,這裡有很多觀光客到訪。大家都來這裡享用飲料及沙拉,小孩則是吃冰淇淋。
T Yeah.	是的。
S But that always wasn't so. This was actually quite a **shady**[19] place.	但並非一向如此。這裡曾是相當惡名昭彰的地區。

NYHAVN 新港

Nyhavn 字面意思是 New Harbor，在一六七〇至一六七三年間，由國王克里斯欽五世（King Christian V）下令興建，原來的目的是要讓船隻貨物可以進到市區而興建的人工運河，後來發展成商業最繁榮的地區，甚至一度成為混亂的紅燈區。

現今的新港已經煥然一新，從新國王廣場（King's Square）一路到丹麥皇家劇院（Royal Danish Playhouse）南邊的港邊區，林立著五彩繽紛的十七、八世紀連棟房屋、咖啡館、酒吧和餐廳，港邊也停靠著許多具有歷史的高桅木船，吸引許多觀光客慕名前來，更是當地人休閒散步的好去處，並且贏得了「全世界最長吧台」的美名。

有人說到哥本哈根，就絕不能錯過新港，這個地方也因為安徒生而聲名遠播。安徒生非常喜歡新港，曾在這裡住了近二十年，或許有機會到哥本哈根，除了細細品味此地的風華，還可遙想童話大師當年的生活。

欲瞭解更多哥本哈根的訊息，可上網查詢：www.visitcopenhagen.com

Vocabulary

18. **touristy** [ˈtʊrəsti] *adj.* 遊客眾多的；吸引觀光客的

19. **shady** [ˈʃedi] *adj.* 不正當的；（樹）成蔭的

對
話

S : *Samantha Brown, Hostess*　　**T** : *Trine Steffensen, Guide*

T No, it wasn't. It was a red-light **district**[20] almost until twenty years ago. Because this was a place where ships came in from all over the place, even the Far East or the Virgin Islands or Africa. **Sailors**[21] would come aboard . . . come into land . . . and then they would do whatever sailors do when they walk ~~in~~ [on] land after half a year [at sea].

沒錯，過去這裡是名聲不好的地區。約二十年前，這裡還是紅燈區。因為當時有很多船隻從世界各地來到這裡，甚至是遠東地區、維京群島或是非洲。水手們上岸時，他們會去做半年來在海上想做而沒有做的事情。

S Those **clean-shaven lads**[22] just out for a good night on the town.

鬍子刮乾淨的男人們到鎮上享樂一晚。

T Yes.

沒錯。

S So do you know what I have found most surprising about being here in Copenhagen?

你知道我在哥本哈根，發現最令我驚訝的是什麼事情嗎？

T No.

是什麼。

S The number of hot dog **stands**.[23] This . . . this is incredible to me. And there's like another one just twenty feet away.

超多的熱狗攤。我簡直無法想像。就像是這裡二十呎外就有另一攤。

學習重點

clean-shaven 鬍子刮乾淨的；未蓄鬍的

clean-shaven 是由 adj. + p.p. (過去分詞) 構成的複合形容詞，表示「鬍子刮乾淨的」。其他例子包括：

- a free-spoken man 一個直言無諱的人
- a soft-boiled egg 一顆半熟的蛋

【延伸學習】

除了形容詞，過去分詞也會與名詞或副詞構成複合形容詞。

用法一 N. + p.p.

- a test-oriented education → an education that is oriented toward tests
  以考試為導向的教育
- a flower-filled park → a park that is filled with flowers 開滿花的公園
- a love-struck girl → a girl who is struck by love 陷入愛河的女孩

用法二 adv. + p.p.

- the best-kept secrets → the secrets that are kept best 嚴守的祕密
- a frequently-asked question → a question that is asked frequently
  常被詢問的問題
- a long-awaited gift → a gift that is awaited long 期待已久的禮物

Vocabulary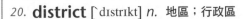

20. **district** [ˈdɪstrɪkt] *n.* 地區；行政區
21. **sailor** [ˈselə] *n.* 水手；船員
22. **lad** [læd] *n.* 年輕人、小伙子；兄弟
23. **stand** [stænd] *n.* 攤位

對話

S : Samantha Brown, Hostess　　**T** : Trine Steffensen, Guide

T Yeah, that's right. We have a lot . . .	對，沒錯。我們有很多……
S You like your hot dogs here, huh?	你們還真愛吃熱狗對吧？
T We love hot dogs.	我們超愛吃熱狗的。
S All right.	很好。
T You can have them with ~~and~~ [or] without the bun. You can actually have the bun only, if you want to.	你可以配麵包吃，或者可以單吃。如果你想的話，單吃麵包也沒什麼不行。
S Why would you want to do that?	為何會有人只吃麵包呢？
T I don't know. If you're a **vegetarian.**[24] You can't afford it. You can, you know, it can be the end of the month and it's that. It doesn't cost very much just to have the bun.	不知道。也許是素食者吧。或是沒錢。你知道的，有時候在月底就可能只得這樣吃。只吃麵包的話不用花很多錢。
S OK. And . . . and the **toppings**[25] look a little different as well.	那……上面的醬料似乎也不太相同。
T It's the ketchup and the mustard and then you've got cucumber salad.	那是番茄醬和芥末，還有黃瓜沙拉。

DANISH HOT DOG TOPPINGS
丹麥熱狗知多少

丹麥的熱狗攤非常普遍，在物價非常高昂的丹麥，熱狗可說是當地的平民美食，最有名的熱狗攤有三家，包括 Tulip、Steff 及 Dansk。

丹麥熱狗通常包含紅辣椒（red sausage）、番茄醬（ketchup）、丹麥芥末（Danish mustard）、炸洋蔥（fried onion）、生洋蔥絲（raw onion），有時還會有蛋黃醬（rémoulade），這是一種以美奶滋（mayonnaise）作為基底的醬料，搭配甜碎漬瓜（sweet relish），上面再加上醃黃瓜（dill cucumber）。

bun
小麵包

sausage
火腿

raw onion
生洋蔥絲

rémoulade
蛋黃醬

cucumber
小黃瓜

ketchup
番茄醬

Vocabulary

24. **vegetarian** [ˌvɛdʒəˋtɛrɪən] *n.* 素食者

25. **topping** [ˋtɑpɪŋ] *n.* （添加在食物上作裝飾或增添風味的）配料

對話

S : *Samantha Brown, Hostess*　　**T** : *Trine Steffensen, Guide*

S Oh, so it's not **pickles**.[26]	喔，所以那不是酸黃瓜？
T Not really like pickles. No, it's not pickles. It's made with **vinegar**[27] and sugar, so it's a little different than pickles.	不是。不是酸黃瓜。它是用醋和糖做的，味道和酸黃瓜不太一樣。
S What should we **wash it down** with?	這該搭什麼飲料來喝呢？
T A couple of chocolate milks.	配著巧克力牛奶。
S Chocolate milk?	巧克力牛奶？
T Yes.	是的。
S I love you guys. You're the best. Hot dogs and chocolate milk. I'm, like, twelve **all over again**.	我愛死你們了。你們真厲害。吃熱狗竟然搭巧克力牛奶喝。我就像是回到童年一般。
T Yes.	沒錯。
T Do you like it? It's good.	喜歡嗎？味道很棒。
S Oh yeah. Who doesn't like a hot dog?	當然。誰不愛吃熱狗呢？
T No, that's right.	沒錯。

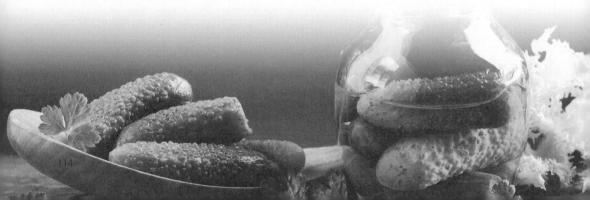

wash down （用水）吞嚥食物

wash down 有兩種意思：

A. 藉由喝水（或其他液體）來幫助吞嚥食物。

- Rachel washed down her breakfast with a cup of coffee.
  瑞秋早餐配一杯咖啡。

B.（以大量的水）沖洗。

- Hank washed down his car before he went on his date.
  漢克去約會之前洗了車子。

(all) over again 重新；再一次

此副詞片語用來表示「從頭再來一次」的意思，前面可加上 all 作為強調，亦可用來指讓人不快、厭煩的事情一而再地發生。

- If I were living my life over again, I wouldn't have wasted my time doing something I don't like.
  如果生命可以重來，我就不會把時間浪費在我不喜歡的事情上面。

- I want to leave now because they started to argue the same thing all over again.
  我現在想離開了，因為他們又重新開始爭論同樣的事情了。

【延伸學習】

over and over (again) 一再；反覆

- Before the concert, the piano player practiced the work by Mozart over and over again.
  在音樂會開始之前，鋼琴師一遍又一遍地練習莫札特的曲子。

Vocabulary

26. **pickle** [ˈpɪkl̩] *n.* 醃黃瓜

27. **vinegar** [ˈvɪnɪgɚ] *n.* 醋

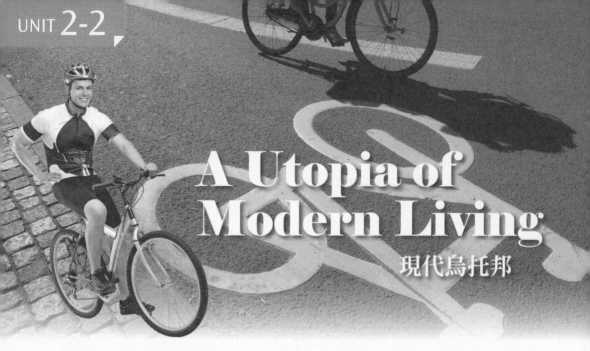

A Utopia of Modern Living

現代烏托邦

🎞 影片原音 06　🎧 課文朗讀 30

自述

[The] Best way to see Copenhagen is on a bicycle. Just do as the Danes do. These are the city bikes, and there are stands all over the city. Simply go up to one, put a coin in, and when you return it at the end of the day, you get the coin back, so it's free. Now, because it's such a good deal, these are actually really hard to find, and so you may have to rent a bike at a shop. But I always try to **assimilate**[1] into a culture. Would you look at how obvious this bike is that I'm a visitor? It's like I should have plastic **pom-poms**[2] coming out of the **handlebars**[3]—a **flag**[4] coming up from my **banana seat**.[5]

探訪哥本哈根最好的方法就是和當地人一樣騎腳踏車。這些是城市單車，到處都有租車點。只要選定一輛腳踏車，投入錢幣，最後還車時還能拿回錢幣，所以這是免費的。由於這真的很划算，所以這些免費腳踏車其實很難找到，也許你還是必須向店家花錢租車。但我總喜歡融入當地文化。不過光看車子就知道我是遊客，我似乎應該在把手上，掛上塑膠彩球，在座椅後面插根旗幟。

COPENHAGEN:
THE BICYCLE-FRIENDLY CAPITAL
幸福的單車首都──哥本哈根

　　哥本哈根以對單車友善聞名於世，每天有超過四成的民眾騎單車去上班或上課。有這麼多民眾利用單車通勤，主要的原因當然是因為自行車道的規劃相當完善，與主要的交通幹道分離，有時甚至有自行車專用的號誌系統，在在都吸引更多的民眾善加利用單車作為交通工具。

　　哥本哈根最為人稱道的還有 CityBike 這項服務，你只要投入二十元克朗（kroner）就可以騎著單車到處遊覽這個迷人的城市，在你還車時，錢幣會自動退還。換句話說，這項服務是免費的。

Vocabulary

1. **assimilate** [əˋsɪməˌlet] *v.* 融入；同化

2. **pom-pom** [ˋpɑmpˌpɑmp] *n.* （裝飾性的）絨球

3. **handlebar** [ˋhændḷˌbɑr] *n.* 把手；（自行車）車把

4. **flag** [flæg] *n.* 旗幟

5. **banana seat** [bəˋnænə] [sit] *n.* （自行車）細長而後部翹起的車座

自述

 Everyone in Copenhagen has a bicycle, and they know how to use it. As a **pedestrian**,[6] you should be very aware of the bike-only lanes. Just a ten-minute ride from the Town Hall Square is the neighborhood of Christianshavn. It's a lovely place set on a peaceful canal. Wait a minute. We're in Denmark, right? The people from Denmark are called the Danes. Things that are from Denmark are considered Danish. Danish!

This is another tip I got from the tourist office: if you're looking for Danish **pastry**[7] in Christianshavn, you can't go wrong in this place. I can't believe I have only now just thought of this. All right, let's see what the system is here. Oh, we got to get a number. Where do you get a number? Oh, here we go.

I got a number. Now I'm looking at the signs here and nothing actually says Danish. So do they call it Danish here? I don't know.

Excuse me. Excuse me. Do you call your pastries here Danish?

哥本哈根每個人都有一部腳踏車,而且他們很懂得如何利用它。身為行人,必須熟知這裡的腳踏車道。從市政廳廣場騎十分鐘,就能來到克里斯欽港區。這是很迷人的地方,座落在寧靜的運河旁。等等,我們是在丹麥吧?來自丹麥的人叫做丹麥人,丹麥的東西也會被冠上丹麥的名號。我想起丹麥麵包!

這是我在旅客中心取得的另一個旅遊秘訣:如果你想在克里斯欽港區尋找丹麥點心,來這裡就對了。真不敢相信我現在才想到這一點。看看這裡是如何運作的。喔,我們要抽號碼牌。要在哪裡抽呢?找到了。

我拿了號碼牌。我看了四週的牌子,卻沒看到丹麥麵包。他們稱這是丹麥麵包嗎?我也不知道。

不好意思。你們這裡的點心是叫做丹麥麵包嗎?

圖片來源：Wikipedia / Karri Huhtanen

TOWN HALL SQUARE
市政廳廣場

奧爾森天文鐘
Jens Olsen's World Clock

　　市政廳廣場位於市政廳前面，由於市政廳位於市中心，且面積廣大，因此經常是各種活動的舉辦地點。哥本哈根市政廳建於一九〇五年，是一座結合古丹麥與義大利文藝復興時期風格的紅磚結構建築。從新港區旁邊的新國王廣場，沿著徒步購物街直走就可以來到市政廳廣場，在這裡，你也可以看見安徒生的雕像，經過時別忘了跟他打聲招呼。

　　市政廳廣場遊客絡繹不絕，在高一〇五點六公尺的鐘塔上可以欣賞到廣場的全景，這裡還有一座天文鐘，據說，這座天文鐘不但會報時，還可以計算行星的位置，是由一名技藝精巧的鎖匠暨製錶工匠奧爾森（Jens Olsen）花費四十年所製造。

Vocabulary

6. **pedestrian** [pəˋdɛstriən] *n.* 行人

7. **pastry** [ˋpestri] *n.* 糕點

119

對話

S : *Samantha Brown, Hostess*　　**M** : *Man with White T-shirt, Pastry Shop Customer*

M	No, we call it the *wienerbrød*.	不，我們稱作是維也納麵包。
S	*Wienerbrød*.	維也納麵包。
M	Yeah. The right **translation**[8] is **Vienna**[9] bread.	是，翻譯過來就是維也納麵包。
S	Vienna bread. You **give someone else credit for your pastry**.	維也納麵包？你們的點心竟冠上別地方的名字。
M	Yeah, we do. That's . . . that's Danish to the, you know . . .	是啊。其實它是丹麥的。
S	So what is your favorite type of Danish?	你最喜歡的是哪一種呢？
M	Something called the dream cake.	那個夢幻蛋糕。
S	Dream cake?	夢幻蛋糕？
M	Yeah.	沒錯。
S	That sounds good. Let me ask you this: Do you wash it down with some chocolate milk?	聽起來很好吃的樣子。我可以問你：你會搭著巧克力牛奶一起吃嗎？
M	Oh, of course.	當然。
S	I love that. They drink chocolate milk. So this is all Vienna bread. This is . . . I'm glad this **fence**[10] is here.	真棒。他們真愛喝巧克力牛奶。所以這些都是維也納麵包。幸好這裡設了圍欄。
M	Yeah.	是呀。

學習重點

---
give sb credit for sth 把某事（讚譽、功勞）歸於某人
---

credit 為不可數名詞，在此用法中有「讚揚；稱讚；功勞」的意思。另一個片語 take credit for sth 則表示「將……歸功於自己」。

- You should give Arthur credit for making a huge deal with that big company.
  和那間大公司談成了一筆大生意，你應該給予亞瑟肯定。

- Gary took credit for winning the basketball game when he made a three-point shot at the last second.
  蓋瑞在最後一秒投進了一顆三分球後，便把贏得籃球比賽的功勞歸給自己。

DANISH PASTRY　丹麥麵包

背景知識

　　丹麥麵包（Danish Pastry）特點是分很多層，外皮則是酥狀的，吃起來口感酥軟、層次分明，充滿濃郁的奶香味。然而世界著名的丹麥麵包為什麼在丹麥叫維也納麵包呢？

　　多處記載顯示這個名稱起源於一八五〇年前後。當時，丹麥麵包師傅因為罷工，麵包店就雇用來到丹麥的奧地利維也納師傅，這些來自維也納的麵包師傅按照自己的配方做麵包，後來當丹麥學徒利用他們的配方加入更多的奶油和雞蛋，使維也納來的配方變成了丹麥人的麵包，但維也納麵包的名字就一直沿用至今。

Vocabulary

8. **translation** [træns`leʃən] *n.* 翻譯
9. **Vienna** [vɪ`ɛnə] *n.* 維也納
10. **fence** [fɛns] *n.* 圍欄；欄杆

對
話

S : *Samantha Brown, Hostess*   **M** : *Man with White T-shirt, Pastry Shop Customer*

S That's incredible. So what's your dream cake?	真是棒極了。夢幻蛋糕是哪一種？
M That's the dream cake.	那就是夢幻蛋糕。
S Now what is that topping?	上面的餡料是什麼？
M I think that's what angels **are made of.**	我想那就是天使的化身。
S You're getting all **misty-eyed.**[11]	你的眼神都迷濛了。
M Yeah.	沒錯。
S My dentist would be very happy if I ate that . . .	如果常吃這種蛋糕，我的牙醫一定會很開心。
M Yeah.	是的。
S . . . **on a regular basis.** Now, that right there is what I know as Danish.	基本上，那才是我所知道的丹麥麵包。
M Yeah. It's what we call the *bagerens dårlige øje*. In English it would be "the bakery's bad eye."	我們稱它為貝洋斯多里亞，英文翻譯就是「麵包店之惡眼」。
S The bakery's bad eye.	麵包店之惡眼。
M Yeah.	是的。
S All right. Sam gets to know the Danish. Oh.	好吧。我要來品嚐丹麥麵包了。

be made of 製成

成品製作過程本質不變，且看得出原料時，句型為：「A + be + made of + B」，表示「A 由 B 製成」。

- All of the bowls on this shelf are made of wood.
  這個架子上所有的碗都是木製的。（看得出是木製）

比較：be made from 製成

成品和原料看起來不同，或本質已改變時，句型為：「A + be + made from + B」，表示「A 由 B 製成」。

- The wine is made from grapes.
  這種酒是葡萄製成的。（葡萄的本質已改變）

on a regular basis 定期地；經常地

on a . . . basis 意思是指「以……為基準」，on a regular basis 就表示「定期地；經常地」，與 regularly 意思相同。

- You should get some exercise on a regular basis to stay healthy.
  你應該定期運動以保持健康。

看其他例子：

▶ on a daily basis	每天
▶ on a weekly basis	每週
▶ on a monthly basis	每月
▶ on a yearly basis	每年

- Mary calls her boyfriend on a daily basis after she gets home from work.
  瑪莉每天下班回到家後都會打電話給她的男朋友。

● 名為「麵包店之惡眼」
the bakery's bad eye
的丹麥麵包

Vocabulary

11. **misty-eyed** [ˈmɪstɪˌaɪd] *adj.* 淚眼朦朧的；感傷的

自述

So, right off of Town Hall Square, where we began our visit, is Copenhagen's main shopping street, which is actually five streets **pieced together**. Now, this is a seriously long pedestrian-only thoroughfare and major shopping experience. You really shouldn't come here **cold**;[12] you need to . . . to get to your local mall, do some **laps**,[13] **build up** an **endurance**,[14] because this is **ambitious**.[15]

在我們出發的市政廳廣場旁邊，就是哥本哈根的主要購物區，範圍包括五條街。這條行人專用通道非常長，這個購物區域非常廣大，真的不該毫無準備就前來，你得在家鄉的購物中心逛個幾圈，養成逛街的耐力，因為這裡實在大得不得了。

On this street you have it all from the inexpensive to the more **high-end**[16] **establishments**.[17] This street is so filled with both visitors and locals, it can feel like you're part of a **cattle**[18] call being pushed through. But the streets do eventually open up to include huge squares that become a perfect rest stop for ice cream and coffee.

這條街上什麼都有，從便宜商品到較高檔的商店，路上到處都是觀光客和當地人，就像聽見鈴聲的牛群，爭相推擠地向前進。但街道發展最後會延伸遍及大型廣場——最佳的休憩之處，在此可以來點冰淇淋和咖啡。

學習重點

piece together 拼湊、湊集起來

piece 在此作動詞，表「拼湊」之意。piece together 也可用來表示將原本零碎的訊息或事物拼湊起來，以理出頭緒或使事物完整。

用法
> **piece together + N.**
> **piece + N./代名詞 + together**

• Julia's quilt was made of five fabrics pieced together.
  茱莉亞的棉被是由五種布料拼製而成的。

• The police tried to piece together what had happened before the crime took place.
  警方試圖將案發前的經過拼湊起來。

build up 增進；鍛鍊

build up 也可表示「增強；增進；逐漸積聚」等意思。

• I want to build up my English-speaking skills.
  我想要加強我的英語口語能力。

Vocabulary

12. **cold** [kold] *adv.* 毫無準備地

13. **lap** [læp] *n.* （游泳池、操場等的）一圈

14. **endurance** [ɪn`durəns] *n.* 耐力

15. **ambitious** [æm`bɪʃəs] *adj.* （計畫、目標）規模宏大的；艱鉅的

16. **high-end** [`haɪ.ɛnd] *adj.* 高檔的；高級的

17. **establishment** [ɪ`stæblɪʃmənt] *n.* 營業場所；企業機構

18. **cattle** [`kætl] *n.* 牛群；牲畜

自述

So, **at some point**, you want to leave the mall and **explore**[19] the side and **parallel**[20] streets here; it's . . . it's much more quiet. It's a softer, slower pace, and the shops are more independent. Do you see that scene behind me? How the . . . the **medieval**[21] buildings sort of **curve**[22] around?—just sort of Copenhagen at its most charming.

One store you have to **drop in on**, if only because you are not going to find it anywhere else, is a store called Illums Bolighus. Illums Bolighus is considered to be a **temple**[23] to design—a **utopia**[24] of modern living. So, while you are here in Denmark, you are going to be hearing about Danish or Scandinavian design that makes you think, "Well, what exactly is that?" Basically, as far back as the 1920s, designers here said, "We are going to **intensely**[25] study the function of an object before we create its form." And if you are thinking, "Well, yeah. I mean, doesn't that always happen?" let me ask you this: Just how comfortable was that airline seat on your flight over here?

這時你就會想離開購物中心，並仔細探訪這些平行的街道，這裡比較安靜、步調比較緩慢，商店也比較獨立，看見我後面的景象了嗎？中古時代的建築蜿蜒成巷，這就是哥本哈根最迷人之處。

有一家店是大家必得造訪的，因為在別的地方絕對找不到，那就是伊路姆斯·波利弗斯傢飾店。伊路姆斯·波利弗斯是設計業界的朝聖地，也是現代生活的烏托邦。身處丹麥，會常聽人談到丹麥或斯堪地那維亞設計，而讓你不禁想那到底是什麼？基本上要追溯到一九二〇年代，這裡的設計師說：「我們要在設計新品的外型前，先深入研究它的實用性。」也許你心想：「不都是如此嗎？」讓我問你一個問題：帶你飛來這裡的飛機座椅是否舒適？

學習重點

at some point 在某個時間點

point 在此指「時間點；發展階段」。at some point 與 someday、sometime 意思相同。

- I'll be very busy for the next six months, but at some point I'd like to start taking pottery classes.
  我之後半年會很忙，不過我想找個時間開始上陶藝課。

drop in on 順道走訪、拜訪

drop in on 後面可加上地方或某人，與 drop by 意思相同，drop by 之後接地方。同義的用法有 drop by + a place。

- Kate dropped in on her grandmother on her way home from school.
  凱特放學後順路去探望祖母。

- Matt dropped by the office this morning.
  麥特今天早上順道來了辦公室一趟。

Vocabulary

19. **explore** [ɪkˋsplɔr] *v.* 探索

20. **parallel** [ˋpærəˏlɛl] *adj.* 平行的

21. **medieval** [miˋdivəl] *adj.* 中世紀的；中古的

22. **curve** [kɝv] *v.* 使彎曲

23. **temple** [ˋtɛmpl̩] *n.* 朝聖地；聖殿

24. **utopia** [juˋtopiə] *n.* 烏托邦

25. **intensely** [ɪnˋtɛnsli] *adv.* 深入地；強烈地

自述

Not everything here is Scandinavian; there are international designers as well. But everything sort of follows the same theme: very **functional**[26] but cool looking at the same time. Now, this is a great idea; look at this, **folks**.[27] This is a chop block, basically. You chop your onions and now just fold it and slide it into the pot. That's a great idea. It is not all modern and **hip**;[28] they also have the world famous Royal Copenhagen **porcelain**.[29] I love, love Scandinavian design. Like, look at this. This is a **mortar**[30] and **pestle**.[31] Isn't that beautiful? And again, it actually works. It is not just simply cool looking; it is actually very functional. Ooh, and this is actually at my hotel. I am so excited. This is a cheese cutter. You put a big block of cheese in, right? And then it just makes these perfect slices with each rotation, [and] goes down the block of cheese. Just **peel**[32] them off. It is perfect. I am going to buy this.

並非一切都是斯堪地那維亞風格，也有來自各國的設計。但每樣東西多少都依循相同的主題：實用並有著酷炫的外觀。真是個好主意，你們看看，基本上這是塊砧板，你在上面切洋蔥，然後折起兩側，直接倒進鍋裡。真是個好主意。這裡的東西不僅是現代流行的，還有舉世聞名的皇家哥本哈根手繪名瓷。我愛死斯堪地那維亞式的設計了。這是杵和臼，很漂亮吧？而且真的很好用，不只是有漂亮的外表而已，其實非常地實用，我的旅館裡也有這玩意，我好興奮。這是切乳酪的工具，把一大塊乳酪放進去，每轉一次，就能切出一片片的完美乳酪，由上而下地將乳酪削成片。太棒了，我要把它買回家。

ROYAL COPENHAGEN
皇家哥本哈根手繪名瓷

皇家哥本哈根手繪名瓷（Royal Copenhagen）是全世界最古老的公司之一，創立於一七七五年，是由當時的皇太后茱莉安 · 瑪莉（Queen Juliane Marie）批准贊助下成立，「只製造真正的精品」為瓷器廠創始的宗旨，至今仍維持工藝傳統來製造餐瓷與餐桌裝飾品。

皇家哥本哈根商標圖騰為象徵丹麥皇室的皇冠，而三條波紋線則代表包圍丹麥的三個海峽，其手繪名瓷最富盛名的即是代表丹麥的藍白瓷，製造和手繪皆由手工製作。

Bing & Grøndahl 的 Fanny Garde 於一八九五年所設計的餐瓷，名為 seagull（海鷗）

皇家哥本哈根以藍白圖紋為特色的瓷器

圖片來源：（左圖）Wikipedia / Gryffindor

Vocabulary

26. **functional** [ˈfʌŋkʃənl] *adj.* 功能性的；實用的

27. **folk** [fok] *n.* 大夥、諸位；大家

28. **hip** [hɪp] *adj.* 流行的；新潮的

29. **porcelain** [ˈpɔrslən] *n.* 瓷器

30. **mortar** [ˈmɔrtə] *n.* 臼；缽

31. **pestle** [ˈpɛsəl] *n.* 杵

32. **peel** [pil] *v.* 削去或剝去（水果、蔬菜等）皮

自述

You'll be happy to know that the Danes love to eat. And they're not these, you know, two-hour-lunch types either. When they're hungry, they want to eat now. With that **mentality**,[33] they have perfected the art of the sandwich. Now, if you think your sandwich shop has the best sandwiches with the most toppings, **you ain't seen nothing yet.**

This is the famous Ida Davidsen sandwich shop. It's like the Carnegie Deli of Copenhagen but with more pleasant service. The first thing you'll notice is how busy it is in here. It's probably the only sandwich shop in the world where you need reservations. This has been a family business since 1888, and Oscar Davidsen is fifth generation.

你們聽到丹麥人很愛吃，一定很高興。他們也沒有固定的用餐時間，當他們感覺飢餓，就想立刻進食。基於這種思維模式，他們發展出完美的三明治藝術。如果你認為你常去的三明治店有著最棒的三明治及餡料，那表示你沒看過真正棒的三明治。

這是著名的伊達戴維森三明治店。它就像是哥本哈根的卡內基熟食店（美國知名熟食店），但服務更加親切。首先注意到的是店裡繁忙的生意，這大概是全世界唯一需要事先訂位的三明治店。這是從一八八八年開始的家族企業，奧斯卡戴維森是第五代傳人。

伊達戴維森（Ida Davidsen）三明治店位在哥本哈根市中心，鄰近新國王廣場，提供的菜單近三百種，深受觀光客和當地人的歡迎。

圖片來源：Wikipedia / Nillerdk

SMØRREBRØD
開放式三明治

在丹麥，到處可見販售開放式三明治（smørrebrød, open face sandwich）的店家。所謂開放式三明治與我們熟知的三明治不同之處在於前者只有底部一片麵包，通常是塗上奶油的裸麥麵包或黑麥麵包。至於餡料的部分，則有烤牛肉、火雞肉、火腿、鮭魚等冷盤菜餚（cold cut）、起司等，由於上面沒有麵包蓋住，所以所有的餡料都一覽無遺，甚至有各種不同的造型。

學習重點

you ain't seen nothing yet　最棒、最精彩刺激的還沒到來

在這個用法中，固定會用 ain't 來表示，ain't 在此是用來代替 haven't。

- If you think James is a great golfer, you ain't seen nothing yet.
  如果你認為詹姆士高爾夫球打得很好的話，那表示你還沒見識過真正的高手。

Vocabulary

33. **mentality** [mɛn`tæləti] *n.* 心態；思維方式

131

對
話

S : Samantha Brown, Hostess　　**O** : Oscar Davidsen, Deli Owner

O Hi. Welcome.	嗨。歡迎光臨。
S Thank you. I'm here to try my very first *smørrebrød*.	謝謝,我要來試試生平第一個開放式三明治。
O It's very close yeah. Very close.	你的發音已經很接近了。
S Close but no cigar.	但還是差一點。
O It's called *smørrebrød*.	應該是唸作開放式三明治。
S *Smørrebrød*.	開放式三明治。
O Yeah.	對。
S A Danish sandwich.	也就是丹麥三明治。
O Yeah. The Danish open face sandwich. We have our fish section here, and down here we have the . . . the meat.	是的。丹麥開放式三明治。這裡是魚肉區,這裡是熟肉區。
S Is there a menu to choose from as well?	這裡有菜單供人選擇嗎?
O Yes. We have between 270 ~~to~~ [and] 280 different kinds.	有。我們有二百七十到二百八十種三明治。
S You have close to 300 different types . . .	你們有近三百種……
O Yes.	沒錯。
S . . . of sandwiches.	……的三明治。
O Yes.	是。

close but no cigar 差一點

此說法源自遊戲攤位上射飛鏢等遊戲，因為獎品通常是 cigar（雪茄），差一點射中標靶時就會這麼說，後來可用於各種「差一點就達到目標」的情況。類似的說法還有：

- Almost got it.
- Pretty close.

旅遊小幫手

Ida Davidsen 伊達戴維森三明治店

從一八八八年開始，伊達戴維森三明治店即為知名的丹麥開放式三明治店。將近三百種的三明治可供選擇，三明治可放的食材有：鮭魚、螃蟹、馬鈴薯、鰻魚、魚子醬等等。

Monday–Friday: 10:30 a.m.–5:00 p.m.
Saturday and Sunday: Closed

(45) 33 91 36 55

http://www.idadavidsen.dk

對話

S : *Samantha Brown, Hostess*　　**O** : *Oscar Davidsen, Deli Owner*

S Do you . . . do you have . . .　　你有，你有沒有……

O And I can also explain to you a little bit [about] all our different kinds of open face sandwiches.　　我也可以稍微向妳介紹一下各式各樣的開放式三明治。

S Yeah. Please.　　好，麻煩你了。

O This is fresh raw salmon. Fresh bought crayfish tails. **Lumpfish**[34] caviar, [with a] slice of lime, and a special **dill**[35] **dressing**[36] **on the side**.[37] Princess Alexandra is fresh raw salmon with a light balsamic cream inside.　　這是新鮮生鮭魚。這是剛購買的蝦尾肉。圓鰭魚、魚子醬、萊姆片，和特製的蒔蘿醬料作為配菜。「亞力珊卓公主」裡有新鮮生鮭魚，佐清淡巴薩米克奶油醬。

Vocabulary

34. **lumpfish** [ˈlʌmpˌfɪʃ] *n.* 圓鰭魚科

35. **dill** [dɪl] *n.* 蒔蘿；茴香

36. **dressing** [ˈdrɛsɪŋ] *n.* 調味醬料

37. **on the side** [ɑn] [ðə] [saɪd] *phr.* 作為配菜

BALSAMIC CREAM VS. BALSAMIC VINEGAR
巴薩米克奶油醬與巴薩米克醋

背景知識

balsamic 義大利文為 balsamico，意思是 balsam-like（像香脂一樣的），帶有能恢復健康、具有療效的意思，故中文亦有人將巴薩米克醋翻成義大利香醋。

2-2

現代烏托邦

圖片來源:（左圖）Wikipedia / Festival della Scienza from Genova、（右下）Wikimedia Commons / Rainer Zenz

巴薩米克醋（balsamic vinegar，義大利文 Aceto Balsamico）主要可分成三種:

一、**傳統巴薩米克醋**:只有產於摩德納（Modena）和雷吉歐‧艾米利亞（Reggio Emilia）、選用當地生產的 Lambrusco、Ancelotta、Trebbiano 三種葡萄品種、依照傳統工法經過壓榨、木桶發酵、再存放在專屬木桶裡經過至少十二年熟成的醋，才能標上 ABTM 或 ABTRE，兩者的命名同時受到官方保護。

摩德納的傳統巴薩米克醋（Traditional Balsamic Vinegar of Modena，義大利文為 Aceto Balsamico Tradizionale di Modena, ABTM）

雷吉歐‧艾米利亞的傳統巴薩米克醋（Traditional Balsamic Vinegar of Reggio Emilia，義大利文為 Aceto Balsamico Tradizionale di Reggio Emilia, ABTRE）

二、**調味品級巴薩米克醋**:標示為condimento balsamico、salsa balsamica 或 salsa di mosto cotto，意為調味巴薩米克醬。其熟成時間、產地等未達到官方規定而無法標示成傳統的巴薩米克醬。

三、**摩德納巴薩米克醋**（Balsamic Vinegar of Modena，義大利文為Aceto Balsamico di Modena, ABM）:為前兩種傳統巴薩米克醋的仿製品，價格較低廉，常與油混合作為沙拉醬使用

至於巴薩米克奶油醬（balsamic cream）又稱為巴薩米克濃縮葡萄醋，將巴薩米克醋以小火濃縮讓醋的酸味揮發，濃縮成膏狀的葡萄醋，常淋在食物上增添風味，或是作為盤飾。

對話

S : Samantha Brown, Hostess   **O** : Oscar Davidsen, Deli Owner

O The Millennium is fresh tomatoes, home smoked potatoes, **poached**[38] egg, and caviar. Roast beef with Piccalilli sauce. Fresh bought Alaska king crab. Our lovely fresh smoked herring. Roast beef with tomato and cucumber salad.

「千禧年」裡有新鮮番茄，煙燻馬鈴薯，水煮蛋和魚子醬。烤牛肉佐皮卡利利醬（辣泡菜汁）。剛選購的阿拉斯加帝王蟹。美味的新鮮燻鯡魚，烤牛肉夾番茄和黃瓜沙拉。

Fresh baked fish cakes. Caviar and fresh green asparagus. Then, we have three different kinds of liver pâté. Two different kinds of fresh smoked eel. Union Jack is made like the English flag with shrimps. This one is called Uffe Ellemann-Jensen, our former Foreign Minister of Affairs. Hansen Frederick. Hans Christian Andersen. You will have to find out what you like and we will try to make it for you. What would you like?

現烤魚片，魚子醬還有綠蘆筍，另外還有三種肝醬，兩種新鮮的煙燻鰻魚，「聯合傑克」是用蝦肉做的英國國旗三明治。這是以前外交部長艾蒙・傑森為名的三明治、還有名為「佛德瑞克」和「安徒生」三明治。看妳喜歡吃什麼，我們會立刻為妳製作，妳想吃哪一種？

S OK. So it's traditional to wash this all down with a beer, a local beer. So I'm going to do that. Now to try my **creation**.[39]

好了。傳統吃法是搭配當地啤酒，我也要入境隨俗。現在來嚐嚐我自己創作的三明治。

S That is really good. I mean, I'm serious.

太好吃了，我是說真的。

背景知識

WHAT GOES IN AN OPEN FACE SANDWICH
開放式三明治好好「加」

開放式三明治的餡料主要是一些冷盤類，
來看看文中介紹的食材：

Alaska king crab
阿拉斯加帝王蟹

raw salmon
生鮭魚

crayfish
小龍蝦；淡水蟹蝦

caviar
魚子醬

lime
萊姆

dill
蒔蘿

herring
鯡魚

asparagus
蘆筍

liver pâté
肝醬

smoked eel
煙燻鰻魚

roast beef
烤牛肉

Vocabulary

38. **poach** [potʃ] *v.* 水煮

39. **creation** [krɪˋeʃən] *n.* 創作物

UNIT 2-3

Going for a Spin

洗衣店飄來咖啡香

🎬 影片原音 07   🔊 課文朗讀 31

自述

I'm in Copenhagen, the capital of Denmark. It's a **compact**[1] city, which makes it very easy to get around on foot, and most everybody does. In the city's center is where you'll find just about all the **accommodations**,[2] and they **run the gamut** from luxury hotels, major **chains**,[3] all the way down to hostels. Standard room rates in Copenhagen . . . very expensive as you'll find in all of Scandinavia, actually. Best thing to do is find a few hotels that you like, then call them directly—see if you can **bring** their price **down**, and if they have rooms available, they will. Good news is, the weekend rates are actually cheaper. It's about 25 percent less.

這裡是丹麥的首都哥本哈根。這是個小巧的城市,所以很容易以步行的方式觀光,多數人都這麼做。在市中心能找到各式的住宿設施,從奢華旅館、連鎖旅店、到青年旅館都有。哥本哈根的旅館房價非常昂貴,整個斯堪地那維亞地區皆是如此。最好的方法是找一些喜歡的旅館,直接致電給他們——看看是否能把房價壓低,如果他們有空房也許就能成功。好消息是週末的房價事實上是較便宜的,大約少了約百分之二十五的費用。

run the (whole/full) gamut . . . 涉及……的全部範圍

gamut 表示「全部；全部的範圍」，the gamut of sth 意思是指「某事物全部、整個範圍」，常搭配動詞 run、之後可接 of sth 或 from . . . to。

- The questions on the math test ran the gamut from very easy to incredibly difficult.
  這個數學測驗的問題從很簡單到非常難的都有。

bring down 降低；減少

用法　bring down + N.
　　　bring + N./代名詞 + down

- As the song ended, the singer brought down the volume of his voice.
  歌曲結束時，那位歌手放低了他的音量。

【延伸學習】

bring down 的其他用法：

A. 擊落（人或物）；使（人）倒下

- The hunter brought down two birds with a single shot.
  獵人一槍便擊落了兩隻鳥。

B. 推翻（政府、統治者等）

- The government of Germany was brought down after the Allies won the war.
  同盟國贏得戰爭後，德國政府遭到推翻。

Vocabulary

1. **compact** [kʌmˋpækt] *adj.* 小巧的；小型的
2. **accommodation** [əˌkɑməˋdeʃən] *n.* 住所、住處（作此義時常用複數）
3. **chain** [tʃen] *n.* 連鎖商店或飯店

自述

I'm staying at The Square, named because it's located right off Town Hall Square. Outside it looks a bit **nondescript**. Inside is where it all changes. The Square is one of the few hotels, surprisingly enough, here in Copenhagen that has a strong Danish design **aesthetic**.[4] If you've never seen Danish design in full force, this is it. It's very **sleek**,[5] **non-fussy**, clean, **crisp**,[6] and I love the big red egg chairs—just makes things pop. I love the fact that this hotel is one of the few hotels I've stayed at where the check-in desk actually **segues**[7] **effortlessly**[8] into a full bar. And when you're here at eight-thirty in the morning, that bar is open.

There are 268 rooms, which is surprising for a hotel that has a more **intimate**[9] **boutique hotel**[10] feel. If street noise is an issue for you, request a room on one of the higher floors.

我下榻於廣場飯店，飯店名稱如此命名是因為它就座落在市政廳廣場旁。外觀看起來並不特別，裡面卻全然不同。廣場飯店是哥本哈根少數令人驚艷的旅館，因為其設計有著強烈的丹麥美學風格。如果你從未見過所有的丹麥風的設計，那這就是了。非常明亮簡潔，不拖泥帶水，我很喜歡那張紅色大蛋型椅，讓整體更具現代感。我還喜歡另一特點，這是我住過的旅館中，少數把大廳櫃檯巧妙融合在整個酒吧裡的，當你在早上八點半來到這裡，酒吧就已經開始營業了。

這裡有二百六十八間房間，令人驚訝的是，它有類似精品旅館溫馨怡人的感覺。如果介意街上的喧鬧聲，就要求較高樓層的房間來住吧。

non- 字首 non- 的用法

字首 non- 多與形容詞或名詞連用，表示「非；不；缺乏」。有些常見的用法或已收錄在字典中的單字則不加連字號，如文中的 nondescript 是 non- 加上 describe 的拉丁文過去分詞而來，表示「毫無特色的；毫不具吸引力的」。但若非常見的用法則會加上連字號，如 non-fussy 則表示「不會過於繁鎖的；不會過於講求裝飾的」，其他像專有名詞或字首為 n 時，也會加上連字號。

【延伸學習】

non + fat = nonfat 脫脂的

non + fiction = nonfiction 非小說類作品；紀實文學

non + profit = nonprofit 非營利（的）

non + American = non-American 非美國人；非美國的

non + native = non-native 非原生的；非本土的

Vocabulary

4. **aesthetic** [ɛsˋθɛtɪk] *n.* 美學

5. **sleek** [slik] *adj.* 流線的；造型優美的

6. **crisp** [ˋkrɪsp] *adj.* 簡潔乾脆的

7. **segue** [ˋsɛgwe] *v.* （直接）接入、轉到……（之後通常會接 into + N.）

8. **effortlessly** [ˋɛfətləsli] *adv.* 輕鬆地；毫不費力地

9. **intimate** [ˋɪntəmət] *adj.* 溫馨怡人；親密的

10. **boutique hotel** [buˋtik] [hoˋtɛl] *n. phr.* 精品旅館

自述

 So, now I thought we'd head out [and] discover a part of Copenhagen that we'd been missing by staying so close to the . . . the city's center. We're now in the neighborhood called Nørrebro.

Now that's . . . how it looks like it's pronounced, but I'm . . . I'm sure they say it a little differently, but I'm just going to go with that. It's about a twenty-minute bus ride from Town Hall Square. And I just got off the bus myself, but already I can tell that this is a much more **diverse**[11] and independent place to be.

This was one of the local tips that I got online at the tourism center. Remember Fleming? And I've also brought my laundry with me. Like when you do laundry in a hotel, it's like twelve dollars for a pair of pants. So when you've got a whole **load**, you'll travel far.

Well, it says **Laundromat**,[12] so it must be here. Wait a minute. Where are the washing machines, the **bleach dispensers**?[13] Why is it so nice? Hi, excuse me.

現在我們要離開市中心，去發掘哥本哈根市中心裡常被忽略的另一面。我們現在來到了諾布羅區。

看起來像是這樣發音，跟他們說的還是不太一樣，我就先暫時這樣說吧。從市政廳廣場到這裡，約是二十分鐘的巴士車程。我才從巴士下車，就已發現這裡是更多元、且與其他地方毫無關聯的地方。

這裡是我在旅客中心的網站上，查到的當地旅遊秘訣。記得富蘭明嗎？還有我也把要洗的衣服帶來了，就像是要在飯店洗衣服般。在飯店洗一件褲子約要十二美元，當你有一堆衣服要洗時，就只好跑遠一點了。

上面寫著自助洗衣店，一定就是這裡了。等一下，洗衣機和漂白粉販賣機呢？這裡怎麼這麼漂亮？你好，不好意思。

學習重點

load 的不同詞性與用法

A. 當名詞

可指「大量」，常用 **a load of N.** 指「一堆……」。也可用來指「（精神）負擔」。

- The woman carried a load of fruit in a basket on her head.
  那女人頭上頂著籃子，裡頭裝了一堆水果。

- Knowing that Jean got home safely was a load off my mind.
  得知琴平安到家讓我卸下心頭重擔。

B. 當動詞

指「裝載；使裝滿」，常用 **load A with B** 表示「把 B 裝到 A；用 B 把 A 裝滿」。

- The waitress loaded her tray with the dirty plates.
  女服務生把髒盤子裝到她的托盤上。

Vocabulary

11. **diverse** [dəˋvɝs] *adj.* 迥異、不同的；各式各樣的（也可唸成 [daɪˋvɝs]）

12. **Laundromat** [ˋlɔndrəˏmæt] *n.* 自助洗衣店

13. **bleach dispenser** [blitʃ] [dɪˋspɛnsə] *n. phr.* 漂白粉（劑）販賣機

對話

S : Samantha Brown, Hostess　　**I** : Ingvi Olafsson, Laundromat Owner

I	Hi.	你好。
S	Do you have any laundry machines here?	這裡有洗衣機嗎？
I	Yes, just right around the corner [is where] we have the Laundromat.	有，洗衣機就在那個角落。
S	Oh, I see them, great. If I can get a cappuccino.	喔，我看到了，太棒了。可以的話，請給我一杯卡布奇諾。
I	Yes, of course.	沒問題。
S	All right. I'll be right back.	我馬上回來。
I	Right away.	馬上來。
S	It's not doing anything.	完全沒反應。
S	Maybe I'll just have dirty clothes. At this point, who cares, right? Ooh, it's starting. All right. Man, I need a coffee.	也許我只能穿髒衣服了。這時候反正也沒人在意，對吧？喔，機器在動了。好了，我真的需要一杯咖啡。
S	Oh, perfect.	太好了。
I	Here's your cup of coffee.	這是你的咖啡。
S	Thank you.	謝謝。
I	Would you like some chocolate **sprinkles?**[14]	要灑點巧克力碎片嗎？

LAUNDROMAT　自助洗衣店

　　Laundromat為西屋電子公司
（Westinghouse Electric Corporation）
的通用商標，現在則用來泛指自助洗衣
（self-service laundry），在美加等地自
助洗衣通稱為 Laundromat，而在英國則
稱為 launderette。

　　大多數的自助洗衣店沒有店員，舉凡
購買洗衣粉、兌幣、洗衣、乾衣等操作流
程皆採自助式。一般來說，自助洗衣店裡
會提供下列設備：

洗衣機　washer, washing machine
烘乾機　dryer, drying machine
自動販賣機　vending machine

Vocabulary

14. **sprinkle** [ˈsprɪŋkl]] *n.* 灑在甜食（如冰淇淋）上的小餅乾或糖花碎片
　　（作此義時會用複數形）；少量、少數

對話

S : *Samantha Brown, Hostess*　　**I** : *Ingvi Olafsson, Laundromat Owner*

S I'd love some. So is this your place?	當然好。所以，這店是你的嗎？
I Yes, it is. Well, one of three owners.	是的。不過我是其中一位，總共有三人。
S I'm Samantha.	我是珊曼莎。
I Hi, **nice to meet you.** I'm Ingvi.	幸會。我是英維。
S Ingvi?	英維？
I Yeah.	是的。
S Oh, this is just wonderful. I mean, usually Laundromats are places you want to avoid.	喔，這裡真是太棒了。洗衣店通常是大家不愛來的場所。
I Yes.	沒錯。
S When you're traveling, they're not very nice.	旅行時去的洗衣店都不是太好。
I Exactly. It's a meeting place down here for meeting family and friends. We have a . . . a library—about four thousand books for while you are doing . . .	沒錯。這裡是和親朋好友會面的好去處。我們有自己的藏書櫃約四千本書，供在你洗衣的時候……
S Color **coordinated**[15] I see.	以顏色分類編排，沒錯。

nice to meet you 幸會；很高興認識你

nice to meet you 主要用於初次見面的打招呼用語，相當於 hello 的意思。
至於原本已認識的人之間可用 hello 或 nice to see you 來打招呼。
其他用於初次見面打招呼的用語包括：

- It's a pleasure to meet you. • Pleased to meet you.

- How do you do?（主要是用於正式的場合，朋友間通常不會用這麼正式的說法）

- Jim: Helen, let me introduce you to Jane Hausen, the company president.

    海倫，我來介紹你跟董事長珍‧霍森認識。

  Jane: How do you do, Helen?

    幸會，海倫。

  Helen: Hello, Ms. Hausen. It's a pleasure to meet you.

    哈囉，霍森小姐妳好。很榮幸認識妳。

【延伸學習】

初次見面後告別時，一般會說 Nice meeting you.，至於原本熟識的人則會說
Good-bye!、Nice seeing you. 或是 See you soon.

旅遊小幫手

The Laundromat Café 自助洗衣咖啡館

你可以在這裡同時洗衣服、喝咖啡、吃東西或是看書，並且供應三餐以及點心。

🕐 Monday–Friday: 8:00 a.m.–midnight　　Saturday–Sunday: 10:00 a.m.–midnight

📞 (45) 35 35 26 72

🌐 http://www.thelaundromatcafe.com

Vocabulary

15. **coordinated** [koˋɔrdəˌnetəd] *adj.* 和諧的；協調的

對話

S : *Samantha Brown, Hostess*   **I** : *Ingvi Olafsson, Laundromat Owner*

I Color coordinated. So a lot of people come down here to wash their clothes, have a **bite**[16] to eat, and do a lot of work on their computers. And, so, it's **multitasking** here.

用顏色分類編排。所以很多人會來這裡洗衣服、吃東西、用電腦工作。這裡可說是一間複合式的洗衣店。

S I've really enjoyed being out in this neighborhood because being in the center of Copenhagen you get the feeling that it's sort of an all-white **monoculture**.[17]

我很喜歡這個地區的感覺,因為在哥本哈根市中心,感覺上多少有點全白人文化。

I Yeah, when you come out to this, out to the **suburbs**,[18] and especially around here, ~~and~~ you see the . . . the **melting pot**[19] actually that Copenhagen is. A lot of different cultures from, you know, the Middle East and Africa, Eastern Europe, all over.

當你來到郊區,尤其是這裡,就能見識到哥本哈根融合其他文化的部分。有許多來自中東、非洲、東歐等不同地方的文化。

S Well, thank you so much. It's amazing what you learn between the **rinse**[20] and the **spin**[21] cycle.

非常感謝你,在洗衣時還能學到這些真好。

I Yes. That's really good to hear.

很高興聽到妳這麼說。

學習重點

multi- 字首 multi- 的用法

字首 multi- 有「多重的；數倍的」之意。文中 multitasking 就是 multi- 加上 task 的動名詞構成的，表示「同時處理多重任務的；多工的」。

【延伸學習】

multi- + purpose = multipurpose 多用途；多重目的

multi- + cultural = multicultural 多元文化的

multi- + function = multifunction 多重功能

multi- + color = multicolor 多色

multi- + lane = multilane 多線道

multi- + level = multilevel 多層次（的）

multi- + media = multimedia 多媒體

- Cars were stopped on the multilane road because of an accident.
  因為一起事故，多線道上的車子都被攔了下來。

Vocabulary

16. **bite** [baɪt] *n.* 少量的食物或點心

17. **monoculture** [ˈmɑnəˌkʌltʃɚ] *n.* 單一文化

18. **suburbs** [ˈsʌbɝbz] *n.* 近郊；城鎮周圍（常用複數）

19. **melting pot** [ˈmɛltɪŋ] [pɑt] *n.* 熔爐

20. **rinse** [rɪns] *n., v.* 沖洗、清洗；漱（口）

21. **spin** [spɪn] *n., v.* 脫水；（用洗衣機）將……脫水

The Mermaid and the Roller Coaster
心中永遠的童話

 影片原音 08　　 課文朗讀 32

自述

So, I'm **about to** take you to the number one attraction in Denmark. It's a place where the mere mention of its name alone causes every Dane in Denmark to get all misty-eyed. This is Tivoli, an old-time **amusement park**[1] right in the center of the city. This has been a favorite Copenhagen destination since 1843.

我將帶大家前往丹麥首選的觀光景點。只要一提到這個地方,所有丹麥人的眼睛就會變得迷濛。這是蒂沃利,位於市中心的古老遊樂園。從一八四三年開始,這裡就一直是哥本哈根最受歡迎的地方。

150

學習重點

be about to V. 將要……; 即將……

be about to 指「即將要發生；接下來就要進行……」，與 be going to 意思相同。而否定的 be not about/going to 則強調「某人不打算……；某事還不會……」。

- We are about to start the movie, so sit down and be quiet.
  我們電影即將要開始了，所以坐下來且保持安靜。

- Jack is not going to give you money. He doesn't even like you.
  傑克不會給你錢的。他甚至就不喜歡你。

比較：be about to 和 will 都可用來表示未來的事件，但意思稍有不同，will 主要是指「未來的任何一個時間點」，be about to 較接近 will be V-ing 的意思。

- These new fashions will hit the stores next spring.
  這些新款流行服飾明年春天就會上市。

旅遊小幫手

Tivoli 蒂沃利遊樂園

這座一八四三年開幕的遊樂園歷史悠久，就位於哥本哈根市中心。

- $ Adult: DKK 95.00
  Group (min. 15): DKK 90.00
  Child (ages 0–7): free
- ☎ (45) 33 15 1001
- 🌐 http://www.tivoli.dk/en/

圖片來源：Wikipedia / Malte Hübner

Vocabulary

1. **amusement park** [ə`mjuzmənt] [pɑrk] *n.* 遊樂園

對話

S : *Samantha Brown, Hostess*　　**M** : *Maya Bjørnsten, Guide*

S Showing me **the sights and sounds of** this beloved attraction is Copenhagen **native**[2] Maya Bjørnsten. When was the first time you came here?

帶我去此景點大開眼界的是哥本哈根的當地人，瑪雅・碧洋斯頓。妳第一次來這裡是什麼時候？

M I think I was about two years old . . . I think.

我想，大概是我兩歲的時候吧。

S You were two years old?

兩歲？

M Yeah. Yeah.

對呀。

S And when was the last time you came here?

那妳最近一次來這裡是什麼時候？

M Three weeks ago.

三週前。

S But it's interesting because if you walk around Copenhagen, the city is so design **forward**,[3] the people are very **conscious**[4] style-wise, and yet this is very old-fashioned.

哥本哈根真的很有趣，當你走在這裡時，會發現城市的設計很先進，大家都非常注重流行，然而這裡卻充滿了懷舊的氣氛。

M Old-fashioned, yeah.

懷舊的氣氛。

S So you guys are kind of **mushy**,[5] aren't you?

所以你們其實很念舊，是吧？

the sights and sounds of N. ……的所見所聞

sight 是指「景象；見到的事物」，sound 是指「聲音」，the sights and sounds 常搭配使用，用來表示「所見到、體會到的事物」。

● We enjoyed the sights and sounds of the beach and had a good time.
我們很享受海水浴場的一切，玩得很開心。

style-wise 就流行而言

-wise 這個字尾除了常見的「朝……方向（clockwise 順時針的）或「和……相同（likewise 同樣地）」意思之外，也常和名詞搭配指「就……而言；就……考量」，用來代替語氣較正式的 in terms of，常見的搭配有：

location + wise = location-wise 就地點而言

time + wise = time-wise 就時間而言

money + wise = money-wise 就金錢考量

weather + wise = weather-wise 就天氣而言

Vocabulary

2. **native** [ˋnetɪv] *n.* 本地人

3. **forward** [ˋfɔrwəd] *adj.* 向前的；前瞻性的

4. **conscious** [ˋkɑnʃəs] *adj.* 特別感興趣的；關注的

5. **mushy** [ˋmʌʃɪ] *adj.* 多愁善感的；感傷多情的

對話

S : Samantha Brown, Hostess　　**M** : Maya Bjørnsten, Guide

M Yeah. Yeah. We . . . we like to keep or to restore our old-fashioned places.	是的。我們喜歡保留或是修復具有古早味的地方。
S Everyone comes here to be with each other . . .	大家都和朋友……
M Yeah.	是呀。
S . . . and have a good time.	來這裡遊玩。
M [It is a] **Supreme**[6] spot in . . . in the city—in the center. Lots of people just come here also just to hang out, relax, and . . .	這裡位於市中心最棒的地點。許多人會來這裡閒晃、放鬆……
S I'm not going to hang out and relax. Roller coaster. Maya, how about a roller coaster?	我可不是來閒晃放鬆的。我要去坐雲霄飛車。瑪雅，陪我去坐雲霄飛車，好嗎？
M I'm not. I'm not. I'm going just to sit quiet[ly].	我不要。我不要。我只想靜靜地坐在這裡就好。
S One roller coaster, that's it. Just one roller-coaster ride with me.	就坐一次，一次就好，跟我一起吧！
M No, ~~not~~ [no] more. No. No.	不，我不想再坐了。
S No, yes, you are. You're coming with me.	不，妳想的，妳當然想坐。跟我來吧！

AMUSEMENT PARK RIDES
圖解遊樂園設施

free-fall ride
自由落體

spinning teacup ride
旋轉咖啡杯

bumper car
碰碰車

Ferris wheel
摩天輪

chair swing ride/
chair-o-plane 旋轉飛椅

roller coaster
雲霄飛車

merry-go-round/
carousel 旋轉木馬

Vocabulary

6. **supreme** [sʊˋprim] *adj.* （權位、程度、特性）最高的

對
話

S : Samantha Brown, Hostess　　M : Maya Bjørnsten, Guide

S	I think I just **swallowed**[7] a bug. We grabbed a front row seat from one of the old **workhorses**[8] of the park, and it dates back to 1914. This is one of the world's oldest roller coasters. Yeah. One more time. I think Maya **is more of** a Ferris wheel kind of woman.	我想我剛才吞了一隻蟲。我們搭上了園中最古老雲霄飛車的前座,其於一九一四年就開始啟用。這是世上最古老的雲霄飛車之一。再來一次。我想瑪雅比較像是那種喜歡坐摩天輪的女生。
S	So is this one of the oldest rides here?	這是這裡最古老的遊樂設施之一?
M	Yeah, I think so, yeah.	是的,我想是這樣沒錯。
S	This is great. You get a great view of the city, too.	感覺真棒,這裡可以看到很棒的城市景觀。
M	Yeah, it is beautiful.	風景很美。
S	I can't get over that. I mean, it is amazing to be at an amusement park, and up you go, and you see spires and steeples and . . .	這美麗的景色令我久久無法忘懷。這裡很神奇的是,當妳身處遊樂園,搭上摩天輪上升時,看見的是那些尖塔建築……
M	Here in the evening, they have fireworks here. It is beautiful. It is huge.	晚上這裡還會有煙火表演。太美了,這裡真大。

Vocabulary

7. **swallow** [ˈswɑlo] *v.* 吞下;吞沒

8. **workhorse** [ˈwɜkˌhɔrs] *n.* 堪負重荷的人或機器(此文指啟用已久的雲霄飛車)

be more of A (than B) 比較像 A（而非 B）

此句型表示「比較像 A 而非 B；與其說是 B，不如說是 A」，A、B 皆為名詞。

- No matter what the title is, the film is more of a comedy than a horror film.

  不管片名是什麼，這部影片都比較像是喜劇片而不是恐怖片。

背景知識

FERRIS WHEEL
摩天輪知多少

　　一八九三年時，喬治・費瑞斯（George W. Ferris）為了芝加哥世界博覽會（Chicago World's Fair）建造了第一座摩天輪，高約八十公尺，當時的目的是想要和法國的艾菲爾鐵塔（Eiffel Tower）一較高下，而這項偉大的工程也以他命名，稱為 Ferris wheel。

　　傳統的摩天輪又稱為重力式摩天輪，其座艙是掛在輪上，藉著重力來維持水平。另一種稱作觀景摩天輪（observation wheel），其座艙懸在輪子外面，透過機械連桿和主輪連結，主輪轉動時座艙會跟著移動。位於英國泰晤士（River Thames）河畔，於一九九九年開幕的倫敦眼（the London Eye）即為代表，亦是世界上第一座觀景摩天輪。

倫敦眼又稱為千禧之輪（Millennium Wheel）高一百三十五公尺，可乘坐八百人，現已成為倫敦相當受歡迎的景點。

維也納摩天輪（Wiener Riesenrad）是現存建於十九世紀的摩天輪，位於維也納普拉特遊樂場中，目前仍在營運。

自述

But people don't come to Tivoli just for the rides. There are beautiful gardens, an old-fashioned **midway**,[9] and thirty-seven restaurants. In fact, the locals willingly pay the **admission**[10] price just to eat here. Of course, not every food at Tivoli **is aimed at** the **sophisticated**[11] **gourmet**.[12]

Look at that. It's like Marge Simpson hair. There's no doubt that for everyone this is **a trip down memory lane**. While most old-fashioned amusement parks have been replaced by their super modern **counterparts**,[13] the Danes like their Tivoli just the way it is.

You can't come to Copenhagen and not see The Little Mermaid. Actually, OK, you can. She's kind of a **trek**[14] to get to because she's not in the city's center, and honestly, I would have completely missed her if it hadn't been for all the people taking pictures and the boats coming up. I was like, "Oh, **what's all the fuss?** Oh, that's The Little Mermaid."

人們來這裡不只是玩遊樂設施，這裡還有美麗的花園、舊式的遊樂園，還有三十七間餐廳。事實上有些當地人甚至願意付門票入園，就為了進來用餐。當然園區裡不是所有的食物都是精緻美食。

你們看，這就像是瑪姬‧辛普森的頭髮。這裡對大家來說，無疑是懷念舊日時光的好地方。當多數舊式遊樂園都被超級先進的設施所取代時，丹麥人卻喜歡蒂沃利保有原來的樣子。

來到哥本哈根，絕不能錯過知名的美人魚。其實，錯過也無妨，因為她不在市中心裡，你還得走上一段路才能見到她，老實說，我很有可能會錯過她，還好有這些拍照的人和來往的觀光船隻。我心想：「他們在看些什麼？喔，原來是小美人魚。」

be aimed at/for sth/V-ing 針對……; 旨在……

aim 在此作動詞，意思是「致力於；以……為目標」，之後可接介系詞 at 或 for。

- The advertisements were aimed at attracting people who have young children.
  這則廣告的目標族群是家有幼童的人。

- I was aiming for a B on my test, but I was happy to see that I got an A.
  我這次考試成績的目標是 B，但我很開心看到我得到 A。

a trip down memory lane 懷念舊日時光

以字面意思「到回憶的小巷裡一遊」來比喻「回憶起往事；懷舊」的意思。也可以寫成複數 trips down memory lane「回憶往事；舊地重遊」。

what's all the fuss 有何大驚小怪

fuss 在此作名詞，指「大驚小怪」。what's all the fuss 用來詢問發生什麼事，其他類似說法包括：

- What's the big fuss?
- What's the big problem?
- What's all the fuss about?

Vocabulary

9. **midway** [ˋmɪd͵we] *n.* 遊樂場（美語用法）

10. **admission** [ədˋmɪʃən] *n.* 入場費；准許進入

11. **sophisticated** [səˋfɪstə͵ketəd] *adj.* 精緻的

12. **gourmet** [ˋgur͵me] *n.* 美食

13. **counterpart** [ˋkauntə͵part] *n.* 互相對應的人或物；極相像的人或物

14. **trek** [trɛk] *n.* 長途跋涉；遠距離行走

自述

 If you want to visit this statue, you should **beware**[15] there's not much else to see in this area, so you may not want to build a whole day trip around her.

Surprising that this is the city's symbol. Actually, I think she's quite beautiful. I mean, **underwhelming**[16] as a city symbol, yes, but they don't call her The Little Mermaid for nothing.

I think there are two ways to discover Copenhagen. One is simply enjoying its unending **charm**.[17] You've got that picture postcard in your mind, and all you want to do is sit alongside one of the historic canals and drink a beer. You should know [that] if you're interested in discovering a real city, one that is diverse, **intriguing**,[18] and full of surprises, then that experience is here for you, too.

如果你想來看這座雕像，要知道這附近並沒什麼景點，所以不需花一整天在它身邊閒晃。

沒想到這就是哥本哈根的象徵。其實我覺得她還挺美的。我是說要作為全市象徵，也許還不夠特別，但美人魚的盛名可不是平白而來的。

我認為探訪哥本哈根，共有兩種方法：一是單純地享受當地源源不絕的魅力。腦海中想著明信片上的風景，坐在歷史悠久的運河邊，享用一杯啤酒。如果你喜愛發掘城市的多變、有趣、充滿驚喜的真實風貌，那這裡正是你該來體驗的好地方。

Vocabulary

15. **beware** [bɪˋwɛr] v. 當心；注意

16. **underwhelming** [ˏʌndəˋhwɛlmɪŋ] adj. 未留下深刻印象的；不熱烈的

17. **charm** [tʃɑrm] n. 魅力；魔力

18. **intriguing** [ɪnˋtrigɪŋ] adj. 有趣的；引人入勝的

自述

I never felt as I sometimes do with these picture-perfect cities that I had seen it all. In fact, as I leave it, I think how I'd love to come back. This is a great city—a lot of unknowns here. Copenhagen is a dream city, absolutely, but once you've been told the fairy tale, you want to see how the real story ends.

我從不覺得在這些美麗的城市中,我已看見全部面貌。事實上當我離開後,我還會想再度造訪。這是個很棒的城市,仍有許多不知道的事情。哥本哈根絕對是個夢幻城市,然而一旦你聽到童話故事,你就會想知道真實故事究竟是如何結束的。

2-4

心中永遠的童話

一分鐘速寫

法國

FRANCE IN ONE MINUTE

　　法國位於西歐，全名為「法蘭西共和國」，受歡迎的程度可從二〇一二年的旅遊數據中看得出來。光是這一年，法國就吸引了八千三百萬名遊客，可說是世界數一數二的觀光業國家。以美食著稱的法國，其中又以里昂——法國第二大城市（以人口數計算）號稱為美食之都。珊曼莎不免俗地介紹傳統的里昂餐廳和法式家常料理，還要帶我們一探究竟隱密的串廊以及引人入勝的巨幅藝術壁畫，最後還要親自會會這位深受人們喜愛的傳奇人物——吉尼奧爾。

首都：巴黎
CAPITAL: PARIS

官方語言：法語
OFFICIAL LANGUAGE: FRENCH

貨幣：歐元（€）
CURRENCY: EURO (EUR)

人口：65,950,000（2013 年統計）
POPULATION (2012): 65,950,000

國際電話區碼：+33
CALLING CODE: +33

UNIT 3

3-1 通往美食的捷徑

珊曼莎來到了里昂的舊市區，走進串廊，四百多條連接各地的祕密通道，讓探訪城市變得更容易，接著珊曼莎將帶您一同體驗道地法式家常美食。

3-2 非看不可的里昂

眼見為憑？！在里昂，我們看見了巨幅錯視壁畫，壁畫建築為城市帶來了趣味。珊曼莎還到了有二百五十年歷史的絲綢工廠，除了了解絲綢歷史，還親自嘗試織圍巾。

3-3 前進吧！口袋美食！

珊曼莎在美食之都里昂學做法式口袋料理，接著到了里昂的半島區，這裡與里昂其他地方大異其趣，由於地勢平坦，很適合單車旅遊。

3-4 隨處可見的吉尼奧爾

里昂最有名的木偶人物非吉尼奧爾莫屬了，它會如此受歡迎，其實有個精采的故事。珊曼莎要帶我們去一探究竟。

A Shortcut to Good Food
通往美食的捷徑

🔊 影片原音 09　　🔊 課文朗讀 33

自述

 If I told you that I was in the **culinary**[1] capital of France, where do you think that would be? Paris, of course. No. Close. I'm in Lyon, France, which gets this very **weighty**[2] title by being the **hub**[3] of surrounding **regions**[4] famous for award-winning wine, meat, **poultry**,[5] cheese, produce. And right now, I'm in this wonderful open market right along the Saône River. This is every single day, you know? This is just normal business here in Lyon. There is no doubt that people take their food very seriously here. But really, isn't that something we assume about all of France, no matter what city you are in? So, I was wondering, you know, what makes this different than any other in France? And today, that is what we are going to discover, the **unexpected**[6] Lyon, France.

若説我身在法國的美食之都，你會認為是哪裡？想必是巴黎。不對，很接近了。這裡是法國里昂。這裡因匯集了周圍各地區的精華而頗負盛名，有得獎的葡萄酒、肉類、家禽、乳酪與農產品聞名遐邇，這裡是頌恩河畔一處很棒的露天市場。每天都是這番景象，這是里昂本地的日常事務，當地居民毫無疑問地相當重視飲食，但不論在哪一個城市，所有法國人不都該是如此？所以我想知道，這裡與其他法國城市有何不同？今天我們就要來探索法國里昂令人驚艷的面貌。

award-winning 獲獎的；得獎的

award-winning是複合形容詞，複合形容詞有多種形式，award-winning 屬於「N. + V-ing」，類似例子有 peace-loving（愛好和平的）、eye-opening（大開眼界的）等。

- The peace-loving man tried to stop the two women from fighting.
  那個愛好和平的人試著阻止那兩位女子爭吵。

- Our visit to the poor village was an eye-opening experience.
  探訪那個貧窮村落是一次令我們大開眼界的經歷。

take sth/sb seriously 認真地看待某事 / 某人

take 在此為「看待、接受」的意思。take sth/sb seriously 表示「認真看待……；把……看得很重要」，相反詞為 take sth/sb lightly，表示「不把……當一回事」。

- You always need to take your studies seriously if you want to get into a good university.
  你如果想上好大學，就一定要把課業當一回事。

- Tom was angry when he spoke to you, so take what he said lightly.
  湯姆跟你說話時還在氣頭上，所以他說什麼你都不要理會。

Vocabulary

1. **culinary** [ˈkʌləˌnɛri] *adj.* 烹飪的；食物的

2. **weighty** [ˈweti] *adj.* 有份量的；重要的

3. **hub** [hʌb] *n.* 中樞；核心

4. **region** [ˈridʒən] *n.* 地區；區域

5. **poultry** [ˈpoltri] *n.* （總稱）家禽；家禽肉

6. **unexpected** [ˌʌnɪkˈspɛktəd] *adj.* 意想不到的；出乎意料的

自述

Lyon is a beautiful city. It has not one but two rivers that flow through it, the Rhône and the Saône. There are also two hills that give its landscape a bit of **oomph**.[7] The hill that is **capped**[8] by the cathedral is known as the hill that **prays**,[9] and ahead is the hill that works. This is where the silk **weavers**[10] set up shop in the 1800s, and the making of fine silk is what gave Lyon its wealth and **prestige**.[11]

Lyon is France's second largest city after Paris, and yet I have found this city to have an **intimacy**[12] that makes it very easy to be in. Lyon is **at ease**[13] with itself. And it is that, combined with its river-reflected beauty, that makes this a city to relax in and **savor**.[14] So let us savor it, shall we?

里昂是個美麗的城市，不只有一條，而是有兩條河流貫其中，即隆河與頌恩河。還有兩座山丘，讓這片美景更添引人入勝之處。上頭有教堂的山丘，稱為「祈禱之丘」，前方則是「工作之丘」，十九世紀的絲織工人就是在此設立工作坊，精絲製造業替里昂帶來了財富與聲望。

在法國，里昂是僅次於巴黎的第二大城，然而我認為這城市散發的親切感讓人感到非常自在，里昂本身就相當不拘束，再加上倒映在河上的美景，能令人放鬆並盡情品味，就讓我們來好好品味吧！

露天市集買菜去
OPEN MARKETS IN FRANCE

露天市集是法國居民購買食材的好去處，這種市集通常就在街區的小廣場、人行道或者河邊，搭上棚架擺上攤位就開賣了。不同街區的市集營業時間也不相同。在法國，人們並不習慣殺價，尤其露天市集的價格已比較便宜。其實攤販也常隨興計價，常常少算個幾分或者多送個蔬果。有趣的是攤販的叫賣聲，通常離市場大老遠就會聽見攤販扯開嗓子飛快地喊著 "cinq euros le kilo, cinq euros le kilo"（一公斤五歐元）。隨著時間越晚，價格越便宜，就會慢慢聽見 "deux euros, deux euros . . . un euro, un euro . . . "（兩歐元⋯⋯一歐元），這時可能已不是以公斤計，而是以籃或箱計，所以一個不小心就會買回成山的蔬果。

Vocabulary

7. **oomph** [ʊmf] *n.* 活力；熱情、吸引力

8. **cap** [kæp] *v.* 由⋯⋯覆蓋頂端

9. **pray** [pre] *v.* 祈禱；禱告

10. **weaver** [ˋwivə] *n.* 編織者；織布工

11. **prestige** [prɛˋstiʒ] *n.* 聲望；威信

12. **intimacy** [ˋɪntəməsi] *n.* 親密；親近

13. **at ease** [æt] [iz] *phr.* 安逸；自在、不拘束

14. **savor** [ˋsevə] *v.* 品味；盡情享受

對話

S : Samantha Brown, Hostess　　**F** : Francois Gonzales, Guide

F All right. Let us go down. We are falling. We are going . . .	好，我們往下走，要跌下去了。我們要……
S Showing me around is Lyon native Francois Gonzales, who is taking me through this city's most historical district: Vieux Lyon, or Old Town.	我的導遊是里昂當地人，法蘭西‧岡澤拉斯，他帶我參觀里昂最具歷史背景的地區，里昂舊城區。
F And now we reach the oldest street in Vieux Lyon, Rue du Boeuf. Do you know what a *traboule* is?	這條就是舊城區最古老的路，牛路。妳知道「串廊」是什麼嗎？
S No.	不知道。
F No?	不知道？
S No.	不知道。
F OK. **Passageways**[15] that **link**[16] two parallel streets.	好。是連接兩條平行街道的通道。
S Yes?	然後？
F A network, **labyrinth-like**,[17] and we use them as **shortcuts**.[18]	就像網狀通道，迷宮一般的，我們當作捷徑來用。
S Oh, yes.	真的？
F Would you like to play with the labyrinth of Vieux Lyon?	妳想走走看里昂的迷宮嗎？
S Yes, certainly.	當然想。

漫談 TRABOULE

　　「串廊」建築發展於西元四世紀,當時為了取水方便,因而築起從山丘直達河岸的建築。traboule 來自 transambulare,指「穿越」,而後用來指貫穿街道兩側穿堂的走道。文藝復興時期,因為絲綢業成了里昂經濟的重要支柱,這些串廊可供搬運絲綢的工人穿過大街小巷,節省搬運時間,並且也可防止絲綢在下雨天運送時被淋濕。目前里昂還保有這些串廊,但因為大部分的老房子還是有人居住,所以不是全部都開放給大眾參觀。

旅遊小幫手

Vieux Lyon　里昂舊城區

里昂最古老的城區,這裡有超過四百年的地下通道,作為區域之間的捷徑。

Adult: EUR 12　Student: EUR 5　Child (8 and under): free

http://www.en.lyon-france.com/Guided-Tours-Excursions/Unmissable/Vieux-Lyon-and-its-Traboules

Vocabulary

15. **passageway** [ˈpæsɪdʒ‚we] *n.* 通道;走廊

16. **link** [lɪŋk] *v.* 連接;聯繫

17. **labyrinth-like** [ˈlæbə‚rɪnθˈlaɪk] *adj.* 像迷宮一樣的;迷宮一般的

18. **shortcut** [ˈʃɔrt‚kʌt] *n.* 捷徑

對
話

S : Samantha Brown, Hostess　　　**F** : Francois Gonzales, Guide

F All right. Let us go for it. It's very easy. The door. Press a button. ~~Put~~ [Turn] the lights on. *Et voilà*.

好，我們出發吧。其實非常簡單，這是門，然後按個鈕，再把燈打開就好了。

S Oh, my goodness. So these are passageways?

我的天啊，所以這些是通道？

F These are passageways. We use them as shortcuts to go from one street to the other, and during the silk trade, weaving[s] ~~these~~ were carried from one place to the other without getting wet on rainy days.

對，我們利用這些通道當作往來街道間的捷徑，在絲織貿易時期，絲藉由這些通道來往運輸在雨天就不會被淋溼了。

S Wow.

哇！

F Of course, in the morning, you will also be protected from ~~receiving the pot on top of your head~~ [getting a pot dumped on your head]. Remember?

當然在早上也能避免被傾倒的排泄物淋到，記得嗎？

S Oh, when they would dump out the **chamber pot?**[19]

當人們把夜壺往外倒的時候？

Vocabulary

19. **chamber pot** [ˋtʃembə] [pɑt] *n.*（舊時的）夜壺、尿壺

對話

S : *Samantha Brown, Hostess*   **F** : *Francois Gonzales, Guide*

F Yes.	對。
S Nice.	很好。
F So we need to continue. And of course, since we are in houses which are lived with people . . .	所以我們得繼續前進，既然這些房舍有人居住。
S Uh-huh.	嗯。
F . . . you have to keep quiet because some of them might still be asleep. So let us ~~put~~ [turn] some lights on.	我們要安靜點，因為可能有人還在睡覺，現在我們把燈打開。
S So people live up above?	所以樓上有人住？
F Yes, they are living here.	對，他們住在這裡。
S Wow. But today, people use them to, you know, have their groceries and . . . and not get wet.	但今日人們通過這裡去買日用品，以及躲雨。
F Exactly.	沒錯。
S So, people still use these today?	所以到今日仍在使用？
F Yes. Here we are.	出來了。
S All right. That is great.	很好。太棒了！
F Isn't it?	很棒吧！
S So, how many *traboule* are there?	總共有多少條串廊？
F More or less, 400.	四百條左右。

3-1

通往美食的捷徑

對話

S : Samantha Brown, Hostess   **F** : Francois Gonzales, Guide

S	400.	四百條。
F	Yeah.	是的。
S	We have got a lot of work to do.	那今天我們還有得忙。
F	You bet.	沒錯。
S	Do we have **access** to all of them?	每一條都能進去嗎？
F	No, not quite. Some of them are actually private.	不一定，有些是私人財產。
S	Yes.	是的。
F	But quite a lot of them are open.	但大多都開放大眾進入。
S	That is great.	很好。
F	But you can also get a good map from the . . .	你可以去拿地圖參考，從……
S	I was going to say, because I would never know that that doorway led to those passageways.	我正想說我根本不會知道那扇門可以通往那些通道。
F	Definitely not.	沒錯。
S	Are we going to see more? Because now I'm sort of **impressed**.[20]	要多走幾條嗎？因為我現在深受吸引。
F	Yeah, sure. Would you like to try another one?	沒問題，要去走另一條嗎？
S	Yes.	要。

access 進入權；使用……的機會或權利

A. 作名詞，可指「使用權、進入權；接近某人或使用某物的機會或權利」，常用 **have access to N.** 表示「能夠使用、接觸某人事物」。

- This white card will give you access to the whole building.
  這張白色卡片會讓你擁有這整棟大樓的進入權。

- Only teachers have access to this restroom, but students can use the one over there.
  這間洗手間只有老師可使用，學生則可用那邊那一間。

B. 作動詞，表示「使用；存取（電腦資料）」。

- To access this computer, you need to know the password.
  你需要知道密碼才能存取這台電腦的資料。

Vocabulary

20. **impress** [ɪmˋprɛs] *v.* 給……留下深刻印象

對
話

S : Samantha Brown, Hostess　　**F** : Francois Gonzales, Guide

S OK. Oh, let us try here.	好。試試這條吧！
F No.	不行。
S No?	不行？
F It's . . . no.	這條不行。
S No? You don't want me to wake the people up, do you?	你怕我吵醒裡面的人吧！
F No. Actually, there is no way to tell. Either you know or you don't.	不是，其實這無法判斷，不知道的話就別進去。
S Really?	真的？
F Or you have a good map, and that is it.	除非你有張好地圖！
S OK.	好。
F OK. Try this one.	試試看這一條！
S This one, is it?	這一條？
F Yes.	對。
S OK. I recognize this. So we want to look for this.	我認得這個。所以我們要找這個。
F Yeah. Well, you were lucky ~~on~~ this time.	這次算妳運氣好。
S So you press that little button there and turn on the light. Voilà.	所以按那個鈕，把燈打開，就可以進去了。瞧！

對話

S : *Samantha Brown, Hostess*　　**F** : *Francois Gonzales, Guide*

F After you.	妳先請。
S Oh, this one's pretty. Nice colors.	這條好漂亮，顏色很美。
F Yes, it's very pretty.	非常漂亮。
S So this is absolutely gorgeous. So . . .	實在太美麗了！
F Yes.	是的。
S . . . some *traboules* must be nicer than others.	一定會有些比較漂亮的串廊。
F Indeed. This one is fifteenth century, for example, and one of the prettiest in the old section.	的確如此，例如這條建於十五世紀，是舊市區最美麗的串廊之一。
S So, this was all built during the **Renaissance**[21] period, which is . . .	所以這些全建於文藝復興時期……
F Yes. Mostly fifteenth, sixteenth century. Second largest environment of buildings from that period, after Venice, in the world.	對，大部分是在十五或十六世紀，是當時世界上僅次於威尼斯的第二大建築區。
S And yet we are in France.	而我們還身處法國。
F And we are still in France.	依舊身在法國。

3-1

通往美食的捷徑

Vocabulary 🔊

21. **Renaissance** [ˌrɛnəˋsɑns] *n.* 文藝復興

自述

The journey down each *traboule* is short, but they **reveal**[22] inner **courtyards**,[23] **arched**[24] **porticos**,[25] even a large **spiral**[26] staircase called the Pink Tower. Walking through a *traboule* gives you the feeling of being deep within the city, but it's never too long before you are out on the street again.

每條串廊的路程很短，但途經內部庭院、拱型門廊，甚至有稱為「粉紅塔」的大型螺旋階梯，走在串廊之間，給人置身城市深處的感覺。但很快地，就又回到大街上。

Being the culinary capital of France, Lyon has many **top-rated**[27] restaurants. But if you want to eat with the locals, you have to go to an establishment known as the *bouchon*. Blandine, Michael, and I are having lunch at Café des Fédérations. **It's believed to be** the city's oldest *bouchon*.

身為法國的美食之都，里昂市內有許多一流餐廳，但若想和當地人共享美食，就得去所謂的「家常菜餐廳」，布蘭汀、麥可和我正在「聯邦咖啡廳」吃午餐，一般相信這裡是全市歷史最悠久的家常菜餐廳。

對話

S : *Samantha Brown, Hostess*　　**M₁** : *Male, Bouchon Owner*

M₂ : *Michael, American in Lyon*　　**B** : *Blandine Thenet, Michael's Friend*

M₁ (*speaking in foreign language*) Bon appétit.	（法語） 祝你胃口大開！
S Merci.	謝謝。
M₂ Merci beaucoup, monsieur.	謝謝你。
B Merci.	謝謝。

It is believed to be . . . 一般相信……；據信……

在此 it 為代名詞，指稱前面提到的 Café des Fédérations，此句型用來表達客觀的立場，表示「據信……」，亦可改用虛主詞 it 或 people believe that . . . 的句型來表示：

> 用法
> S. + be believed to V.
> = It is believed that S. + V.
> = People believe that S. + V.

- Killer whales are believed to be the travelers and keepers of the sea.
↳ It is believed that killer whales are the travelers and keepers of the sea.
↳ People believe that killer whales are the travelers and keepers of the sea.
據信殺人鯨被認為是遨遊海洋的守護者。

【延伸學習】

這類句型常用的動詞還包括：think、say、report 等。

- Sea bears such as Miga are thought to have evolved from killer whales.
↳ It is thought that sea bears such as Miga evolved from killer whales.
↳ People think that sea bears such as Miga evolved from killer whales.
像米加這樣的海熊被認為是由殺人鯨演化而來的。

Vocabulary

22. **reveal** [rɪˋvil] *v.* 顯示、展示；揭露

23. **courtyard** [ˋkɔrtˏjɑrd] *n.* 庭院；中庭

24. **arch** [ɑrtʃ] *v.* 成弓形彎曲；拱起（文中 arched 為過去分詞作形容詞，表示「拱形的」）

25. **portico** [ˋpɔrtɪˏko] *n.* 柱廊；有圓柱的門廊

26. **spiral** [ˋspaɪrəl] *adj.* 螺旋的

27. **top-rated** [ˋtɑpˏretɪd] *adj.* 一流的

圖片來源：Wikipedia / Trishhhh

對話

S : *Samantha Brown, Hostess*　　**M₂** : *Michael, American in Lyon*

B : *Blandine Thenet, Michael's Friend*

S What did he say?	他説什麼？
M₂ I think he called this *andouillette*. This is actually **chitlins**,[28] like we call them in the South. It's pig **intestines**,[29] OK?	他説這道菜是腸肚包，在南方我們稱此為豬腸，就是豬腸！
S OK. OK.	好。
M₂ And actually, here, what was . . . what was the French name again?	法文這道則是叫什麼？
B *Gras-double.*	*Gras-double*。
M₂ *Gras-double.* That is actually pig intestines also.	其實也是豬腸。
S Oh, but just finely chopped, I see.	只是切碎了，我懂了。
M₂ Finely chopped.	切碎的。
S Lovely.	真棒！
M₂ And your dish here is chicken **à la**[30] vinegar.	你吃的這道是醋醃雞肉。
S Thank you. Yeah. Order the chicken for the American.	謝謝，替美國人點雞肉絕對不會出錯。
M₂ Yeah.	對。

背景知識

看懂法文菜單

HOW TO READ A FRENCH MENU

L'Apéritif 開胃酒	**Menu/Carte** 套餐／單點
Entrées 前菜	**Légumes** 蔬菜料理
Plats 主菜	**Fromages** 起士
Viandes 肉料理	**Desserts** 甜點
Poissons 魚料理	**Boissons** 飲料

3-1

通往美食的捷徑

Vocabulary

28. **chitlins** [ˈtʃɪtlənz] *n.* 豬腸

29. **intestine** [ɪnˈtɛstən] *n.* 腸

30. **à la** [ˈɑˌlɑ] *prep.* 按照……方式的

179

對
話

S : *Samantha Brown, Hostess*　　M₂ : *Michael, American in Lyon*

B : *Blandine Thenet, Michael's Friend*

S	Safe choice.	安全的選擇。
M₂	And my lovely dish here is *boudin* in French, and what we call blood sausage.	我這道美味的菜餚是法國豬血香腸。
S	*Boudin.* You know, it just sounds so lovely in French, doesn't it? And then they are like, yeah, it's **stomach lining**.³¹ But this is traditional *bouchon* **fare**.³²	用法文唸實在很優美吧！不像我們直接叫它做胃壁。這是家常菜餐廳的傳統料理。
B	Yes, it is. It's a really nice atmosphere. The tables are very close to each other so that everybody can talk together and . . .	沒錯，這裡的用餐環境很好，每張餐桌的距離都很近，大家可以一起聊天。
S	Mm-hmm.	嗯。
B	. . . the boss of the restaurant is never very far from you. He's always . . .	餐廳老闆也從不會離客人太遠。他總是……
S	But that was the man who served us, right?	上菜的人就是老闆嗎？
B	Yes, that is right.	對，就是他。
S	He's the owner.	他是老闆。

180

品「腸」法國料理
MEAT IN FRANCE

le saucisson
saucisson
臘腸

la saucisse
pork sausage
香腸

la merguez
merguez
辣味香腸

le tartare de bœuf
steak tartare
生牛肉

l'andouillette
andouillette
內臟香腸

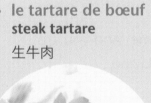

la galantine
galantine
肉凍

le boudin
blood sausage
豬血香腸

Vocabulary 🛍️

31. **stomach lining** [ˈstʌmək] [ˈlaɪnɪŋ] *n. phr.* 胃黏膜；胃壁

32. **fare** [fɛr] *n.* 餐點；飯菜

對
話

S : Samantha Brown, Hostess　　**B** : Blandine Thenet, Michael's Friend

M₂ : Michael, American in Lyon

B And he's, yes, definitely. And he can advise you and tell you what could be the best for you according to your tastes and everything. So it's a really, really good atmosphere and really good food for very cheap. It's very cheap.	對。他可以給你意見，依照你的口味，告訴你哪道菜最適合你。因此這裡的用餐氣氛非常好，食物也物美價廉。很便宜。
S Right. And you were saying that people come here to . . . to eat. You know, eating is very important here.	你說人們來這裡用餐。飲食在法國是重要的一環。
B Yeah.	是的。
S They take their time. And you are American, Mike. Living . . .	他們慢慢地享用餐點。麥克，你是美國人。
M₂ Yeah.	是。
S . . . now in Lyon for how many years?	你在里昂住了多久了？
M₂ Three years now.	三年了！
S Three years.	三年。
M₂ Yeah.	是。
S So what is the difference? Because I'm sure you know.	你一定對兩者的差異非常瞭解。

開動啦！BON APPÉTIT!

　　法國人飯前要說〝Bon appétit!〞，先祝福有好胃口才開始用餐，然而繁複的禮節和極長的用餐時間常讓人有吃到天荒地老之感。其實，吃飯隱含了法國人慢活的生活態度。平日用餐可以簡單、不拘小節，但如有宴客就必須注意禮節和程序。

　　首先，在等待賓客到來時，先在客廳喝開胃酒。等賓客到齊，待女主人邀請，就移駕到餐桌旁準備用餐，這時桌上已經擺好了所有餐具以及切片棍子麵包。原則上吃完一道菜就收一次盤，接著才上下一道。有時菜的最後處理工作在前一道收盤後才進行，所以等待是常事，閒談就變成用餐的重點。也因此一餐差不多要三、四個小時才能結束，但這種馬拉松式的用餐時間是星期天或假日才會出現的情況。

　　在餐廳吃飯的順序大致相同，但如何點菜就是一門學問了。在餐廳裡通常會拿到菜單及酒單，如不需要開胃酒，就直接點菜。甜點一般是用完主菜後才點，有些餐廳將乳酪歸在甜點下。但在高級餐廳，乳酪是獨立的選項，選取的方式也很特別，由服務生推著餐車到桌邊，顧客挑選後才切。除了套餐，也可以單點。最常見的是兩道或三道菜的套餐，通常就是前菜加主菜，或主菜加甜點，或是前菜、主菜加甜點。飲料必須另外點，如果不點飲料，就跟服務生要個免費的桌邊水（de l'eau en carafe / de l'eau plate）囉。

對話

S : Samantha Brown, Hostess　　**M₂** : Michael, American in Lyon

B : Blandine Thenet, Michael's Friend

M₂ Oh, well, it's amazing. Actually, the biggest thing that I noticed in France is that people spend all their evening at the table. You know, in ~~French~~ [France] we . . . we spend the night with our friends, like you say . . .

差異很大，我注意到最大的不同就是，人們在餐桌上度過整個晚上。嗯，在法國，我們整晚會和朋友在一起，像你説⋯⋯

S Mm-hmm.

嗯。

M₂ . . . and we really savor the food and the wine, actually. And we really appreciate a little bit more, I think, here.

品嚐佳餚美酒，我們的確更懂得品味生活。

B Definitely.

沒錯。

S Wonderful. A good French meal at a good price.

太好了！物美價廉的法式美食。

B Yes.

對。

M₂ With good friends.

與朋友共享。

S With good friends.

與好朋友共享。

M₂ Excellent.

太好了！

📖 影片原音 09   📖 課文朗讀 33

對話

S : *Samantha Brown, Hostess*   **M₂** : *Michael, American in Lyon*

B : *Blandine Thenet, Michael's friend*

S Bon appétit.	祝胃口大開！
M₂ Bon appétit.	祝胃口大開！
B Bon appétit. Cheers.	祝胃口大開！乾杯！
S Cheers.	乾杯！
M₂ Cheers.	乾杯！
B *Santé.*	乾杯！
S *Santé.*	乾杯！
M₂ *Santé.*	乾杯！

Seeing Is Unbelieving

非看不可的里昂

📖 影片原音 10　　📖 課文朗讀 34

自述

I'm in the city of Lyon, France, where things aren't always as they seem. Ooh, an ATM. What? No. Don't be surprised if you are fooled by a **mural**.[1] There are 150 buildings here that give Lyon an **eccentric**[2] **radiance**[3] around every corner. Most are painted in the trompe l'oeil style, which means "to fool the eye." And it works. This is the Silk Workers Wall. It is the largest mural painting of its kind in Europe, and what it depicts is actually quite simple: just everyday life here on Croix-Rousse, which is a neighborhood located on one of the two hills in Lyon. Being on a hill, of course, there are lots of steps, and people are working—they are doing their banking and shopping. The purpose of these murals is to **spur**[4] a . . . a local pride—strong residential **identity**.[5]

這裡是法國里昂,凡事不盡如表面所見。喔,看見一台提款機。什麼?不是。若被壁畫矇騙也別太訝異,這裡共有一百五十棟建築物,讓里昂每個角落,無不散發出異乎尋常的光芒。大部分壁畫是以錯視畫風繪製,意思是「愚弄雙眼」,而且確實如此。這是絲織工人之牆,是全歐洲最大型的錯視壁畫,畫裡描述的主題其實很簡單,就是克魯胡斯的日常生活景象。這是位於里昂兩座山丘其中一座之上的社區,既然位於山丘上當然有很多階梯,人們在工作:出入銀行、購物,這些壁畫的目的是激發當地居民的驕傲——對居住社區的強烈認同。

FOOL YOUR EYES — TROMPE L'OEIL
看得到卻摸不到的「錯視風格畫」

    trompe l'oeil [tromp`lə͵i] 法文指「欺瞞眼睛」，即在平面圖像描畫出一些乍看起來立體的物件。這種畫風會讓觀賞者誤以為看見真的風景或物品。錯視畫風最早出現在古希臘藝術中，至古羅馬時期更加精緻，流行於文藝復興時代。文藝復興時期錯視畫最常出現的地方是在教堂裡的濕壁畫（fresco），最有名的是維也納的耶穌會教堂（Jesuit Church），平面的教堂天花板上，呈現出圓頂屋頂的立體效果。這類的繪畫後來還包括整棟建築物外觀及地面，例如法國里昂，到處可見錯視畫風的壁畫。

圖片來源：（上）張夢純、（下）Wikipedia / Alberto Fernandez Fernandez

Vocabulary

1. **mural** [`mjʊrəl] *n.* 壁畫（通常指大型壁畫）

2. **eccentric** [ɪk`sɛntrɪk] *adj.* 怪異的；不尋常的

3. **radiance** [`rediəns] *n.* 光輝、閃爍（指從某物上所投射的溫暖、柔和的光）

4. **spur** [spɜ] *v.* 激勵；推動

5. **identity** [aɪ`dɛntəti] *n.* 身份

自述

Also, all the murals together create this wonderful open-air museum, with no entrance fee and no waiting in long lines. Oh, look at this. This is a silk-weaver shop, and silk weaving is exactly the reason why we are in Croix-Rousse. Good doggy.

而且所有壁畫形成令人讚嘆的露天美術館，不收門票，也不必大排長龍，你瞧瞧，這是一間絲織店，而我們來到克魯胡斯的目的就是為了絲織品。乖狗狗。

對話

S: Samantha Brown, Hostess　　**G**: Guillaume Verzier, Prelle Owner

S We have been granted access into Prelle, a 250-year-old silk-weaving factory. Its clients range from France's Palace of Versailles to New York's Metropolitan Museum of Art. Guillaume Verzier is the owner of Prelle. My goodness. These machines are absolutely incredible. They are just **massive**.[6]

我們獲准進入普瑞爾，這是一家擁有二百五十年歷史的絲織工廠，客戶包括巴黎的凡爾賽宮到紐約的大都會藝術博物館。吉庸‧維西爾是普瑞爾工廠的老闆，我的天啊，這些機器真是太不可思議了，實在是巨大無比！

G ~~This is~~ [These are] **looms**.[7] They are . . . this is what we call Jacquard looms, with this card made by Jacquard.

這些是織布機。我們稱為甲卡提花織機，這張卡片就是甲卡製作的。

JACQUARD 甲卡提花織機

　　甲卡提花織機是由法國人約瑟夫·馬利·甲卡（Joseph Marie Jacquard, 1752–1834）於西元一八〇四年在法國所發明的。利用可交替的穿孔卡來控制布料的織法，如此可自動織出任何想要的樣式。甲卡提花織機成為現代自動化織布機的基礎，也對現代電腦和資料處理的發展，產生了相當深遠的影響。第一位發明並製造電腦的查爾斯·巴貝奇（Charles Babbage），就是以甲卡為靈感來源，將穿孔卡改造在他所構想的分析機輸入－輸出媒介中。赫爾曼·何樂禮（Herman Hollerith）則是改造穿孔卡，發明了穿孔卡片製表機，是電腦的前身。

旅遊小幫手

Prelle 普瑞爾絲織工廠

創立於一七五二年，為法國里昂最古老的工廠。此工廠不對外開放，欲參觀者需事先來信預約：info@prelle.com。

📞 (33) 472 10 11 40

🌐 http://www.prelle.fr/en/

Vocabulary

6. **massive** [ˈmæsɪv] *adj.* 巨大的；龐大的

7. **loom** [lum] *n.* 織布機

影片原音 10 　　 課文朗讀 34

對
話

S : Samantha Brown, Hostess 　　 **G** : Guillaume Verzier, Prelle Owner

S	So the . . . the . . . the actual weave follows the holes of those cards?	所以是沿著紙卡上的洞織絲?
G	Exactly, yes.	沒錯。
S	That exactly is what an old computer is like.	和舊式電腦一模一樣。
G	It was created by Jacquard . . .	這是由甲卡……
S	Uh-huh.	嗯。
G	. . . at the beginning of [the] nineteenth century. It's like a computer, in fact.	在十九世紀初製造,其實和電腦差不多。
S	And what are they making right now? What is she making?	他們現在在製作什麼?她在織什麼?
G	She's weaving handmade velvet.	她正在織手工絲絨。
S	Ooh.	喔。
G	We still continue to use this kind of ~~looms~~ [loom] to make this **fabric**.[8] There is no other way.	我們仍沿用這種紡織機生產這種織品,不用其他方法。
S	So even your modern **machinery**,[9] which I know you have, can't **reproduce**[10] what is handmade?	所以即使你有那些現代新型機器,也無法取代手工織品?
G	This kind of velvet? No.	對,這種手工絲絨不行。

背景
知識

DIFFERENT TYPES OF FABRICS
布料種類九宮格

denim
牛仔布（斜紋粗棉布）

velvet
絲絨

flannel
法蘭絨

cashmere
羊毛

linen
亞麻

cotton
棉布

lace
蕾絲

silk
絲綢布

polyester
聚酯纖維；人造纖維

Vocabulary 📖

8. **fabric** [ˋfæbrɪk] *n.* 織物；布料

9. **machinery** [məˋʃinəri] *n.* 機器、機械設備（總稱）

10. **reproduce** [ˌriprəˋdjus] *v.* 複製

191

對
話

S : Samantha Brown, Hostess　　**G** : Guillaume Verzier, Prelle Owner

S So you must have an amazing fabric sort of **archived**[11] somewhere.

不行，所以想必這裡儲藏了許多織品。

G Yes, we have a large **archive**[11] because we keep one sample of every ~~production we made~~ [product we've made].

對，存量很多，因為我們會為每組產品保留一件樣本。

S So may I see some of these old fabrics? Do you still have them archived somewhere?

我可以看些老布料嗎？你還存放在某處嗎？

G Yes. We ~~have not~~ [don't have] the original piece, but we have one sample of the ~~production~~ [product] we made forty years ago. ~~No.~~ So I will show you the . . . the curtain.

對，我們沒有原本的，但我有一組大約四十年前的產品樣本。那我帶你去看窗簾。

S The curtain he's talking about is a piece of recreated silk made originally for the Palace of France's most **infamous**[12] queen, Marie Antoinette. How long would it take to make just this piece?

他口中的窗簾，是一片經過重新製作的絲綢，原是為法國宮廷內最惡名昭彰的瑪麗·安東娃妮特皇后所製造，只製作這片窗簾要花多久時間？

MARIE ANTOINETTE
凡爾賽拜金女　瑪麗皇后

　　瑪麗・安東妮（Marie Antoinette）是一位奧地利公主，年輕時嫁入法國皇室，成了政治聯姻下的犧牲品。安東妮成了法國皇后後，揮金如土、熱衷於玩樂和慶宴，奢侈無度，同情外敵，而不被法國民眾喜愛。法國大革命爆發後，王室出逃的懦弱行為，令不少支持王室的民眾大感失望，瑪麗皇后本有機會逃回奧地利，但她拒絕離開。一七八九年皇后代夫提出法國仿傚英國君主立憲制，希望挽救危急存亡的皇室地位，體現出一位皇后的尊嚴與驕傲。爾後，法國宣布廢除君主制，安東妮被控叛國罪，判處死刑，享年三十七歲。直到現今，安東妮的名聲仍評價兩極，許多書籍及電影皆改編自她的傳奇故事。

圖片來源：（左圖）Wikipedia

非看不可的里昂

Vocabulary

11. **archive** [ˋɑrˏkaɪv] *v.* 存檔　*n.* 檔案文件；史料

12. **infamous** [ˋɪnfəməs] *adj.* 惡名昭彰的；聲名狼藉的

對話

S : Samantha Brown, Hostess　　**G** : Guillaume Verzier, Prelle Owner

S In the . . . in the old times, not new **computerized** machines.	在古代，而不是用新的電腦化機器。
G Oh, in the old time[s].	在古代。
S Yeah.	對。
G But we still continue to produce . . . if we have to reproduce it, we will reproduce it by hand.	我們至今仍持續生產，若有必要重新生產，我們也採用手工。
S Oh, that is right. Right.	對。
G So the [amount of] time will be the same. There is no machine to produce, so . . .	所以花的時間其實一樣，我們不使用機器，所以……
S Because you could not produce this on a . . . a computerized machine.	因為無法採用電腦化機器生產。
G No, absolutely not.	不能，絕對不行。
S You have to use the originals.	必須用原本的製法。
G Yes.	嗯。
S It's too difficult.	這太困難了。
G So maybe, to weave that, we would need four months—something like that.	所以織這一片窗簾需要四個月左右。
S Four months?	四個月？

對話

S : *Samantha Brown, Hostess*　　**G** : *Guillaume Verzier, Prelle Owner*

G Yes.	對。
S To do this one piece.	就為了織這片窗簾。
G Yes.	對。
S Wow. That is a lot of time.	哇！好長一段時間！
G It's a very, very sophisticated . . .	這是非常精緻的
S My goodness.	我的天呀。
G . . . fabric.	織品。

3-2

非看不可的里昂

學習重點

computerized　經電腦處理的

字尾 -ize 表示「使……；以……方式處理」，常與名詞或形容詞結合形成動詞。如文中的名詞 computer（電腦）+ -ize = computerize [kəmˋpjutəˌraɪzd] 文中 computerized 為過去分詞作形容詞用，指「經電腦處理的」，其他帶此字尾的字包括：

final 　　+ **ize** = **finalize** 　使完結；定案

special 　+ **ize** = **specialize** 　專門從事

summary + **ize** = **summarize** 　總結

memory 　+ **ize** = **memorize** 　熟記

- Diana and Tim met to finalize their plans for the school show.
  戴安娜和提姆見面要為學校表演計畫定案。

- For the English test, you will need to memorize this list of words.
  要準備這個英文測驗，你需要熟記這張表上的單字。

自述

Prelle isn't open to the public, but if you wanted to buy something silky in Lyon, well, that's no problem. In my travels, I'm always looking for that perfect souvenir, right? Something, hopefully, that won't weigh down the luggage as well, and in Lyon, just perfect: buy silk.

普瑞爾工廠不對外開放，但你若想在里昂買絲織品，絕對不用煩惱，我在旅途中，總是不斷尋找完美的紀念品，也希望那東西不會佔用太多行李重量，在里昂，一切都正合我意，買絲織品就對了！

對話

S : Samantha Brown, Hostess　　**M** : Male, Artisan

S Great shop. I mean, who in your life wouldn't love a beautiful silk scarf? And when you buy one of these scarves, you can tell the person that you bought it for that this was made by a monsieur who had his own workshop in the back of the shop. See him working there? He is a true **artisan**[13] **in residence**,[14] and this makes the shop actually an **atelier**,[15] a workshop. Gorgeous, gorgeous pieces. Oh, that is neat. Bonjour, monsieur.

好漂亮的商店！有哪個人會不喜歡一條精美的絲織圍巾？當你買了這些圍巾，可以告訴對方，圍巾是由擁有私人工作坊的師傅親手織成，工作坊就在商店後方，看見他在那工作沒？他是駐店的一流織工，整家商店等於是他的工作室，好漂亮的織品！真精美！你好！先生。

M Bonjour.

你好！

對話

S : *Samantha Brown, Hostess*　　**M** : *Male, Artisan*

S *Qu'est-ce que c'est?* What is this?　　這是什麼？

M This is [a] machine to . . .　　這機器是用來⋯⋯

S It's a machine to . . .　　這個機器是用來⋯⋯

　　OK.　　好。

　　So I am making this?　　所以我正在織？

M Yes. It's magic.　　對，很神奇吧。

S *Magique.* And now you can say, "Actually, I made you this scarf."　　很神奇，現在你可以説：「這是我為你織的圍巾」。

S Ah, merci, monsieur.　　謝謝你，先生。

M Merci.　　謝謝。

S Au revoir.　　再見。

M Merci. Au revoir.　　謝謝你，再見。

S Yay! I just shopped for five people, and look how small and light the bag is. It's a traveler's dream.　　我替五個人買了禮物，但你瞧瞧這個袋子又小又輕巧，簡直是每個旅人的夢想！

3-2

非看不可的里昂

Vocabulary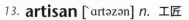

13. **artisan** [ˈɑrtəzən] *n.* 工匠

14. **in residence** [ɪn] [ˈrɛzədəns] *phr.* （作家、藝術家）常駐（某地）的

15. **atelier** [ˌætlˈje] *n.* （藝術家）工作室；畫室（源自法文）

The Little Beggar's Purse. Ride On!

前進吧！口袋美食！

🧳 影片原音 11　🧳 課文朗讀 35

自述 It is very popular now to take a cooking class while in any part of Europe. The idea of going to a **stiff**[1] culinary **institute**[2] didn't really **appeal**[3] to me, so I found out about a woman who teaches in her home.

無論你身在歐洲何處，參加烹飪課程都是很受歡迎的。我沒興趣去嚴格的烹飪學校，因此我找到一位在自家開課的婦女。

對話

S : *Samantha Brown, Hostess* **A** : *Aurelle, Cooking Teacher*

A Oh, yes, Samantha.	你好！珊曼莎！
S Bonjour.	你好！
A Bonjour, Samantha. How are you?	你好！珊曼莎你好！
S How are you?	你好！
A It's nice to meet you.	幸會！

ON SE FAIT LA BISE?
法式招呼這樣打

在法國打招呼不是說聲〝Bonjour〞就結束了，而必須進行〝faire la bise〞（吻頰禮）。

la bise 通常見於女性之間，而男性及不熟的異性則行握手禮。關係較親近的家人或是朋友，才會不分男女行吻頰禮。吻頰禮其實就是輕碰臉頰，並發出「啾」的親吻聲兩次或四次（次數有此兩種說法）至於要先從左臉還是右臉開始呢？這是不少法國人也充滿疑惑的問題。其實各地習慣不同，最好的方法是先觀察對方的行動再配合。

旅遊小幫手

Plum Lyon Teaching Kitchen 里昂烹飪廚房

里昂最受歡迎的烹飪教室，提供了各式各樣的甜點及料理課程，詳情可上網查詢喔！

$ Herbs in French Cooking EUR 75.00
　La Religieuse: A French Pastry Experience EUR 75.00
　Croissants: A-Z EUR 75.00
　Macaron Workshop EUR 75.00

🌐 www.plumlyon.com

Vocabulary 🧳

1. **stiff** [stɪf] *adj.* 嚴厲的；拘謹的

2. **institute** [`ɪnstə͵tut] *n.* （教育或研究）機構；協會

3. **appeal** [ə`pil] *v.* 引起興趣；對……有吸引力

對話

S : Samantha Brown, Hostess　　**A** : Aurelle, Cooking Teacher

S	It's nice to meet you, too. This is Aurélle. She holds a cooking course from her own kitchen, something you don't often see in Lyon.	我也是！她是歐若莉，在自家廚房開設烹飪課，這在里昂並不常見。
A	So we are going to cook autumn foods and sugar **almond**[4] pastries.	我們要製作秋季的食物，與糖漬杏仁派。
S	Ooh, yum.	喔，好吃。
A	Yes. So we will use apples . . .	要使用的材料是蘋果……
S	Mm-hmm.	嗯。
A	. . . **pears**,[5] sugared almonds, and **phyllo**[6] pastry. All right? So we first peel using a **peeler**[7] . . .	梨子、糖漬杏仁和薄酥皮，明白嗎？首先我們用削皮器削皮。
S	OK.	好的。
A	. . . we will peel the apples and pears, right?	將蘋果和梨子削皮，對嗎？
S	Right.	好。
A	So.	嗯。
S	I think people really assume Paris to be the culinary **core** of France, but really it is Lyon.	很多人認為巴黎是法國的美食中心，但其實是里昂吧！
A	Yeah, I think, really, it's Lyon.	對，我認為其實是里昂才對。

---

core 要點；中心

core [kɔr] 原本指「果核；果仁」，後常被喻為事物的「核心；要點；中心」。

• Love is at the core of the new movie.
愛情是這部新片的核心。

【延伸學習】

to the core 徹底地；完全地

• The apple is rotten to the core.
那顆蘋果爛透了。

Vocabulary

4. **almond** [ˋɑmənd] *n.* 杏仁

5. **pear** [pɛr] *n.* 梨子

6. **phyllo** [ˋfilo] *n.* （製作酥點時）桿成極薄一層的生麵

7. **peeler** [ˋpilɚ] *n.* 削皮器

對話

S And, Clotille, you are from Lyon?	柯蒂爾，妳來自里昂嗎？
C I am, yes.	對！
S Does everyone here know how to cook?	這裡每個人都懂烹飪？
C Absolutely.	沒錯。
S Yes, that is important?	這點非常重要嗎？
C It is very important.	非常重要！
S Obviously, because you . . . you are taking lessons; we are **brushing up**.	很明顯你必須來上烹飪課，來磨練、精進廚藝。
C Yeah, basically it is important to improve all the time and to . . . to make sure you are . . . you know more and more things about cooking.	不斷追求進步很重要，以便學習到更多關於烹飪的知識。
S A little **competitive**[8] here, is it?	這裡的競爭很激烈吧？
C Absolutely. It is somewhat.	沒錯。可以這麼說。
S Very competitive here.	這裡的競爭很激烈。
S Why is the chef world so male **dominated**?[9]	為何廚師界都由男性主導呢？

LES DESSERTS
甜在心法式甜點 PART 1

le crêpe
crepe
可麗餅

la tarte Tatin
apple tart
反烤蘋果塔

la galette des rois
French king cake
葡式帝王蛋糕

la mousse au chocolat
chocolate mousse
巧克力慕斯

le Far Breton
Far Breton
布列塔尼奶油蛋糕

les meringues
meringue
蛋白甜餅

3-3

前進吧！口袋美食！

學習重點

brush up　練習；精進

brush 意思是「擦拭」，brush up (on) sth 引申指經由練習來增進以前學過的技能或知識。

- All of the students needed to brush up on their math skills before learning the new material.
  所有學生在學習新內容之前要先練習精進數學能力。

Vocabulary

8. **competitive** [kəm`pɛtətɪv] *adj.* 競爭的；好勝的

9. **dominate** [`dɑmə͵net] *v.* 佔主要地位；控制、支配

對話

S : Samantha Brown, Hostess　　**A** : Aurelle, Cooking Teacher

A Because, you know, it is difficult for a woman to have a restaurant and have her children. You know, you have to work in the evening, you have to work during the weekend, and [it's a] very hard job. You have to carry heavy dishes, and you work in a hot atmosphere. It is very difficult, so I think it is impossible to have a restaurant and to have children.

因為女性有了小孩後，要經營餐廳就很難。在晚上和週末都得工作，這是很困難的，還必須拿很重的碗盤，在炙熱的環境中工作是很不容易的。我認為餐廳和小孩要兼顧，根本是不可能的！

S After the fruit has been peeled and diced and the candied almonds have been completely pulverized, the **mixture**[10] is cooked for a few minutes into a nice, pink **filling**.[11] Now it is time to make puff pastry purses to hold it in.

將水果削皮和切片，糖漬杏仁也被搗碎之後，就全部混合起來，煮個幾分鐘，直到成為粉紅色的餡料，接著將酥皮做成袋狀，以便包住餡料。

A More of this. So, then you take this . . .

再放一點，然後把這個拿起來……

S Mm-hmm.

嗯嗯。

A . . . and make a nice little purse.

包成漂亮的小袋子。

S Oh, like a little beggar's purse.

像個小錢包一樣。

LES DESSERTS
甜在心法式甜點 PART 2

le bugne
angel wings
油炸甜甜圈

le clafoutis
cherry clafoutis
水果布丁蛋糕（克拉芙緹）

le soufflé
soufflé
舒芙蕾

la crème brûlée
crème brûlée
法式焦糖布丁

le mille-feuille
napoleon
法式千層酥

l'éclair au chocolat
chocolate éclair
巧克力閃電泡芙

le macaron
macaron
馬卡龍

la madeleine
madeleine
瑪德蓮蛋糕

moelleux au chocolat
lava cake
岩漿巧克力蛋糕

3-3

前進吧！口袋美食！

Vocabulary

10. **mixture** [ˈmɪkstʃɚ] *n.* 混合料；混合

11. **filling** [ˈfɪlɪŋ] *n.* 餡料；填充物

影片原音 11   課文朗讀 35

<table>
<tr><td>對
話</td><td>S : Samantha Brown, Hostess</td><td>A : Aurelle, Cooking Teacher</td></tr>
<tr><td></td><td colspan="2">F : Female with White Shirt</td></tr>
</table>

A	Yes. Now with the toothpick, make a cross.	再用一根牙籤把開口封起來。
S	And now we bake it.	然後放進烤箱烤？
A	Yes. For three minutes. It should become brown and **crisp**.[12]	對，烤三分鐘。要烤得金黃酥脆。
F	It's great.	真好吃！
S	Mmm. Oh, that is . . . that is very good.	非常美味！
A	Oh, nice. I'm happy. But not [with] your peeling.	太好了，我很高興。但妳皮削不好。
S	I did a fantastic job, if I do say so myself.	我做得太棒了，我自己會這麼説。

Vocabulary

12. **crisp** [krɪsp] *adj.* 酥脆的

烹飪「動」起來
FOOD PREPARATION VERBS

dice 切丁

candy 糖煮的

pulverize 磨成粉

bake 烤

sprinkle 撒

wrap 包

toss 拌

crack 打（蛋）

peel 剝；削皮

自述

We are now in what is considered the heart of Lyon, an area called Presqu'île, which means "almost island." And that is because it's a **peninsula-shaped**[13] piece of land between the Rhône and the Saône rivers. Now, while this is a very walkable city, public transportation here is excellent. There are buses, trams, subways, and something you don't see every day: bicycles. And you rent them from these machines here and, oh, no. It's all in French. That is because we are in France, Samantha.

這裡被認為是里昂的中心，這個地區稱為「半島區」，意思就是「近似島嶼」，因為這是片半島形狀的陸地，位於隆河與頌恩河之間。儘管這座城市很適合步行，但這裡的大眾交通工具非常便利，有巴士、電車、地下鐵，還有一種不是天天會看到的交通工具：腳踏車。而你可以用這些機器來租車。喔！不！全都是法文。珊曼莎！這是因為我們在法國。

里昂綠色微笑行
VÉLO'V —THE PUBLIC BICYCLE SYSTEM OF LYON

　　一印象中的法國交通工具，應該就是地鐵了。但是在法國罷工已是一種常態，對大眾運輸系統的使用者來説，罷工成了一項難題，因為對乘客來説，會花上比原本多上幾倍的交通時間。為了因應此問題，部分法國人選擇自備交通工具，譬如滑板車或自行車，或者使用公用租借系統。

　　法國從二〇〇七年開始公用自行車系統，最早在里昂，稱為 Vélo'v。後來巴黎也效法，稱為 Vélib（Vélos en libre-service），即可以自由使用的自行車之意。因為自行車站數量多，自動售票系統操作簡單，又提供甲地借乙地還的服務，只要找到有空位的自行車站就可以還車，再加上各個城市積極規劃自行車專用道，提供騎士更安全的使用空間，因此成為一種便利的選擇。

旅遊小幫手

Vélo'v Bike Stations　公用自行車站

在里昂有三百四十個自行車站，提供短期和長期的租賃。

$ First Thirty Minutes: Free　First Additional Thirty Minutes: EUR 1.00
　　Additional Thirty Minutes: EUR 2.00

🌐 http://www.velov.grandlyon.com

Vocabulary 🧳

13. **peninsula-shaped** [pə`nɪnslə`ʃɛpt] *adj.* 半島形狀的

對話

S : *Samantha Brown, Hostess*　　　**M** : *Male with Mustache*

S No, really, usually these machines are multilingual, but I don't know what to do because it's . . . pardon, monsieur.	其實這種機器通常有多國語言解説，但我不知道要怎麼操作，因為……不好意思，先生。
S *Parle vous Anglais?*	你會説英文嗎？
M Of course.	會。
S Can you help me? I was wanting to rent a bike, but I don't . . .	你能幫我嗎？我想租腳踏車，但是我看不懂。
M Yeah, yeah.	好的。
S . . . I don't read **fluent**[14] French.	我的法文不好。
M You want to . . . to . . . to . . . to take a bike. OK. So . . .	妳要租腳踏車，好的。
S Put in my credit card there?	把我的信用卡插進這裡？
M Yeah, put [in] your credit card [there].	對。把你的信用卡放進這裡。
S All right.	好的。
M Yeah. And after that, you take this.	然後把這張卡拿出來。
S Oh, excellent.	太棒了！
M You have a card like this, and it's a card for one week.	這種卡的有效期限是一週。

影片原音 11 課文朗讀 35

對話

S : *Samantha Brown, Hostess*   M : *Male with Mustache*

S	All right.	好。
M	After you get your card, put your card here.	拿到卡片之後，就把卡片放這裡。
S	You will definitely have to ask for help on this. There is just no way you are going to know how to do this on your own.	你絕對需要找救兵，光靠自己絕對不知道該怎麼辦。
M	So ~~after~~ [afterward], you can take this one.	之後，你可以用這一部。
S	OK. These bike stands are all over town, and the first half hour is free. After that, it's about two dollars and fifty cents per hour. All right. *Merci beaucoup.*	好。這些腳踏車租用機隨處可見，前半小時完全免費，之後大約是每小時兩塊五美元，太好了，非常感謝！
M	You are welcome. Bye.	不客氣，再見！
S	Au revoir.	再見！
M	Au revoir.	再見！

3-3

前進吧！口袋美食！

Vocabulary

14. **fluent** [ˋfluənt] *adj.* 流利的

自述

The look of Presqu'île is very different from the rest of Lyon. Cross the bridge from the tight **maze-like**[15] quarter of the old city and you will find wide **boulevards**[16] and pedestrian-only streets, grand open squares **framed**[17] by **stately**[18] **mansions**[19] **peeking**[20] out over the tops of tall trees. And don't worry about steep hills. Presqu'île is completely flat.

Presqu'île is also where most of the serious shopping is. And when you need a break, there are tons of cafés and *bouchons*. Or head to Place des Terreaux. Two buildings that define this city happen to be right next to one another: the **ornate**[21] City Hall, and the Opera House, which is also home to the ballet. Here is where you will also find lots of **innovative**[22] modern dance. The modern, almost hip addition of this Opera House is a surprise for this **conservative**[23] city. It's a true symbol of the **evolution**[24] of the arts.

半島區的風貌與里昂其他地區大異其趣。從擁擠如迷宮般的舊市區過橋，就能看見寬廣的大街，與行人專用的道路，廣闊的廣場由富麗堂皇的宅邸包圍，宅邸從高聳的樹木頂端探頭而出，別擔心陡峭的山丘，半島區地勢完全是平坦的。

半島區同時也是最著名的購物天地，逛累時還有許多咖啡廳與家常菜餐廳讓你歇腳，也可以前往泰爾烏廣場，本市兩棟地標建築恰巧就比鄰而建，壯麗的市政廳與歌劇院，也是芭蕾舞演出的地點，同時還能在此欣賞許多創新的現代舞蹈。這座歌劇院中添加了摩登又時髦的舞蹈表演。在此保守的城市中，令人感到驚訝，這確實是藝術演進的象徵。

Vocabulary

15. **maze-like** [ˋmezˋlaɪk] *adj.* 如迷宮一般的

16. **boulevard** [ˋbuləˏvɑrd] *n.* 林蔭大道

17. **frame** [frem] *v.* 將⋯⋯圍繞；給⋯⋯鑲邊

18. **stately** [ˋstetli] *adj.* 宏偉的；高貴優雅的

19. **mansion** [ˋmænʃən] *n.* 宅邸；大廈

20. **peek** [pik] *v.* 偷看；窺視

21. **ornate** [ɔrˋnet] *adj.* 裝飾華麗的

22. **innovative** [ˋɪnəˏvetɪv] *adj.* 創新的；革新的

23. **conservative** [kənˋsɝvətɪv] *adj.* 保守的

24. **evolution** [ˏɛvəˋluʃən] *n.* 演進；演化

213

自述

I'm visiting Lyon late in November. I have had gorgeously sunny days, but it is quite chilly. It's that chill and all this hill climbing that has **kept my appetite very healthy.** You will be eating a lot in Lyon, so you need that appetite. I'm staying at a hotel that is midway at the top of this hill. It's quite a hike, but well worth it.

It's the Villa Florentine, a Relais and Châteaux property located on a perfect **wedge**[25] of land **overlooking**[26] Lyon. When I first walked into this lobby, it just, I mean, it **took my breath away.** It is in a former eighteenth-century chapel, and there are **fresco**-like[27] paintings and **panels**[28] that hang like **tapestries**[29] from the ceiling.

我在十一月底來到里昂，這時有著陽光普照的好天氣，但還是有點涼意，涼颼颼的天氣和爬坡的運動讓我保持好胃口。在里昂，你會享用很多美食，因此食欲要好！我住的這間旅館位於半山腰，得走上好一段路，但很值得。

這是佛羅倫汀別墅飯店，隸屬於城堡飯店集團，座落在完美的楔形狀上的地段，可以俯瞰里昂市，我第一次走進大廳時，簡直讓我嘆為觀止，它位於一座十八世紀的教堂中，有壁畫般的繪畫，天花板上掛的鑲板也宛如繡帷。

214

keep one's appetite very healthy 保持好胃口

appetite 指「胃口；食欲」，healthy 指「顯示健康的」，引申指「大量的」而「胃口好」的英文可以說 have a healthy appetite。

 【延伸學習】

| 用法一 | have an appetite for sth | 渴望；想要 |

| 用法二 | lose one's appetite | 對⋯⋯失去興趣 |

- All good athletes have an appetite for victory.
  所有優秀運動員都渴望奪冠。

- Smelling the rotting fish by the beach made me lose my appetite.
  聞到海邊腐魚的味道讓我倒盡胃口。

take one's breath away 使某人歎為觀止

breath 是「氣息；呼吸」，take one's breath away 是「形容某事物極其壯觀、美麗，讓人屏氣凝神、歎為觀止」的意思。

- The sight of so many stars in the night sky took my breath away.
  夜空中繁星點點的景色令我屏息。

Vocabulary

25. **wedge** [wɛdʒ] *n.* 楔形物

26. **overlook** [ˌovɚˋluk] *v.* 俯瞰；眺望

27. **fresco** [ˋfrɛsˏko] *n.* （塗在濕的灰泥壁上的）壁畫

28. **panel** [ˋpænl̩] *n.* 鑲板；嵌板

29. **tapestry** [ˋtæpəstri] *n.* 繡帷；掛毯、壁毯

圖片來源：（左）Hall d'accueil © Groupe Métropole、（右）Dîner en terrasse © N Calluaud

自述

The original chapel windows let in the light that just **illuminate[s]**[30] the space. I mean, it makes it positively heavenly. And it's hard to believe that in this **opulent**,[31] grand lobby, that this is actually an intimate hotel—only twenty-eight rooms. So let me show you mine. I have a classic room. Out of the twenty-eight rooms here, no two are alike. One thing they do all have in common is a very large size, especially the bathrooms—very **spacious**.[32] And most of the rooms have a really lovely view. Look at this. I have one of almost all of Lyon. You have the old city down there, the hill with the Croix-Rousse neighborhood—just . . . just gorgeous. One week you absolutely want to avoid coming to Lyon is towards the end of August, beginning of September, and that is when the largest **lingerie**[33] and swimsuit **convention**[34] is held, so there are no hotels or restaurant reservations to be had. But I don't know. That is, for a lot of you, could be reason enough to come to Lyon. But if that is true, make your reservation now.

光線從原本的教堂窗戶灑入，照亮整個空間，讓這裡有如人間天堂。很難想像在這寬敞氣派的大廳背後，其實是一間很私密的飯店，只有二十八個房間，我帶你去參觀我的房間。我的是經典房，這裡總共有二十八間房，每一間設計都不同，唯一的共同點是空間都很大，特別是浴室非常寬敞，多數房間都擁有美麗景觀，你看！從我這一間幾乎可以俯瞰全里昂，舊市區在那裡！還有山丘以及克魯胡斯區，實在非常美麗！最好避免在八月底九月初來里昂，因為最大型的內衣與泳裝大會就在那時登場，因此旅館和餐廳都將客滿。可是我不知道，可能很多人就是衝著這點來到里昂吧！若真是如此，現在就著手訂房吧！

旅遊小幫手

Villa Florentine 佛羅倫汀別墅飯店

Relais & Châteaux 豪華精品飯店聯盟，成立於一九五四年，由 Marcel 及 Nelly Tilloy 兩人創立。目前連鎖飯店已經遍佈六十個國家和地區。想要納入它們齊下品牌，其中一項條件是，需滿足五個 C：charm（魅力），calm（寧靜），character（獨特），courtesy（殷勤）and cuisine（美食）。由其可知，它們將豪華生活的藝術完全應用在飯店經營當中。

$ 房價每晚二百八十元歐元到四百九十元歐元左右；高級套房一晚房價則是五百八十歐元到九百六十元歐元。

☎ (33) 4 72 56 56 56

🌐 http://www.villaflorentine.com/

Vocabulary

30. **illuminate** [ɪˋlumə͵net] *v.* 照亮；照射

31. **opulent** [ˋɑpjulənt] *adj.* 豪華的；富麗堂皇的

32. **spacious** [ˋspeʃəs] *adj.* 空間寬敞的

33. **lingerie** [͵lɑndʒəˋre] *n.* 女性貼身內衣

34. **convention** [kənˋvɛnʃən] *n.* 大會

圖片來源：（上）Vue de la Villa Florentine © JC Dortmann、（下）Piscine panoramique © E Saillet

Guignol Is Everywhere
隨處可見的吉尼奧爾

🎬 影片原音 12　🔊 課文朗讀 36

自述

 You know, the biggest celebrity in Lyon **happens to** be a 200-year-old **puppet**.[1] His name is Guignol, and he is everywhere in this city. He's in **storefronts**.[2] His image is on posters. He's painted on murals on buildings. There is a great story of how he came to be, so let us go see.

你知道嗎？里昂最紅的名人，是個兩百歲的木偶，它名叫吉尼奧爾，市內隨處可見它的蹤影，他出現在店家門前、海報上、被繪製在建築物的壁畫上，它會如此受歡迎，有個精采的故事，我們去看看吧！

對話

S : *Samantha Brown, Hostess*　　**P** : *Patrice Cardelli, Puppeteer*

S Where is Guignol? Where is Guignol? Guignol!	吉尼奧爾在哪裡？吉尼奧爾究竟在哪裡？
P I am here.	我在這裡！
S Guignol!	吉尼奧爾！
P (*speaking in foreign language*)	（法語）

happen to 剛好、碰巧……

用法一 **sb + happens + to + V.** 某人碰巧做某事

- I happened to see Vicky while I was walking into the post office today.
  我今天走進郵局時碰巧看到了薇琪。

用法二 **sth + happens + to + sb** 某事發生在某人身上

- I haven't heard from David in months; who knows what has happened to him?
  我幾個月沒聽到大衛的消息了；誰知道他發生了什麼事嗎？

旅遊小幫手

Théâtre La Maison de Guignol 吉尼奧爾劇院

$ Sunday: 2:00 p.m.–6:00 p.m.
Monday: Closed
Tuesday–Thursday: 10:00 a.m.–6:00 p.m.
Friday–Saturday: 10:00 a.m.–11:30 p.m.

☎ (33) 4 72 40 26 61

🌐 http://www.lamaisondeguignol.fr/

隨處可見的吉尼奧爾

Vocabulary

1. **puppet** [ˈpʌpɪt] *n.* 木偶
2. **storefront** [ˈstɔrˌfrʌnt] *n.* 店門口；（臨街）店面

對
話

S : *Samantha Brown, Hostess*　　**P** : *Patrice Cardelli, Puppeteer*

S Guignol, Guignol.	吉尼奧爾！吉尼奧爾！
P (*speaking in foreign language*)	（法語）
S Guignol, we would like to know the story of how you came to be.	吉尼奧爾！我們想知道你成名的經過。
P (*speaking in foreign language*)	（法語）
S Yep.	好的。
P (*speaking in foreign language*)	（法語）
S Towards the 1800s, Laurent Mourguet was a **professional**[3] tooth puller.	在十九世紀時，羅朗·洛格是職業拔牙師傅。
P (*speaking in foreign language*)	（法語）
S To **distract**[4] his clients that were **aching**[5] in pain, and also to attract more people, he wrote little **sketches**[6] to entertain them. Right? Is that how it goes?	為了讓病患分心，忘卻牙痛帶來的苦楚，同時吸引更多顧客，他就寫下好笑的短劇取悅他們，對不對？是這樣的嗎？
P Yes.	對。
S OK.	好。

轉角遇見小王子
CORNER WITH THE LITTLE PRINCE

里昂的名人除了木偶吉尼奧爾之外，還有一位無人不知、無人不曉的「小王子」。童書《小王子》(*The Little Prince*)於一九四三年出版，作家安東尼·聖艾修伯里(Antoine de Saint-exupéry, 1900–1944)，出生於法國里昂，《小王子》展現了聖艾修伯里童心未泯與對現實世界的批判，陸續被翻譯成兩百五十種語言，迄今在全球已售出逾兩億冊，成為家喻戶曉的文學經典。

3-4

隨處可見的吉尼奧爾

The Little Prince《小王子》

《小王子》(一九四三)既是一本關於愛情、友情與孤獨的童書，也是一本老少咸宜的寓言小說。墜機的飛行員與來自另一個星球的小王子在沙漠中相遇，展開了一段相知相惜的友誼。故事中的每個角色都帶有象徵意義，對畫中富含人生哲理，令人回味無窮。

Vocabulary

3. **professional** [prəˋfɛʃənl] *adj.* 專業的；專職的

4. **distract** [dɪˋstrækt] *v.* 轉移（注意力）；使分心

5. **ache** [ek] *v.* 疼痛

6. **sketch** [skɛtʃ] *n.* 幽默短劇

對話

S : *Samantha Brown, Hostess*　　**P** : *Patrice Cardelli, Puppeteer*

P ~~I play to you Gnafron~~ [I will show you Gnafron].	現在我來介紹涅馮!
S Oh, Gnafron. We have not met Gnafron.	涅馮?我們還沒見過涅馮!
P Gnafron?	涅馮?
S Gnafron?	涅馮?
P Gnafron. Oh, yes, yes. But do you speak English, Gnafron?	我來了!你會説英文嗎?涅馮!
S You speak English?	你會説英文嗎?
P No. But . . . but . . . but you . . . you . . . Oh, a little bit. I like the **Beaujolais**.[7]	不會。但是,只會一點點。我最愛喝薄酒萊。
S Oh, he likes the Beaujolais a lot. So two hundred years later, Laurent Mourguet could not have possibly imagined that his puppets, Guignol, Gnafron, and Madelon, would still be here in Lyon with their own puppet theater. **Encore**![8]	他非常喜歡薄酒萊,因此兩百年之後,羅朗·洛格做夢也想不到,他的戲偶,吉尼奧爾、涅馮和瑪德琳,仍舊在里昂演出,而且擁有自己的木偶劇院。安可!
P Hey!	嘿!
S Oh, the French.	法國人!

背景知識

法國葡萄酒產區
MAJOR WINE REGIONS OF FRANCE

法國葡萄酒有以下幾大產區：

Alsace
阿爾薩斯

3-4

隨處可見的吉尼奧爾

Bourgogne 勃艮地
&
Beaujolais 薄酒萊

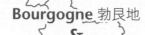

Bordeaux
波爾多

Rhône 隆河

　　法國原產地管理證明：原產地管理證明 A.O.C.（全名 Appellation d'Origine Contrôlée）會載明於酒瓶的標籤上，通常在 Appellation 和 Contrôlée 兩字中間會加進原產地名。例如：波爾多產區會標示為 Appellation Bordeaux Contrôlée。

Vocabulary

7. **Beaujolais** [ˌbodʒoˋle] *n.* 薄酒萊

8. **encore** [ˋɑnˌkɔr] *n.* 安可；再來一曲

Provence
普羅旺斯

223

自述

 Every night, the city of Lyon uses creative design **schemes**[9] to light up its best-known buildings and **monuments**.[10] The idea is that light can reveal elements of a city's character that you might not have noticed during the day. And I notice that there are a lot of these unexpected **revelations**[11] throughout the city, which **on the whole** is a very **affluent**[12] and conservative one, yet there are these wonderful hidden surprises.

Like I said before, Lyon is a city at ease with itself, and that allows you to relax and savor the unexpected.

每晚里昂市都以匠心獨具的設計巧思，照亮聞名遐邇的建築物與紀念碑，概念是光線能映照出那些，或許在白天被你所忽略的特色。而且我注意到里昂有著許多令人意想不到的發現！整體看來，這裡是座繁榮而保守的城市，然而隨處隱藏著美好的驚喜。

如我之前所說，里昂是座悠哉的城市，這讓你跟著放鬆、並且一同享受這城市帶來的驚喜！

學習重點

---

on the whole 整體來說；大體上而言

on the whole 為副詞片語，與 generally、in general 意思相同。

- There are a few problems with your plan, but on the whole, it is pretty good.
  你的計畫有一些問題，但大體來說相當不錯。

- The dove is generally regarded as a symbol of peace.
  鴿子通常被認為是和平的象徵。

- Steve is a bit careless, but he is a good man in general.
  史提夫有點粗枝大葉，但是大致上是個好人。

【延伸學習】

as a whole 整體而言的；總體上的

as a whole 常接在名詞後作形容詞用，表「整體的、一起的」。

- The singing in the church is quite loud when the choir as a whole is singing.
  合唱團一起歌唱時的歌聲在教堂裡很響亮。

Theatre des Celestins,
Lyon, France 塞爾斯丁劇院

Vocabulary

9. **scheme** [skim] *n.* 計畫；方案

10. **monument** [ˈmɑnjəmənt] *n.* 紀念碑；歷史遺跡

11. **revelation** [ˌrɛvəˈleʃən] *n.* 意想不到的事物；揭露

12. **affluent** [ˈæfluənt] *adj.* 富裕的；豐富的

瑞士

SWITZERLAND IN ONE MINUTE

　　瑞士正式名稱為「瑞士聯邦」，位於西歐，共有二十六州。瑞士是一個特別的國家，從一八一五年後就未曾捲入國際戰爭，且由德語、法語、義大利語三個主要的語言及文化所組成，雖然瑞士德語人口居多數，但並未形成單一民族及語言國家，再加上瑞士人對共同歷史背景及價值觀的認同而產生國家歸屬感。

　　瑞士風景明媚，主要是以阿爾卑斯山脈的山景為特色，北邊有侏羅山脈（Jura Mountains），中部為瑞士高原（Swiss Plateau），而日內瓦就位在瑞士高原及日內瓦湖西南角匯入羅納河之處。這一集中，珊曼莎要帶我們去看這個高度國際化的都市，精品、核子物理、乳酪鍋，一起來吃喝玩樂、增長知識吧！

聯邦首府：伯恩
FEDERAL CITY: BERN

國家最高行政機構：聯邦委員會
HEAD OF STATE: FEDERAL COUNCIL

官方語言：德語、法語、義大利語、羅曼什語
OFFICIAL LANGUAGES: GERMAN, FRENCH, ITALIAN, ROMANSH

貨幣：瑞士法郎（**SFr**）
CURRENCY: SWISS FRANC (CHF)

人口：8,014,000（2012 年統計）
POPULATION: 8,014,000 (2012)

國際電話區碼：+41
CALLING CODE: +41

UNIT 4

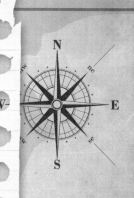

Hi, Geneva!
哈囉！日內瓦

 影片原音 13　　 課文朗讀 37

對話

S : *Samantha Brown, Hostess*　　**D** : *Dogsled Driver*

S　Whoo. Hey, everybody! It's me, Samantha. I'm here in Switzerland, a country known as being an outdoor **paradise**,[1] 365 days out of the year.

大家好，我是珊曼莎。這裡是瑞士，一個被公認是全年無休的戶外活動天堂。

D　OK, **halt**.[2]

好，停下來。

Vocabulary

1. **paradise** [ˈpɛrəˌdaɪs] *n.* 樂園；像天堂般的地方
2. **halt** [hɔlt] *v.* 暫停；停止；終止

從日內瓦出發～到處都好玩
HAVE FUN IN SWITZERLAND

西庸城堡（法語：Château de Chillon）

位於沃州蒙特勒（Montreux）附近的維托（Veytaux）鎮，西庸城堡座落在日內瓦湖（Lake Geneva）湖畔，是瑞士最有名的古蹟之一。十六世紀時，城堡為監禁囚犯的監獄，最有名的囚犯是因支持日內瓦獨立而遭到囚禁的彭尼華（Banivard）神父。一八一六年，英國詩人拜倫（Lord Byron）到此參觀後，有感而發寫下著名的長詩《西庸的囚徒》，如今在城堡內還可看見拜倫簽名的字跡。詳情可見：http://www.chillon.ch/en/

格呂耶爾（法語：Gruyères）

格呂耶爾這個瑞士小鎮是著名的乳酪產地，這裡生產的是硬質、沒有孔的乳酪。到此參觀乳酪工廠，你會發現傳統乳酪製作的祕密及歷史，當然還有不能錯過新鮮美味的瑞士乳酪鍋！乳酪工廠詳情可見：www.lamaisondugruyere.ch

圖片來源：Wikipedia / Cjeiler

蒙特勒（Montreux）

瑞士最大的聖誕市集在法語區的蒙特勒，為期一個月的聖誕市集從每天早上十一點開始到半夜，持續到十二月二十四日結束。想要來感受濃厚的聖誕氣氛，一定要親自走一趟！詳情可見：http://montreuxnoel.com/

229

對話

S : Samantha Brown, Hostess　　**D** : Dogsled Driver

S　Did you know that a **whopping**[3] 80 percent of visitors to Switzerland come here specifically to vacation? But this country has a very famous city where it is actually just the opposite. Seventy percent only come to work. Of course, I'm talking about Geneva, known for banking and **bureaucracy**.[4] So, the reputation of the people is that they're very serious—all business, absolutely no fun at all!

你知道來訪瑞士的旅客，有高達八成是專程來度假的嗎？但這個國家有座著名的城市，卻完全相反，有七成訪客是為工作而來。當然，我指的就是，以銀行業和官僚體制而聞名的日內瓦。所以，當地人的風評就是他們非常認真，只談正事，一點都不有趣。

But there's another side to Geneva. It's one of Europe's most **cosmopolitan**[5] cities, with an incredible location on a **pristine**[6] lake surrounded by mountains. It also **boasts**[7] a **magnificent**[8] mix of people from 173 countries from all corners of the world. So, I ask you, do you find the world boring? No? Then, you won't be bored by Geneva. Can you **drop me off** in the city center?

但日內瓦也有另外一面，它是歐洲最具國際化的城市之一，座落於純淨的湖畔、群山環繞，當地還有來自世界各地多達一百七十三個國家的人。所以我問你，你覺得這個世界很無聊嗎？不會？那麼日內瓦也肯定不會讓你覺得無聊。可以送我到市中心嗎？

D　Yes, sure.

好的，沒問題。

drop sb/sth off 讓某人中途下車；中途卸貨

drop off 在文中是指「在……讓某人中途下車」，受詞可為人或事物，作此義時也可以只用 drop 來表示。

用法一 drop + 名詞/代名詞 + (off) + 地點

- I will drop the dry cleaning off on my way to work and pick it up on the way home.
  我上班途中把乾洗的衣物送去，回家時再去拿。

用法二 drop (off) + 名詞 + 地點

- The bus dropped off several passengers at a bus stop near the park.
  公車在公園旁的一處站牌讓一些乘客下車。

Vocabulary

3. **whopping** [ˈhwɑpɪŋ] *adj.* 龐大的

4. **bureaucracy** [bjʊˈrɑkəsi] *n.* 官僚制度；官僚作風

5. **cosmopolitan** [ˌkɑzməˈpɑlətən] *adj.* 世界性的；國際化的

6. **pristine** [ˌprɪsˈtin] *adj.* 純淨的；原始狀態的

7. **boast** [bost] *v.* 以……自豪；擁有（值得驕傲的成就）

8. **magnificent** [mægˈnɪfəsənt] *adj.* 宏偉壯麗的；令人印象深刻的

自述

Switzerland is a very small country surrounded by Europe's **heavy hitters**.[9] We've got France, Germany, Austria, Italy. Now, it's in Europe, but it's not a part of the European Union. So they've kept their own currency: the Swiss franc. They, however, don't have their own language. People here just sort of take from whatever country they are closest to. In Geneva's case, it's France. And, actually, when you arrive here in Geneva, you've got a decision to make: you can either go to France or you can go to Switzerland. It's that close.

One of the key things about Geneva is its **accessibility**.[10] You can get from the airport to your hotel in about twenty minutes, and be in the **spectacular**[11] French or Swiss mountains in not much longer.

So, I dropped my bags at the hotel and headed out to see the city.

瑞士是一個很小的國家，被歐洲幾個重量級大國包圍，包括了法國、德國、奧地利和義大利。它雖是歐洲的國家，卻不屬於歐盟，所以仍然沿用自己的貨幣——瑞士法郎。不過他們沒有自己的語言，這裡的人只好使用最鄰近國家的語言。對日內瓦來說，那就是法國了。其實當你抵達日內瓦後，就得做個決定：你可選擇前往法國或瑞士，它們就是那麼近。

日內瓦最大的特色之一就是它的交通便利，從機場到飯店只需約二十分鐘，前往壯麗的法國或瑞士山脈時間也多不了多久。

所以我把行李放在飯店後，就出發一覽市區面貌了。

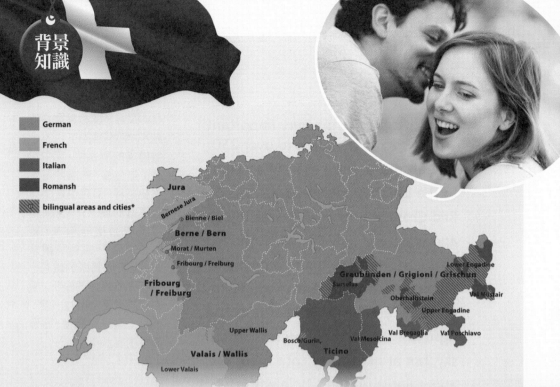

German
French
Italian
Romansh
bilingual areas and cities*

Jura
Bernese Jura
Bienne / Biel
Berne / Bern
Morat / Murten
Fribourg / Freiburg
Fribourg / Freiburg
Graubünden / Grigioni / Grischun
Surselva
Lower Engadine
Oberhalbstein
Val Müstair
Upper Engadine
Upper Wallis
Val Bregaglia
Val Poschiavo
Bosco/Gurin
Val Mesolcina
Ticino
Valais / Wallis
Lower Valais

4-1

哈囉！日內瓦

瑞士的官方語言
THE LANGUAGES OF SWITZERLAND

　　瑞士有四種官方語言，分別是：德語、法語、義大利語及羅曼什語。有六成多的人使用德語，兩成的人說法語，剩下少數人說義語及羅曼什語。德語區有蘇黎世州（Zurich）、亞本塞州（Appenzell）及聖加侖州（St. Gallen），而伯恩州（Bern）、佛立堡州（Fribourg）、瓦萊州（Valais）則是德法兩種語言通用的區域。法語區有日內瓦州（Geneva）、侏羅州（Jura）等等。義語區有提契諾州（Ticino），但自從一九七〇年之後，說義語的人口數漸漸減少了，主因是移民到瑞士的義大利人減少的緣故。格勞賓登州（Graubunden）是主要的羅曼什語區，雖然羅曼什為小眾語言，但是在瑞士仍被視為官方語言之一。

圖片來源：（地圖）Wikipedia / Marco Zanoli

Vocabulary

9. **heavy hitter** [ˋhɛvi] [ˋhɪtɚ] *n.* 有影響力的政客或商界人士（在此指具影響力的國家）

10. **accessibility** [ɪkˏsɛsəˋbɪləti] *n.* 易到達；便利性

11. **spectacular** [spɛkˋtækjəlɚ] *adj.* 壯觀的；引人注目的

自述

Geneva is a very important city. It's home to over 250 organizations, from the United Nations to the International Headquarters of the Red Cross. It's also a very wealthy city, and you need only to look at the tops of the buildings to figure out why. Banks and watches. Banks you've heard of. Banks you've never heard of. And right now they sort of **blend**[12] into the sky, but at night they light them up, and it lights up the whole **waterfront**.[13]

Geneva is a **visually**[14] **striking**[15] city, and it's immediately **apparent**[16] that most of its citizens enjoy a very high standard of living. Lake Geneva, or Lac Léman, **bisects**[17] the city and is a major center of activity. And the celebrated symbol of this city is called Jet d'Eau which is a jet that sprays eight thousand **gallons**[18] of water per minute, five hundred feet in the air. Today, it's out of order. Sorry about that.

日內瓦是一座相當重要的城市，它是超過二百五十個機構的所在地，其中包括了聯合國，到國際紅十字會總部，而且也是個非常富有的國家，你只要看看各棟大樓的頂端，就知道原因了。銀行和鐘錶業，有著你聽過的銀行，也有從沒聽過的銀行，現在它們與天空融為一體，但晚上燈光點亮後，將照亮整個濱水區。

日內瓦是座在視覺上引人注目的城市，可想而知這裡多數的居民生活水準都非常高。日內瓦湖或稱雷夢湖，將這座城市一分為二，也是主要的活動中心，這座城市最著名的象徵，叫做大噴泉。這座噴泉每分鐘會噴出八千加侖的水，水柱高達五百呎。今天，它故障了。真是抱歉。

背景知識

日內瓦隨處可見的地標：大噴泉
JET D'EAU

　　日內瓦湖上可見一柱擎天、宛若鯨魚噴出的水柱，這就是日內瓦的大噴泉，每次可噴出高一百四十公尺，五百公升噴水量的噴泉，由一百三十馬力的電力推動，此為世界上最大的人工噴泉。當水柱被風吹動時，就宛如水做成的白帆，而白帆又會跟著風向改變，景象非常奇特，遠看好似一把長劍直衝天際。壯觀的景象讓大噴泉成了日內瓦最具代表性的地標。

Vocabulary

12. **blend** [blɛnd] *v.* 與……融合；混合

13. **waterfront** [ˋwɔtɚˏfrʌnt] *n.* 濱海區

14. **visually** [ˋvɪʒʊəli] *adv.* 視覺上；可見地

15. **striking** [ˋstraɪkɪŋ] *adj.* 顯著的；引人注目的

16. **apparent** [əˋpɛrənt] *adj.* 明顯的；顯而易見的

17. **bisect** [ˋbaɪˏsɛkt] *v.* 將……一分為二

18. **gallon** [ˋgælən] *n.* 加侖（美制 1 加侖約等於 3.8 公升）

圖片來源：（下）李政娟

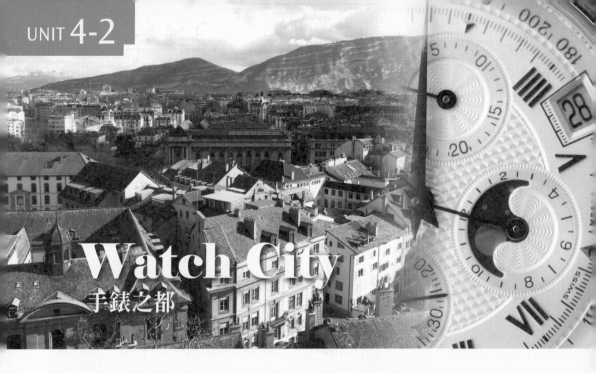

Watch City
手錶之都

影片原音 14　　課文朗讀 38

自述

So, if this is a wealthy city, then it must have **fabulous**[1] shopping, right? Oh, oh, does Geneva ever. What are you **in the market for**? **Pearls?**[2] Nice jackets? One hundred thousand dollar diamond necklace? Yeah, it's that kind of shopping here. I'm on the Rue du Rhône, a street known for having the world's most **luxurious**[3] **brands.**[4] So, of course, the number one luxury item to get here is the watch. I'm sorry, I'm sorry. The Swiss watch, right? All the major Swiss **watchmakers** are represented in Geneva. In fact, Geneva is called "Watch City."

既然這是一座富有的城市，那一定會有很棒的購物場所吧？來日內瓦準沒錯。你想要買什麼呢？珍珠？漂亮的外套？價值十萬美元的鑽石項鍊？沒錯，這裡專賣這種商品。我正置身隆河大道，這條街以雲集世上最奢華的品牌而聞名。當然，這裡最受歡迎的奢侈商品就是手錶。對不起。應該是瑞士手錶？所有主要瑞士手錶製造商在日內瓦都有設點。其實日內瓦也叫做「手錶之都」。

in the market for　有意購買

in the market for sth 是口語用法，表示「對某事物有興趣想買進」的意思。

- Carrie just moved to the city, so she's in the market for a new apartment.

  凱莉剛搬到都市裡，所以有意買間公寓。

watchmaker　手錶製造商

名詞 maker 表「製作人；製造者」之意，常與其他名詞結合形成複合名詞，表示「製作……的人」，常見的例子包括：

film　　　+　maker　=　filmmaker　製作影片者（可指導演或製作人）

law　　　+　maker　=　lawmaker　立法者

peace　　+　maker　=　peacemaker　調解者；和事佬

trouble　+　maker　=　troublemaker　製造麻煩的人；惹是生非的人

- A few of the lawmakers want to make major changes to the country's criminal codes.

  有幾位立法者想大幅改革國內的刑法。

4-2

手錶之都

Vocabulary

1. **fabulous** [ˋfæbjələs] *adj.* 極好的；絕妙的
2. **pearl** [pɝl] *n.* 珍珠
3. **luxurious** [lʌgˋʒʊriəs] *adj.* 奢侈的；奢華的
4. **brand** [brænd] *n.* 品牌

自述

Now, when it comes to buying a watch, from what I've been told, prices are better here, but not necessarily. One thing that would guarantee you 15 to 20 percent off the listed price is just to bring cash. Then, you're going to have to get one of those little black **attaché cases**[5] with the **handcuffs**.[6] That would be fun. You know, what's pretty **ironic**[7] about Geneva is here you don't even need a watch. There are **clocks** everywhere.

Of course, there's a museum for watches. Patek Philippe is one of the most esteemed Swiss watchmaking companies since 1839.

就選購手錶而言，據我所知，這裡的價格比較便宜，但卻不是必然的。只有付現能保證讓你享受標價八折到八五折優惠，那你就必須帶著一個黑色公事包，外加一副手銬，那一定很好玩。而在日內瓦最諷刺的是，你根本不需要手錶。這裡到處都有時鐘。

當然，這裡也有鐘錶博物館，百達斐麗從一八三九年起就是最受敬重的瑞士鐘錶製造商之一。

clock　與時鐘有關的用語

英文中有許多與 clock 有關的用語，列舉如下：

▶ **around the clock　日以繼夜**

- The robbers couldn't steal the valuable necklace because it was guarded around the clock.

  小偷無法偷走那條貴重的項鍊，因為項鍊不分晝夜都有人看顧著。

▶ **against the clock　搶時間；與時間賽跑**

- We raced against the clock to turn in our homework on time.

  為了準時交作業，我們努力跟時間賽跑。

▶ **turn back the clock　時光倒轉**

- I wish I could turn back the clock and live my life over again.

  我真希望時光能倒轉，再想重新好好活過一次。

▶ **beat the clock　提前完成任務**

- I beat the clock by turning in my project one day earlier than expected.

  我比預期早一天將企畫案提交出去。

4-2

手錶之都

Vocabulary

5. **attaché case** [ˌæˌtæˈʃe] [kes] *n.*　公事包

6. **handcuff** [ˈhændˌkʌf] *n.*　手銬

7. **ironic** [aɪˈrɑnɪk] *adj.*　諷刺的；具有諷刺意味的

對話

S : *Samantha Brown, Hostess*　　**S₁** : *Suzanne Rumphorst, Guide*

S Suzanne Rumphorst, a guide in Geneva, gave me a tour. So why did Geneva become the center of . . . of watchmaking?

日內瓦的導遊蘇珊·蘭佛斯特帶我入內參觀。為什麼日內瓦會成為鐘錶的製造中心？

S₁ That was in about the sixteenth century, when the **refugees**[8] from France, the Huguenots, were **fleeing**[9] France because of [the] **persecution**[10] of **Protestants**.[11] And then they came to Geneva, and they brought their kinds of early handwork, which was lace making and **goldsmith**.[12]

約在十六世紀，當法國的難民胡格諾派教徒，由於受到新教徒的迫害而逃離法國，來到日內瓦帶來了他們早期的手工藝品，就是蕾絲製作以及金匠工藝。

S Having time—the ability to tell time—was that something only for the wealthy? Because that's what it looks like here.

擁有辨別時間的能力，是有錢人的專利嗎？在這裡看似如此。

S₁ Oh, yes! It was a very direct sign of your wealth, of your position, your status in life.

沒錯，那非常直接地象徵著你的財富、職務和身分地位。

Have you heard about this? Watch **mechanisms**,[13] which were developed for the blind.

妳有聽說過這個嗎？這種手錶的機械裝置是專為盲人而研發的。

S No, no, no.

沒聽過。

Patek Philippe Museum 百達斐麗博物館

百達斐麗可說是高級名錶的代名詞，最早是由百達和斐麗兩位製錶師傅合作所創立的品牌。他們所製作的鐘錶手工精密，因此在鐘錶界有相當崇高的地位。位在日內瓦的百達斐麗博物館於二○○一年成立，欲多了解日內瓦傳統製錶的過程，及一窺珍貴名錶的廬山真面目，來到日內瓦，千萬不能錯過這裡！

$ Adult: CHF 10.00   Senior: CHF 7.00
  Disabled: CHF 7.00   Unemployed: CHF 7.00
  Student (18-25): CHF 7.00 Group (10 or more): CHF 5.00
  Child (under 18): Free

☎ +41 (0) 22-807-0910

🌐 http://www.patekmuseum.com/

4-2

手錶之都

Vocabulary

8. **refugee** [ˌrɛfjʊˋdʒi] *n.* 難民

9. **flee** [fli] *v.* 逃離；逃避

10. **persecution** [ˌpɝsɪˋkjuʃən] *n.* 迫害

11. **Protestant** [ˋprɑtəstənt] *n.* 新教教徒（指十六世紀脫離羅馬天主教之基督教團體或後來由其形成的教派成員）

12. **goldsmith** [ˋgoldˌsmɪθ] *n.* 金匠；金器商

13. **mechanism** [ˋmɛkəˌnɪzəm] *n.* 機械裝置

對
話

S : Samantha Brown, Hostess　　**S₁** : Suzanne Rumphorst, Guide

S₁ Yeah.	是。
S Is that the **arrows**[14] there?	就是那些箭頭嗎？
S₁ Yes, exactly, that's it. Obviously, to allow one to feel the time.	沒錯，那讓人可以用觸覺來確認時間。
S Oh, it doesn't have a glass piece over it.	它上面並沒有玻璃蓋。
S₁ Exactly. It's a living industry and it's a **blooming**[15] industry. Much of . . .	沒錯。這是一個活躍且興盛的產業。
S Still to this day?	到現在還是？
S₁ Still to this day. And new watchmakers open up all the time and, obviously, find a living.	到現在還是。而且常常會有新的鐘錶製造商出現，顯然這行還是可以維持生計。
S And they've got to start in Geneva to be serious.	在日內瓦開店需要非常地認真。
S₁ And they find a **clientele**,[16] also. People come specifically to Geneva to buy watches and really don't want to leave without buying a watch here.	同時也可以找到客源。人們專程到日內瓦購買手錶，絕對不想空手而回。

瑞士著名的鐘錶品牌
SWISS WATCHES

日內瓦聚集了瑞士鐘錶界的精英，知名品牌如百達斐麗（Patek Philippe）、勞力士（Rolex）、Piaget（伯爵）、Chopard（蕭邦）、江詩丹頓（Vacheron Constantin）、弗蘭克·穆勒（Franck Muller）等，都是源自於日內瓦。

瑞士如今成了世界上最大的鐘錶製造地之一，全球約有一半的鐘錶都是在瑞士製造。即使大多數知名品牌鐘錶價高昂貴，但也有平價又暢銷的超薄塑膠腕錶「帥奇錶」（Swatch）。Swatch 錶靠著出色的技術能力，生產出可當滑雪場入場券的 Swatch Snowpass錶款，以及具有網際網路時間功能的 Swatch Beat，公司不斷發展，至今仍是最成功且最有活力的製錶公司。

4-2
手錶之都

Vocabulary

14. **arrow** [ˋæro] *n.* 箭頭

15. **blooming** [ˋblumɪŋ] *adj.* 興盛的；容光煥發的

16. **clientele** [ˏklaɪnˋtɛl] *n.* 顧客、客戶（總稱）

The Most Expensive Garage Sale
連二手貨都好貴

🎧 影片原音 15　　🎧 課文朗讀 39

對話

S : *Samantha Brown, Hostess*　　**H** : *Holli Schauber, Professor*

S	I'm in Geneva, Switzerland, a city with an unusual combination of both natural beauty and international **flair**.[1] It makes for a great weekend **getaway**;[2] that is, if you can afford it. Now, being a visitor to Geneva . . .	這裡是瑞士的日內瓦,這裡獨特地結合了自然美景和國際都市的氣息,造就了週末度假的好去處。當然如果能負擔得起的話,身為日內瓦的訪客……
H	Right.	是。
S	. . . I'm constantly shocked by the prices here.	這裡的價格常常讓我震驚。
H	Well, being a resident here, I'm equally shocked by the prices here.	身為日內瓦的市民,這裡的價格也常常讓我震驚。
S	Really?	真的嗎?
H	Yeah.	真的。
S	Holli Schauber, a professor here in town, showed me around.	荷莉·史考伯是城裡的一位教授,她帶我到處參觀。

認識日內瓦
GENEVA'S COST OF LIVING

日內瓦是世界上十大高消費城市之一。因為日內瓦的產業以金融業居多,而金融業的薪資較高,因此也帶動了日內瓦的生活水準。一般而言,平均稅後月薪約 5,600 瑞士法郎(折合台幣約 181,818 元)。

飲食

在一般餐廳用餐,一餐約 25.00 瑞士法郎(折合台幣約 812 元)

點一份麥當勞套餐約 13.00 瑞士法郎(折合台幣約 422 元)

一杯可樂約 4.00 瑞士法郎(折合台幣約 130 元)

一杯啤酒約 6.00 瑞士法郎(折合台幣約 195 元)

交通

公車單程票價為 3.50 瑞士法郎(折合台幣約 114元)

計程車起跳資費 7.00 瑞士法郎(折合台幣約 227 元),每公里以 3.00 瑞士法郎(折合台幣約 97 元)跳錶。

居住

在城市裡租套房,每個月約 1,862.50 瑞士法郎(折合台幣約 60,470 元)

在郊外租屋,每個月花費 1,600 瑞士法郎(折合台幣約 51,948 元)

匯率計算:1 瑞士法郎 = 32.47 台幣(二〇一三年十月)

4-3

連二手貨都好貴

 Vocabulary

1. **flair** [flɛr] *n.* 吸引人的特質、氣息

2. **getaway** [ˈgɛtəˌwe] *n.* 適合週末渡假的去處;短暫的假期

對話

S : *Samantha Brown, Hostess*　　**H** : *Holli Schauber, Professor*

H And you sort of live in **denial**[3] about how expensive everything is. Otherwise, you wouldn't be able to function properly. You . . . you get sick or shocked wherever you go.

你多少得拒絕承認這裡的物價非常貴，否則就無法正常生活了。不管你到哪裡，你都會病倒或嚇昏。

S But . . . so here we are at the **flea market**.[4]

但這裡是跳蚤市場。

H Yeah.

是。

S Are things going to be cheaper?

東西會比較便宜嗎？

H This is probably the most expensive **garage sale**[5] you'll ever go to.

這裡大概會是妳所去過價格最昂貴的車庫拍賣會。

S The flea market is held from eight to two on Saturdays and Wednesdays.

Why Wednesdays?

跳蚤市場的開放時間是每週六和週三的八點到兩點。

為什麼是每週三呢？

H Because there's no school on Wednesdays in Geneva at the public schools. There's no school on Wednesdays.

因為日內瓦的公立學校週三是不用上課的。週三不用上課。

S There's no school on Wednesdays?

週三不用上課？

H No, no, no.

不，不，不用。

S Do they go to school on Saturday and Sunday?

週六和週日要上課嗎？

THE SCHOOL SYSTEM IN GENEVA
日內瓦的學校制度

瑞士的教育系統不同地區有不同標準，即使如此仍大同小異。每個人都享有免費九年的義務教育，包括外籍人士。日內瓦各中小學每周上課二十八到三十小時，週三及週末兩天是不上課的，每年有八周左右的假期。

每個小孩上小學前，可先上一至兩年的學前課程。學前課程是免費的，且可依個人意願選擇是否就讀，不過在日內瓦年滿四歲就必須上一年的義務性學前教育。義務教育階段結束後，根據老師和家長的建議，瑞士初中畢業生開始選擇各自發展方向。一些學生會選擇進入以上大學為目的的會考高中，其他大部分學生則選擇普通職業高中和各類技術職業學校。

日內瓦教育系統如下所示：

Preschool 學前教育	1-2 years
Primary School 小學	6 years
Lower Secondary 中學	3 years
	以上屬於義務教育
Upper Secondary 高中	3-5 years
Tertiary 大學專科等高等教育	3-5 years (8 for PhD)

4-3

連二手貨都好貴

Vocabulary

3. **denial** [dɪˋnaɪəl] *n.* 否認；拒絕

4. **flea market** [fli] [ˋmɑrkət] *n.* 跳蚤市場

5. **garage sale** [gəˋrɑʒ] [sel] *n.* 舊物出售；車庫拍賣會（指在自家車庫前的空地上廉價出售家中舊物，或稱 yard sale「院子拍賣會」）

247

對話

S : Samantha Brown, Hostess　　**H** : Holli Schauber, Professor

H No. Just four days a week, yeah. So . . .

不用，一週只上四天課，就是這樣。

S And whether or not you're looking for a tribal mask, it's a place where you can see the cultural mix of the people, among the **bric-a-brac**[6] and the used furniture.

不論你是否想買個部落面具，透過這裡的小飾物和二手傢俱，你可以看到不同民族的文化。

H Oh, wow! Look at this map! I collect antique maps.

哇！你看這張地圖！我平常有在收集古代地圖。

S You do?

真的？

H Yeah.

沒錯。

S And what is the year?

這是哪個年份的？

H And this is from 1715. *Plan de Genève*. Plan of Geneva.

這是一七一五年的，日內瓦的地圖。

H Two hundred francs! Wow!

二百法郎？哇！

S Is that . . . is that expensive?

這樣算貴嗎？

H Oh, that . . . that seems to be pretty expensive for a . . . a map that's sitting out here, folded and **wrinkled**.[7]

對一張放在外頭，折過的皺地圖來說，算是很貴了。

S You ask him how much this is.

你問他這個要多少錢。

ANTIQUES 古物珍奇尋寶去

在二手市集，可發現許多珍奇的古董物品：

購物小提醒：在市集中若看到箱子上有 "Cadeau" 或 "Servez–vous, gratuit!" 法文字樣的話，表示這些東西是免費贈送的。

古董地圖
antique map

古董打字機
antique typewriter

古董花瓶
antique vase

古董留聲機
antique phonograph

古董家具
antique furniture

4-3

連二手貨都好貴

Vocabulary

6. **bric-a-brac** [ˋbrɪkəˌbræk] *n.* 小擺設；小玩意（源自法文）

7. **wrinkle** [ˋrɪŋkəl] *v.* 有皺痕；起皺紋

對話

S : Samantha Brown, Hostess　　**H** : Holli Schauber, Professor

M : Male at the Stall

H Fifty.	五十塊。
M No, sorry.	不，對不起。
H That's fifty?	那個要五十塊。
S Fifty? Can you . . . do you **haggle** here?	五十塊？這裡能殺價嗎？
M Fifty.	五十塊。
S Thirty. I'll give you thirty.	三十塊，我出價三十塊。
M Thirty? Thirty?	三十塊？三十塊？
S Cash.	現金。
M Well, d'accord. OK.	好，成交了。
S D'accord? All right!	成交？太好了！
M All right. Yes.	好，沒問題。
H Terrific.	太棒了。
S That is beautiful. I love that.	真漂亮，我好喜歡。
H Yes. OK.	對啊。
S Maybe we can get this down to thirty. I'm a good haggler. Thirty!	或許這個能殺到三十塊，我是殺價高手。三十塊！
H Maybe we'll get this down to thirty.	或許這個能殺到三十塊。
M Sorry. No.	對不起，不行。

haggle 討價還價

haggle 指「（為條件或價格）爭論；討價還價」，與 bargain 意思相同。

用法一 haggle with sb over/about sth

用法二 bargain with sb for sth

- Jane haggled with a vendor at the night market over the price of a shirt.
  珍在夜市和一名攤販為了一件襯衫在討價還價。

- Katie likes to bargain with the street vendors for good deals on clothes.
  凱蒂為了買到便宜的衣服，喜歡跟路邊攤老闆討價還價。

【延伸學習】

Haggling in English 用英語殺價

- A: This old typewriter costs thirty dollars.
  這台舊的打字機要價三十元。

  B: That's a little too expensive. Can you do any better?
  有點太貴了。可以算我便宜一點嗎？

- A: It's sixty-five dollars for the CD player.
  這台 CD 播放機要價六十五元。

  B: That's a little steep. How about fifty dollars?
  有點太貴了。五十元如何？

- A: I'll give you twenty dollars for the knife set.
  這組刀我出價二十元。

  B: I'm sorry. Twenty-five dollars is my final offer.
  很抱歉。二十五元是最低價了。

自述

 There have been humans in Geneva since 3000 BC. It was once **defended**[8] by Julius Caesar. But to get a feel for Geneva's history, you head up the hill into Old Town.

What strikes me is that compared to most cities' old towns, the . . . the architecture reflects its **struggle**,[9] right? The city is coming to its own. But here in Geneva, the Old Town is just, I don't know, the buildings are perfect, stately, grand—**gives you the impression** that Geneva has always been a successful city from day one.

I tell you what, Old Town is definitely an **upscale**[10] residential neighborhood. The stores sort of **reflect**[11] that, don't they? It's got galleries, incredible home-interior shops, antique shops. And even the . . . the restaurants appear to be really for the locals as well. I always like that, when there's still **authentic**[12] city life. It's not just taken over by tourism.

在西元前三千年，日內瓦就有人類居住了，凱撒大帝曾在此防守過，但想感受日內瓦的歷史，就得走上山坡進入舊城區。

讓我驚訝的是，跟多數城市的舊城比較起來，建築物應該會反映出過去的奮鬥史吧！市貌會留下歲月的痕跡，但日內瓦的舊城，卻是建築物依然完好、宏偉和華麗，讓你感到日內瓦好像從一開始就是座繁榮的城市。

讓我告訴大家舊城顯然是一個高級住宅區，看店家就可以知道了，對不對？這裡有畫廊，極佳的家飾店和古董店，甚至是餐廳，顯然也是為本地人而設的。我一直都喜歡，這種道地的城市生活，而不是一切都以觀光業為主。

give sb an/the impression . . . 給某人……的印象

impression 表示有「印象；感想」的意思，前面可加 good、favorable 或 poor 等形容詞來修飾。與 leave/make/have an impression on sb（讓某人留下印象）意思相同。

- The book gave us a dark impression of the city.
  這本書讓我們對這城市留下負面的印象。

- The man made a poor impression on Jane, so she is not going to hire him.
  那名男子給珍的印象不好，所以她不會雇用他。

旅遊小幫手

St. Pierre Cathedral 聖彼得大教堂

此間位於日內瓦舊城的教堂興建於十二世紀，爬上一百五十七個階梯可到達北塔的塔頂。在北塔可以眺望整個城市和日內瓦湖，風景獨一無二。

- $ Adult: CHF 16.00　Group (15 or more): CHF 10.00
  Child (7–16): CHF 8.00　Child (under 7): Free

- ☏ (41) 22 310 29 29

- 🌐 http://www.site-archeologique.ch/

4-3

連二手貨都好貴

Vocabulary

8. **defend** [dɪˋfɛnd] *v.* 防禦；防守

9. **struggle** [ˋstrʌgəl] *n.* 掙扎；奮力

10. **upscale** [ˋʌpˋskel] *adj.* （口）高檔的；優質高價的

11. **reflect** [rɪˋflɛkt] *v.* 反映；反射

12. **authentic** [ɔˋθɛntɪk] *adj.* 真正的；道地的

自
述

Crowning[13] the hill is the cathedral of Saint Pierre, where Geneva became the center of the Reformation during the 1500s, giving it the nickname "Protestant Rome." Its welcoming of religious refugees during this time is what began its reputation as an international city.

座落於山頂的是聖彼得大教堂，日內瓦在一五〇〇年代成了宗教改革的重心之後，這裡就多了個綽號，叫做「新教徒的羅馬」，在此期間這裡接受了各地的宗教流亡人士，從此就成了一座國際性城市。

Oh, my gosh! Come here. Let me show you something. I want to show you something. I think I've found, actually, a cheap meal here in Geneva. You get a half a chicken, potatoes Provençal, and salad for 13.90. That's about ten dollars and fifty cents. When you eat here in Geneva, you're paying at least twice as much for that. We're eating chicken.

天啊，過來，過來看看，我要讓大家看一下，我想我在日內瓦找到供應便宜餐點的地方了，包括了半隻雞，普羅旺斯薯條和沙拉，只要十三塊九，大約是十塊半美元。在日內瓦用餐，價格一般都比這裡貴一倍，我們去吃雞肉吧。

Chez Ma Cousine offers only three entrées, all with chicken, plus one vegetarian dish. Ah, this is incredible! Look, I got a **roasted** chicken, **a pile of** crisp fries, and a salad all for about ten bucks. OK, with the soda it's about twelve dollars.

這間「家庭料理餐廳」只供應三款主菜，全都是雞肉料理，另外還有一道素食，真是太棒了！看，有烤雞肉、一疊酥脆的薯條和沙拉，全部只要約十美元，再加一杯汽水就是約十二元。

roast 烘烤

roast 和 grill 都有「烤」的意思，差別在哪裡呢？

roast	grill
v. 以烤箱燒烤 *n.* 烤肉；烤肉野餐	*v.* 以烤架燒烤、炙烤 *n.* 烤架
• Peg roasted the potatoes for thirty minutes. 佩葛烤洋芋烤了三十分鐘。	• We grilled some steak and vegetables at the barbeque. 我們烤肉時烤了些牛排和蔬菜。

a pile of 一堆；一疊

pile 意思是「堆；疊」，piles of 或 a pile of 之後接名詞時都表示「大量；一大堆」的意思，常用於金錢、紙張、衣服等。

• There is a pile of toys in the corner of the children's room.
小孩子房間的角落有一堆玩具。

旅遊小幫手

Chez Ma Cousine 家庭料理餐廳

在日內瓦有三家分店（分別位於 Vieille ville、St Gervais、Petit-Saconnex），餐點費用從 12.90 至 15.40 瑞士法郎，並且也提供兒童餐。

📞 (41) 22 310 96 96

🌐 http://www.chezmacousine.ch/

Vocabulary

13. **crown** [kraʊn] *v.* 形成或覆蓋在……的

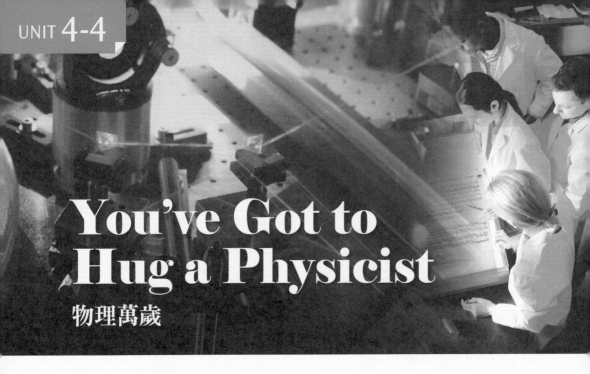

You've Got to Hug a Physicist

物理萬歲

🎧 影片原音 16　🎧 課文朗讀 40

自述

Geneva is a very walkable city, but public transportation is excellent. There are buses and **trams**.[1] There's even a boat that takes you from one side of the lake to the other. And get this, there's a certain place in this city where some of the most brilliant people on the planet **deliberately**[2] stage **collisions**.[3]

This is the **headquarters**[4] of CERN, the European Organization for Nuclear Research. It's a **particle**[5] physics **laboratory**[6] right within Geneva. And visitors can take a three-hour guided tour.

日內瓦是個非常適合步行的城市，但它的公共運輸系統也很完備，這裡有公車和電車，甚至還可以搭船到湖的對岸。還有，在這座城市的某處，有一群地球上最傑出的人才正蓄意引起碰撞。

這裡是 CERN，歐洲核子研究委員會的總部。這是位於日內瓦的一座粒子物理學實驗室，遊客可以來這參加三小時的導覽之旅。

旅遊小幫手

CERN 歐洲核子研究委員會

是世界上最大的粒子物理學實驗室，也是全球資訊網的發源地。免費入場參觀。參觀入口在瑞士，但實驗室大部分是在法國境內，故進入之前要先確認是否持有有效護照及簽證。

🕐 Monday–Friday: 8:00 a.m.–5:45 p.m.   Saturday: 8:30 a.m.–5:15 p.m.
Sunday: Closed

📞 (41) 22 767 84 84

🌐 http://home.web.cern.ch/

圖片來源：（上）CERN、（下）Wikipedia / Adam Nieman

Vocabulary

1. **tram** [træm] *n.* 有軌電車

2. **deliberately** [dɪˋlɪbərətli] *adv.* 故意地；蓄意地

3. **collision** [kəˋlɪʒən] *n.* 碰撞；相撞

4. **headquarters** [ˋhɛdˏkwɔrtəz] *n.* （公司的）總部

5. **particle** [ˋpɑrtɪkəl] *n.* （物理）粒子；微粒

6. **laboratory** [ˋlæbrəˏtɔri] *n.* 實驗室

對話

S : *Samantha Brown, Hostess*　　**Fi** : *Female on Bike, CERN Guide*

S So, right now I am in the largest underground scientific facility in the world, traveling through a **tunnel**[7] seventeen miles long—goes through two countries: France and Switzerland. And what is this tunnel going to be used for?

現在我正置身於世上規模最大的地下科學研究機構，穿過長達十七哩的隧道——跨越法國和瑞士這兩個國家。這條隧道有什麼用途？

Fi In this tunnel, we will have an **accelerator**[8] where particles will travel at the speed of light; they will hit a **detector**,[9] and we're going to recreate the beginning of time.

在這條隧道中有一個加速裝置，讓粒子以光速行進，它們會碰撞到偵測器，讓我們重建時間的源頭。

S Wow! What? The beginning of the universe? Wasn't that like 13.7 billion years ago? Just how were they going to do that? With this! What **in the world** is that?

什麼，宇宙的開端？那不是一百三十七億年前的事嗎？怎麼能辦得到？就憑這個，這個到底是什麼？

Vocabulary 🎧

7. **tunnel** [ˋtʌn!] *n.*　地道；隧道

8. **accelerator** [ækˋsɛlə͵retɚ] *n.*　加速器；油門

9. **detector** [dɪˋtɛktɚ] *n.*　偵測器；檢測器

in the world　到底；究竟；怎麼會這樣

in the world 接在疑問詞之後作為強調用，意思是「到底；究竟」，也可用 on earth 來表示。

- What in the world is going on here?!
  這裡究竟發生了什麼事呀？！

- Where on earth were you able to find tickets to the sold-out game?
  你到底是在哪裡弄到那個已售完場次比賽的門票？

背景知識

4-4

物理萬歲

大型強子對撞機
LARGE HADRON COLLIDER

大型強子對撞機 LHC（Large Hadron Collider）為一對撞型粒子加速器，作為國際高能物理學研究之用，由近百個國家的八千多名科學家合作興建而成。LHC 大到需要一個周長達二十七公里、橫跨法國與瑞士兩國的地底隧道。事實上，這裡所使用的纜線，如果你拉直的話，總長大概可以繞地球六圈。希格斯玻色子（又稱上帝粒子）就是在這裡發現的，從理論提出到驗證花了共四十八年的時間。比利時物理學家弗朗索瓦・恩格勒和英國物理學家彼得・希格斯因成功預測希格斯玻色子（又稱上帝粒子）而榮獲二〇一三年諾貝爾物理學獎。

圖片來源：（右上及右下）CERN、（上圖）Wikimedia Commons / Muriel

對話

S : *Samantha Brown, Hostess*　　**M₁** : *Male at CERN, Physicist*

M₁ Well, this is the world's largest particle detector. Right down there, where you see those gentlemen down there, there are going to be collisions from **protons**[10] that are going to recreate the environment that existed at the beginning of time.

這是世上最大的粒子偵測器。就在這下方,有幾位男士正在下方,利用質子進行碰撞,以便重建宇宙形成時的環境。

We're going to hope to create some of the particles that existed at that time. They're going to come out into this giant detector called Atlas, and we're going to measure those particles and hope to understand through that the **fundamental**[11] **building blocks** of the universe.

我們希望能創造出一些在當時存在的粒子,粒子會進入這座巨型的偵測器,它叫做「阿特拉斯」。我們會測量那些粒子,希望透過模擬宇宙生成的過程,瞭解其中的原理。

S So the **formation**[12] of the . . . the stars, the mountains, the air.

包括了星星、山脈和空氣的形成。

M₁ Everything. Maybe even more than that. We don't know.

所有一切,或許還有更多。我們還不知道。

S I think it's fascinating also that people can take a tour of this. It's free, one . . .

這裡真的是很棒,大家也可以進來參觀。觀光客可享有免費導覽。

M₁ Oh, yeah.

是的。

building blocks 基本材料；必要元素

building block 原指「建築使用的砌磚；玩具積木」，可引申指「（事物的）構成元素」。

- Addition and subtraction are two of the building blocks of mathematics.
  加法和減法是兩種基本數學運算。

旅遊小幫手

International Red Cross and Red Crescent Museum
國際紅十字會和紅新月會博物館

國際紅十字會的發源地，也是全球唯一的紅十字會博物館。

⑤ CHF 15.00

🕐 10:00–18:00 April to October,
   10:00–17:00 November to March,
   Closed on Monday

🌐 http://www.redcrossmuseum.ch/

The United Nations Office at Geneva
聯合國日內瓦辦事處

聯合國日內瓦辦事處是規模僅次於美國紐約聯合國總部的聯合國機構，其辦公場所即為前國際聯盟的總部萬國宮（Palais des Nations）每年有超過十萬人到此參觀，提供十五種語言導覽。

⑤ Adults: CHF 12.
   University students, senior citizens and disabled persons: CHF 10.
   School children and youths (aged 6 to 18): CHF 7.
   Groups (minimum of 20 adults): CHF 10.

🌐 http://www.unog.ch/

4-4

物理萬歲

Vocabulary

10. **proton** [ˈproˌtɑn] *n.* （物理）質子

11. **fundamental** [ˌfʌndəˈmɛntl] *adj.* 基本的；主要的

12. **formation** [fɔrˈmeʃən] *n.* 形成；結構

對話

S : Samantha Brown, Hostess　　**M₁** : Male at CERN, Physicist

S . . . and visitors can come . . .	觀光客可以來此……
M₁ How . . . how could you not come here to take a tour of this? If I was in Geneva, for sure I would come here to take a tour of this.	沒錯，怎能不來參觀這裡呢？如果我來日內瓦，我一定會來這裡參觀。
S Absolutely.	絕對會。
M₁ You want to see where all the action is going to be at in the next couple of years.	你要知道未來幾年重要的研究趨勢。
S You might not have heard of CERN, but they are responsible for creating something you simply could not live without.	你或許沒聽過 CERN，但他們卻負責製造一種，我們賴以維生的東西。
M₁ You might know one of the most important **inventions**[13] that has come out of this place **had nothing to do with** particle physics. It was **due to** the fact that ~~us~~ [we] physicists wanted to communicate with each other. We used the **network**[14] that was existing at the time. Well, that's called the World Wide Web.	妳或許知道這裡最重要的發明之一，跟粒子物理學一點關係也沒有。它的誕生是因為我們這些物理學家需要彼此聯繫，我們使用了一種當時存在的網路系統，就叫做全球資訊網。

have nothing to do with 和……毫無關連

have to do with . . . 指「與……有關」，可視關係密切的程度，加上
nothing、something、much 等字來修飾：

用法	
A + **have nothing to do with** + B	A 與 B 沒有關係
A + **have something to do with** + B	A 與 B 有點關係
A + **have much to do with** + B	A 與 B 有很大的關係

- For me, happiness in life has nothing to do with how much money I make.

  對我來說，生活快不快樂和我賺多少錢一點關係也沒有。

- The doctor said that my skin problem might have something to do with the soap I was using.

  醫生說我的皮膚問題可能和我用的肥皂有關。

due to 由於；因為

due to 為片語介系詞，之後接名詞或 V-ing，若接子句需先接名詞同位語，如
文中的 the fact。due to 與 owing to、because of 意思相同，但語氣較
because of 正式。

- Due to the extra weight it was carrying, the airplane had a hard time taking off.

  飛機由於超載所以很難起飛。

Vocabulary

13. **invention** [ɪnˋvɛnʃən] *n.* 發明；發明物

14. **network** [ˋnɛt͵wɜk] *n.* 網絡；網狀系統

對話

S : *Samantha Brown, Hostess*　　M₁ : *Male at CERN, Physicist*

| S | Can I give you a hug for that now? | 我可以為此抱你一下嗎？ |

| M₁ | Oh, I'm glad you like it. | 我很高興妳喜歡。 |

| S | Because that has changed my life. | 因為那改變了我的生活。 |

| M₁ | I'm glad. I'm glad you like it. You're welcome, anytime. | 真的很開心妳喜歡。不客氣。 |

| S | Just, you know, and **on behalf of** the entire world, you know, you got to hug a physicist. | 我必須代表全人類，給物理學家一個擁抱。 |

| M₁ | Oh, yeah. Yeah. We're important. | 沒錯，我們很重要的。 |

白述

 Here in Geneva, life certainly **revolves**[15] around this lake. And the city itself **wraps**[16] around it **in a horseshoe**[17] **fashion**. On the left side of the lake is where you'll find the excellent shopping streets and the steep hill of Old Town. Here on the right . . . here along the lakefront is where you'll find the city's most well-known hotels. And I'm staying at one of them, Hotel D'Angleterre.

在日內瓦這裡，生活確實以這座湖為中心，而城市本身像個馬蹄鐵般將它包圍住，在湖的左邊，有高級的商店街，和位於陡坡上的舊城。而在右邊這裡的濱水區，可以找到市內最有名的飯店，而我入住的就是其中一家，德恩格列特飯店。

> ## on behalf of sb　代表某人

behalf 指「代表；利益」，主要用於 in/on behalf of 的片語中。

- On behalf of his late grandfather, the grandson accepted the award.
  這名孫子代表剛過世的祖父領獎。

> ## in a . . . fashion　以……方式；以……的樣子

fashion 作名詞，在此表示「方式；樣子」。in a horseshoe fashion 就是指「以馬蹄的方式」，與 in a . . . way/manner 意思相同。

- The woman wore a long dress, and all of the young girls were dressed in a similar fashion.
  那名女子穿了一件長洋裝，而所有年輕女孩也都是類似穿著。

4-4

物理萬歲

Vocabulary

15. **revolve** [rɪˋvɑlv] v.　以……為主要中心；圍繞

16. **wrap** [ræp] v.　緊繞；圍住

17. **horseshoe** [ˋhɔrsˌʃu] n.　馬蹄

自述

 D'Angleterre has been a hotel since 1891. This is a luxury boutique hotel with only forty-five rooms and suites. It has been selected as one of the finest hotels in Europe by Leading Hotels. The **exquisitely**[18] and **individually**[19] decorated rooms range from 520 to 1,800 Swiss francs.

So this is my room. I have a junior suite with the lake view. And all the rooms here are just the finest that you are going to find anywhere in the world. It **makes sense** because their clientele here are people of the world—people that are certainly used to the finer things in life. So, the attention to detail here, from the furniture to the **upholstery**,[20] the artwork on the walls, the all-marble bathrooms—just absolutely exquisite.

Now, hotel prices in Geneva? Oh, they are very expensive. A good way to save money is to come here on the weekends, where prices are a good 20 percent cheaper. I do have something special to show you—one more thing. Come here.

德恩格列特飯店，從一八九一年開始營業，它是一家高級的精品旅館，一共只有四十五個房間和套房，它被「最佳飯店」挑選為全歐洲最高級旅館之一，客房裝飾精緻又具獨特性，價位為五百二十到一千八百瑞士法郎。

這就是我的房間，這是一間具備湖景的小套房，這裡所有的房間，都可以算是全世界最高級的，這點很合理，因為這裡的客人來自世界各地，都是慣於享受較高級事物的人，所以這裡對細節的關注，從傢俱到椅套，牆上的藝術品和全大理石的浴室，全都非常地精緻。

日內瓦的飯店價格如何？真的是非常昂貴，省錢的好方法是選在週末來此，可以享受八折的優惠。我還要給大家看個很特別的東西，跟我來吧！

make sense 有道理；合乎情理

make sense 以事物作主詞時，指事物「合乎情理；可以理解」，主詞為人時，用法為 make sense of sth，表示「理解、弄懂某事物」。

- It makes sense to check your car's oil before a long road trip.
  在長途開車前先檢查車子機油是很合理的。

- Can you make sense of these strange characters carved in the stone?
  你看得懂刻在石頭上的這些奇怪文字嗎？

旅遊小幫手

Hotel D'Angleterre 德恩格列特飯店

Hotellerie Suisse Rating: ★★★★★

$ Premium Room: From CHF 650.00
Exclusive Lake Room: From CHF 870.00
Junior Suite: From CHF 1,100.00
Bellevue Suite: From CHF 2,400.00
Presidential Suite: From CHF 4,500.00

☎ (41) 22 906 55 55

🌐 http://www.dangleterrehotel.com/

Vocabulary 📖

18. **exquisitely** [ɛkˋskwɪzətli] *adv.* 精緻地；精美地

19. **individually** [ˌɪndəˋvɪdʒuəli] *adv.* 獨特地；單獨地

20. **upholstery** [ʌpˋholstəri] *n.* 椅套；座套

圖片來源：Wikimedia Commons / Moumou82

自述

Whoo! OK, well, it's winter, so let's just say I'm not taking any breakfast out here on my balcony. But from here you can see how close we are to the lake, and there's the left side of the city. It's just so disappointing because what I really wanted to show you is, see those sort of, you know, gray clouds that are over there? Well, those are the mountains of France, and on a clear day I have a perfect view of Europe's highest mountain, Mont Blanc. I mean, what a special view to have. But, you know the weather; what can you do? Bad weather happens to the best of us, doesn't it?

Luckily, though, the weather soon cleared, giving me the chance to **investigate**[21] those oh-so-**tempting**[22] mountains.

好，因為現在是冬天，所以我不會在陽台上享用早餐，但從這裡可以看到，我們跟湖的距離有多近，還可以看到城市的左側。真是令人失望，因為我真正想讓大家看的是，有沒有看到那一大片烏雲，那裡其實是法國的山區，在天氣晴朗時，歐洲最高的山脈白朗峰，就可以一覽無遺，那是多麼特別的景觀啊！但遇上這種天氣能怎麼辦？運氣再好也會遇上壞天氣，對吧？

不過幸好天氣很快就放晴了，讓我有機會可以細察，這幾座引人入勝的山脈。

Vocabulary

21. **investigate** [ɪnˋvɛstəˌget] *v.* 探究；調查（真相、原因）
22. **tempting** [ˋtɛmptɪŋ] *adj.* 吸引人的；誘人的

MONT BLANC 白朗峰

　　白朗峰（法語：Mont Blanc，義大利語：Monte Bianco，意為白色之山）海拔四千八百一十公尺，坐落在法國阿爾卑斯山靠近瑞士和義大利邊界之處，是歐洲及阿爾卑斯山的最高峰。白朗峰是一九二四年第一屆冬季奧運的舉辦地，世界性的滑雪教練訓練中心也在這裏，這裡不僅僅是登山客的極限挑戰，更是滑雪客的最愛。

　　位於阿爾卑斯山白朗峰下的白山隧道（Mont Blanc Tunnel）（又稱為白朗峰隧道）是一條連接法義的跨國公路隧道，全長十一點六公里，耗時八年興建完工。

圖片來源：（義大利入口）Wikipedia / Nicolas Sanchez、（法國入口）Wikipedia / Kristoferb、
　　　　　（隧道內側）Wikipedia / Leon petrosyan

法國端的入口　　　義大利端的入口

自述

Geneva makes a perfect base in which to explore the surrounding countryside and mountain towns that Switzerland is so famous for. Right now I'm about two hours outside of the city. There's a gorgeous drive along Lake Geneva up a **winding**[23] mountain road to this town, known as Les Diablerets, "Little Demon," and as you can see, it doesn't get more Swiss than this. It's just perfect. It's a little quiet right now in Les Diablerets. That's because everyone's on the mountain. So, let's go.

There's, of course, skiing and snowboarding, but also **dogsledding**.[24] You can get out of town, ski all day, year-round, and be back in time for dinner.

日內瓦是個非常棒的出發點,方便人們前往探索周邊的鄉間,和瑞士非常著名的山間城鎮,這裡距離市區約兩小時車程,沿著日內瓦湖欣賞美景,駛過蜿蜒的山路進入這座小鎮——萊迪亞布勒雷,是「小精靈」的意思,如你所見,沒有比這裡更具瑞士風情的了。真是完美,現在的萊迪亞布勒雷有點安靜,因為大家都到山上去了,所以,我們走吧!

這裡當然可以滑雪、玩滑雪板,以及狗拉雪橇可以坐。在一年當中,你隨時都能離開城市,到這滑整天的雪,再及時趕回去享用晚餐。

Vocabulary

23. **winding** [ˋwaɪndɪŋ] *adj.* 彎曲的;蜿蜒的
24. **dogsled** [ˋdɔɡˏslɛd] *v.* 以狗拉雪橇

WINTER ACTIVITIES
認識冬季活動

1. skiing
滑雪

2. snowboarding
滑雪板運動

3. skating
溜冰

4. ice hockey
冰上曲棍球

5. sleigh
大雪橇
（通常會以馬來拉車）

6. sled
小雪橇

4-4

物理萬歲

對
話

S : Samantha Brown, Hostess　　G : Group

M2 : Male Wearing Glasses, Web Site Member

S From my trip to Les Diablerets, I met up with a group of friends who were all from around the world but live in Geneva. They all met through an online organization that gets people with similar interests together.

在我前往萊迪亞布勒雷的途中，認識了一群來自世界各地，但全都住在日內瓦的朋友，他們是透過網路上一個幫助集結同好的組織而認識彼此。

G *Santé!*

乾杯！

M2 Welcome to Geneva!

歡迎來到日內瓦！

S So, Geneva is an international city. Does that make it easier or harder to meet people?

日內瓦是一座國際都市，認識朋友會比較容易還是困難？

M2 It's mixed: easier and harder. ~~There's~~ [There are] two groups of people in Geneva. There ~~is~~ [are] all the Swiss people that are great, and **with all due respect** to them, the international folks don't mix around with them. Because the Swiss don't really need us; they have their set of friends. They know we're going to be pulling out after two years. They're saying, "Listen, I've already got my friends; why should I make the efforts?"

不一定，兩者都有。日內瓦有兩大群人，其中一群全部是很棒的瑞士人，恕我冒昧，外籍人士不太和他們打交道，因為瑞士人不需要我們，他們有自己的朋友，他們知道我們可能兩年後就會離開。他們會說：「聽著，我自己已經有朋友了，何必再白費力氣呢？」

with all due respect　恕我冒昧；恕我直言

此為正式用法，用於將提出對某人不表認同的看法時。

• With all due respect, I don't think you understand my question.
恕我冒昧，我想你沒聽懂我的問題

背景
知識

瑞士人的性格
SWISS MENTALITY

　　位處特殊的地理環境及文化背景，面對法國人的浪漫、德國人的嚴謹，其下的瑞士人，性格又是如何呢？

低調

　　低調的瑞士人不喜歡炫耀、誇大其辭，且他們認為「小即是美」，從他們的語言中即可嗅出端倪，像是他們喜好在名詞後面加上li，li 在德語中表示「小」。

守時誠信

　　瑞士人注重準時，不論上班或是社交場合都講究守時。大眾交通工具也鮮少誤點。另外，跟瑞士人約會一定要事先約好，他們往往在一兩個月前就會先約好時間、地點。

勤奮節儉

　　瑞士人每週的工作時數在歐洲來說算是很多。他們開源節流，勤儉持家，因為生活消費很高，所以非必要情況，他們不會花錢。

對話

S : *Samantha Brown, Hostess*　　**M₂** : *Male Wearing Glasses, Web Site Member*

F₂ : *Female with Blonde Hair, Web Site Member*

F₃ : *Female Wearing Red Shirt, Web Site Member*

S And this is where you came in.	所以你就上場了。
M₂ This is where we came in.	所以我們就上場了。
S Because you created the Web site.	你建立了一個網站。
M₂ We all had the same problem. We set up a Web site called GenevaOnline.ch, where people can just log on, mainly **expats**,²⁵ and meet other people and get together. Not a dating site; just for fun.	我們遭遇相同的難題，所以建立了「日內瓦線上」網站，大家可以登入，通常是外籍人士，認識新朋友，聚在一起。這不是約會網，只是尋求樂趣。
F₂ Yeah, you can go ~~to ski~~ [skiing] during the weekend, or you can go sailing during the summer. You can eat chocolate.	可以在週末相約去滑雪，在夏季一起出海，還可以吃巧克力。
You can eat chocolate. It is a good hobby.	可以吃巧克力。是不錯的嗜好。
S I want to sign up for that activity.	我也想參加這項活動。
F₂ Or you can eat *le fondue*.²⁶	也可以吃巧克力鍋。
F₃ *Le fondue.*	巧克力鍋。

4-4

物理萬歲

GLOCALS.COM 全球在地化網站

　　Glocals.com 提供一個外籍人士和當地人的互動平台，在這網站上，可以使用英語溝通，結交各地的朋友。此外網站上還有論壇，大家可以在此留下需求、建議或協助回答問題。這裡還提供刊登廣告，包括：找工作、找房子、語言交換、二手物品交易等等。過去網站名稱為 GenevaOnline.ch，但後來改名為 Glocals.com。

　　其他類似的網站有：在台灣有 Taiwanease.com，在韓國有 Waygook.org，在日本則有 gaijinpot.com。

Vocabulary

25. **expat** [ˋɛksͺpæt] *n.* 移居國外的人；僑民

26. **fondue** [fɑnˋdu] *n.* 瑞士火鍋；起士鍋（融化的起士或巧克力當鍋底，再用麵包或水果等沾來吃）

對
話

S : Samantha Brown, Hostess　　F4 : Female Wearing Pink Shirt, Web Site Member

F3 : Female Wearing Red Shirt, Web Site Member

F2 : Female with Blonde Hair, Web Site Member

S	But you were saying that Geneva itself really isn't a terribly exciting city with . . . **in terms of** nightlife.	但你們認為日內瓦的夜生活，並不怎麼刺激精彩。
F4	Well that's the thing about Geneva; it's really the city that sleeps, like, a lot. So there isn't much of a nightlife, and it's hard to figure out ~~what to~~ . . . [where] to go ~~out~~ and [what] to do in the evening. So it's really helpful when you have an online community like Geneva Online to . . . to show you what to do, and to have stuff to go out and . . .	日內瓦的確是個睡眠時間很長的城市，所以沒什麼夜生活可言。晚上沒什麼地方可去，也沒什麼事可以做，所以有像日內瓦線上這樣的線上社群是很有幫助的……可以告訴你該做什麼，出門要帶什麼東西以及……
F3	People are friendly; they just want to meet you.	大家都很親切，他們只是想認識你。
S	And I've noticed you . . . you are all from different areas of . . . of Europe. Well, you're from Canada, which I'm pretty sure is not Europe.	我發現你們是來自歐洲不同的國家，而你來自加拿大，我頗確定那不是歐洲。
F4	No.	不是。
S	But. You're from southern France?	你來自法國南部？
F2	And I'm French. Yes.	是的，我是法國人。

對話

S : *Samantha Brown, Hostess*　　**F₃** : *Female Wearing Red Shirt, Web Site Member*

M₂ : *Male Wearing Glasses, Web Site Member*

M₃ : *Male with Blonde Hair, Web Site Member*

M₄ : *Male Wearing Green Shirt, Web Site Member*　　**G** : *Group*

F₃	Portugal.	葡萄牙。
M₂	Israel.	以色列。
S	America.	美國。
M₃	I'm from Denmark.	我來自丹麥。
M₄	And Belgium.	比利時。
S	So, amazing. So, then, if you go online, you're not going to find a̶ [the] Spanish, say, sticking with only the Spanish people.	太棒了，那麼，你們在線上會只找同國籍的人嗎？比方說只找西班牙人。
G	No.	不會。

4-4

物理萬歲

學習重點

---

in terms of N.　就……方面來說；就……而言

此片語中的 terms 恆用複數。

• Jane is quite happy with the computer in terms of speed, but she wishes it were smaller.

就速度方面來說，珍對這台電腦很滿意，但她希望可以小一點。

對話

S : Samantha Brown, Hostess　　**M2** : Male Wearing Glasses, Web Site Member

S ~~Or,~~ everyone ~~is~~ just comes together. That's great. Is this something that a visitor coming to Geneva can **log on to** and say, "Hey, I'm coming for only two, three days. Can I be a part of something?"

大家集合在一起，真的很棒。來日內瓦的遊客能不能上網留言詢問如果只待兩三天，有沒有什麼活動可以參加？

M2 Sammy, if you come, you'll be a VIP member.

珊曼莎，如果是妳要來的話，就是我們的貴賓級會員。

S No, but really, is it . . . do . . . do tourists, visitors for only a few days, take advantage of what you do?

説真的，只逗留兩三天的遊客，也能利用你們的網站嗎？

M2 Oh, yeah, yeah. We had people posting stuff saying, "Listen, I'm visiting Geneva on this and this date. What's going on in town?" or "I'm visiting Geneva. Who's **up for a** drink with me?"

有人會留言問説要在哪幾天來日內瓦，這裡有什麼好玩的？或説我要來日內瓦，誰能陪我喝一杯？

S Right, right. Well, they missed out on a great day of dogsledding, right?

那樣就會錯失搭乘狗雪橇，趣味十足的一天吧？

M2 Oh, yes, indeed!

沒錯！

M2 Cheers.

乾杯！

log on to sth 　登入（電腦、網路等）

log on 是指藉由輸入帳號、密碼或其他指令登入電腦或網路等系統，後面須先加介系詞 to 再接受詞，且 on to 常會合寫成 onto。log on to 與 log in 意思相同。而「登出」電腦或網路，則會說 log out/off of。

* You must log in before you can use that computer.
  你必須先登入才能開始使用那台電腦。

* Rachel logged on to Skype to chat with her friends.
  瑞秋登入通訊聊天軟體，跟她的朋友聊天。

* Make sure you log out of the database before you leave for the evening.
  晚上離開時，要確認你已經登出資料庫。

be up for 　想要……；有……的興致

此片語表示「想要、願意參加某活動」，之後接名詞或 V-ing。

* I'm not really up for a movie tonight. I'd rather just go to bed early.
  我今晚不是很想看電影。我寧願早點睡覺。

* Gareth is always up for playing computer games with his friends.
  加雷思總是想要跟朋友玩電動。

Cheese! Cheers!

狂歡吧，日內瓦

🎒 影片原音 17　🎒 課文朗讀 41

對話

S : *Samantha Brown, Hostess*　　**M** : *Michael Doser, Physicist*

S We are exploring the Swiss city of Geneva—about to experience its **vibrant,**[1] **party-until-you-drop** nightlife, which Geneva is not really known for. In fact, its reputation is that it's quite **dull.**[2]

我們正在探索瑞士城市——日內瓦，我們即將體驗此地活躍且任人盡情狂歡的夜生活，而日內瓦在這方面不太出名。事實上，日內瓦的夜生活並不精彩。

M And it's a well-deserved reputation because in Geneva it's really hard to find something lively. If anything is happening in Geneva, it's in this part of town, in The Pâquis. This is where there are bars, cafés, jazz restaurants. It's actually one of the few places in Geneva where you can have a fun time in the evening here and in the Old Town.

這樣的說法是名符其實的，因為日內瓦的晚上沒什麼娛樂。如果真有什麼好玩的，那就一定是在帕奎斯這裡。這裡有酒吧、咖啡廳和爵士餐廳。這裡是日內瓦少數幾個能找到夜間娛樂地方之一，在舊城這裡。

Vocabulary 🎒

1. **vibrant** [`vaɪbrənt] *adj.* 充滿生氣的；活躍的
2. **dull** [dʌl] *adj.* 枯燥乏味的；色彩晦暗的

party-until-you-drop 盡情狂歡

party-until-you-drop 為複合形容詞，由 party until you drop（盡情狂歡到累垮為止）而來，在這個片語中，party 做動詞，意思是「盡情歡樂；縱情狂歡」，而 drop 也是動詞，意思是「累倒；累垮」。party 也可換成其他動詞，常見的有 shop、dance、run 等。

背景知識

日內瓦夜晚的好去處～露天電影院
GENEVA'S OPEN-AIR CINEMAS

如果在夏天來到日內瓦，一定要試試戶外的露天電影院。這裡有兩間露天電影院，放映時間皆到八月中旬左右。

CinéTransat

這是在公園旁邊設置投影大螢幕，看電影不收費，但是租椅子要五瑞士法朗。電影在日落時開始播放，會配上法文字幕。除此之外，這裡還會安排具主題性的電影之夜，例如：殭屍夜，大家就會裝扮成殭屍，一起看恐怖片。

$ FREE

http://www.cinetransat.ch/2013/

OrangeCinema

OrangeCinema 露天電影院在瑞士各大城市都有，環境比 CinéTransat 要精緻些。日內瓦的電影院位於日內瓦港口邊，可看見日內瓦湖的風景，提供酒吧及餐飲。主要提供兩種播放方式：原音配上法文字幕，以及法語配音。購票前可先問清楚。

$ CHF 19.00

　　Child (under 14) & Student: CHF 15.00

http://www.orangecinema.ch/en/geneve.html

4-5

狂歡吧，日內瓦

對話

S : *Samantha Brown, Hostess*　　M : *Michael Doser, Physicist*

S By the way, this is Michael Doser. He's a physicist at CERN, and he assures me that we can actually find fun places here in Geneva for nighttime fun!	對了，這位是麥可・杜沙，他是 CERN 的物理學家，他向我保證晚上在日內瓦也能找到好玩的地方。
M I will try to **convince**³ you of that.	我會試著讓你相信的。
S A lot of restaurants here.	這裡有很多餐廳。
M Yeah, all the . . . all kinds of restaurants.	沒錯，各種餐廳都有。
S Yeah, good **ethnic**⁴ mix.	算是一種很好的民族融合。
M Chinese, Indian—you can find pretty much everything. But to get a **reasonably**⁵ priced meal . . .	中國菜，印度菜，幾乎什麼都找得到，但如果想吃到平價的餐點……
S Yeah.	嗯。
M . . . it's going to be really, really hard. And if . . .	那就是一大難事了。而且如果……
S Yeah, I've noticed that. Even though we're sort of in this **offbeat**⁶ area, prices are still expensive.	我注意到了，就算在這麼非主流的地區，價格還是很貴。
M It's Geneva.	這就是日內瓦。
S It's Geneva.	這就是日內瓦。

OVALTINE
瑞士的國民飲料——阿華田

　　阿華田是來自瑞士的天然麥芽飲品，後來銷售到世界各地。最初名為 Ovomaltine，ovom 意指「蛋加上麥芽」。一九〇九年出口到英國時，商標誤拼成 Ovaltine，後來也就以 Ovaltine 之名販售至今，這項飲品陪伴著許多人的成長，至今仍受到大眾喜愛。

　　阿華田最受歡迎的口味是巧克力麥芽。其他還有：麥芽口味、濃巧克力口味。阿華田除了以飲料粉販售外，還製成了其他商品如：巧克力棒、餅乾、麥片等等。

　　阿華田因為有來自美國廣播電視節目的贊助，所以聲名遠播。尤其是香港，多數餐廳皆有販售阿華田的飲品。在巴西，人們喜歡將阿華田加入香草冰淇淋，最受歡迎的速食店也拿阿華田來製成奶昔及聖代。到瑞士玩的時候，別忘了阿華田抹醬也是不錯的伴手禮選擇喔！

4-5

狂歡吧，日內瓦

Vocabulary

3. **convince** [kən`vɪns] *v.* 使確信、信服；說服

4. **ethnic** [`ɛθnɪk] *adj.* 有民族特色的；種族的

5. **reasonably** [`riznəbəl] *adv.* 合理地

6. **offbeat** [`ɔf⹁bit] *adj.* 非主流正統的；不尋常的

對話

S : Samantha Brown, Hostess　　**M** : Michael Doser, Physicist

M	Yeah, this is the place I was talking about. Why don't we go in here?	這就是我所說的地方。為什麼我們要進去這裡？
S	This is one of your favorites?	你最愛的地方之一嗎？
M	Yeah, one of my favorites. Why don't we go in here before dinner?	沒錯，我們在晚餐時間前進去吧！
S	So this is Café Art's?	這就是藝術咖啡廳？
M	Café Art's, yeah.	是藝術咖啡廳，沒錯。
S	And artists come here? I mean, is it one of . . .	會有藝術家來嗎？我是說，有一位……
M	That's . . .	這是……
S	A true art café?	這是真正的藝術咖啡廳嗎？
M	Yes, sort of. There are exhibitions. You can see pictures on the walls. The artists are regular customers here. And, again, it's a mix of different kinds of people.	可以這麼說。這裡還有展覽，可欣賞牆上的畫作，有些藝術家是這裡的常客，這裡也同樣融合了各式各樣的人。
S	Yeah. Looks like an interesting crowd.	這群人似乎很有趣。
M	Yeah. It's lively. And one can feel at ease here, and it's really comfortable—the drinks, the people.	沒錯，氣氛很活潑，這裡的人和飲料，會讓人感到很輕鬆自在。

當地山區牧民的傳統樂器
阿爾卑斯長號 ALPHOIN

阿爾卑斯長號（Alphoin）為長約三到四公尺、重達四公斤的木質號角。過去阿爾卑斯山民就是利用這種長號，在不同的高山牧場之間聯繫，傳播婚喪喜慶之類的訊息。目前這種樂器雖然早已不再作為聯絡工具，但也常出現在傳統節慶活動當中，成為牧民的象徵。如今阿爾卑斯長號如同雪絨花（Edelweiss）一樣，儼然成了瑞士的象徵。雪絨花（或譯作高山火絨草）生長於阿爾卑斯高山地帶，開白花，為瑞士及奧地利的國花。

狂歡吧，日內瓦

旅遊小幫手

Café Art's 藝術咖啡廳

這間位於帕奎斯區的熱門咖啡廳，除了提供美味餐點及酒飲之外，亦為當地藝術家聚集的地方。店裡以藝術品裝飾，美輪美奐。

🕐 Monday–Friday: 11:00 a.m.–2:00 a.m.
　　Saturday and Sunday: 8:00 a.m.–2:00 a.m.

📞 (41) 22 738 07 97

Museum of Modern and Contemporary Art (MAMCO) 日內瓦當代藝術館

瑞士最大的當代藝術館，場館位於Plainpalais區，從一座五〇年代的工廠，變身成日內瓦當代藝術館，四千平方公尺的空間，展出世界各地的當代藝術，是喜愛藝術的您，不能不去的地方。

🕐 Tuesday–Friday: 12:00 p.m.–6:00 p.m.　　Saturday and Sunday: 11:00 a.m.–6:00 p.m.
　　Monday: Closed

💲 CHF 8.00

🌐 http://www.mamco.ch/

對話

S : *Samantha Brown, Hostess*　　**M** : *Michael Doser, Physicist*

S How late will a place like this be open until?

像這樣的店會營業到多晚?

M Well, you'd better be finished by eleven because that's pretty . . . midnight, if you are lucky.

最好在十一點之前喝完,但幸運的話有時也會到午夜。

S So at twelve o'clock things are done, we go home.

所以十二點一切就結束,回家了。

M Pretty much over by then. Yes.

到那時就差不多結束了。

S All right, we got to hurry up, then.

那我們要快點喝才行了。

M Yeah, yeah.

沒錯。

S After drink[s], we headed to a restaurant to enjoy a certain Swiss dish that just can't be missed. Poor Michael; I asked him to show me cool, hip Geneva, but then I said, "You know, I really want to go to Edelweiss to have fondue—listen to traditional Swiss music." And, I'm sorry, this is really what I wanted to do. And where else do you get to actually eat in . . . in a Swiss **chalet**[7] like this?

喝一杯之後我們前往餐廳享用絕不容錯過的瑞士料理。可憐的麥可,我叫他帶我去看酷炫時髦的日內瓦,但後來我卻又説:「我想到小白花餐廳吃火鍋、聽聽傳統的瑞士音樂。」我很抱歉,但這才是我真正想做的事情。哪裡還會有比這裡更傳統的瑞士餐廳呢?

M Absolutely.

對。

SWISS FONDUE 瑞士乳酪鍋

　　乳酪火鍋的做法首見於一六九九年蘇黎世出版的一本食譜書裡。做法提及將乳酪削碎後，加點酒，然後用麵包沾著乳酪吃。直至今日，乳酪鍋已經有各式各樣不同的做法，並且也有各種配料。這裡要來介紹最普遍的瑞士乳酪鍋食譜。

Ingredients 材料

- garlic 蒜頭
- white wine 白酒
- lemon juice 檸檬汁
- cornflour 玉米粉
- kirsch 櫻桃酒
- cubed bread 塊狀的麵包
- emmental cheese 艾門塔爾乳酪
- gruyère cheese 格呂耶爾乳酪

Step by Step　乳酪鍋這樣做

4-5

狂歡吧，日內瓦

Step 1: 先用蒜頭抹於乳酪鍋內側。

Step 2: 倒入酒和檸檬汁，加熱直至滾開。降溫後，陸續將乳酪放進去攪拌，直到呈現液狀，過程中需不停攪拌。

Step 3: 若備有櫻桃酒，可將櫻桃酒拌入玉米粉，酒也可以水取代。拌完後，倒入乳酪中，慢火煮到混合物成綿密狀，注意不要煮滾或焦掉。

Step 4: 用小塊麵包沾取吃即可。

Vocabulary

7. **chalet** [ʃæˋle] *n.* （尤指瑞士山區的）小木屋

對
話

S : *Samantha Brown, Hostess*　　**M** : *Michael Doser, Physicist*

S I mean, this is VIP seating **in my book**. I think I know how to do this. You just, you know, **poke**,[8] right, get a little piece of bread and . . .

這就是我所謂的貴賓席，我想我知道這個要怎麼做，首先用叉子，取一小塊麵包。

M Yes.

沒錯。

S And I've heard that it's actually a pretty big European debate: what goes into fondue? I just figure it's a bit of a cheese and some alcohol.

我聽說歐洲人掀起了一個激烈的爭議，火鍋要用什麼材料？我想裡面應該是乳酪和酒吧。

M Ah, it's very complicated.

其實材料非常複雜。

S It is?

材料有？

M Three different cheeses. Then, you have white wine that goes in there, of course, and **kirsch**,[9] the cherry **liquor**.[10] And then, depending on how good you are and how good the cheese is, you can put a little bit of *maizena*[11] **cornmeal**.[12]

共有三種不同的乳酪，當然，然後再加入白酒，還有櫻桃酒，就你接受的程度和乳酪的品質，也可以加入一些粗玉米粉。

S Cornmeal? Oh, nice **thickener**.[13]

玉米粉？很不錯的芡粉。

M Yeah, exactly.

沒錯，好的。

in one's book　依某人之見

此用法最早出現於十九世紀中，book 是指「名冊」或個人的「手札；筆記」，in one's book 表示「依某人之見；在某人看來」的意思，與 in one's opinion 意思相同。

- Allen thinks he is very smart, but he isn't in my book.
  艾倫覺得自己很聰明，但我不這麼認為。

旅遊小幫手

Restaurant Edelweiss　日內瓦小白花餐廳

為日內瓦市著名的瑞士傳統餐廳，各種瑞士小火鍋都吃得到，而且還可以邊吃飯邊觀賞傳統音樂表演。

🕐 Monday–Sunday: 7:00 p.m.–11:30 p.m.

📞 (41) 22 544 51 51

🌐 http://www.hoteledelweissgeneva.com/en/restaurant-1

4-5

狂歡吧，日內瓦

Vocabulary

8. **poke** [pok] *v.* 刺；戳

9. **kirsch** [kɪrʃ] *n.* 櫻桃酒

10. **liquor** [ˈlɪkɚ] *n.* 酒；烈酒

11. **maizena** [ˌmaɪˈzɛnɑ] *n.* 玉米澱粉

12. **cornmeal** [ˈkɔrnˌmil] *n.* 玉米粉

13. **thickener** [ˈθɪkənɚ] *n.* 增稠劑；稠化劑

對話

S : *Samantha Brown, Hostess*　　**M** : *Michael Doser, Physicist*

G : *Group*

S OK. Do I just go? I'm . . . I'm kind of scared.	好的。就這樣吃嗎,我有點害怕。
M It's hot. You'd better be careful.	這個很燙,你要小心點。
S Oh, that's very nice. It is typical also to have a glass of white wine. Cheers.	味道非常棒。配上一杯白酒吧,也是傳統的吃法吧,乾杯!
M Cheers. And this is probably Swiss white wine, if I'm not mistaken. Yeah, local from Geneva.	乾杯,如果我沒有弄錯的話,這應該是瑞士白酒。沒錯,日內瓦本地出產的。
S And this is good to try because the Swiss actually don't **export**[14] their wine.	這是個品嚐的好機會,因為瑞士的酒是不出口的。
M No.	不出口。
S Really can't get it in the States.	在美國喝不到的。
M They know a good thing; they keep it for themselves.	他們懂得好東西;他們把好東西留給自己。
S Well, we'll just empty that by the end of the night.	我們在今晚結束前就把它喝光吧!
G (cheering)	(乾杯)

4-5

狂歡吧，日內瓦

SWISS WHITE WINE
瑞士白酒

　　在瑞士只有百分之二的酒出口到其他國家（主要出口到德國）。百分之五十八的葡萄多用來製成紅酒，百分之四十二製成白酒。在瑞士，常見的白酒葡萄品種是 Chasselas，在 Valais 又名 Fendant。用 Chasselas 製成的葡萄酒，酒色清澈，呈淡黃色。濃度高、口感濃郁，可作為開胃酒，或加進瑞士乳酪鍋內食用。

Vocabulary

14. **export** [ɛk`spɔrt] *v.* 輸出；出口

291

自述

What people who live here love most about Geneva is its accessibility. Everything seems possible when nature is so close. And many enjoy what they describe as Geneva's small-town feel, which I got to admit, I . . . I didn't pick up on that one right away. But then I found out that the population here is only around four hundred thousand. Geneva, a city with one of the highest international **profiles**[15] in the world, has the population of . . . of a large town. Now, the benefit to that is that it is a comfortable city to be in immediately. **Downside**[16] is, no, you won't be able to walk down just any street and find great bars, music clubs, **happening**[17] restaurants; you got to put a little effort into it, right? Maybe meet a few locals—have them tell you where to go. Luckily, here in Geneva, people are very open and friendly, just as you would find in a small town. A small town where the locals happen to be from 173 countries from all around the world.

居住在日內瓦的人，最喜歡的就是這裡的便利性。跟大自然如此接近，一切都看似可能，有很多人說他們喜歡日內瓦的小城風情，我必須承認，我並未立刻感受到這點。後來我發現了這裡的人口只有大約四十萬，日內瓦這個世上享有國際盛名的城市之一，竟然只有一個大城鎮的人口數。若，好處是這裡成為了令人感到舒服自在的城市。缺點是很難在街上隨意找到很棒的酒吧、音樂俱樂部、熱門的餐廳。你得花點力氣去尋找，對吧？或許可以去認識幾位本地人，請他們指點指點。我很幸運，日內瓦的人都非常坦率和親切，就跟小城鎮裡的人一樣，而這個小城鎮的居民剛好是來自全球一百七十三國的人。

GENEVA ON A BUDGET 精打細算玩日內瓦

這裡介紹一些日內瓦旅遊專家的建議玩法，讓你省荷包又可看見日內瓦不同的風情！

馬丁·博德默基金會—世界文獻博物館
Foundation Martin Bodmer—Library and Museum 早上

馬丁·博德默基金會是世界上最大的私人圖書館之一，有十六萬多件、分成八十種語言的收藏品，藏品中包括古版書籍、古文明遺跡，還有礦物及化石等等。

$ Admission is CHF 15.00 for adults and CHF 10.00 for children.

日內瓦植物園
Jardin Botanique—Villa Le Chêne 中午

裡面有約一萬五千種植物，佔地二十八公頃，有玫瑰、鬱金香、鳶尾草花，還有來自不同地域和國家的植物，還有專門為盲人設計的花園。全日免費開放。

帕奎斯浴場
Bains des Pâquis 晚上

浴場始於一九三二年，當地人稱這裡為城市海灘（city beach），夏天時，你可以在此享受日光浴；冬天時，你可以泡三溫暖，一覽大噴泉和日內瓦湖的美景。

$ Admission to the beach is CHF 2.00 for adults and CHF 1.00 for children.

4-5

狂歡吧，日內瓦

Vocabulary

15. **profile** [ˋproˌfaɪl] *n.* 檔案

16. **downside** [ˋdaʊnˌsaɪd] *n.* 不利；劣勢

17. **happening** [ˋhæpənɪŋ] *adj.* 熱門的；新潮的

義大利

ITALY IN ONE MINUTE

　　義大利文化深具影響力，其中包含古羅馬建築、歌劇、及披薩、義大利麵、咖啡和冰淇淋（gelato）等美食。威尼斯位於義大利東北部，其區域涵蓋亞得里亞海（Adriatic Sea）沿岸的許多小島。威尼斯市內運河（canals）交錯，搭乘水上渡船是主要交通工具之一，最具代表性的是貢多拉（gondola）這種傳統小舟。在本集珊曼莎要帶我們揭開浪漫水都威尼斯的神祕面紗，深入威尼斯人的生活，品嚐小酒館（bacari）的各式各樣小點心，參訪知名的面具商店以及拜師學藝，學習馬賽克藝術畫的製作。想要親見不一樣的威尼斯，千萬不能錯過本集的內容！

首都：羅馬
CAPITAL: ROME

官方語言：義大利語
OFFICIAL LANGUAGE: ITALIAN

貨幣：歐元（€）
CURRENCY: EURO (EUR)

人口：59,685,227（2012 年統計）
POPULATION (2012): 59,685,227

國際電話區碼：+39
CALLING CODE: +39

UNIT 5

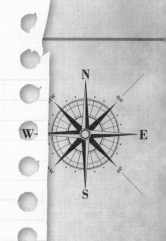

5-1 前進威尼斯

這是一個沒有汽車、公車或摩托車的城市,想要遊覽威尼斯只有靠船或走路。本集要發掘不為人知的威尼斯,所以珊曼莎要帶我們直擊可以親身體驗威尼斯人當地生活的里奧托市場(The Rialto Market)。

5-2 揭開面具,大杯喝酒

珊曼莎到一間叫「蒙多諾沃」的工作坊兼展覽館,揭開了面具的神祕面紗,工作坊的老闆葛瑞諾·路瓦托是世界知名的雕刻家,也被譽為傳統威尼斯面具教父。下一站到了專門供應酒類的卡納萊托餐廳,這裡獨特之處在於他們使用的是一公升半的超大玻璃酒杯,珊曼莎要介紹用此種酒杯喝酒的好處。

5-3 遇見馬賽克藝術大師

珊曼莎介紹威尼斯猶太人區,接著參觀歐森尼的馬賽克工作坊。歐森尼是威尼斯的手工馬賽克藝術大師,珊曼莎在這裡一展身手,學習製作馬賽克藝術畫。

Access to Venice
前進威尼斯

影片原音 18　　課文朗讀 42

自述

 There was a time when the citizens of Venice, Italy, wore masks. Not just for carnival time, but all the time. They wanted to gossip, gamble, and otherwise fool around without fear of recognition or **retribution**.[1] Venice today is still **awash**[2] in secret **hideaways**[3] that travelers never get to see. The city that greets over sixteen million tourists a year hides her most **precious**[4] treasures. Join me as we **unmask**[5] one of Europe's most beautiful and **elusive**[6] cities. Welcome to "Hidden Venice."

Venice is built on over one hundred islands **tucked**[7] in the northeastern corner of Italy in a **lagoon**[8] off the Adriatic Sea. It is, of course, most famous for having the canal as its main thoroughfare rather than a street. I'm sure you have heard that water is rising in Venice, but that is not the only thing that is flooding the city.

曾有一度，義大利威尼斯的居民會戴面具，不只是在嘉年華期間，而是時時刻刻都戴著。他們想說長道短、賭博、或在外胡搞時，就不怕被認出或遭受懲罰。現今的威尼斯仍然充斥著許多不為遊客所知的祕密藏身處。這座每年迎接超過一千六百萬名遊客的城市，隱藏了它最珍貴的寶藏，請跟我們一起揭發歐洲最美麗、也是最難以捉摸的城市之一，歡迎來到「神祕的威尼斯」！

威尼斯是建立在義大利東北部亞得里亞外海超過一百個島嶼的潟湖上。當然，這裡最著名的，就是作為主要幹道的是運河而非街道。我相信你一定聽說過，威尼斯的水位正不斷上升中，但那並不是這座城市唯一氾濫的東西。

VENICE IS SINKING
下沉中的威尼斯

　　威尼斯素有「水都」之稱，然浪漫的背後卻有讓人感傷的一面。早年，威尼斯居民利用水井抽取地下水而造成水平面下降，雖然目前已禁止水井汲水，然全球暖化、海平面上升的結果讓惡化情況以驚人的速度增加當中。根據美國科學家的研究，最近一百年下沉的速度比原本的速度增加了五倍之多。此外，人造衛星拍攝到威尼斯正往東傾斜，隨著亞得里亞海（Adriatic Sea）海面升高，很可能會為威尼斯帶來大災難。

　　二〇〇三年，義大利政府啟動了「摩西計畫」（The MOSE Project），在威尼斯潟湖外圍的三個出海口處建造大型的自動水閘門，以阻擋大浪進入威尼斯。這項頗具爭議性的防洪計畫預計將於二〇一六年竣工，但是否能改變威尼斯的命運仍不可而知。

5-1

前進威尼斯

Vocabulary

1. **retribution** [ˌrɛtrəˈbjuʃən] *n.* 懲罰；報應

2. **awash** [əˈwɑʃ] *adj.* 充滿、充斥的；被水覆蓋著（之後常接介系詞 in 或 with）

3. **hideaway** [ˈhaɪdəˌwe] *n.* 隱匿處；躲藏處

4. **precious** [ˈprɛʃəs] *adj.* 珍貴的；珍稀的

5. **unmask** [ˌʌnˈmæsk] *v.* 揭露；除去面具

6. **elusive** [ɪˈlusɪv] *adj.* 捉摸不定的；難以捉摸的

7. **tuck** [tʌk] *v.* 塞進；藏入

8. **lagoon** [ləˈgun] *n.* 環礁湖；潟湖

自
述

 So, this is St. Mark's Square, or Piazza San Marco. But strangely enough, this and the narrow streets right off of it are where most tourists come to and never leave. When you are in this situation, it's really hard to admire Venice for its beauty because the **stampede**[9] you are caught up in **threatens**[10] to **flatten**[11] you. Now, the good news is that it is very easy, on this tiny island where almost sixty thousand people visit a day, to just take a few corners, take a few turns, and . . . and discover a hidden Venice, a true Venice. It's real important to remember that in Venice there are no cars, buses, or scooters. The only way to get around is by boat or walking. The vaporetto, or water bus, is public transportation, and there are water taxis, but those will **cost you an arm and a leg**, and you are going to need that leg to walk. But there is another form of transportation here that only the locals know about and use: the **gondola**[12] **ferryboat**[13] known as the *traghetto.*

這裡就是聖馬可廣場,但奇怪的是,這裡和附近的狹窄街道是最多遊客前來的地方,而且久久不離去。當你置身這種情境時,就很難欣賞到威尼斯的美麗,因為你被捲入蜂擁人群之中,人多到可能會把你推倒。但好消息是,在這座一天湧入約六萬人的小島上,只要轉幾個角,兜幾個彎,就能輕易發掘威尼斯不為人知之處,真實的威尼斯。最重要的是一定要記得,威尼斯沒有汽車、公車或摩托車。想到處去只能搭船或走路。公共汽艇這種水上巴士是大眾運輸工具,另外也有水上計程車,但將花上你的一隻手臂和一隻腳(比喻所費不貲,將付出極高的代價),而你走路也是需要那隻腳的(意指走路不花任何費用、較划算的意思)。但這裡還有另一種只有本地人才知道的交通工具,就是這種貢多拉渡船。

cost sb an arm and a leg　所費不貲；花費極高

an arm and a leg 並非指字面上的「一隻手臂和一隻腳」，而是引申指「一大筆錢」之意，與 cost 連用即表示「花費極高或代價極高」的意思，與 cost a fortune 意思相同。

- To get my car fixed after the accident cost an arm and a leg.
  車禍後的修車費用花了我很多錢。

- This Armani suit cost me an arm and a leg, but I think it looks great on me!
  這套亞曼尼西裝花了我一大筆錢，不過我覺得穿在我身上看起來很帥！

- If you don't have health insurance and you get sick, it can cost a fortune.
  如果你沒健保又生病的話，可能會花一大筆錢。

5-1

前進威尼斯

Vocabulary

9. **stampede** [stæm`pid] *n.* 爭先恐後的現象；蜂擁

10. **threaten** [`θrɛtn̩] *v.* （壞事）將要發生、可能發生（之後會接 to + V.）

11. **flatten** [`flætn̩] *v.* 推倒；弄倒

12. **gondola** [`gɑndələ] *n.* 威尼斯平底狹長小船（俗稱「鳳尾船」；貢多拉）

13. **ferryboat** [`fɛrɪˌbot] *n.* 渡船

自述

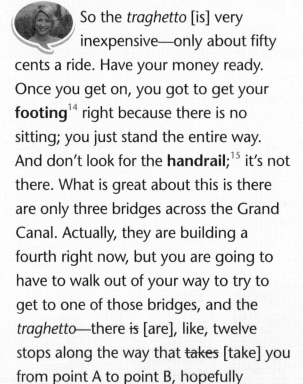

So the *traghetto* [is] very inexpensive—only about fifty cents a ride. Have your money ready. Once you get on, you got to get your **footing**[14] right because there is no sitting; you just stand the entire way. And don't look for the **handrail**;[15] it's not there. What is great about this is there are only three bridges across the Grand Canal. Actually, they are building a fourth right now, but you are going to have to walk out of your way to try to get to one of those bridges, and the *traghetto*—there ~~is~~ [are], like, twelve stops along the way that ~~takes~~ [take] you from point A to point B, hopefully without falling into the canal. I'm getting off at a spot where even Marco Polo **disembarked**[16] over seven hundred years ago, and what happened here then, happens to this day.

貢多拉渡船的費用非常便宜，一趟只要大約五角美元，先把錢準備好，上船之後你要馬上站穩，因為上面沒有任何座位，整趟路程都必須站著。而且不用找欄杆，因為沒有欄杆。最棒的地方是，跨越大運河的橋樑只有三座，其實目前正在興建第四座，但必須走上好遠的路，才能走到其中一座橋，但若搭乘渡船，全程共有十二站，能將你從甲地載往乙地，但願不會掉進運河裡。我要下船的地方，甚至是七百年多前馬可波羅也在這裡下船，而當時這裡的景況和現在一模一樣。

FOUR BRIDGES ACROSS THE GRAND CANAL
橫跨大運河的四座橋

Ponte di Rialto　里亞托橋

一五九一年改建完成的石造拱橋，連接了聖馬可（San Marco）和聖保羅（San Polo）兩區。在學院橋建立之前，里亞托橋是唯一可以通過大運河的橋樑。

Ponte degli Scalzi　赤足橋

一九三四年完成的石造拱橋，連接卡納雷吉歐區（Cannaregio）和聖十字區（Santa Croce）。

Ponte dell'Accademia　學院橋

學院橋原本是鋼構建築，不過在遭到破壞之後，於一九一三年重建成一座木橋。後來這座重建的學院橋因為結構不穩，所以在一九八五年再度重建。這座橋連接了多爾索杜羅區（Dorsoduro）和聖馬可區（San Marco），因為位在學院美術館（Gallerie dell' Accademia）正前方，故名為學院橋。

Ponte della Costituzione　憲法橋

憲法橋以鋼和鋼筋混擬土製成，是四座橋當中最新的一座橋，在二○○八年九月十一日開放供市民使用，連接了聖塔露西亞車站（Stazione di Santa Lucia）和羅馬廣場（Piazzale Roma）。

5-1
前進威尼斯

Vocabulary 🧳

14. **footing** [ˋfʊtɪŋ] *n.* 立足點；站穩

15. **handrail** [ˋhænd͵rel] *n.* 扶手；欄杆

16. **disembark** [͵dɪsəmˋbɑrk] *v.* 登陸；下（車、船、飛機等）

自述

So we are now in the . . . the heart of Venice, the Rialto Market. And I know we are trying to get away from the center of things—see what is hidden; however, the Rialto Market does attract something that goes **virtually**[17] **undetected**[18] by the casual visitor here, and that is Venetians. They are everywhere. They are selling their goods; they are shopping. This is where they come to buy their fish and beautiful produce, lovely vegetables, and . . . and you see real life here. I mean there is a big **controversy**[19] right now because Venice is actually too expensive for Venetians. They are leaving in droves, but if . . . if these people leave, then who is going to cook you their wonderful food? Who is going to talk to you about their wine? What **craftsmen**[20] are going to make you their Venetian crafts? I mean without these people, Venice has no soul, right, and it just becomes an empty theme park.

這裡是威尼斯的中心，里亞托市場。我知道我們設法要遠離一切核心——要去瞧瞧不為人知的事情，但里亞托市場的確吸引了一般遊客所不以為意的一群人——那就是威尼斯人。他們無所不在，有的販賣自己的商品，有的購物，他們會到這裡來購買魚類、優良的農產品，和漂亮的蔬菜，在這裡可以看到真實的在地生活。目前發生很大的爭議，因為威尼斯的物價太高，所以威尼斯人一批一批離開，但如果這些人離開了，要由誰替我們烹煮道地的美食呢？誰會向你介紹他們的酒？什麼工匠會替你做手工藝品？如果沒有了這些人，威尼斯就會失去靈魂，只剩下一座空洞的主題公園。

in droves 成群結隊地

名詞 drove 表示「人群；（被驅趕或向前移動的）畜群」，in droves 表示「成群地；數量眾多地」，在此 droves 通常用複數。

- When the product finally went on sale, customers showed up in droves at the department store.

  這項產品終於特賣時，成群的顧客湧入百貨公司。

- When my flowers bloomed, bees were soon coming in droves to feed off them.

  我種的花盛開時，不久就有成群地蜜蜂來吸花蜜。

旅遊小幫手

The Rialto Market 里亞托市場

里亞托市場是威尼斯最熱鬧的蔬果、魚市場，甚至在莎士比亞的《威尼斯商人》（*The Merchant of Venice*）作品中也提及這個市場。許多義大利人喜歡來這邊喝杯小酒，度過下班後的休閒時光，所以這裡是能一窺威尼斯人生活的好地點。

☑ Rialto Fish Market: Monday–Sunday: 7.00 a.m.–2.00 p.m.

☑ Rialto Fruit and Vegetable Market: Monday–Sunday: 7.00 a.m.–8.00 p.m.

🌐 http://www.veniceconnected.com/content/markets-venice

Vocabulary

17. **virtually** [ˋvɝtʃʊəli] *adv.* 事實上；幾乎、差不多

18. **undetected** [ˌʌndɪˋtɛktəd] *adj.* 未被察覺的；未被發現的

19. **controversy** [ˋkɑntrəˌvɝsi] *n.* 爭論；論戰

20. **craftsman** [ˋkræftsmən] *n.* 工匠（複數為 craftsmen）

自述

And consider this: when you spend a few cents on a piece of fruit in this market, you are standing on the exact same spot where the merchants of Europe and Asia traded luxury goods over seven hundred years ago.

Contrary to popular rumor, the people in these gondolas are not on their way to the famous Harry's Bar here in Venice to enjoy a Bellini cocktail, although many visitors to this city do. But if you want to find out where the locals **unwind**,[21] you need to seek out the neighborhood *bacari*, or wine bar. At this one, Gia Schiavi, I'm meeting Tizziana Ferrari. She's a **Londoner**[22] who has called Venice her home for eighteen years.

請你想想：當你在這個市場，花幾分錢買一顆水果時，你腳下所站的位置，正是七百多年前，歐、亞商人交易昂貴貨品的地方。

跟盛傳的傳聞相反，這些貢多拉上的乘客，並非要前往威尼斯著名的哈利酒吧品嚐貝里尼雞尾酒。雖然許多前來這裡的遊客都會這麼做。但如果你想知道本地人會去哪裡放鬆休息，那你就要尋找一下附近地區的小酒館或酒吧了。在這間「奴隸酒莊」，我會見到蒂吉安娜・法拉利，她來自倫敦，在威尼斯生活了十八年。

來到威尼斯，不能錯過的傳統小酒館
THE TYPICAL VENETIAN BAR

威尼斯的傳統小酒館叫做bacaro（複數形bacari），這裡是大家聯繫感情、認識新朋友的好地方。小酒館介於酒吧和小餐館之間，類似西班牙小酒館（tapas bar），在十七世紀開始就已經存在。直至現在，整個城市裡到處都有這樣的小酒館。

這裡人潮尖峰時間為午餐和傍晚時間，傳統小酒館不設桌椅，當地人常常在下班後過來喝點小酒、吃點小點心（cichetti 或譯作下酒小菜）就離開了，小點心種類口味琳瑯滿目，每一份份量只有兩三口，僅作為正餐前解饞之用，屬於精緻的小點心。

Cantinone Gia Schiavi 奴隸酒莊

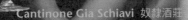

Monday–Saturday: 8:00 a.m.–8:00 p.m. Sunday: Closed

Cichetti: EUR 1–3.00 Wine: EUR 1–3.00
Venetian Spiritz: EUR 2.00 Coffee: EUR 1.00

(39) 041 523 0034

5-1
前進威尼斯

Vocabulary

21. **unwind** [ˌʌnˈwaɪnd] *v.* 放鬆
22. **Londoner** [ˈlʌndənɚ] *n.* 倫敦人

對話

S : *Samantha Brown, Hostess*　　　**T** : *Tizziana Ferrari, Londoner*

T Hi.	你好。
S Tizzi. Hello. Nice to see you again.	蒂吉安娜，很高興再見到妳！
T Yes, you made it.	我也是，妳真的找到了！
S Yeah, right.	對呀。
T Found it.	找到了！
S This place is fabulous. So is this the *cicchetti* . . .	這個地方好棒！這些就是小點心？
T Yes, it is.	沒錯。
S . . . little snacks?	小點心？
T Yes.	沒錯。
S This is fabulous.	真棒！
T Fresh bread with, *si*, with everything.	新鮮的麵包，是的，加上所有的東西。
S Various cheeses—typical Venetian.	各式各樣的起士，典型的威尼斯料理。
T Yes, very typical, yes.	沒錯，非常典型的威尼斯料理。
S Oh, look at, what is . . .	這個叫做什麼？
T Ricotta and rucola Parmesan.	這是義大利鄉村軟酪加上芝麻菜和帕馬森乳酪。

認識義大利乳酪
ITALIAN CHEESE

乳酪（亦稱作起士）在義式料理中是很重要的食材之一，所以了解乳酪的使用方式，就能做出好吃的義式料理。以下列出四種義式料理中常見的乳酪。

瑞可塔乳酪 Ricotta

義大利鄉村軟酪色白質軟，用乳清製成，乳清也就是牛奶凝結成凝乳塊後分離出的液體。這種乳酪呈白色狀，帶點甜味。常用於甜點，像是起士蛋糕和瑞可塔起士捲（cannoli）。除此之外也可用在義大利麵、千層麵（lasagna）及義大利餃（ravioli）。

莫札瑞拉乳酪 Mozzarella

源自義大利南部坎帕尼亞和那不勒斯的淡起士，主要是用水和牛奶製成。多用在沙拉中，與切片番茄和羅勒搭配食用，或用在開胃菜（如莫扎瑞拉乳酪條）、或焗烤、披薩中。

帕瑪森乳酪 Parmigiano-Reggiano

硬式乳酪，以牛乳烹煮，壓榨後製成方形筒狀，常被磨成粉末，用於義大利麵食、湯或與巴薩米克醋搭配食用。

哥岡卓拉藍紋乳酪 Gorgonzola

藍黴乳酪，為世界三大藍乳酪之一。以牛奶製成的藍紋乳酪，乳酪上的藍綠紋條，是盤尼西尼菌的標誌。產區在義大利北部的皮埃蒙特（Piedmont）和倫巴底（Lombardy），常用於義式燉飯（risotto）和玉米粥（polenta）。

對話

S : Samantha Brown, Hostess　　T : Tizziana Ferrari, Londoner
F : Female with White Shirt

S	Oh, I love this one, the **fig**[23] with the Grana cheese. Oh this is just **delectable**.[24]	我喜歡這個，無花果加乳酪粉（格拉娜起士常用作精磨的硬質起士），真是太好了！
T	Yes.	對。
S	And Venetians, they just come here for one or two of these just to . . .	威尼斯人會來這吃一兩個……
T	Yeah, just before their lunch or their dinner.	沒錯，就在午餐或晚餐之前。
F	We got Gorgonzola, we got *baccalà*—typical **Veneto**.[25]	我們有哥岡卓拉藍紋乳酪、巴卡拉，典型的威尼斯料理。
S	So, she's saying it's typical of Venice?	她是說這是威尼斯特有的？
T	This is a Gorgonzola with nuts.	這是哥岡卓拉藍紋乳酪配堅果。
S	Mm-hmm.	嗯嗯。
T	And this is *baccalà*, which is the . . . the salt[ed] fish.	而這是巴卡拉，也就是鹽漬鱈魚。
S	So do we just take [it]?	我們就這樣拿起來嗎？
T	Yes, just take [it].	沒錯。就是拿起來。
S	Oh.	喔。
T	They are her own recipes.	這些是她自創的菜餚。

義大利的美食拼圖
ITALIAN FOOD

想到義大利，就會想到美味的義式料理，像是義大利麵、披薩、甜點等等。以下四種為義式料裡常見的道地調味餐點，來到義大利，一定要親嚐一番。

義式蔬菜湯 Minestrone

蔬菜濃湯，通常湯裡會放義大利麵或是米飯。常以豆子、洋蔥、芹菜、紅蘿蔔以及番茄做成。

青醬 Pesto

青醬據說在羅馬時代從北非引進義大利，起初是由羅勒、大蒜、鹽、橄欖油做成，後來才加入松子及乳酪。現今青醬也演變成許多版本，像是用芝麻菜（rucola）取代羅勒（basil）等等。使用 pesto 最有名的一道餐叫做 Pesto pasta alla genovese，就是我們所稱的青醬麵。

義式烤大蒜麵包
Bruschetta

抹上橄欖油的烤大蒜麵包，上面配番茄、莫札瑞拉乳酪、肉、羅勒等料食用。

義大利餛飩 Tortellini

這是一種戒指狀的義大利麵食，外表與中國的餛飩相似，麵皮內餡包有碎肉和乳酪，常搭配牛肉或雞肉湯做成不同口味的義大利餛飩食用，在歐洲及美國非常受到歡迎。

5-1

前進威尼斯

Vocabulary

23. **fig** [fɪg] *n.* 無花果

24. **delectable** [dɪˋlɛktəbəl] *adj.* 美味可口的；令人喜愛的

25. **Veneto** [ˋvɛnɛˏto] *n.* 威尼托區（位於義大利東北部，首府為威尼斯）

對
話

S : *Samantha Brown, Hostess*　　**T** : *Tizziana Ferrari, Londoner*

T	Oh, it's . . . it's a passion . . . lifelong passion.	這是她一輩子最大的興趣。
S	*Grazie.*	謝謝！
T	The specialty of the house.	這是店裡的招牌菜！
S	Venetians stop into their *bacari* two times a day: late morning for a little snack before lunch, and then again before dinner, and whether it's ten in the morning or six p.m., wine or **grappa**²⁶ is always served.	威尼斯人一天會光顧小酒館兩次，上午在午餐前來點小點心，晚餐前再一次，不管是早上十點或下午六點，都會供應酒類和格拉巴白蘭地。
T	Let me get you a Spritz Aperol.	我替你點一杯艾普羅香甜酒。
S	~~This a what?~~ [What is this?]	這是什麼？
T	Spritz Aperol.	艾普羅香甜酒。
S	It's only like twelve of the day.	現在才中午十二點而已。
T	Yeah, but this is pre-**aperitif**²⁷ lunch drink.	但這是午餐前喝的餐前酒。
S	You do . . . you do drink at lunch?	你們午餐時也會喝酒？
T	Oh, definitely.	沒錯！
S	Before lunch?	在午餐之前？
T	Oh, yes, definitely.	沒錯。
S	What is this?	這是什麼？

威尼斯的澄色魅力
SPRITZ APEROL & BELLINI COCKTAIL

　　艾普羅香甜酒（Spritz Aperol）起源於義大利威尼斯，因酒精濃度較低，故用做開胃酒。在威尼斯的威尼托區（Veneto）區流行這種飲料。義大利除了咖啡之外，最常見的即是這種帶點苦味的橙色氣泡酒。二〇〇四年，世界前五大酒廠 Campari（金巴利）以重金收購 Aperol，使 Aperol 成為義大利開胃酒的明星品牌。此調酒是以三份 Prosecco（氣泡酒）加上二份艾普羅利口酒加上一份蘇打水調製而成，最後可加上少許冰塊及一片柳橙切片。

　　另外一種著名的威尼斯調酒為貝里尼雞尾酒（Bellini Cocktail），混合了白桃果泥（peach purée）與義大利 Prosecco 氣泡酒，是義大利極受歡迎的雞尾酒。最早出現於一九三四年到一九四八年，義大利威尼斯一家知名的 Harry's Bar 的調酒師 Giuseppe Cipriani 發明的，一開始此酒並沒有名字，後來在一九四八年因為 Giuseppe 看到知名畫家 Giovanni Bellini 的一幅畫，畫中人物穿的粉紅色外袍與這種酒顏色很像，於是 Giuseppe 將此酒命名為 Bellini。此酒原本僅在威尼斯喝得到，後來傳到美國紐約，至今已經傳遍世界。

5-1

前進威尼斯

Vocabulary

26. **grappa** [ˋɡrɑpə] *n.* 格拉巴酒（義大利以葡萄果渣製成的白蘭地）

27. **aperitif** [əˏpɛrəˋtif] *n.* 餐前酒；開胃酒

對話

S : Samantha Brown, Hostess　　T : Tizziana Ferrari, Londoner

T This is white wine with soda water and Aperol, which is like a herb-based **syrup**.[28]

這是白酒加蘇打水和艾普羅香甜酒，就像是以香草為底做成的糖漿。

S You know . . . and you look around—it looks like everyone is very Venetian. I mean, people are here drinking, you know?

環顧四周大家似乎都是威尼斯人，都是來這裡喝酒的。

T That is right. It's typical. I mean there is [are] not so many left now.

沒錯，這是一大特色，但現在所剩不多了。

S Mm-hmm, of these *bacari*?

你是說這種小酒館？

T Yeah, these you will find like off the . . . **off the beaten track**, and you won't find them in the major, like, tourist centers.

沒錯，這些店只能在隱密巷道中找到，在主要的觀光勝地是找不到的。

S Right, you won't. You know, you don't because I have been looking around and I haven't seen anything like this.

沒錯，的確如此，的確找不到，因為我到處參觀都沒看過這種店。

T And these you will find, like, in small **alleys**[29] or . . . yeah.

只在小巷裡才有。

S Right, so the darker the alley . . .

所以你必須走進較暗的小巷……

T Exactly.

沒錯。

對話

S : *Samantha Brown, Hostess*　　**T** : *Tizziana Ferrari, Londoner*

S . . . you go down it because . . .	你走進去因為……
T Oh yeah.	對。
S . . . there is probably something fascinating . . .	這樣才能找到迷人的……
T Definitely.	沒錯。
S . . . and very local there. Well, thank you, this is wonderful.	又富有地方色彩的店。謝謝妳，真的太棒了！

學習重點

off the beaten track　人跡罕至的；偏僻的

beaten 在此指「（路）踩出來的；常有人行走的」，字面意思為「遠離常有人走的路」，即表示「偏遠的；窮鄉僻壤的」。

• The beaches that we found in the Philippines were definitely off the beaten track.
　我們在菲律賓發現的海灘絕對是很少人會去的地方。

【延伸學習】

off the beaten track　不落俗套的；脫離常軌的

• Some breakthroughs in science have come from researchers wandering off the beaten track.
　有些科學上的突破來自於研究人員推陳出新。

Vocabulary 📖

28. **syrup** [ˋsɪrəp] *n.* 糖漿

29. **alley** [ˋælɪ] *n.* 巷道；小巷

I Drank
Only One Glass

揭開面具，大杯喝酒

🔊 影片原音 19　　🔊 課文朗讀 43

自述

We are in Venice, Italy, trying to find the city behind the city. We are **uncovering**[1] hidden Venice. The mask is an **icon**[2] of Venice and **synonymous**[3] with the once-a-year, pre-Lent **blowout**[4] called Carnival. Today you see these masks for sale by the thousands. The problem is, they aren't Venetian, but made in Korea or China, and it has just about **suffocated**[5] the real art of the mask. But a workshop and gallery called Mondonovo is where you see the true **seduction**[6] of the mask. *Buongiorno.*

這裡是義大利的威尼斯，我們試著發掘它不為人知的一面。我們要揭開威尼斯不為人知的一面，面具是威尼斯的代表，也等同於一年一度大齋期之前的盛事，就是嘉年華會。現今有數以千計地面具待售，但問題是它們並不是本地生產的，而是在韓國或中國製造，因此扼殺了面具真正的藝術性。但在這間叫「蒙多諾沃」的工作坊兼展覽館中，能見識到面具的真正魅力。哈囉！

CARNIVAL OF VENICE
威尼斯嘉年華會

　　許多人認為嘉年華會的慶祝活動起源於古代歐洲的異教儀式，當時人們認為寒冷黑暗的冬天是惡魔的傑作，所以要在春天初臨時舉辦喧鬧的慶祝活動來嚇退惡魔。這項年度盛事並不因基督教而式微，反而融入基督教曆法中，變成了「懺悔星期二」（Shrove Tuesday, Mardi Gras）之前的慶祝活動，懺悔星期二這天即是「四旬齋」或稱「大齋期」（Lent）前的最後一天，而所謂四旬齋就是復活節前的四十天基督徒需齋戒，以紀念耶穌基督曾在曠野四十晝夜禁食並戰勝惡魔試探的事蹟。至於 carnival（嘉年華）這個字來自拉丁文，意思是「向肉說再見」（farewell to meat）。

　　威尼斯嘉年華會起於一一六二年，靠著悠久的傳統、精緻的面具製造技術、十八世紀風格的化妝舞會服裝，成為目前最時髦的嘉年華會。在傳統上，面具和服裝讓與會者可以自由地在城市漫遊而不被認出來，模糊了社會階級藩籬，而如今，面具和服裝的設計則讓人留下深刻印象。

　　威尼斯在嘉年華會期間，處處可見炫麗妝扮的男女，喬裝成各式各樣的角色，在街頭巷弄穿梭著。遊客來此也會融入情境，買張喜愛的面具，置身華麗的慶典當中，而嘉年華會最後也會以燦爛的煙火劃下美麗的句點。

5-2

揭開面具，大杯喝酒

Vocabulary

1. **uncover** [ʌnˋkʌvɚ] *v.* 揭露；揭發

2. **icon** [ˋaɪˌkɑn] *n.* （某事物的）代表；圖標

3. **synonymous** [sɪˋnɑnəməs] *adj.* 等同於……的；同義的

4. **blowout** [ˋbloˌaʊt] *n.* 盛宴；大餐

5. **suffocate** [ˋsʌfəˌket] *v.* 窒息；扼制、束縛

6. **seduction** [sɪˋdʌkʃən] *n.* 吸引力；誘惑

對話

S : *Samantha Brown, Hostess*　　**T** : *Tizziana Ferrari, Guide*

G : *Guerrino Lovato, Shop Owner*

T	*Buongiorno.*	你好！（義大利語）
G	*Buongiorno.*	你好！（義大利語）

S Guerrino Lovato is the owner of the shop and is famous throughout the world as a **sculpture**[7] and **restorer**[8] of lost Venetian treasures. Lovato is considered the godfather of traditional Venetian masks. He even designed and built the ones used in the Stanley Kubrick film *Eyes Wide Shut*. Beautiful.

葛瑞諾・路瓦托是這間店的老闆，是聞名全球的雕刻家，也專門修復失落的威尼斯珍寶，路瓦托被譽為傳統威尼斯面具的教父。他甚至為史丹利・庫布利克的電影《大開眼戒》設計並製作面具。真漂亮！

S *Grazie.* That is wonderful. And Venetians wore these on a daily basis, and we always think of them just wearing them at Carnival . . . but every day.

謝謝。真的好棒！威尼斯人過去每天都會配戴面具，我們都一直以為只在嘉年華會才會戴……原來是每天戴的。

T Oh yes.

沒錯。

S Some masks had a purpose beyond **disguise**.[9] This one was worn by doctors during the plague. The **beak-shaped**[10] nose was filled with **medicinal**[11] herbs to protect them. So, now is he one of the last left?

有些面具的用途不只是偽裝，這個是瘟疫時期醫師專用的面具，鳥嘴形狀的鼻子填滿了草藥，來保護他們。現在僅存他一人嗎？

背景知識

PLAGUE DOCTOR
鳥嘴醫生

瘟疫醫生（Plague Doctor）顧名思義是專門治療瘟疫病人的醫生。在十七、十八世紀時，部分瘟疫醫生因戴著鳥嘴面具（Medico della Peste）替人看病，所以亦被稱作鳥嘴醫生。特別的是，在鳥嘴面具內，裝有琥珀、薄荷、樟腦、丁香等，用來過濾空氣，以保護醫生。除此之外，瘟疫醫生還會穿戴過蠟的大衣、帽子、木質手杖。手杖是為了檢查病情時不用與病人直接接觸。即便如此，作為瘟疫醫生仍是一件高度危險的工作。在黑死病期間，威尼斯有十八位瘟疫醫生，只有一位存活下來。

圖片來源：Wikipedia

5-2

揭開面具，大杯喝酒

Vocabulary

7. **sculpture** [ˋskʌlptʃɚ] *n.* 雕像；雕刻作品

8. **restorer** [rɪˋstɔrɚ] *n.* 修護者；修補者

9. **disguise** [dɪsˋgaɪz] *n.* 偽裝物；掩飾；假扮

10. **beak-shaped** [ˋbik͵ʃept] *adj.* 鳥嘴形狀的

11. **medicinal** [məˋdɪsn̩əl] *adj.* 藥用的；有藥效的

影片原音 19　 課文朗讀 43

對
話

S : *Samantha Brown, Hostess*　**T** : *Tizziana Ferrari, Guide*
F : *Female with Ponytail*

T	There is [are] two left: himself and another gentleman.	一共剩下兩個人：他和另一位男士。
S	Oh. They are the only ones left that . . .	現在只剩他們……
T	Yes.	是的。
S	. . . truly make masks in the real sense. *Buongiorno.*	能夠創造出真正道地的面具。你好！
F	*Buongiorno.*	你好！
T	*Buongiorno.*	你好！

自
述

Each one of Maestro Lovato's masks is handmade in his workshop. Layers of paper and glue are pasted into a **mold**[12] and dried. It's not unlike **papier-mâché**,[13] but it was never like this in my art class.

路瓦托大師的所有面具，都是在工作坊以手工製成的。層層的紙張和膠水黏在模型上，再晾乾。它的做法跟紙糊沒有兩樣。但在美術課中，我可做不出這種藝術品。

Vocabulary

12. **mold** [mold] *n.* 模子；模具
13. **papier-mâché** [ˌpepəməˋʃe] *n.* （法文）紙糊、混凝紙漿

318

VENETIAN CARNIVAL MASKS
華麗的假面

　　威尼斯傳統面具可用皮革或紙糊方式製作，紙製（papier-mâché）面具重量較輕。現在的面具選擇越來越多，製作上也較為繁複。除了大型面具，也有不少小面具，可供遊客輕鬆購買回家當紀念品。

　　嘉年華會期間，常見的面具種類：

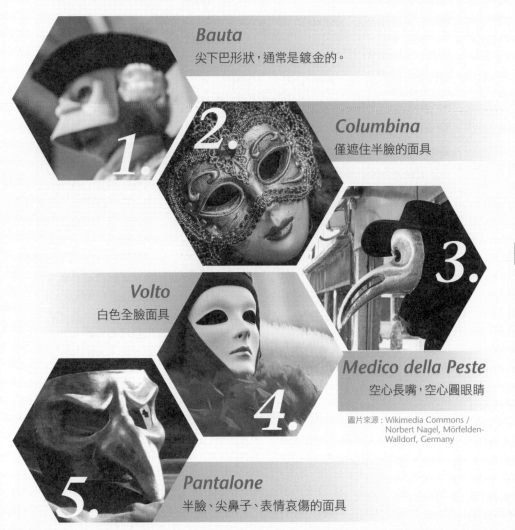

Bauta
尖下巴形狀，通常是鍍金的。

Columbina
僅遮住半臉的面具

Volto
白色全臉面具

Medico della Peste
空心長嘴，空心圓眼睛

圖片來源：Wikimedia Commons /
Norbert Nagel, Mörfelden-
Walldorf, Germany

Pantalone
半臉、尖鼻子、表情哀傷的面具

5-2

揭開面具，大杯喝酒

自述

Traditional mask making is an art that has almost dried up. Guerrino Lovato is one of a very few who is [are] trying to keep the tradition alive by encouraging new generations to discover the beauty and craftsmanship of the Venetian mask.

Even though there are lots of opportunities to **sample**[14] small **treats**[15] in the wine bars and markets of Venice, when it comes to really nice dining, most restaurants are designed for the passing-through or we-will-never-see-you-again crowd. But in hidden Venice there is a quiet street off St. Mark Square where you will find a completely different mood in the Restaurant Canaletto. Now, Canaletto is a restaurant where they specialize in serving wine, which you know, we are in Italy, that is not such a big deal, right? What is a big deal are the glasses they serve it in. I have found my home.

製作傳統面具是一門幾乎要失傳的技藝。而葛瑞諾‧路瓦托是少數致力於保留這項傳統的人之一，鼓勵著新一代去發掘威尼斯面具的美麗和藝術性。

雖然在威尼斯的小酒館或市場中，有很多機會可以品嚐到小吃，但說到想要享受高級的晚餐，大多數的餐廳都是針對過客，和一面之緣的顧客所設計的，但不為人知的是在聖馬可廣場旁，有一條安靜的街道，那裡有一間卡納萊托餐廳，具備截然不同的用餐氣氛。卡納萊托是一間專門供應葡萄酒的餐廳，既然這裡是義大利，這也沒什麼特別的吧，其實最特別的，是他們所使用的玻璃酒杯，我真是來對地方了。

MONDONOVO MASCHERE
摩多諾沃——面具博物館

葛瑞諾・路瓦托（Guerrino Lovato）是威尼斯著名的面具之父，他是首位開始製作並販售面具的人。由於他的面具店深受歡迎，多數競爭者開始爭相效仿，以機械化方式製造出許多華麗且色彩豐富的面具，但是只有路瓦托堅持傳統手工製作面具，他甚至為史丹利・庫布利克的電影《大開眼戒》設計並製作面具，他的面具工坊現已變身成為面具博物館，成為遊覽威尼斯必訪之處。對路瓦托面具有興趣的讀者可上網購買（www.maskedart.com）。

$ Venetian Masks: from EUR 190.00 – 650.00
Eyes Wide Shut Masks: from EUR 280.00 – 460.00
Merchant of Venice Masks: from EUR 250.00 – 270.00

☏ (39) 041 520 0698

🌐 http://www.maskedart.com/

圖片來源：www.maskedart.com

旅遊小幫手

Ristorante Cantina Canaletto　卡納萊托餐廳

卡納萊托位於威尼斯市中心，是一間專門供應葡萄酒的餐廳，這裡最特別的是你可以像珊曼莎在節目當中一樣，用超大酒杯喝酒。

☏ (39) 041 241 1016

🌐 http://www.cantinacanaletto.it/

Vocabulary 🎁

14. **sample** [ˈsæmpəl] *v.* 品嚐；試吃

15. **treat** [trit] *n.* 點心

對話

S : Samantha Brown, Hostess　　**Si** : Silvio, Restaurant Owner

S	Silvio, this is really the glass you are going to pour me a glass of wine in?	希爾維奧,倒酒吧,這真的要給我用來喝酒的嗎?
Si	Yes, for the red wine.	沒錯,用來喝紅酒的。
S	The red wine. Now, if I wanted, say, [to] fill it up to the top, how many bottles of wine would that be?	喝紅酒。如果要把杯子倒滿,一共需要多少瓶酒?
Si	This is one liter and a half—one **magnum**.[16]	這容量是一公升半。
S	Well, I'm not going to take that much today; maybe just down to here.	我今天不打算喝這麼多,或許到這裡就行了!
Si	OK.	好,沒問題。
S	And, looking around, this is such a beautiful room. You have hundreds upon hundreds of bottles of wine.	環顧四周發現這裡真是漂亮。這裡擺了無數瓶的酒。
Si	618 different kind[s] of wine.	六百一十八種不同的酒。
S	And, so, I can get a glass from any bottle I want in your collection?	所以你所收藏的酒,我都可以任意喝上一杯嗎?
Si	No problem.	沒問題。
S	Even the most expensive bottle of wine here?	即使是這裡最昂貴的酒?

WINE TASTING TERMS
品酒詞彙這樣說

背景知識

品酒通常會根據不同的口感做出評論，對於酒的外觀（appearance）、香氣（nose）、餘味（finish）等都是評比會注意的部份，至於要如何形容酒品，確實也是一門學問。以下列出常用的形容詞：

Aromatic 果香、有香氣的：
形容酒含有果香，由其是花香和香料味。

Crisp 酸爽、爽脆：
形容新鮮、年輕具有好酸度的酒，通常用來描述白酒清新、突出的酸味。

Delicate 嬌貴的：
形容輕身至中等身型的酒，具有很好的香味、溫和、誘人的特質，通常用在稀有葡萄品種釀造出來的好酒上。

Dry 完全不甜的：
形容酒在製程中，釀酒師謹慎地讓酒沒有任何甜分，或是保留極少量的含糖量，通常低於 0.5%。

Earthy 泥土香：
通常形容紅酒，指酒含有母土壤（mother-earth）的香味。

Fruity 水果香：
形容一種酒的身型和豐穎，表示品嚐出酒中葡萄的風味，通常表示在新鮮葡萄或酒中有額外的糖分存在。

Heady 酒精濃度高的：
形容酒含有高酒精度。

Nutty 有堅果味的：
一種暴露在空氣中的酒，表現出和雪利酒相同的氣味。一般是有裂痕的紅酒，或是一些白酒也有此現象。

Velvety 醇和：
含有富足的香味及如絲般柔軟的質感。

Woody 木質香：
形容在木桶儲存過久，除了吸收了橡木香味外，也吸收了其他木質香味。同義的說法還有 Oaky。

5-2

揭開面具，大杯喝酒

Vocabulary

16. **magnum** [ˈmæɡnəm] *n.* （容量約 1.5 公升的）大酒瓶

對
話

S : Samantha Brown, Hostess　　**Si** : Silvio, Restaurant Owner

Si ~~The Gaja fee around 300 euro to the top.~~ [It costs 300 euros to fill your glass to the top with Gaja.]	歌雅酒一杯的價格為三百歐元。
S I don't think I have the money for a glass of that, actually, so I'll just go with the . . . the Valpolicella, right. That is the wine of the region. Ah.	事實上，我想我付不起那種酒，我喝華普里契拉紅酒就行了，那是這個地區出產的紅酒。
S So, do I **swirl**[17] it around? Do I drink it? Smell it? The whole thing?	要先搖晃一下才喝嗎？還是要先聞一下？
Si Yes.	沒錯！
S I'm going to have to use two hands.	我還是用雙手喝好了。
S Oh, very nice. I lost my head in that for a second, but I came back up. I could drown in this glass. Do a lot of people order a glass of wine and have it in this glass?	非常好喝。我感到一陣飄飄然，恢復之後，甚至願意跳進這杯酒裡面。很多人會用這種杯子來喝酒嗎？
Si Yes.	很多。
S They do?	真的嗎？

Vocabulary

17. **swirl** [swɝl] *v.* （使）旋轉

GAJA 歌雅酒廠

歌雅 GAJA 酒廠由 Giovanni Gaja 創立於一八五九年，至今已傳至四代，目前由 Giovanni Gaja 的曾孫 Angelo Gaja 管理，傳承家族事業的他以創新改革著稱，有義大利紅酒教父之稱。

歌雅家族釀酒歷史開始於 Barbaresco 產區。（Barbaresco 是一個小村的名稱，位於義大利東北部 Piedmont 行政區的 Langhe 地區。）

歌雅酒廠生產的 Barbaresco 酒被認為是世界上最好的酒之一，酒齡必須至少兩年以上，酒精濃度必須是百分之十二點五。典型的 Barbaresco 酒有玫瑰色澤，散發出果實、甘草、礦物、咖啡的芳香，口感複雜細緻。知名的 GAJA Barbaresco 酒不僅僅代表了 GAJA 家族的光榮傳承，亦被視為是 Angelo Gaja 先生對傳統的最高敬意。

圖片來源：Wikimedia Commons / Renzo Grosso

VALPOLICELLA
華普里契拉產區

華普里契拉（Valpolicella）位於義大利北部威尼托區加爾達湖（Lake Garda）東岸的一個葡萄酒產區，是義大利第二重要的 DOC。當地主要的紅葡萄品種是科維納（Corvina），有酸櫻桃或草藥的風味，有時也會和其他品種進行混合，像是 Negrara。根據義大利以及歐盟的法規，Valpolicella 法定產區出產的葡萄酒在酒標上都可以使用 Valpolicella 的字樣。它既是產區又是一種義大利典型葡萄酒的名字。

Valpolicella 的基礎酒具有輕度酒體和一種不太讓人喜歡的酸度和苦味；但是品質更好一些的 Valpolicella 葡萄酒在夏季冷卻之後會散發出非常好的櫻果般味道。精選 Valpolicella 經過一年的熟化，一般表現得更加豐滿，酒精度更高以及更圓潤的口感。

圖片來源：Wikimedia Commons / FotoosVanRobin

對話

S : *Samantha Brown, Hostess*　　**Si** : *Silvio, Restaurant Owner*

Si	Because you know that usually the old wine you open three or four hours before. With this glass, [it] is not necessary because the wine here [is] open and it take[s] **oxygen.**[18]	因為品嚐陳年酒，必須在三、四小時之前開瓶，但用這種杯子就不必了，因為酒杯的開口較大，吸收氧氣的量較多。
S	So we are just speeding up the process?	所以我們只是加速那個過程？
Si	And then it is also nice to see.	沒錯，可以這麼說！
S	It is very nice to see. So are there any other benefits to drinking in a big glass like this?	可以這麼說！用這種大酒杯還有別的好處嗎？
Si	Yes. When you go home . . .	有，回家之後。
S	Yeah?	什麼？
Si	. . . you can say, "I ~~drink~~ [drank] only one glass of wine."	你可以說你只喝了「一杯」酒而已！
S	*Salute.*	乾杯！
S	*Grande.*	敬大杯！

Vocabulary

18. **oxygen** [ˋɑksədʒən] *n.* 氧氣

326

ITALIAN CLASSIFICATIONS OF WINES
義大利的酒類分級制度

原產地管制暨保證法

原產地管制暨保證法。義大利最高等級的葡萄酒,生產條件嚴格,包括特定的酒瓶大小、較低的產量許可、需要試飲檢查以及深入化學分析。

原產地管制法

原產地管制法。明定酒的法定產區,包括整個區域內的所有葡萄園或者僅限其中的幾處葡萄園。對於每種列入 DOC 的酒及其衍生種類〈紅酒、玫瑰紅酒、氣泡酒等〉,所用的葡萄品種、顏色、香味、滋味、酒精含量、酸度、成熟期長短以及最高產量都必須合乎一定的標準,等同於法國的 AOC。

DOCG

DOC

IGT

VDT

特定地理標示

特定地理標示。指明某種酒是產自某特定區域,可能是某一區或某一省,通常比 DOC 的區域大。這類酒必須使用核可的葡萄品種,但是對於色澤、滋味與產量的規定不如 DOC 嚴格。

普級餐酒

佐餐酒,標籤上通常不指明葡萄品種、年份或原產地。

The Mosaic Maestro

遇見馬賽克藝術大師

🎬 影片原音 20　　🔊 課文朗讀 44

自述

 Venice **is made up of** six districts, or *sestieri*, and a small part of the district known as Cannaregio is a place where the Venice landscape changes.

It feels like we have walked into a **compound**,[1] doesn't it?—sort of a **fortification**.[2] And really, that makes sense because here is where, back in the 1500s, the city of Venice **confined**[3] its entire **expanding**[4] Jewish population to live. It was growing at an **alarming**[5] rate, so that is why you see these tall buildings, because there was nowhere else to go. They had to live here. It is an island. There were only two bridges at the time to connect it to the rest of Venice, and those bridges would be cut off at night and guarded. So again, they could not leave.

威尼斯由六個行政區組成,而在卡納雷吉歐區中的一小部分,可以看到景貌截然不同的威尼斯。

好像走進了一座大宅院吧,有點像一座堡壘。其實這點很有道理,因為在十六世紀,限制人口數不斷攀升的猶太人居住在這裡,人口增加的速度驚人,才會興建這些高樓,因為他們根本無處可去。他們必須住在這裡,這裡是一個島,當時只有兩座橋,可以通往威尼斯的其他區域,而那些橋在夜間是禁止通行,而且設有守衛,所以他們無法離開。

圖片來源:(上方)Orsoni Mosaici

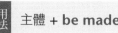

be made up of 由……所組成

用法 **主體 + be made up of + 組成份子**

指「某物由……組成」，類似的說法還有 be composed of。

- The group is made up of six women and three men.
  這個團體由六女三男所組成。

- The baseball team is composed of the school's best players.
  這支棒球隊是由學校最優秀的選手組成。

● Cannaregio（卡納雷吉歐），在
義大利文中是指「運河區域」的
意思。（位於威尼斯的最北邊）

5-3

遇見馬賽克藝術大師

Vocabulary

1. **compound** [ˋkɑmˏpaʊnd] *n.* 大宅院；有圍牆的建築群

2. **fortification** [ˏfɔrtəfəˋkeʃən] *n.* 堡壘；要塞

3. **confine** [kənˋfaɪn] *v.* 限制；侷限（在有限範圍內）

4. **expand** [ɪkˋspænd] *v.* 擴展；擴大

5. **alarm** [əˋlɑrm] *v.* 使驚恐；使擔心

自述

This is the Venetian ghetto, and the word *ghetto*, as we know it today, actually originated here in Venice, because before all these buildings were built, this is where the metal **foundries**[6] were. Foundries were called *ghèto*, so back then it had a very different meaning but has now grown to sort of **signify**[7] the **segregation**[8] and confinement of the Jewish population.

Today, the Venetian Jewish population numbers around six hundred faithful, and there is a storefront yeshiva, or mission school, for the foreign **rabbinical**[9] students from America and Israel. But there is another reason that brings me to the Cannaregio District.

OK, so I am really excited to take you to our next destination. It's a place that I have been coming to every day since I've been here in Venice and working on something extremely special, and I know you are going to like it. And why this place is so special, is no one knows it's here. It just, well, come here and you will see.

這裡是威尼斯的猶太人居住區,現在我們所知道的「猶太人居住區」這個名詞其實起源於此。因為在這些大樓蓋好之前,這裡原本是金屬鑄造工廠的集中地,而兩者發音相似,所以那時候「猶太人居住區」有著截然不同的意思,但現在對猶太人來說,多少有隔離和限制的意味。

現今居住在威尼斯的猶太人人口約六百人,設有臨街的猶太學校,即教會學校,接受來自美國和以色列的研究拉比教義的學生,但我來卡納雷吉歐區是另有原因的。

好,帶大家前往下一個讓我感到非常興奮的目的地。自從來到威尼斯之後,我每天都會到那裡去做一件非常特別的事情,我知道你們會喜歡它,為什麼這麼特別的地方,卻沒有人知道它在這裡呢!跟我來你就知道了!

VENETIAN GHETTO
威尼斯的猶太區

　　威尼斯的卡納雷吉歐區（Cannaregio District）有一個最古老的猶太區（ghetto）。過去猶太人（Jews）被迫住在一座被運河圍繞的五角形小島上，島上設有金屬鑄造廠在義大利文是 *ghèto*，因此此區就被稱作 ghetto，ghetto 這個字後來也就拿來指「猶太人區」。

　　由於此區不大，但猶太人口數不斷增加，因此這裡的建築物就往上發展，越蓋越高，成了威尼斯罕見的高樓大廈區。一直到現在，仍有許多猶太人住在這裡，因此來到這裡仍可嗅出濃濃的猶太味，你會發現處處可見猶太人留下的足跡及文化，像是猶太學校（yeshiva）、猶太食材店、猶太藝品店以及一些猶太教會堂。

5-3

遇見馬賽克藝術大師

Vocabulary

6. **foundry** [ˋfaʊndrɪ] *n.* 鑄造廠

7. **signify** [ˋsɪgnəˏfaɪ] *v.* 意味；表示

8. **segregation** [ˏsɛgrɪˋgeʃən] *n.* 隔離；隔離政策

9. **rabbinical** [rəˋbɪnɪkəl] *adj.* 拉比教義的（拉比 rabbi 是猶太教的宗教領袖，有資格講授猶太教義）

對話

S : *Samantha Brown, Hostess*　　**M** : *Maestro Orsoni, Mosaic Maker*

F : *Female in Yellow Shirt*

F Hi, Sam.	珊曼莎，妳好！
S Lianda, nice to see you again. This is the house of Orsoni, the only maker of mosaic **tiles**[10] in Venice. I have been making my own mosaic. Isn't that beautiful? It's my favorite flower, the **anemone**,[11] and this is **Maestro**[12] Orsoni. He's my teacher. So, the first thing we need to do is actually cut our pieces that we are working with.	莉安達，很高興再見到妳！這裡是歐森尼的家。他是威尼斯唯一會製作馬賽克瓷磚的人，我在製作我的馬賽克瓷磚，漂亮嗎？這是我最喜歡的花——秋牡丹。這位就是歐森尼大師，也是我的老師。第一個步驟就是把它切成小塊狀。
M Yes.	沒錯。
S It's actually . . .	就像這樣。
M Cut a little more of this one.	這個還要多切掉一點。
S A little smaller?	還要更小嗎？
M Yeah.	是的。
S It's hard. Ooh, all right, not bad.	真難。沒錯。
M Yeah. Yeah.	對，對。

旅遊小幫手

Orsoni Mosaici　歐森尼馬賽克工作坊

世界各地許多地方都有歐森尼的馬賽克作品，像是在倫敦的西敏寺、泰國曼谷的佛像、沙烏地阿拉伯的宮殿、上海的外灘十八號樓等等。來到威尼斯，最好的活動之一就是學習製作馬賽克畫，對馬賽克藝術的歷史及技巧想要多瞭解者，或從事藝術工作的人，來此必定會受益良多。

$ Three-Day Workshop: Euro 500　Micro-Mosaic Class: Euro 900
One-Week Master Class: Euro 780　Two-Week Master Class: Euro 1,400

🌐 http://www.orsoni.com/

Vocabulary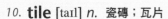

10. **tile** [taɪl] *n.* 瓷磚；瓦片

11. **anemone** [əˋnɛməni] *n.* 秋牡丹；銀蓮花

12. **maestro** [ˋmaɪstro] *n.* 藝術大師

圖片來源：（all）Orsoni Mosaici

對話

S : *Samantha Brown, Hostess*　　**M** : *Maestro Orsoni, Mosaic Maker*

S OK. So we have our pieces and it's just ~~painstakingly putting them~~ [**painstaking**[13] to put them] together. This is actually a two-week course in mosaic craft, and you don't need any experience. You can even stay in the bed-and-breakfast they have set up here. The rooms are brilliantly **accented**[14] in, what else, Orsoni tile. And it's only sixty euro per person per night. Working with these tiles, it's amazing because they are actually handcrafted, right, all handmade, these tiles.

M Yeah.

我敲對了嗎,很好!準備好小塊的瓷磚後,再小心地把它拼湊起來,其實這是為期兩週的馬賽克工藝課程。你不必具備任何經驗,你甚至可以入住他們在此設立的民宿。房間裡美麗的裝飾,還會是什麼,當然是歐森尼的瓷磚!每人每晚的收費只要六十歐元,這些瓷磚真的非常特別。因為它們全是手工製的,對吧?這些瓷磚全是手工製的。

沒錯。

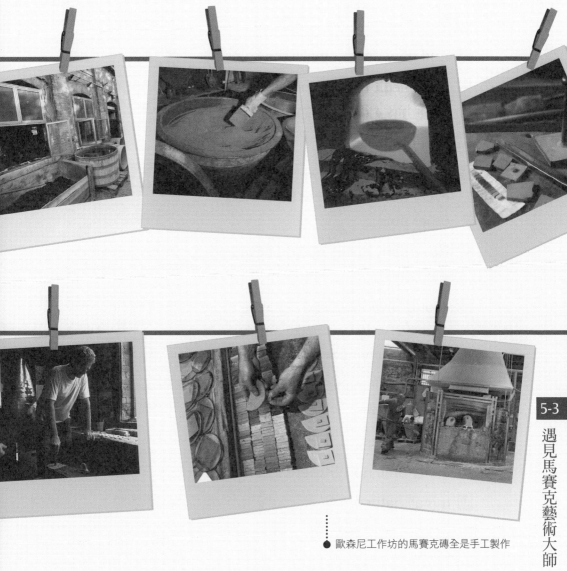

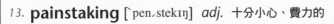
● 歐森尼工作坊的馬賽克磚全是手工製作

5-3

遇見馬賽克藝術大師

Vocabulary

13. **painstaking** [ˈpenˌstekɪŋ] *adj.* 十分小心、費力的

14. **accent** [ˈækˌsɛnt] *v.* 強調；標重音

圖片來源：Orsoni Mosaici

335

對話

S : *Samantha Brown, Hostess*　　M : *Maestro Orsoni, Mosaic Maker*

S And how do you make the color?	顏色是怎麼做出來的？
M It's difficult to explain because every color has a **different story**.	這很難解釋，因為不同的顏色有不同的做法。
S Mm-hmm.	嗯。
M It's like music, like [a] musical note; every note is different from every other note.	它就像音符一樣，每個音符都是獨一無二的。
S How many colors do you have here, thousands?	這裡共有幾種顏色，幾千種？
M Four or five thousand—maybe more. And every day we make a new color—many new color[s].	四、五千種吧，或許更多！每天都會製作新的顏色，許多新的顏色！
S They are all made using **minerals**,[15] though, right?	不過全部都是由礦物製成的，對吧？
M Minerals, yes.	沒錯！
S All natural, no **synthetics**.[16]	完全天然，沒有合成物！
M It is all natural.	全是天然的！

a different story　另一回事；不同情況

a different story 用來指所提到的狀況，與原本的情況不同。另一個常聽到的說法 but that's another story（那是另一回事）用於說法者不想對所提到的主題進一步說明的情況。

- Harrison also went to Jane's house, but that's another story.
  哈理遜也去了珍家，不過那是另一件事了。

- Working at home is a whole different story from working in an office all day.
  在家工作和整天在辦公室工作完全不同。

 歐森尼工作坊的馬賽克磚
顏色上千種

5-3

遇見馬賽克藝術大師

Vocabulary

15. **mineral** [ˈmɪnərəl] *n.* 礦物
16. **synthetic** [sɪnˈθɛtɪk] *n.* 合成物

對話

S : *Samantha Brown, Hostess*　　M : *Maestro Orsoni, Mosaic Maker*

S It's almost hard to believe that this little factory has provided mosaic glass for some of the greatest cathedrals and monuments in the world. Paris, London, Barcelona, and, of course, here in Venice. When you see the . . . the mosaics of Venice, you know, St. Mark's **Basilica**[17] and the . . . and the **façades**[18] on the **palazzo**,[19] it's amazing how vivid the colors are in a mosaic. I mean, it's much more powerful than seeing say a . . . a painting or façade of . . . of a fresco.

實在很難想像這間小工廠為世上一些最大的教堂和紀念碑提供馬賽克玻璃，包括巴黎、倫敦、巴塞隆納，當然還有威尼斯。當你看到威尼斯的馬賽克裝飾，例如聖馬可大教堂（正式名稱為「聖馬爾谷聖殿宗主教座堂」），以及氣派建築的外觀，馬賽克中顏色鮮明的程度，實在令人驚訝。它比油畫或壁畫更具有震撼力。

M Well, I always say that when you want to make mosaic, you have to think mosaic, because mosaic is not painting or sculpture or other things. Mosaic is a very big art, and they ~~make for that for~~ [last] forever, you know? Because the mosaic of St. Mark ~~are~~ [is] still there, and [the] fresco [has] disappear[ed] during the . . . the many, many years.

我常對那些想製作馬賽克的人說，必須以馬賽克的方式思考，因為馬賽克並不像油畫或雕刻之類的東西。馬賽克是一種大型的藝術，而且是永存不朽的，明白嗎？像是聖馬可教堂的馬賽克仍然完好如初，而壁畫會隨著歲月而消失。

FAMOUS MOSAICS FROM AROUND THE WORLD
環遊世界看馬賽克藝術

Jesus at Saint Catherine's Monastery (Egypt)
埃及聖凱瑟琳修道院：被列為世界文化遺產

Jameh Mosque (Iran)
伊朗星期五清真寺：伊朗最古老的清真寺

Casa Batlló (Barcelona, Spain)
西班牙巴特略公寓：二〇〇五年被擴充入世界遺產安東尼·高第·科爾內特的建築作品中。

Florence Baptistry (Italy)
義大利佛羅倫斯聖若望洗禮堂：佛羅倫斯現存最古老的建築之一

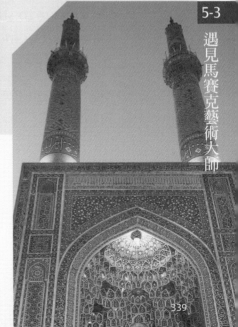

5-3

遇見馬賽克藝術大師

Vocabulary

17. **basilica** [bə`sɪlɪkə] *n.* 長方形的大教堂或大會堂

18. **façade** [fə`sɑd] *n.* 建築物的正面；外表

19. **palazzo** [pə`lɑtso] *n.* （尤指義大利的）氣派建築（如博物館）

339

對
話

S : *Samantha Brown, Hostess*　　**M** : *Maestro Orsoni, Mosaic Maker*

S But it's really all about the . . . the eye. I'm looking to see which piece is going to go next.	重點在於眼力，我必須尋找下一片適合的小磚塊。
M You are better than our student that stay[ed] here for two weeks.	妳已經比那些學過兩週的學生厲害了。
S Really?	真的嗎？
M Really.	真的。
S Wow, it's pretty amazing hearing a maestro **compliment**[20] you.	聽到大師的稱讚，感覺還真不錯呢！
M No, no, here.	不，應該是這裡。
S No, no, no. No, no. So I think this is going to take me a while, so why don't I meet you back at the hotel. I may have to stay in Venice for at least another month. What do you think?	不對。我想我還要一陣子才會完成，不如我們回頭飯店見吧。我或許得在威尼斯，至少再待一個月，你認為如何？
M Yes, you can make many other flowers.	好，妳可以再多做很多花。

來自義大利文的藝術詞彙
ENGLISH WORDS BORROWED FROM ITALIAN

　　從古代到十六世紀為止，義大利都是西方文化的核心，因此義大利藝術對西方藝術深具影響，許多英文的藝術詞彙其實是源自於義大利文，常見的有：

saic 馬賽克；鑲嵌圖案

tempera
蛋彩畫
（盛行文藝復興時期的繪畫方式，主要是將雞蛋加入繪畫顏料中）

graffiti 塗鴉

fresco 濕壁畫

relievo 浮雕

caricature
諷刺畫

5-3

遇見馬賽克藝術大師

圖片來源：（諷刺畫）Wikipedia

Vocabulary

20. **compliment** [ˈkɑmpləˌmɛnt] *v.* 稱讚；恭維

自述

 The hotel I'm staying at is five minutes from St. Mark's Square, but it's hidden from the crowds. Turn a few corners and you will find it located in a quiet and private square. This is the Westin Europa and Regina.

Now, when I think of the Westin Hotel, I think "big and new." And so this is very different. It was actually made by joining five historic family palaces. These were homes, don't you know? So it has a very intriguing **layout**[21] of . . . of marble steps that lead up to other rooms and long marbled **corridors**.[22] It allows you to . . . to **wander**[23] about the place, right, pretending you are of Venetian **nobility**.[24]

我下榻的飯店距離聖馬可廣場只有五分鐘路程，但卻遠離塵囂，轉過幾個街角後你就會發現，它就位於一座安靜隱密的廣場上。這裡是威斯汀歐洲女王飯店。

一提到威斯汀飯店，就會聯想到又大又新，但這裡卻截然不同，這裡其實是由五座歷史悠久的家族豪宅所組合而成的，這裡曾是住家，你不知道嗎？所以這裡佈滿迷人的大理石台階，帶領你到達其他的廳室。還有長長的大理石走廊，讓你可以四處逛，假裝自己就是威尼斯的貴族。

● 馬賽克藝術最著名的是建於一〇八四年的威尼斯聖馬可大教堂（St. Mark's Basilica），教堂的牆面和屋頂全都以鑲金馬賽克藝術來裝飾。

聖馬可廣場
PIAZZA SAN MARCO

　　聖馬可廣場（St. Mark's Square；義大利語：Piazza San Marco）曾被法國皇帝拿破崙稱讚為「歐洲最美的客廳」，是威尼斯最大的廣場，也是威尼斯的地標。廣場四周有聖馬可大教堂（St. Mark's Basilica），還有總督宮（Doge's Palace）、鐘樓、新舊行政官邸大樓等建築，廣場四周皆是文藝復興時期的優美建築。而今聖馬可廣場遊客絡繹不絕，四周也有許多露天咖啡廳，是一個享受浪漫景點的好去處。

5-3

遇見馬賽克藝術大師

Vocabulary

21. **layout** [ˋleˏaʊt] *n.* 設計；布局

22. **corridor** [ˋkɔrədə] *n.* 走廊；通道

23. **wander** [ˋwɑndə] *v.* 閒逛；漫遊

24. **nobility** [noˋbɪlətɪ] *n.* 貴族

圖片來源：（左頁）Julia Lin

自述

So this is my room, which I really like a lot because, I don't know, it has a feminine touch to it, and just a little bit of Venetian **opulence**[25]—not too much. Unlike a lot of the Westins we know, every single room here is unique, just, you know, little jewels unto themselves. Now before we head out again, [there's] just one more thing I want to show you. You are going to like this. Come here.

Now, in my bathroom I have a pretty interesting view. See, everybody wants the canal, right? Well, look at this, the city of Venice. And listen, if . . . if you want one of those rooms with the grand balcony overlooking the canal, I mean, like, you are right on it, they have got them. And there is a good reason why they have rooms overlooking the canal. You see, this is the **rear**[26] entrance to the hotel. Take a look at the main entrance. Look at this. We are right on the Grand Canal. I am so close to the Santa Maria della Salute, I could kiss it.

這就是我的房間，我真的非常喜歡，因為很有女性化的感覺，也有一點點威尼斯的貴氣，但不會太多。跟其他的威斯汀飯店不同的是這裡每個房間都是獨一無二的，個自都有一些小珠寶。我們再次出發前，我要給大家看一樣東西，你們一定會喜歡的，跟我來。

從浴室能看到很有意思的景觀，大家都想要看到運河吧？請看！整個威尼斯市！如果你想入住那種具備大陽台，能俯瞰運河的房間，這裡也有，而他們具備能俯瞰運河的房間，其實是有原因的。這是飯店的後門，看看這個大門，你看，我們現在就站在大運河的上方，我跟安康聖母教堂距離很近，甚至可以親它一下了。

安康聖母教堂
SANTA MARIA DELLA SALUTE

一六八七年完工的安康聖母教堂簡稱 Salute，位於威尼斯大運河和聖馬可內港之間，建造這座教堂光是打地基就用了十七萬根木樁。正堂為八角形柱體，八根立柱圍繞巨大的圓頂，周圍有六座禮拜堂環繞。教堂內主祭壇上有「聖母驅走瘟疫」雕刻，聖母左邊那位懇求跪姿的高貴婦人象徵威尼斯，而右邊代表瘟疫的醜惡老嫗則在天使的驅趕下逃竄。安康聖母教堂的建築為巴洛克風格，充滿神聖寂靜的氛圍，是到威尼斯不能錯過的景點之一。

5-3

遇見馬賽克藝術大師

Vocabulary

25. **opulence** [ˈɑpjələns] *n.* 富麗堂皇；豪華

26. **rear** [rɪr] *adj.* 後面的；後部的

圖片來源：（左）Wikipedia / Wolfgang Moroder

自述

Here you can just sit on the **terrace**,[27] you know, were it not 40 degrees out, and watch the fascinating activity of the Grand Canal and how it opens up to the lagoon—just endless pleasure watching the city that basically lives on the water.

So, Venice was built on over one hundred islands, and it is sort of charming to know that every time you cross over a bridge you are in fact stepping onto a different island. There are around 409 bridges in Venice, and most of them are these really friendly, lovely structures, and then there is the Rialto, which is this, you know, **muscular**[28] Greek temple of a thing that **stretches**[29] over the Grand Canal. Now, just looking at it you can tell [it is a] very, very important bridge, and up until 1854 this was the only bridge across the Grand Canal.

你大可以坐在平台上，如果不是外頭氣溫只有華氏四十度，你可以欣賞大運河迷人的風情，以及它如何向潟湖開展開來，欣賞一座基本上是位在水上的城市，真的是樂趣無窮！

威尼斯建立在超過百座的島嶼之上，迷人之處是每當你跨越一座橋，就踏上了另一座小島。威尼斯一共大約有四百〇九座橋，多數橋構造都非常友善又可愛，但里亞托橋，卻像是一座宏偉的希臘神殿，橫跨大運河的兩岸，光看外表你就會知道，它是一座非常重要的橋。直到一八五四年為止，它都是唯一橫跨大運河的橋樑。

旅遊小幫手

Westin Europa and Regina 威斯汀歐洲女王飯店

這是一間五星級飯店，位於聖馬可廣場附近的大運河畔。

$ Classic Room: from EUR 350.00　　Grand Canal Room: from EUR 1,000.00
Canal Terrace Room: from EUR 1,100.00　　Deluxe Terrace: from EUR 4,000.00

📞 (39) 041 240 0001

🌐 http://www.westineuroparoginavenice.com/

Vocabulary 🛍

27. **terrace** [ˈtɛrəs] *n.* （屋外）平台；階梯看台

28. **muscular** [ˈmʌskjələ] *adj.* 肌肉的；強壯的

29. **stretch** [strɛtʃ] *v.* 伸展；延伸

圖片來源：（右）Flickr / brianandjaclyn

自述

Now, I'm sure you have heard the small fact that Venice is sinking, which, I'm sorry, that has got to be the most **ridiculous**[30] thing I have ever heard. I mean, this place has been around for like 1,500 years. Now it's sinking?

Seriously, Venice is sinking and the water is rising. Venetians experience dozens of days of flooding each year. They call it *acqua alta*, or high water, and that is bad news as Venice is already suffering heavily from water damage. Now, many experts feel that this city will not be around forever, which is definitely not the hidden Venice we have been seeking out.

My favorite time in Venice is in the early evening when the **day-trippers**[31] have gone and people here are slowly, quietly making their way back home, and the streets are so silent that the only sound I hear is that of my own footsteps echoing off the buildings.

你一定聽説過,威尼斯正在下沉這種説法。對不起,這是我聽過最荒謬的事情了。這個地方已經存在一千五百年了,現在卻正在下沉?

説真的,威尼斯確實正在下沉中,而水位正不斷上升。每年威尼斯都會經歷幾次的淹水,他們稱之為漲潮水位,而這真是個壞消息,因為淹水已對威尼斯造成非常嚴重的破壞了。而今,許多專家認為這座城市將不可能永遠存在。而我們可不想揭開威尼斯的這種祕密。

我最喜歡威尼斯的傍晚時分,一日觀光客都離開了,這裡的人慢慢地、安靜地準備回家。街道非常地安靜,唯一能聽到的聲音,就是我那迴盪在建築間的腳步聲。

自述

 For me, there is something about that sound that just . . . it **elicits**[32] Venice's **eternal**[33] mystery. You know that even though the city has seen over a thousand years of visitors, no one completely knows her. And it's in this moment of silence that I imagine I am not **merely**[34] Venice's one billionth customer, but a person who has the incredible fortune of having an intimate moment with one of the most beautiful cities the world has ever known.

對我來說，這種聲音也意味著，威尼斯永恆的神秘感。雖然千年來，有無數的遊客造訪過此地，但卻沒有人完全瞭解她。在這個寂靜的時刻，我想像自己並不只是威尼斯十億遊客中的一份子，而是能跟這座世上最美麗的城市共享這種親密時光的超級幸運兒。

5-3

遇見馬賽克藝術大師

Vocabulary

30. **ridiculous** [rə`dɪkjələs] *adj.* 荒謬的；可笑的

31. **day-tripper** [`de͵trɪpə] *n.* 當天往返的短途旅客

32. **elicit** [ɪ`lɪsət] *v.* 引出；套出

33. **eternal** [ɪ`tɝn̩l] *adj.* 永恆的；不朽的

34. **merely** [`mɪrli] *adv.* 僅僅；只有

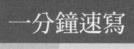

希臘

GREECE IN ONE MINUTE

　　希臘乃西方文明的發源地，歐洲文化來自愛琴海（Aegean Sea）上的基克拉澤斯群島（the Cyclades）。聖托里尼為基克拉澤斯群島最南端的一個島嶼。聖托里尼又稱為錫拉島（Thíra），昔日稱作 Thera，是著名的旅遊勝地。聖托里尼的城鎮上可眺望破火山口。聖托里尼以自製的酒和令人嘆為觀止的景觀聞名，在本集當中珊曼莎要帶我們航向愛琴海、介紹當地的餐廳，一嚐道地希臘美食，想要一睹希臘的迷人風采，千萬不能錯過本集內容。

首都：雅典
CAPITAL: ATHENS

官方語言：希臘語
OFFICIAL LANGUAGE: GREEK

貨幣：歐元（€）
CURRENCY: EURO (EUR)

人口：10,815,197（2011 年統計）
POPULATION (2011): 10,815,197

國際電話區碼：+30
CALLING CODE: +30

UNIT 6

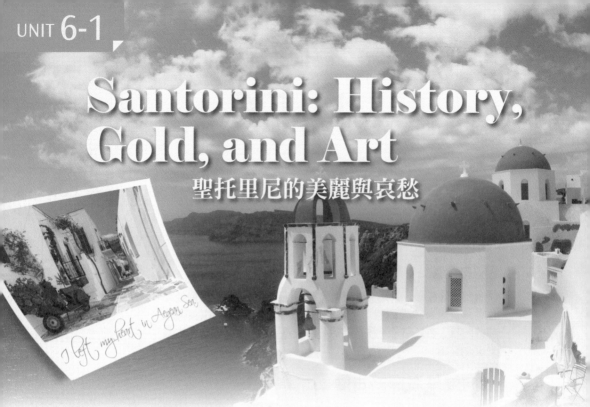

Santorini: History, Gold, and Art

聖托里尼的美麗與哀愁

🔖 影片原音 21　　🔖 課文朗讀 45

自述

 Today we are on an island where, every day, vacationers, visitors, and locals alike stop what they are doing, [and] point themselves west to watch the sun **take** its daily final **bow**.[1] The scenery is very **dramatic**,[2] but standing here on this cliff, all I need to do is turn in the opposite direction and see a scene even more dramatic. Floating islands [and] **soaring**[3] cliffs that together form a **basin**[4] of blue. You may not realize this, but what you are **peering**[5] down into is the largest volcanic crater in the world.

今天我們來到一個小島上，這裡的遊客與居民，每天都會停下手邊的事，遠眺西方，望著太陽西沉。景色優美，令人印象深刻，但是站在這懸崖上，我只需轉過身，就能欣賞更激動人心的景觀。漂浮的島嶼、高聳的懸崖共築一個藍色的盆地，你也許沒意識到，但你現在所俯瞰的，正是世界上最大的火山口。

BULGARIA
保加利亞

ALBANIA
阿爾巴尼亞

GREECE
希臘

Aegean Sea
愛琴海

TURKEY
土耳其

ABOUT SANTORINI
聖托里尼二三事

背景知識

聖托里尼為基克拉澤斯群島（the Cyclades）最南端的一個島嶼，位在希臘本島東南方兩百公里的愛琴海（Aegean Sea）上，由火山環所組成。聖托里尼又稱為錫拉島（Thíra），昔日稱作 Thera。

二〇一三年 CNN 票選了全球十二處最佳觀賞夕陽的地點，位於聖托里尼北邊的山頂小鎮伊亞（Oia）入選其中，這裡有「歐洲最美日落」的美譽，其特色便是依山而建的藍白房子。此外，欣賞落日在這裡可算是一種社交活動，每到下午，餐廳以及絕佳的拍攝地點都會擠滿人，攝影師忙著按下快門，而其他人則在夕照美景下，享受著佳餚美食。

Oia
Imerovigli
Thirasia
Firostefani
Fira
Kamari

圖片來源：Bonnie Chen

6-1

Vocabulary

1. **take a bow** [tek] [ə] [baʊ] *v. phr.* （演員向觀眾）鞠躬致意；謝幕

2. **dramatic** [drə`mætɪk] *adj.* 讓人印象深刻的；激動人心的

3. **soaring** [`sɔrɪŋ] *adj.* 高聳的

4. **basin** [`besn̩] *n.* 盆地；窪地；大碗盆

5. **peer** [pɪr] *v.* 凝視；盯著看

聖托里尼的美麗與哀愁

自述

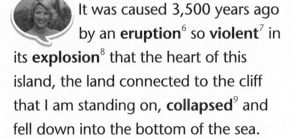

It was caused 3,500 years ago by an **eruption**[6] so **violent**[7] in its **explosion**[8] that the heart of this island, the land connected to the cliff that I am standing on, **collapsed**[9] and fell down into the bottom of the sea.

Now, today we're going to be finding out why people travel here from all around the world and what makes the people and culture here different than any other island in Greece. It's an island the Greeks call Thíra, but we know it as Santorini.

Santorini is located southeast of mainland Greece and is the most southern of the group of islands known as the Cyclades. Centering itself is a group of islands that form the volcanic caldera.

這個火山口是三千五百年前一場劇烈火山爆發所造成的，在爆發中，小島的中心，也就是連接著我此刻站上的這座懸崖的土地崩垮了，掉進了深深的海底。

今天我們將探索世界各地的遊客來此的原因以及此地人民與文化不同於其他希臘島嶼的原因，它是個名叫錫拉的小島，但我們熟悉的名字是聖托里尼。

聖托里尼位於希臘本島的東南方，也是基克拉澤斯群島的最南端。島嶼環繞，形成巨火山口。

從伊莫洛維里（Imerovigli）所見到的聖托里尼破火山口全貌

圖片來源：Bonnie Chen

VOLCANIC ERUPTION
破火山爆發

聖托里尼的藍白建築洋溢著浪漫、幸福的氛圍，然而，這裡並不是一直都這麼平靜。大約三千五百年前，這裡曾爆發史上規模數一數二大的火山爆發，稱為米諾斯錫拉島火山爆發（The Minoan Eruption of Thera），考古學家推測這次事件還間接促成了克里特島（Crete）上米諾斯文明的滅亡。

發生在一八六六年的火山爆發還成了文學名著《海底兩萬浬》（*Twenty Thousand Leagues under the Sea*）小說中尼莫船長（Captain Nemo）和船員們親眼目睹的事件。還好對今天的遊客而言，聖托里尼在一九五〇年最後一次火山爆發後就平靜下來，愛探險的遊客不但可以去爬山，還可在當地的天然溫泉中泡湯。

Caldera 破火山口

caldera 可稱為破火山口、火山臼、陷落火山口，其外形為碗狀的凹地，直徑面積從數百公尺到數公里不等。破火山口依形成的原因分成三類：噴發火山臼、沈降火山臼和複式火山臼，大多是第三種，即在火山噴發之後，由於底下原本支撐的岩漿房（magma chamber）因噴發流失，而使得火山錐頂部陷落造成火山口（volcanic crater）擴大，聖托里尼島便是由破火山口所構成的島環。

圖片來源：Bonnie Chen

Vocabulary

6. **eruption** [ɪˋrʌpʃər̩] *n.* （火山）爆發；（岩漿）噴出

7. **violent** [ˋvaɪələnt] *adj.* 猛烈的；強烈的

8. **explosion** [ɪkˋsploʒən] *n.* 爆炸

9. **collapse** [kəˋlæps] *v.* 坍塌；倒塌

6-1

聖托里尼的美麗與哀愁

自述

So, when you're standing on these cliffs and feeling the powerful Greek wind, it's pretty cool to think that you're actually standing on the **rim**[10] of a volcano. And that's it right there. And it's still active, so if you start to see smoke coming up or maybe large bubbles coming up to the surface, I just want to say it's been a pleasure and an honor being your host.

So, I thought we would begin our trip here in Fira. This is the capital of the island as well as the major hub. If you need to be where all **the action**[11] is, this is where you would stay. And it's here in Fira that you will see evidence of the commercial explosion which rocked this island. And it's hard to believe, looking around, that in the 1960s there were no tourists—no travelers. And now you walk around and it's just shop after shop. One thing you will see a lot of is jewelry, especially gold. There's even a gold street. In ancient times, Santorini was known for its master goldsmiths.

當你站在懸崖上，感受希臘的勁風時，其實你是站在火山邊緣，光想到這點就覺得挺酷的。火山就在那裡，它仍是座活火山，所以如果你看到白煙開始竄出，或是水面冒出大泡泡的話，我只想說真的很高興也很榮幸能夠在此擔任各位的主持人。

我想我們的希臘之旅就從費拉開始吧。這是島上的重鎮，也是主要樞紐。如果你需要去熱鬧刺激的地方，就是這裡了。你會在費拉見到令小島熱鬧滾滾的蓬勃商業，看看四周，很難相信在一九六〇年代，此地渺無觀光客芳蹤，如今到處商店林立，你會見到很多珠寶，尤其是黃金，甚至還有黃金街。古早時期，聖托里尼曾以金匠工藝聞名。

shop after shop　商店林立

用法 **N. + after + N.**　某事物接連地出現;一個接一個的

名詞不需加冠詞。文中 shop after shop 就表示「一家店接著一家店」的意思,其他用法包括:

- ▶ day after day　日復一日
- ▶ fight after fight　接連地爭吵、起衝突
- ▶ story after story　一個故事接一個故事地
- ▶ year after year　年復一年

- Day after day I watched the weather turn colder.
  我看著天氣一天一天地變得愈來愈冷。

【延伸學習】

用法 **N. + by + N.**　逐……地(指事物的逐漸變化)

常見的搭配有:

- ▶ bit by bit / little by little　一點一點地;逐漸地
- ▶ one by one　一個接一個地;逐一地
- ▶ page by page　逐頁地

- Sally memorized her lines word by word for the school play.
  莎莉將學校話劇的台詞逐字背下來。

Vocabulary

10. **rim** [rɪm] *n.* 邊緣

11. **the action** [ði] [ˋækʃən] *n.* (某地所發生)最熱鬧、刺激的活動(作此義時要加 the)

自述

Today, the shops sell jewelry from all over the world, so there is an incredible variety. Variety is the key word here in Fira. You will find shops selling everything, and the **twisting**[12] streets that seem to **dangle**[13] over the caldera make Fira a shopping experience like no other.

而今店裡販售世界各地的珠寶，種類繁多，多樣化正是費拉的賣點。商店販賣五花八門的物品，彷彿懸在火山口上的蜿蜒小徑讓在費拉購物成為獨一無二的經驗。

對話

S : *Samantha Brown, Hostess*　　C : *Christoforos Asimis, Artist*

S One of the treasures of this city is artist Christoforos Asimis. His art gallery Phenomenon is right on the main thoroughfare. But I caught up with him in, **shall we say**, his outdoor studio. Christoforos.

其中一個鎮城之寶是藝術家克理斯多佛羅・阿司米，他的藝廊「風潮」就在主要通道上。但我找到他的地方，可說是他的戶外工作室。克理斯多佛羅。

C Hello, Samantha.

你好，珊曼莎。

S Nice to see you. This is wonderful.

幸會，這真漂亮。

C How are you today?

妳好嗎？

S Excellent. What are you sketching? Is this the . . .

很好！你在畫什麼？這是……

C This is the Santorini church. [It] is the symbol of the Fira town.

這是聖托里尼教堂，是費拉城鎮的象徵。

shall we say 可以說

shall we say 或是 shall I say 用於提醒對方，接下來所要說的事情可能會讓人震驚或是會冒犯對方。

- Her performance last night was, shall we say, underwhelming.
  她昨晚的表演，可以說，並不是很熱烈。

旅遊小幫手

AK Asimis Kolaitou Art Foundation

克理斯多佛羅·阿司米（Christoforos Asimis）是希臘聖托里尼著名的藝術家，他善用當地的色彩和光線來表現周遭環境的美。AK Asimis Kolaitou Art Foundation 這家藝廊展示克理斯多佛羅不凡的作品，也陳列他夫人依蓮妮·寇蕾朵（Eleni Kolaitou）的珠寶和雕刻作品，以及他們兒子卡多那斯（Katonas）的繪畫。你可以到這間藝廊參觀，或許還可以遇見這位藝術家和他的家人。

更多的訊息可以上網或打電話詢問：

📞 (30) 6983 096771

🌐 https://www.facebook.com/AkAsimisKolaitouArtGalleries
　　http://www.ak-galleries.com

圖片來源：AK ART FOUNDATION

6-1

聖托里尼的美麗與哀愁

Vocabulary

12. **twisting** [ˋtwɪstɪŋ] *adj.* 曲折的；盤旋蜿蜒的

13. **dangle** [ˋdæŋgəl] *v.* 懸盪；吊掛

對話

S : *Samantha Brown, Hostess*　　**C** : *Christoforos Asimis, Artist*

S This is the symbol of Fira.	這是費拉的象徵。
C Yes.	正是。
S What is it about Santorini that inspires you? Is it the light? Is it the landscape?	聖托里尼哪一點激發了你?是光線還是景色?
C It's the light. Look [at] this building. The light is a little yellow, and those others are blue and gray. The colors change every moment.	是光線。你看這棟建築,光線有點偏黃色,其餘的是藍與灰,色彩每一刻都在變化。
S Right.	是的。
C Every moment.	每一刻。
S See. This is why you're an artist and I'm not, because I only see white. Christoforos took me to see his **yet** unfinished **masterpiece**[14] at the Orthodox Metropolitan Cathedral.	看吧!所以你是藝術家而我不是,因為我只看到一片白色。克理斯多佛羅帶我去看他在基督正教都會大教堂尚未完成的傑作。
S This is you?	這是你的作品?
C This is my life['s] work.	這是我畢生的傑作。
S This is your life's work.	這是你畢生的傑作。
C Yes.	是的。

yet 的用法

yet 可作副詞，也可作連接詞，以下整理幾個常見的用法。

A. 作副詞用時：

① 表示「還；尚」，用於否定句或疑問句，搭配否定時常寫成 **have not + p.p. + yet** 或 **have yet + to V.**。

- I haven't finished my homework yet, so I can't play video games right now.
  我的功課還沒寫完，所以我現在不能玩電動。

② 表示「再；又」，常和 **another** 連用作強調用。

- The company will be adding yet another employee to the factory this month.
  該公司這個月將再增加一名工廠員工。

③ 表示「截至目前為止」，通常與最高級連用。

- The singer onstage right now is the best one yet to perform this evening.
  現在台上的那位歌手是今晚到目前為止表現最棒的一個。

B. 作連接詞用：

表示「然而；但是」，引導意思相對的字詞或子句，意思相當於 **but**，但語氣較為強烈。

- Charles has plenty of friends, yet he still feels lonely.
  查爾斯有很多朋友，可是他還是感到寂寞。

6-1

聖托里尼的美麗與哀愁

___

Vocabulary

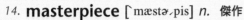

14. **masterpiece** [ˈmæstəˌpis] *n.* 傑作

對話

S : *Samantha Brown, Hostess*　　**C** : *Christoforos Asimis, Artist*

S Oh, my goodness. Twenty-five years ago, Christoforos walked into an all-white cathedral. Now it is **alive with**[15] color.

哇，二十五年前，克理斯多佛羅走進的是一片空白的教堂，而如今這教堂色彩繽紛。

C Every year, I painted some part. [It] ~~Cost~~ [cost] so much painting, and this is real gold.

我每年畫一部分，有許多畫作要完成，而這是真的黃金。

S This is . . .

這是⋯⋯

C This is **gold leaf**,[16] 24 **karats**.[17]

是二十四 K 金的金箔。

S Now this is a very different style from the rest of your paintings.

這和你其他的畫作風格很不同。

C Exactly. Exactly. This is a religious painting. It's **Byzantine**[18] style.

沒錯，這是宗教畫，是拜占庭風格。

S Christoforos is one of the very few to actually have a set of keys to the cathedral so that he may paint whenever he is inspired. Now, there's a . . .

克理斯多佛羅是少數擁有教堂鑰匙的人，如此一來，他一有靈感便能進來繪畫。現在，有⋯⋯

ORTHODOX METROPOLITAN CATHEDRAL
基督正教都會大教堂

背景知識

位於費拉市中心的 Orthodox Metropolitan Cathedral 是一座基督正教會的教堂，最早興建於一八二七年，但是在一九五六年的大地震中遭到嚴重毀損，因而大規模重建。教堂內的壁畫（frescoes）富麗堂皇，主要是由聖托里尼當地的藝術家 Christoforos Asimis 所繪製。

正教會常稱為東正教（Eastern Orthodoxy），主要分佈在東歐、東南歐、俄羅斯、土耳其一帶，為基督教（Christianity）的主要宗派之一，與天主教（Roman Catholic Church）、基督新教（Protestantism）為基督教的三大宗派。中文所稱的基督教則是指基督新教。

東正教是由稱為「自主教會」（autocephaly）的地方教會所組成，每個自主教會均不受其他教會管轄，目前有十五個自主教會，希臘正教會（Greek Orthodox Church）是其中一個自主教會，建於一八五〇年。

圖片來源：（上圖）AK ART FOUNDATION /（下圖）Bonnie Chen

6-1

Vocabulary

15. **alive with** [əˋlaɪv] [wɪθ] *phr.* 充滿⋯⋯的；滿是⋯⋯而熱鬧活躍的

16. **gold leaf** [gold] [lif] *n.* 金箔

17. **karat** [ˋkærət] *n.* 克拉（carat 為英式拼法，亦可寫作 karat）（一克拉表示合金中有二十四分之一的純金成份，twenty-four karats（二十四克拉）就表示「純金」。）

18. **Byzantine** [ˋbɪzənˌtin] *adj.* 拜占庭風格的

聖托里尼的美麗與哀愁

對話

S : *Samantha Brown, Hostess*　　C : *Christoforos Asimis, Artist*

C Because . . .	因為……
S . . . big white spot there. Is that unfinished or . . .	那裡有一大塊白色，那還未完成嗎？
C Yeah, maybe next year.	是的，也許明年會完成。
S To be here in a cathedral with the artist, I feel like I'm standing with Michelangelo himself.	和藝術家一起站在教堂裡，好像站在米開朗基羅身邊一樣。
C It's my pleasure.	這是我的榮幸。
S This is beautiful.	真是美極了！
C Oh, no, I am smaller: Michelangelito. ~~No, no compare with Michelangelo~~ [No, don't **compare** me **to** Michelangelo]. He was a great, great master.	我渺小多了，我無法和米開朗基羅相比擬，他是大師。
S When you walk in here, how does it make you feel to see . . .	當你走進這裡，看到這情景時有何感想？
C I feel like [it's] my house.	我覺得這裡就像我家一樣。
S Well, you've got the keys.	你是有鑰匙沒錯。
C Yes. I have the keys.	對，我有鑰匙。

compare A to/with B　拿 A 與 B 作比較

片語中的 A、B 可為人或事物，用來比較 A 與 B 之間的異同。

- Jenny compared her real diamond ring to/with a fake one and couldn't notice the difference.

  珍妮拿她的真鑽戒與一枚假鑽戒做比較，卻看不出差別。

- When the photograph was compared to/with the painting, it was hard to tell the two apart.

  這張照片和那幅畫兩相比較之下，兩者很難分辨。

【延伸學習】

用法 **compare A to B**　將 A 比作 B

此用法用來強調兩者的相似處。

- A young opera singer is so good that people are comparing him to Pavarotti.

  那位年輕的歌劇演唱家唱功一流，人們常將他比作帕華洛帝。

文中 Christoforos 說：I am smaller: Michelangelito，這裡他用俏皮的方式說自己頂多只能說是小米開朗基羅（-ito 為西班牙文的字尾，表示「使……變小」的意思），因此要用 compare . . . to 才能將他的原意清楚表達。

來看西班牙文中，加上字尾 –ito 的其他例子：

> ▶ un gato (*a cat*) → un gatito (*a kitten*)
> ▶ hermano (*brother*) → hermanito (*little brother*)

聖托里尼的美麗與哀愁

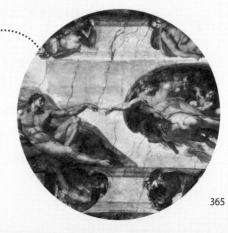

米開朗基羅的壁畫作品：梵諦岡西斯汀教堂（Sistine Chapel, Vatican）天花板壁畫

A Seductive Hotel & a Beautiful Winery

品味希臘

📖 影片原音 22　📖 課文朗讀 46

自述

Here on the Greek island of Santorini, I'm staying on the island's northern tip, in a village called Oia. Many people consider this to be Santorini's prettiest village. And that's because even though there's a lot of **commercialism**[1] here, it **maintains**[2] a lot of its original character. You see, there are shops and restaurants that follow along the **spine**[3] of the cliff, and then the hotels and the various types of accommodation spill down over it. And wait till you see our hotel. Oh.

在希臘聖托里尼島這裡，我正位在島嶼北端的「伊亞」小村落，許多人認為這是聖托里尼最美的村落。原因是即使這裡有許多商業活動，但它仍保持著許多原始風貌，你會見到許多商店與餐廳沿著懸崖隆起地帶而立，然後是飯店和各式各樣的住所沿著山勢灑落下來。現在等著來看我們下榻的飯店吧！

SOMETHING YOU HAVE TO KNOW ABOUT OIA
關於伊亞不可不知

OIA

1. Oia 在希臘文中發音為 Ia，O 不發音，故中文譯成「伊亞」。

2. 每到落日時分，大批遊客湧進伊亞想一睹「日落愛情海」的景致，不過熱門的地點早在一兩個小時前就擠滿了人。建議你如果想要欣賞美麗的夕陽，最好要先佔位子且記得要佔西邊面向阿莫迪港口（Amoudi Bay）的位子。深受攝影愛好者喜愛的拍攝地點就位在古老的廢墟處，即從阿莫迪小鎮延伸的階梯走到底的地方。

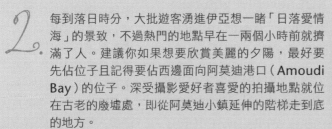

3. 伊亞有許多房子是沿著山壁穿鑿而成的洞穴屋，到這裡別錯過機會去體驗一下這個冬暖夏涼的特殊風情。

4. 在伊亞除了可以悠閒地漫步在蜿蜒的階梯間，或購物、或享受美食，還可以體驗當地特殊的活動：騎驢子。

6-2

圖片來源：Bonnie Chen

品味希臘

Vocabulary

1. **commercialism** [kə`mɝʃəˌlɪzəm] *n.* 商業主義

2. **maintain** [men`ten] *v.* 維持；保持

3. **spine** [spaɪn] *n.* 脊椎；脊柱

自述

Katikies Hotel looks and feels like it is **suspended**[4] over the sea.

It's a **seductive**,[5] **vertical**[6] world, where curving stairways **persuade**[7] you into areas that never let you **take your eyes off** the view. A sun terrace of white love seat–inspired **lounge chairs**.[8] An open-air dining room. And, of course, an **infinity**[9] pool. The pool here is quite famous on its own. It has been **featured**[10] in travel magazines around the world because, my gosh, look at this view. You can look down on massive cruise ships and sailboats. And just think they look like little toys in a big blue tub. Katikies has rooms, suites as well as **villas**.[11] Room prices for this luxury begin at 285 euros for the high season.

卡緹吉斯飯店彷彿懸浮於海上。

那是迷人垂直的天地世界，蜿蜒的階梯帶你進入令你目不轉睛的美景中。陽台上擺放著白色雙人長椅，開放式晚餐區，當然還有無邊際泳池。這泳池本身就非常有名，曾登上全球各大旅遊雜誌，你自己看看這美景，俯瞰巨大遊艇與帆船，它們就像藍色大浴缸裡的小玩具。卡緹吉斯飯店擁有一般房、套房與別墅，享受這份奢華的價碼，在旺季時是二百八十五歐元起跳。

take one's eyes off 將⋯⋯的視線從⋯⋯上移開

take off 字面意思為「把⋯⋯帶走」，此動詞片語即表示「將某人的視線從⋯⋯上移開」。

- You should never take your eyes off your personal property when you are at the airport.
  在機場時你絕不該將視線離開個人財物。

- Samuel couldn't take his eyes off of the new girl in his class.
  山繆無法將他的視線從班上這位新來的女生身上移開。

旅遊小幫手

Katikies 卡緹吉斯飯店

American Academy of Hospitality: ★★★★★

$ Double Room: from EUR 380.00   Junior Suite: from EUR 435.00
  Senior Suite: from EUR 560.00   Superior Suite: from EUR 670.00
  Honeymoon Suite: from EUR 840.00 Katikies Suite: from EUR 1,050.00

☎ (30) 2286 071401

🌐 http://www.katikies.com/

Vocabulary 🧳

4. **suspend** [səˋspɛnd] *v.* 懸掛；懸吊

5. **seductive** [sɪˋdʌktɪv] *adj.* 有魅力的；誘惑的；非常吸引人的

6. **vertical** [ˋvɝtɪkəl] *adj.* 直立式的；垂直的

7. **persuade** [pɚˋswed] *v.* 勸說、說服；使信服

8. **lounge chair** [laʊndʒ] [tʃɛr] *n. phr.* 休閒椅

9. **infinity** [ɪnˋfɪnəti] *n.* 無邊無際；無窮大

10. **feature** [ˋfitʃɚ] *v.* 以⋯⋯為重點介紹；以⋯⋯為主題、特色

11. **villa** [ˋvɪlə] *n.* 別墅

自
述

So, this is my room, and it's just **adorable**.[12] I feel like I'm in this big birdhouse and that it's a small home **perched**[13] above the rest of the property. A really relaxing décor done in an island-y style with some antiques. And look at this ceiling—very **lofty**.[14] Bathroom, just a little thing, but it's completely done in marble. And I love the antique mirror. Let me show you outside.

Now, of course this hotel is just the place for **honeymooners**[15] and couples having the trip of a lifetime. So I sort of have this the-cheese-stands-alone **complex**[16] right now, you know, but don't worry about me. I'll **keep a stiff upper lip**. I'll **gaze**[17] out at this view from my luxury accommodations and think to myself, "I'll get through this."

這是我房間，非常可愛，就像在巨大的鳥舍裡，這是位在最頂端的小窩，裝潢非常舒適，以古董營造出島嶼風格。看這天花板，挑高很高，浴室只是個小地方，但完全以大理石打造，我喜歡這面古董鏡，我們出去瞧瞧吧！

此飯店正適合渡蜜月的小倆口，或進行一趟畢生難忘之旅的伴侶，我現在有單身情結，但別擔心我，我還是會沈著冷靜。從奢華的住所向外凝望並想著：「我會撐過去的。」

THE-CHEESE-STANDS-ALONE
單身

此說法來自一首古老的童謠〝The Farmer in the Dell〞〈山谷里的農夫〉。小孩唱此兒歌的時候通常會圍成一圈，扮演農夫的人開始挑選角色到圈圈裡面，第二輪時，所有的人會再度圍成一圈。最後只剩下起士一人在圈圈裡。故珊曼莎用此說法來表示「別人都有伴了，而自己像是歌謠裡的起士一樣，落得孤單一人」。

** 想聽此曲的話，可以關鍵字 The Farmer in the Dell 上網查詢。

學習重點

keep a stiff upper lip　沈著冷靜

本動詞片語用「保持上唇生硬」的意象來表示某人即使心裡難過也不會透露內心的情緒，即「堅定沈著、冷靜」的意思。

- Although Sandra has been going through a difficult time, she keeps a stiff upper lip.
  雖然珊卓拉一直處在難熬的時期，她卻堅強沈著地面對。

Vocabulary

12. **adorable** [əˋdɔrəbl] *adj.* 討人喜愛的；可愛的

13. **perch** [pɝtʃ] *v.* 在⋯⋯頂部、邊緣

14. **lofty** [ˋlɔfti] *adj.* （房間）屋頂高的；高聳的

15. **honeymooner** [ˋhʌnɪˏmunə] *n.* 渡蜜月的人

16. **complex** [ˋkɑmˏplɛks] *n.* 情結；不正常的精神狀態

17. **gaze** [gez] *v.* 凝視；注視

6-2

品味希臘

自述

 Looking at this land where very few **crops**[18] grow, it's hard to imagine you'll find this: a **winery**.[19]

看著這片作物稀少的土地，很難想像會在這發現釀酒廠。

對話

S : *Samantha Brown, Hostess*　　**E** : *Elli, Guide*

S Santorini is known for producing some of Greece's best wines. And this is Elli. She's giving me a tour of the Sigalas Winery. You know, walking on these big rocks and small stones, it's hard to believe this land has any wine-growing **potential**.[20]

聖托里尼以出產某些希臘頂級酒類聞名。這位是愛莉，由她為我們導覽席加拉斯釀酒廠。你走在這些大大小小的石頭上，很難想像這裡竟有產酒的可能。

E Yes, Santorini has a very big history and culture. Volcanic **soil**[21] helps, and very good grape varieties also. So they say that they are the very same varieties that they had before the eruption, the big eruption of the volcano.

是的，聖托里尼歷史悠久，文化精深博大。火山土壤幫助甚大，再加上有多品種的優良葡萄。據説這些葡萄品種跟火山大爆發前是一樣的。

SIGALAS WINERY
席加拉斯釀酒廠

　　席加拉斯釀酒廠成立於一九九一年。酒廠原本是一處民宅，現在每年生產超過三十五萬瓶的葡萄酒，所使用的葡萄品種為 Assyrtiko（阿司帝寇）、Athiri（阿斯瑞）、Aedani（艾達尼）、Mandilaria（曼迪拉里亞）和 Mavrotagano（美芙羅塔加諾）。釀酒廠內有提供品酒，還有販售食物和飲料，以及提供一個半小時的品酒導覽，每人二十五歐元。詳細的內容可上網或致電洽詢。

April and October
Monday–Friday: 10:00 a.m.–7:00 p.m.
Saturday–Sunday: 11:00 a.m.–7:00 p.m.
May
Monday–Friday: 10:00 a.m.–8:00 p.m.
Saturday–Sunday: 11:00 a.m.–8:00 p.m.
June, July, August, and September
Monday–Friday: 10:00 a.m.–9:00 p.m.
Saturday–Sunday: 11:00 a.m.–9:00 p.m.

(30) 2286 071644
http://www.sigalas-wine.com/english/index.asp
http://www.sigalaswinetasting.com/

圖片來源：Sigalas Winery

6-2

品味希臘

Vocabulary

18. **crop** [krɑp] *n.* 作物

19. **winery** [ˋwaɪnəri] *n.* 釀酒廠

20. **potential** [pəˋtɛnʃəl] *n.* 可能性；潛力

21. **soil** [sɔɪl] *n.* 土壤；泥土

對話

S : Samantha Brown, Hostess　　**E** : Elli, Guide

S And, so, are we looking at descendants[22] of those ancient vines right here?

所以我們所見到是古早葡萄樹的後代？

E Maybe.

也許。

S Maybe. I'm used to seeing vines sort of straight up.

也許？我習慣看葡萄樹是往上生長。

E Yes. As you can see, we give ~~to~~ the plants the shape of a basket, and we are doing this because we want to protect the new plants. The very small plants. So the strong wind takes all the dust and can ~~make a very big~~ [do much] damage.

對，正如你所見，每株葡萄藤都有個籃子之類的東西，這麼做的原因是我們想保護新樹苗，就是那些小樹。強風會帶來一切塵土而造成很大的損害。

S May I ask you, what do you do about no rain?

如果沒下雨要怎麼辦？

E The soil has the ability to absorb[23] the humidity[24] that we have during the night, and then it gives it back to the plant during the day. And this is very relieving[25] for the plants.

這土壤能吸收夜晚的濕氣，然後白天時提供給植物吸收，解除植物的乾渴。

WINE INDUSTRY IN SANTORINI
聖托里尼的葡萄酒工業

聖托里尼島上有一個規模不大卻很興盛的葡萄酒工業，主要的葡萄品種是當地特有的 Assyrtiko（阿司帝寇），以及其他兩種愛情海的品種：Athiri（阿斯瑞）和 Aedani（艾達尼）。阿斯瑞是希臘的白葡萄品種，種植面積廣，常和阿司帝寇混釀，所釀製出來的葡萄酒帶有檸檬味。而艾達尼也是白葡萄品種，所釀製的酒果香濃郁、酸度和酒精含量適中，若與阿司帝寇混合則口味更佳。

阿司帝寇的葡萄枝極為古老，據當地釀酒業者表示，由於火山土壤排水良好，再加上其化學成分有助於對葡萄根瘤蚜（phylloxera）免疫，而得以在十九世紀末此項疾病大流行時免於被移除。

聖托里尼混合的 Assyrtiko 和 Athiri 的葡萄酒
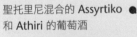

聖托里尼氣候乾熱，其實並不是非常適合葡萄生長的環境，每英畝的產量大概只有法國或加州的一成至兩成。為了適應當地環境，葡萄樹植株之間相隔很大，由於主要的供水來源為露水，因此常被修剪成籃子狀，然後將葡萄懸掛在籃子中以避免風帶來的損害。

圖片來源：Wikimedia Commons / Agne27

6-2

品味希臘

Vocabulary

22. **descendant** [dɪˋsɛndənt] *n.* 後裔；子孫

23. **absorb** [əbˋzɔrb] *v.* 吸收

24. **humidity** [hjuˋmɪdətɪ] *n.* 濕度

25. **relieve** [rɪˋliv] *v.* 緩解；解除

對話

S : Samantha Brown, Hostess　　**E** : Elli, Guide

S So it gets what it needs. Let's go taste some of this wine.	植物因此得到所需的水分。我們去嚐嚐這裡的葡萄酒吧！
E OK.	好的。
S A big part of your trip to Santorini is tasting all of its wines. And even the smallest of markets **have** an entire aisle **dedicated to** the wine. So what are we trying first?	到聖托里尼旅遊的一項重要行程便是品酒。即使是最迷你的超市，也有一整排走道放本地產的酒。我們首先要嚐哪一種呢？
E We will start with Santorini Sigalas. It's made from 100 percent Assyrtiko, which is the main variety here in Santorini.	我們首先品嚐聖托里尼席加拉斯。百分之百由阿司帝寇葡萄製成，那是聖托里尼主要的葡萄品種。
S I like the brightness. It's really lovely.	我喜歡它鮮明的口感，很好喝。
S You know, in a beautiful location with **agreeable**[26] company and a selection of tasty **vintages**,[27] it's amazing how an afternoon can go by in a **blur**.[28]	美景當前，好友相伴，加上精選的葡萄醇釀，下午的時間竟然就這麼飄飄然地過去了。

聖托里尼的土質氣候宜於葡萄生長。小小島嶼上盛產三十六種葡萄，用於釀製紅白葡萄酒。右圖為各種紅白葡萄酒品酒杯。

圖片來源：Wikipedia / Marcelo Costa

have . . . dedicated to N./V-ing　使……作為……的用途

dedicate sth to N./V-ing 在此表示「決定某事物（作為某種用途）」，受詞常用時間、精力、金錢、注意力等，中文常譯為「把（時間、精力等）用於……」；亦常用反身代名詞 oneself，表示「致力於、獻身於……」。

- Eric is a teacher who is dedicated to his students and wants all of them to do their best.
  艾瑞克是個為學生盡心盡力的老師，他希望他的學生都能全力以赴。

- The doctors are dedicated to finding a cure for cancer.
  醫生們全心投入在尋找癌症的療方。

- Mother Theresa dedicated herself to helping the poor people in Calcutta.
  德蕾莎修女獻身於幫助加爾喀達的窮人。

文中用到另一個文法：have + O. + p.p.，have 在此為使役動詞，受詞與補語為被動關係，故受詞補語（dedicated）用過去分詞，表示「使（某事物）或安排（某事物）被……」。

- Sophie and Oscar had their car fixed at the shop around the corner.
  蘇菲和奧斯卡把他們的車交給轉角那間車行修理。

Vocabulary

26. **agreeable** [əˋɡriəbəl] *adj.*　親切的；討人喜歡的

27. **vintage** [ˋvɪntɪdʒ] *n.*　特定年份釀製的葡萄酒；（優質葡萄酒的）產地和年份

28. **blur** [blɜ] *n.*　模糊形狀

對
話

S : *Samantha Brown, Hostess*　　**E** : *Elli, Guide*

S	You know, in America we don't get . . . we don't know a lot about Greek wines. And I think, I mean, look at the **labeling**;[29] it's pretty intimidating to see this.	我們在美國不太買得到，也不太清楚希臘葡萄酒。我要說的是，這上面貼著的標籤，我覺得看起來有點嚇人。
E	In blue letters it says Santorini.	藍色的字寫著聖托里尼。
S	That says Santorini?	那是聖托里尼？
E	Yes. And . . .	對。還有……
S	I would never have guessed that.	我永遠也猜不到。
E	And here it says wine white dry.	然後這裡寫著不甜的白葡萄酒。
S	Wine white dry. I will learn how to read Greek from wine.	不甜的白葡萄酒。我要從品酒來學希臘文。
E	OK.	很好。

Vocabulary 🎧

29. **label** [`lebl] *v.* 用標籤標明；貼上的標籤

WINE-PRODUCING REGIONS
葡萄酒的產地

　　葡萄酒產區主要分布在南北半球緯度三十度至五十度之間，需要有適宜的氣候、陽光、土壤和濕度，才能釀製出高品質的葡萄酒。一般來說，日照過多會太甜、太少會過酸，而土壤則以沙礫般貧瘠的土地為宜，而好的葡萄酒產區通常都會有河川流經。

　　葡萄酒的產地有舊世界與新世界之分，前者主要是指歐洲歷史悠久的國家，包括法國、義大利、西班牙等，而後者則是指美洲、澳洲甚至南非等新興的產酒國。兩者的差別除了釀酒歷史長短不同外，舊世界較強調傳統的釀造技藝，而新世界則多採用新技術來釀造，再加上每個產區的風味、品質都各有千秋。無論是當作投資價值的上等年份酒，或是一般餐酒，都有不同的支持者，就看個人的口味喜好了。

葡萄酒產品分布圖，二〇一一年，世界主要的產酒國依序為法國、義大利、西班牙、美國和中國

圖片來源：Wikipedia / Denkhenk

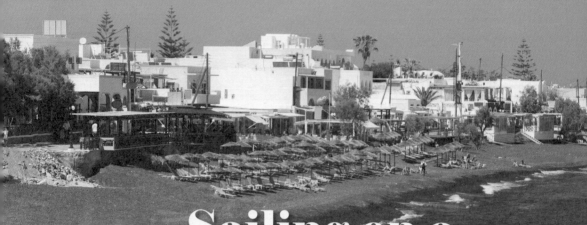

Sailing on a Volcanic Crater

航向愛琴海探訪古厝

 影片原音 23　　 課文朗讀 47

自述

The massive eruption that happened in the 1600s BC may have caused much of this island to meet a violent and **watery**[1] death. However, it did create this lovely black sand beach. This is Kamari Beach. It's one of the most popular on the island. And let me tell you, this is hot. Kamari Beach is **accessible**[2] by bus and is part of the **California-esque** beach town of Kamari.

西元前一六〇〇年發生的大爆發，也許造成島上許多人受傷而死或淹死，但它創造了這片迷人的黑沙海灘，這是卡馬力海灘，島上最熱門的海灘之一。告訴你，這沙超燙的，你可以搭乘巴士到卡馬力海灘，這是卡馬力加州風格的海濱小鎮。

California-esque 加州風格的

字尾 -esque 源自法文，帶有兩種意思：

A. 表示「以……風格的；以……方式的」，接在名詞（常為專有名詞）之後構成形容詞。

> ▶ Faulkneresque 具有福克納風格的
> ▶ New York–esque 帶有紐約風的
> ▶ Romanesque （建築）具有羅馬風格的
> ▶ Michelangelesque 米開朗基羅風格的

B. 表示「像……的；……似的」，接在名詞（尤其是專有名詞）之後構成形容詞。

> ▶ novel–esque 像小說似的
> ▶ statuesque 如雕像般的；高挑、挺拔的
> ▶ picturesque 風景如畫的
> ▶ Gatsbyesque 像蓋茲比般的

Vocabulary

1. **watery** [ˋwɑtəri] *adj.* 充滿水的；水分過多的

2. **accessible** [ækˋsɛsəbl] *adj.* 易接近的；可進入的

自述

 Now, one thing I find surprising about visiting Santorini is that here we are surrounded by the Aegean Sea—endless sunshine—yet going to the beach isn't the main focus here. Really, visitors spend most of their time exploring the villages and, of course, shopping. There also aren't a lot of beaches like this one. That's not to say that the beaches here aren't **out of this world**, but **there was no way** I was getting any closer to this sand.

Taking a break at the beach is one way to experience Santorini, but you don't want to miss a chance to see this island from another **perspective**.³ Good morning.

來聖托里尼旅行，讓我驚喜的是我們被愛琴海與無窮無盡的陽光擁抱，但往海邊跑卻不是主要目的。旅客花上許多時間探索村落與購物。這類的海灘沒有很多，並不是說這海灘不好，但我絕不要再接近那些沙了。

在沙灘上休憩一會是體驗聖托里尼的一種方式，但你可不會想錯過以另一種角度體驗這島嶼的機會。早安！

out of this world 極好的；非常棒的

形容詞片語 out of this world 字面意思為「在這個世界之外」，引申為「非凡的；不俗的；無與倫比的」之意。放在名詞前修飾時須寫成 out-of-this-world。與 wonderful、fantastic 意思相同。

- The scenes in the movie were out of this world, and that is what made it so much fun to watch.

  電影裡的場景精彩極了，所以才會這麼好看。

there's no way 不可能……

there's no way 之後會接子句，用來強調某事是絕對不可能發生的。

用法	there's no way (that) + S. + V.	不可能……

- Had it not been for your help, there is no way I would have finished this project on time.

  若非你的幫忙，我根本沒辦法準時完成這個計畫。

- If you always try your best, then there's no way you can go wrong.

  如果你總是全力以赴的話，就絕對不會出錯。

Vocabulary

3. **perspective** [pɚˋspɛktɪv] *n.* 觀點；思考方法

對
話

S : Samantha Brown, Hostess　　　**C** : Captain Ted, Boat Captain

C How are you?

妳好嗎？

S Just put the shoes here?

鞋子放這嗎？

C Yeah, right in the basket is fine.

對，放籃子裡就行了。

S OK. Meet Captain Ted. He owns Santorini Sailing. You can hire him for a full- or half-day cruise around the island. Thank you. This is just the perfect way to see Santorini. I mean, this . . . you don't get this view, obviously, from the top.

好的，這位是泰德船長，他是聖托里尼遊艇公司的老闆。你可以雇他來趟聖托里尼全日或半日環島遊，謝謝。這是欣賞聖托里尼最棒的方式，顯然地，從高處無法見到這種景色。

C Down below it's something; it's truly amazing. You can really **grasp**[4] what happened here.

從下方看風景真的很迷人，可以將美景一覽無遺。

S Like, you see the **infrastructure** of this entire island.

可以看到整座島嶼的基礎建設。

C Yeah, totally.

沒錯。

S The **layers**[5] are **fantastic**.[6]

那些層次真的太美了。

C Yeah, different **striations**[7] also give way to different historical periods of how many eruptions we've had.

對，不同紋路代表不同時期，表示火山曾爆發過幾次。

infrastructure 基礎建設；基礎設施

infrastructure 是由字首 infra-（在下）加上 structure（系統安排；結構體）所組成，infra- 除了表示「在下方」（below）之外，還可表示「在……之內；在裡面」以及「在某個範圍以下」。其他帶有字首 infra- 的字介紹如下：

infra + human = infrahuman 類人猿的

infra + sonic = infrasonic 聲下的；亞音的

infra + sound = infrasound 次聲波

infra + specific = infraspecific 同物種的

infra + red = infrared 紅外線的

6-3

航向愛琴海探訪古厝

Vocabulary

4. **grasp** [græsp] *v.* 理解、領會；掌控

5. **layer** [ˋleɚ] *n.* 層次

6. **fantastic** [fænˋtæstɪk] *adj.* 極好的；美妙的；精彩的

7. **striation** [straɪˋeʃən] *n.* 紋路；條痕

對話

S : *Samantha Brown, Hostess*　　C : *Captain Ted, Boat Captain*

E : *Evi, Tour Guide*

S	How deep does the crater get?	火山口有多深？
C	The crater gets to about 1,500 feet deep, and in certain parts they weren't able to find **depths**.[8]	約一千五百呎深，有些地方無法探得深度。
S	Oh.	嗯。
C	We've had a lot of explorers come on. For example, Cousteau was here many, many years ago, and he couldn't find depth in certain parts of these holes.	有許多勘測家來到這裡，例如庫斯托多年前來過，他測不出某些洞的深度。
S	Cousteau couldn't find it.	庫斯托也測不出來。
C	Cousteau, yes. Yes.	是的，庫斯托。
S	Wow. There you go. Evi, a tour guide on the island, joined me for the cruise. So, Santorini is actually a grouping of islands.	我們在小島上的導遊艾薇，陪我一同搭船。聖托里尼其實是個群島。
E	Yes.	沒錯。
S	And the main island that I'm on that I think is Santorini is actually . . .	現在這個聖托里尼的主島，其實叫做……
E	Thera.	錫拉。
S	Thera. And straight ahead is the crater itself.	錫拉。而正前方就是火山口。

JACQUES-YVES COUSTEAU
雅克–伊夫 · 庫斯托

　　庫斯托（1910–1997）是一位法國海軍軍官，海洋生態探險家，也是一位電影製片人、攝影師和作家，一生從事的許多工作皆與海洋相關，喜歡稱自己為 oceanographic technician（海洋技術員），留給世人超過一百二十部電視紀錄片、五十本書，以及致力於世界海洋保護的非營利機構——庫斯托基金會。

　　一九四三年時，庫斯托與埃米爾·加尼昂（Émile Gagnan）共同發明了潛水調節裝置（diving regulator），亦稱為水肺裝置，為輔助潛水者在水中呼吸的器具。由於這項發明，帶動了水肺潛水運動的興起，以及讓更多人瞭解、關注海洋的環境生態。

　　誠如文中所提，庫斯托深愛聖托里尼，曾和他的團隊在這裡花費數年的時間探測海底的深度。在他過世後，最小的兒子皮耶–伊夫·庫斯托（Pierre-Yves Cousteau）克紹箕裘，也與聖托里尼這塊地方結下難解的海洋之戀。

6-3

航向愛琴海探訪古厝

Vocabulary

8. **depth** [dɛpθ] *n.* 深度

對話

S : *Samantha Brown, Hostess*　　　**E** : *Evi, Tour Guide*

E Actually the volcano itself, because . . .

事實上是火山，因為……

S The volcano.

火山。

E . . . we are now in the middle of the crater. So that one is called Nea Kameni.

我們在火山口中央，所以它叫做納亞卡美尼。

S On Nea Kameni, boats stop and you can take a short hike to take a closer look at the volcano. When was the last big eruption?

船停在納亞卡美尼，你可以登上火山近看。最近一次大爆發是何時？

E 1950.

一九五〇年。

S Well, that's not a long time ago.

那不是很久以前的事。

E Not at all.

沒錯。

S Are people scared?

人們不害怕嗎？

E Well, I don't know. You don't think about it ~~at the ends~~ [in the end]. Then, the locals say they are able to predict the eruption. They say that the color of the seawater turns into **yellowish, grayish, and whitish** because of the **sulfur**.[9] And then the last day, the very last day, it turns into **vivid**[10] **violet**.[11]

我不知道，終究不會去多想。當地居民說他們有辦法預測火山爆發，他們說海水會因為硫磺，而呈現淡黃色、灰色與白色，最後一天則會變成鮮豔的紫色。

yellowish, grayish, and whitish 淡黃色、灰色、白色

-ish 與形容詞結合，表示「稍為……的；有點……的」。

red　　+ **ish** = red**dish**　微紅色；帶點紅色的

tall　　+ **ish** = tall**ish**　有點高的；偏高的

young + **ish** = young**ish**　略顯年輕的

-ish 若放在名詞或名字之後，表示「像 (某人、事物) 的；有……特徵的」。

girl　　+ **ish** = girl**ish**　像是少女的

Jolin　+ **ish** = Jolin-**ish**　像蔡依林一樣

-ish 若放在時間、日期或年齡之後，表示「 ……左右的」。

Noon　+ **ish** = Noon-**ish**　中午前後的

twenty+ **ish** = twenty-**ish**　二十歲上下的

6-3

航向愛琴海探訪古厝

Vocabulary

9. **sulfur** [ˋsʌlfə] *n.*　硫磺

10. **vivid** [ˋvɪvəd] *adj.*　(色彩) 明亮、鮮豔的；生動逼真的

11. **violet** [ˋvaɪələt] *n.*　藍紫色；紫羅藍色

對話

S : *Samantha Brown, Hostess*　　**E** : *Evi, Tour Guide*

S Violet.	藍紫色。
E Violet. They say.	據説是藍紫色。
S And that's when they got to leave.	這時候他們就得逃跑了。
E Yeah.	對。
S They **theorize**[12] that the **civilization**[13] that did drop down to the bottom of the sea is in fact the lost city of Atlantis. Whether it's true or not, when you look at this landscape and you know that there was a civilization, in fact, that was lost in the sea, it makes . . .	他們推理陷落至海底的文明其實是失落的城市亞特蘭提斯。姑且不論真假，當你看著這片景觀，就知道曾經有文明消失在海底。
E It makes you **shiver**[14] really.	聽起來會讓你發抖吧。
S It really . . . it's just such a **mythical**[15] place, this island.	這島嶼真是個神祕的地方。
E Yeah.	對。

ATLANTIS　亞特蘭提斯－－消失的文明

　　亞特蘭提斯是個北邊有山、南邊是平原的巨大海島，根據傳說，亞特蘭提斯完全沉沒於海底消失了。亞特蘭提斯的存在說法來自於柏拉圖（Plato）的二本對話錄 *Critias*《克里特雅斯》和 *Timaeus*《提邁尤斯》，他並多次提及亞特蘭提斯王國並非是他虛構的。如果柏拉圖所說的確有其事，那麼早在一萬二千年前，人類就已經創造了文明。數千年來，人們對此傳說保有高度興趣，即使多數的學者已證實柏拉圖提出的亞特蘭提斯王國是虛構不實的，但還是有一些學者提出亞特蘭提斯王國可能的沉沒之處。像是地中海域的聖托里尼（Santorini）、克里特島（Crete）、薩丁尼亞島（Sardinia）、西西里島（Sicily）、賽普勒斯（Cyprus）以及馬爾他（Malta）都宣稱亞特蘭提斯這失落的文明國度就在其所在的海底裡，甚至還有研究人員指出南極（Antarctica）也極有可能是這神秘島嶼的消失之處。

6-3

Vocabulary

12. **theorize** [ˈθiəˌraɪz] *v.*　推理；建立理論

13. **civilization** [ˌsɪvələˈzeʃən] *n.*　文明；文明社會

14. **shiver** [ˈʃɪvə] *v.*　顫抖；打哆嗦

15. **mythical** [ˈmɪθɪkəl] *adj.*　神話般的；虛構的

航向愛琴海探訪古厝

自述

The island has been destroyed and recreated twelve times in the last four hundred thousand years. With smoke rising from the volcano and **occasional**[16] earthquakes, the island of Santorini is still a work **in progress**.

So, I wanted to take us to see something that in all of Greece is unique to Santorini. It's really unusual; I think you're going to like it. Problem is, I can't find it.

Supposedly[17] here in this village of Finikia, no travelers really come here. There are no **out-of-the-way tavernas**[18] or shops to see. This is simply a place where Santorinians live and have lived for over three hundred years. It's really a fascinating place, huh?

在過去四十萬年間，這島嶼經過十二次毀壞與重建，從火山口冒出的煙與不時的地震，聖托里尼島的地底活動仍在進行中。

我要帶你去看看對全希臘來說，聖托里尼最獨特之處。那真的很特別，我想你會喜歡。問題是我找不到它。

它應該在非尼奇亞村落裡，很少有遊客來這裡，這裡沒有特殊的酒館與商店，這裡只是當地居民，居住了超過三百年的地方。很不賴的地方吧？

in progress　正在發生；正在進行中

in progress 表示某事物已經開始或持續進行中，與 under way 意思相同。

- We weren't allowed to enter the theater because the play was already in progress.
  我們不被允許進入戲院，因為表演已在進行。

- Betting stops a few minutes before the horse race gets under way.
  賽馬開始前幾分鐘就停止下注。

out-of-the-way　偏遠的；人煙罕至的

out-of-the-way 在文中指「偏遠的；人煙罕至的」，與 off the beaten track 意思相同。

- Up on the mountain, I found an out-of-the-way hotel that has really nice rooms and a great restaurant.
  我在山上找到一間偏遠的旅館，有很棒的客房和餐廳。

- The beaches that we found in the Philippines were definitely off the beaten track.
  我們在菲律賓發現的海灘絕對是很少人會去的地方。

【延伸學習】

out-of-the-way 還可指「不尋常的」，意思相當於 unusual、out-of-the-ordinary。

- She didn't like the coffee because she has out-of-the-ordinary taste buds.
  因為她的味蕾異於常人，所以她不喜歡這咖啡。

6-3

航向愛琴海探訪古厝

Vocabulary

16. **occasional** [əˋkeʒənl] *adj.*　偶爾的；間或的

17. **supposedly** [səˋpozɪdli] *adv.*　理應要；據稱

18. **taverna** [tɑˋvɜnə] *n.*　（希臘的）酒館；餐館

對話

S : Samantha Brown, Hostess　　**R** : Rita Ricci, Home Owner
G : Gabrielle, Home Owner

S Hello, Rita. I found you.	妳好，麗塔，我找到妳了。
R Hi.	妳好！
S Hello. This is the home of Rita Ricci and her husband, Gabrielle. From the outside, the house looks normal, but when you step inside . . .	你好！這裡是麗塔・李奇，與她丈夫蓋布爾的家，房子的外觀普通，但當你一踏進屋內……
S Oh, wow. OK, now I can see that you live in a cave.	我可以看出來你住在洞穴裡。
R Yes.	是的。
G Yeah.	沒錯。
S This is fantastic. How old is your home?	太驚人了。這個家有多久了？
G It would be two, three hundred years.	可能有兩、三百年了。
S Nice.	真的。
G Even more, now, because ~~they're not changed the style since many centuries~~ [the style hasn't changed for many centuries].	也許更久，但數世紀以來，都未曾改變它的風格。
R You see, we had to put [in] the glass window.	你看，我們必須裝上玻璃窗。

CAVE HOME 冬暖夏涼的洞穴屋

　　早期聖托里尼的居民很窮困，無法用木材或是其他建材來建造房子。於是當地人善加利用火山灰土壤的特性，在懸崖邊挖洞建屋居住，之所以選擇懸崖邊，是因為無法種植東西而較便宜之緣故。後來，洞穴屋被證實非常實用，房子通風且採光佳，獨特的建築結構加上冬暖夏涼的特性，以及在洞穴屋的私人陽台上可直接俯瞰海景及破火山口景觀。直至今天，洞穴屋在聖托里尼仍是非常普遍的房屋類型。雖然一間洞穴屋僅包含兩三間房間，但價格相當高貴。

對話

S : Samantha Brown, Hostess　　**R** : Rita Ricci, Home Owner

G : Gabrielle, Home Owner

S So you let all this light in. Now, what was the function of the cave home three hundred years ago?

這樣才能讓光線透進來。三百年前洞穴屋的功用是什麼？

R They were making caves because they were ~~more safe~~ [safer], because **pumice**[19] is a kind of very **flexible**[20] **cement**.[21]

洞穴屋比較安全，因為浮石是種很有彈性的塗料。

S Oh, so it moved.

所以它不會死死固定著。

R So **in case of** earthquake . . .

所以倘若有地震的話……

G Yeah, it is very **elastic**.[22]

它很有彈性。

R Yes. And also because they were warm in winter and cool in the summer.

沒錯，也因為洞穴裡冬暖夏涼。

S And that's because of the pumice.

都是浮石的關係。

R It's very cool in summer because of the pumice and the **lava**[23] stone.

夏天會很涼爽，因為浮石以及火山熔岩的關係。

R You don't feel the wind; you don't feel the noise.

你感覺不到風與噪音。

S Ah, this is a perfect . . .

這是最好的……

R It's a very **protective**[24] place. Yes.

非常安全的地方。沒錯。

in case of 如果;假使

在美語中，in case 可用來引導條件子句，與 if 意思相近，表示「如果、萬一、倘若（某事發生的話）」的意思，有兩種用法：

 用法一 in case of + N.

- In case of fire, never use the elevator.
  要是發生火災，千萬不要搭電梯。

 用法二 in case + S. + V

- In case you need to reach me, here is my cell phone number.
  萬一你需要跟我聯絡，這是我的手機號碼。

【延伸學習】

in case of 也有「以免;以防」之意，同 for fear of。

用法 in case of / for fear of + N./V-ing

- For fear of a power outage, the hospital has a backup power supply.
= In case of a power outage, the hospital has a backup power supply.
  醫院備有緊急供電設備以防停電。

Vocabulary

19. **pumice** [ˋpʌməs] *n.* 浮石;輕石
    （一種可去汙及柔膚的火山石）

20. **flexible** [ˋflɛksəbəl] *adj.* 有彈性的;柔軟的

21. **cement** [sɪˋmɛnt] *n.* 接合劑;黏固劑;水泥

22. **elastic** [ɪˋlæstɪk] *adj.* 有彈性的

23. **lava** [ˋlɑvə] *n.* （火山）熔岩

24. **protective** [prəˋtɛktɪv] *adj.* 防護的;保護的

對話

S : Samantha Brown, Hostess　　R : Rita Ricci, Home Owner

G : Gabrielle, Home Owner

S	Great area for your flat screen TV.	這裡放平面電視剛剛好。
R	It's a good area. Yeah.	是很好，沒錯。
S	Rita and her husband did add the hallways; originally the rooms would not have been connected. Well, **thank you so much for having me.** This is absolutely wonderful. So, it's just such a different way to live. Really. You have to do me one big favor, though.	麗塔與丈夫加蓋了長廊，原本房間彼此並不相連。謝謝你讓我進來參觀，這房子棒極了！這是很獨特的生活空間，真的，但你還得再幫我一個大忙。
G	Yes?	妳說。
S	You have to help me find my way out of the village, because I think there are some villagers back there that . . .	你得幫我走出這個村子，因為那裡有些村民……
G	With pleasure, we will lead you out of the village. Out of the house first.	我們很榮幸，我們會幫妳找到走出村子的路。首先先要走出房子。
S	Out of the house first, right.	首先要走出房子，沒錯。

thank you for having me　謝謝你們的招待

這句話是在離去時向主人表達感謝的禮貌說法。與 thank you for inviting me 意思相同。若同行者不只自己，則可以將 me 改成 us。

- A: Good-bye, glad you could come.

  再見囉，很高興你們能過來。

  B: We had a great time. Thank you for having us.

  我們玩得很開心。謝謝你邀請我們。

- A: I had a good time. Thank you for inviting me.

  我玩得很盡興。謝謝妳的邀請。

  B: Come back again, Sally. It was good talking to you.

  莎莉，要再過來唷。跟妳聊天很開心。

6-3

航向愛琴海探訪古厝

The Mouth of the Grouper
美食大口吃

 影片原音 24   課文朗讀 48

自述

We're back on the Greek island of Santorini. **Being surrounded by the Aegean Sea, fish would be a most appropriate[1] choice for dinner.** And when you ask which restaurant has the best fish, one name keeps popping up, the Sunset Taverna down in Ammoudi Harbor.

我們回到希臘聖托里尼島，這裡被愛琴海所環繞，鮮魚當然是最佳的晚餐選擇。要是你打聽哪家餐廳有最美味的魚，就會不斷聽到一個名字，阿莫迪港口的日落小館。

Dangling Modifier 虛懸分詞構句

修飾的子句在句中找不到可以修飾的對象就稱為「虛懸修飾」（dangling modifier）。一般來說，分詞構句省略了與主要子句相同的主詞，並將動詞改成分詞的形式，主動用 V-ing（現在分詞），被動用 p.p.（過去分詞），若分詞構句省略的主詞與主要子句不同時，則句子會形成虛懸狀況。

文中第二句 Being surrounded by the Aegean Sea, fish . . . 中分詞構句的主詞為 Santorini，但主要子句的主詞為 fish，則這個句子便是虛懸分詞構句。這種句子在口語中雖然很常見，但並不合文法，在書寫中應避免。

- <u>Being surrounded by</u> the Aegean Sea, fish would be a most appropriate choice for dinner.

正確說法為：

- <u>Since/Because Santorini is surrounded by</u> the Aegean Sea, fish would be a most appropriate choice for dinner.

6-4

美食大口吃

Vocabulary

1. **appropriate** [əˋproprɪət] *adj.* 　合適的；恰當的

對話

S : Samantha Brown, Hostess　　**A** : Akis, Son of Restaurant Owner

S Oh, my gosh, what is that? That fish.

我的天，那是什麼魚？

A This is, yeah, this is a **grouper**.[2]

那是石斑魚。

S That is huge. How big is that fish?

好大一條，牠大概多重？

A It's about forty kilos.

大約四十公斤。

S Sunset Taverna is a family-owned business. I'm with the son, Akis. His parents started it over twenty years ago when it was just a little **shack**.[3] His dad would do the fishing, and mom would cook. Now, four boats come to them every day **unloading**[4] their **catch**,[5] so it literally goes from the sea to your plate. *Yiamas*.

日落小館是家族企業，我身邊的是兒子阿奇斯，他的父母二十多年前開了這間餐廳，當時只是間小木屋。父親捕魚，母親下廚，現在一天四班船進來卸魚貨，所以料理確實是直接從海裡進到盤子裡。乾杯！

A *Yiamas*.

乾杯！

S I love the Greek style of eating just **all at once**. Just bring it all out, no waiting.

我喜歡希臘式吃法，一次上完菜，全部端上來，不用等。

A You can eat all of them?

妳可以全部吃完？

S I can eat all of this, absolutely. But tell me what it is first.

我當然可以全部吃完。但先告訴我那是什麼。

(all) at once　同時；一起

(all) at once 在此用來表示許多不同的事情同時發生。

- That's too much information for me to take in all at once!

  資料太多了，我沒辦法一下子全部融會貫通！

- The boat can only hold 500 pounds in weight, so no more than three or four people should ride in it at once.

  這艘船只能負重五百磅，所以一次不能乘坐超過三到四名乘客。

【延伸學習】

at once 也可表示「立即；馬上」，與 right now、right away、immediately、in no time 意思相同。

- We need to leave at once, as we're already late for work.

  我們必須馬上出發，因為我們上班已經遲到了。

6-4

美食大口吃

Vocabulary 📖

2. **grouper** [ˋgrupɚ] *n.* 石斑魚

3. **shack** [ʃæk] *n.* 簡陋的小屋

4. **unload** [ˌʌnˋlod] *v.* 卸（貨）

5. **catch** [kætʃ] *n.* 捕獲總量

對話

S : *Samantha Brown, Hostess*　　**A** : *Akis, Son of Restaurant Owner*

A This is pepper.	那是甜椒。
S Stuffed peppers.	鑲甜椒。
A Yes, stuffed with cheese. This is fava.	對，起士餡。這是蠶豆。
S Those are beans, right?	是豆子吧？
A Yes, like beans. This is grilled **octopus**.[6]	對，類似。這是烤章魚。
S I like that, too. I love grilled octopus.	我也喜歡。我喜歡烤章魚。
A The salad.	沙拉。
S Salad, of course.	是的，沙拉。
A Sunset salad. The color of the sunset. And this is grilled shrimps.	日落沙拉。夕陽的顏色。這是烤蝦。
S The grilled shrimp.	烤蝦。
A This is **eggplant**[7] salad.	這是茄子沙拉。
S That's one of my favorites.	那是我最愛的菜之一。
A Yeah? Everything, we made it. We handmade everything.	真的？每道菜都是自製的，我們自製所有料理。

RECIPE FOR STUFFED PEPPER 鑲甜椒食譜

　　stuffed pepper 泛指將甜椒、青椒或番茄鏤空，加入其他食材做成的一道菜，許多地方都有類似的料理，也都有不同的名稱。在希臘這道菜稱作 yemista，是一道充滿地中海風味的家常蔬菜燒烤料理，裡面添加的食材通常會有米、起司、香料、海鮮魚肉或牛肉、豬肉等絞肉，可隨個人的喜好添加。

食材（約四人份）

4 bell peppers 甜椒四顆	1/2 onion 洋蔥半顆
1 1/2 cups rice 米一杯半（生米或熟飯皆可）	100 grams minced meat 絞肉一百克
1 tomato 番茄一顆	1/2 cup feta cheese 費塔起司半杯
1 teaspoon oregano 奧勒岡葉一小匙	a handful of parsley 巴西利一小把
salt and pepper to taste 鹽和胡椒適量	1 tablespoon olive oil 橄欖油一大匙

以下是簡單的作法：

1. 將甜椒去籽後泡在溫水裡三十分鐘。

2. 起油鍋，將洋蔥丁炒至金黃後再加入絞肉同炒。

3. 炒至出水後加入鹽、胡椒調味，到水分收乾。

4. 加入奧勒岡葉和巴西利，接著加入番茄丁炒到出水。

5. 將米飯加入鍋中至上色（若用生米，需再加一杯水並炒到半熟）後熄火。

6. 加入費塔起司，稍微攪拌後將所有餡料放入甜椒中。

7. 將甜椒置於烤盤中，覆蓋錫箔紙，以一百九十度度烤二十分鐘。

圖片來源：Bonnie Chen

6-4

美食大口吃

Vocabulary

6. **octopus** [ˋɑktəpəs] *n.* 章魚

7. **eggplant** [ˋɛɡˏplænt] *n.* 茄子

對
話

S : Samantha Brown, Hostess　　**A** : Akis, Son of Restaurant Owner

S Did your mom . . .	這些都是你母親……
A Yes.	是的。
S And so these are your mom's recipes?	這些都是你母親的食譜？
A Yes.	是的。
S Oh. Oh, that is gorgeous.	這道好豐盛。
A Yes. This is **lobsters**.[8]	對，這是龍蝦。
S Sure. Is this one of your favorites?	當然了！這是你的最愛之一嗎？
A Yes. I like [it] very much.	對，我很喜歡。
S Me, too. I love it.	我也是。我超喜歡。
A Please, try this one.	請嚐嚐這道。
S Try this one?	嚐嚐這個？
A Yes.	是的。
S That's a very big piece.	這很大一塊。
A Yes? No.	有嗎？還好吧。
S I don't have the mouth of the grouper.	我沒有石斑魚那種大嘴。
A Yeah?	是嗎？

POPULAR GREEK DISHES
受歡迎的希臘料理

希臘飲食受到義大利、巴爾幹各國以及土耳其影響，普遍使用橄欖油、羊奶、香草、蔬菜、穀類以及麵包、海鮮、肉類、葡萄酒等，為典型的地中海飲食。

主要常見的前菜介紹如下：

pita
皮塔餅；烤餅

tiropita
起士派

spanakopita
菠菜起司捲

grilled octopus
烤章魚

Greek salad
希臘沙拉

tzatziki
黃瓜優格醬

avgolemono
地中海檸檬蛋黃雞湯

fasolada
傳統雞豆泥湯

eggplant moussaka
穆薩卡（茄子千層派）

圖片來源：Bonnie Chen

Vocabulary

8. **lobster** [ˋlɑbstɚ] *n.* 龍蝦

6-4

美食大口吃

407

對話

S : Samantha Brown, Hostess　　　**A** : Akis, Son of Restaurant Owner

S No.	我沒有。
A Please try.	請嚐嚐看！
S Oh. That's wonderful. We need to see these because these are the special dish here.	喔。非常可口。我們得介紹一下這個當地特產。
A Yes.	沒錯。
S . . . in Santorini.	聖托里尼的特產。
A In Santorini, yes.	聖托里尼的特產，是的。
S Tomato **fritters**.[9]	番茄炸餅。
A Tomato fritters. Yes.	番茄炸餅，是的。
S They look **unbelievable**.[10]	看起來美味極了。
A Yes. This is without . . . without meat. It's just tomato, pepper, and some other things that I'm not going to tell you.	對，它不含肉類，只有番茄與甜椒，還有其他一些我不打算跟妳説的東西。
S Again, secret.	又是商業機密。
A Yes.	對。
S We can't tell. I noticed that the shrimp are still looking at us. That's something else in Greece that's a little different than in the States.	我們不能洩漏。我注意到蝦子仍在盯著我們看。這是希臘和美國的不同之處。
A I cannot understand you.	我不懂妳的意思。

TOMATO FRITTERS　番茄炸餅

fritter 是指將蔬菜、水果或肉類裹粉低溫油炸的餡餅，tomato fritter 可稱為「番茄炸餅」或「炸番茄球」，在聖托里尼是很常見的一道餐前小點。主要材料包括番茄、洋蔥、甜椒、切碎的薄荷葉等。

聖托里尼所產的小番茄酸味濃郁，搭配薄荷味道相當合適，再加上許多開胃菜和沙拉會淋上的優格沾醬，美味極了。

圖片來源：Flickr / avlxyz

6-4

美食大口吃

Vocabulary

9. **fritter** [ˋfrɪtɚ] *n.*　帶餡的油炸麵團

10. **unbelievable** [ˏʌnbɪˋlivəbl] *adj.*　令人難以置信的；非常棒的

對話

S : *Samantha Brown, Hostess*　　A : *Akis, Son of Restaurant Owner*

T : *Tara, Local Friend*

S	You don't cut the heads off.	你們不把蝦頭切掉。
A	Yes. Yes. ~~Why, to cut it~~ [Why do you cut them off]?	當然，為何要把頭切掉？
S	I don't think we like our food looking at us.	我們不喜歡食物盯著我們看。
A	Why?	為什麼？
S	Because they're looking at me funny. After that dinner, I had a lot to **work off**.[11] I thought we might **take in** a little of Santorini's nightlife.	因為它們看著我的樣子很怪。晚餐後我有很多活動可以來消耗熱量，我們該參與一下聖托里尼的夜生活。
S	My local friend Tara suggested we **cap**[12] the evening with a little Greek music at Santorini Mou, a place to be with the rest of the Santorinians out enjoying a Saturday night, and one musician **in particular**.[13]	當地朋友塔拉建議我們，讓夜晚沉浸在希臘音樂中，就在聖托里尼茂伊，一個與其他聖托里尼居民共享週六夜的地方，尤其是聽某位樂手的演出。
S	So this is Michael's place.	這是麥可的酒館？
T	Yeah.	沒錯。
S	And what's his Greek name?	他的希臘名字是？
T	Mihalis.	米赫利斯。

take in 參觀；欣賞

- We're going to get something to eat and then take in a movie.
  我們要去吃點東西，然後看場電影。

【延伸學習】

A. 表示「理解、消化（資訊）」。

- I was tired, so it was difficult to take in the information in class.
  我很累，所以很難消化課堂上的資訊。

B. 表示「把（衣物）改小」。

- Suzie lost a lot of weight and had to have her clothes taken in.
  蘇西減重了很多，必須請人把她的衣服改小。

C. 受詞為「人」時，指「欺騙」。

- All the girls were taken in by Roberto's smooth charms.
  所有女孩都被羅貝托圓滑精明的魅力騙了。

6-4

美食大口吃

Vocabulary

11. **work off** [wɜk] [ɔf] *v.* （透過消耗體力來）排除解（精力、壓力等）

12. **cap** [kæp] *v.* 以……作為結束

13. **in particular** [ɪn] [pəˋtɪkjələ] *phr.* 特別；尤其

對話

S : *Samantha Brown, Hostess*　　　T : *Tara, Local Friend*

S	Mihalis. And everyone comes here to see him play.	米赫利斯。大家都來看他演出。
T	Yeah. Of course.	當然了。
S	I mean he really brings . . .	他真的是……
T	Everyone loves Mihalis. Whoever comes for the first time continues coming every day.	大家都愛米赫利斯，來了第一次以後就會天天來報到。
S	I look around and it seems like a big local crowd.	我張望了一下，都是當地居民。
T	Yes.	沒錯。
S	These are real Santorinians.	都是些聖托里尼在地人。
T	Yes.	是的。
S	Is that what you call yourself?	你們是這樣自稱的嗎？
T	Yeah.	是的。
S	And he's a wonderful musician.	他是個很棒的音樂家。
T	Yeah. And these are his own songs.	他還自己寫歌。
S	And these are his own songs?	這些都是他寫的歌？
T	Yes.	沒錯。
S	But people know them.	但大家都知道那些歌。
T	Yeah. Yeah.	對。

SANTORINI MOU
希臘小酒館

　　Santorini Mou 是當地一家小酒館（tavern），老闆 Mihalis 很喜歡唱歌，常隨性拿起吉他唱起希臘歌謠，他原本是一位廚師，後來到聖托里尼開了一家餐館，將興趣與職業結合在一起。

　　走進這家餐廳店內牆面貼滿照片，這些都是曾到此用過餐的客人留影，許多名人包括珍妮佛‧安妮斯頓（Jennifer Aniston）、Green Day 主唱比利‧喬（Billie Joe Armstrong）和孫燕姿都到過這家餐廳。除了名人加持之外，小酒館供應的菜色走純樸家常菜風格，雖無精緻的盤飾，但美味絲毫不減，連許多當地人也常到此用餐，是一家想體驗傳統希臘菜的絕佳去處。

6-4

美食大口吃

圖片來源：（右上招牌）Flickr / BluEyedA73

對話

S : *Samantha Brown, Hostess*　　T : *Tara, Local Friend*

S So people keep coming back and they love his music.

顧客一直回籠，又喜愛他的音樂。

T Because he sings them every day.

因為他每天都唱。

S What I love about the whole Greek music tradition is that, you know, where I'm from, generations have their own music, right, and we sort of **roll our eyes at** our parents' music, and we don't like it. And our younger **siblings**[14] don't like our music. But here, everyone loves the same songs.

整個希臘音樂傳統讓我最喜歡的地方是，嗯，在我的國家每個世代有不同的流行音樂，我們對雙親那世代的音樂翻白眼、討厭那些歌。我們的下一代又不喜歡我們的歌，但是在這裡，大家都喜愛相同的歌。

T For Greeks, it's very important to keep the traditions. We really like the music, and the lyrics are unique in every . . . in every Greek song.

希臘人很重視保存傳統文化，我們很喜歡音樂，其中的歌詞也很獨特，每首希臘歌曲都一樣。

S OK. So . . . so what do you mainly sing about?

你們的歌主要在表達什麼？

T About **sentiment**.[15] About sentiment. About love, about pain. About appreciation. About family. About everything.

表達情感。關於愛、痛苦、感恩，關於家庭。各式各樣，包羅萬象。

roll one's eyes (at sb/sth) （對某人或某物）翻白眼

此片語字面意思是「轉動（某人的）眼珠」，引申表示對某人或某事不耐、不以為然或不敢置信，類似中文的「翻白眼；回以白眼」。eyes 在此恆用複數。

- When I told Joe a dumb joke, he just rolled his eyes at me.
  我跟喬說了一個愚蠢笑話，他只是對我翻了個白眼。

- The mother rolled her eyes at the mess the children had made in the kitchen.
  媽媽對孩子們把廚房搞得亂七八糟不耐地翻了白眼。

6-4

美食大口吃

Vocabulary

14. **sibling** [ˋsɪblɪŋ] *n.* 兄弟姐妹

15. **sentiment** [ˋsɛntəmənt] *n.* 感傷；情緒

對話

S : *Samantha Brown, Hostess*　　**T** : *Tara, Local Friend*

S All right, so basic music . . .	所以，基本上音樂就是……
T Yeah, yeah.	是的。
S But mainly about love, I'm sure.	都是關於愛吧。
T Yes, yes, yes. Greeks like . . . like love.	沒錯，希臘人很多情。
S I think it's wonderful . . .	我覺得這地方很棒。
T Yeah.	對呀。
S It's a wonderful environment here. Thank you for taking me.	這裡氣氛好好。謝謝妳帶我過來。
T Yeah, that's nice. Thank you.	很高興妳喜歡。謝謝妳。
S This is fabulous.	這裡好迷人。
T Yeah, thank you for coming.	謝謝妳過來。
S **Bravo.** Bravo. Bravo.	好極了！太棒了！

bravo　好極了；太棒了

bravo 通常用於對某表演大為讚賞的喝采聲，在英文中已變成感嘆詞，可用於對某人的行為表示讚賞，意思是「很棒；太好了」，而 bravo 會單獨使用。其他用來表示讚許的說法還包括：

▸ Awesome　　　▸ Good for you
▸ Good going　　▸ Good job/work
▸ Way to go　　　▸ Well done

6-4
美食大口吃

自述

You just never grow tired of looking at this view. And you feel as though you're seeing something **prehistoric** with absolutely no **ties**[16] to modern times. Santorini's physical beauty is **stunning**[17] and is definitely what attracts visitors to this island, as well as its lifestyle. Music, drink, food. And to taste wine, its flavors **descended**[18] from ancient times. To have fish that comes straight from the sea to your plate. And then there are the villages that spread **thinly**[19] across the rim and dangle over the crater of a volcano. With buildings white, that blend into and absorb one another, all connected by vertical passageways. Corridors into another world you never knew really existed. And you just think, wow. The mythical city of Atlantis? Maybe it was never lost **in the first place**.

這美景真是百看不膩，你會覺得見到了史前的景物，完全和現代沒有關聯。聖托里尼的自然美景令人讚嘆，絕對是吸引遊客來到島上的因素，還有這裡的生活方式。音樂、美酒、美食，品嚐傳承自遠古時代的葡萄酒，享受直接由海上端上盤的鮮魚，以及稀疏散布在外緣和垂懸在火山口的村落，白色建築互相交織，櫛比鱗次，由縱向的小徑互相連結，通往另一個你以為不存在的幻境，你心裡會連聲驚嘆，亞特蘭提斯這謎樣的城市－－也許從來未曾消失。

prehistoric 史前的；遠古的

字首 pre- 表示「先於；事先；在……之前」的意思。其他帶有 pre- 字首的字包括：

`pre` + pay = **prepay** 預付

`pre` + view = **preview** 預先觀看；預習

`pre` + caution = **precaution** 預防措施

`pre` + agricultural = **preagricultural** 農業社會之前的

in the first place 當初；一開始

作此義時通常放在句尾，用來表示最初的情況。

- You should have told me about that rule in the first place.
  你應該一開始就告訴我那個規則的。

【延伸學習】

指「首先；第一」，用來列舉事項的第一點，通常放在句首，以逗號與子句隔開，與 in the beginning、firstly、first of all、to begin/start with 意思相同。

- I don't like this TV show. In the first place, it's not funny. Secondly, the acting is bad.
  我不喜歡這個電視節目。第一，它不好笑。第二，演技很糟糕。

Vocabulary

16. **tie** [taɪ] *n.* 關係；關連

17. **stunning** [ˋstʌnɪŋ] *adj.* 令人吃驚的

18. **descend** [dɪˋsɛnd] *v.* 下降

19. **thinly** [ˋθɪnlɪ] *adv.* （人煙等）稀疏地

6-4

美食大口吃

FOR CORRESPONDENCE

POST CARD

FOR ADDRESS ONLY

FOR CORRESPONDENCE

POST CARD

FOR ADDRESS ONLY

FOR CORRESPONDENCE

POST CARD

FOR ADDRESS ONLY

LIVE PEN 智慧點讀筆

隨點隨聽 是您最佳的語言學習家教!

學習語言時,遇到不會唸的單字或句子,不是問人就是只能拿起翻譯機聽著死板發音,這種學習方式已經落伍了! LiveABC邀請您一起來體驗嶄新的學習模式!

LIVE PEN **智慧點讀筆**,使用高品質的光學感應筆頭,書中的單字、句子、段落都可隨點隨聽,走到哪、讀到哪、聽到哪,不受任何時間地點限制,攜帶方便,外型輕巧時尚,符合現代人講求方便、快速、有效的學習需求,一筆在手,樂趣無窮。

功能說明

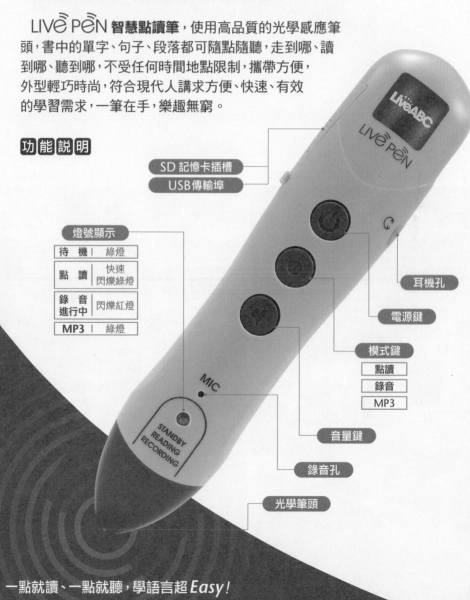

SD 記憶卡插槽
USB傳輸埠

燈號顯示

待 機	綠燈
點 讀	快速閃爍綠燈
錄 音進行中	閃爍紅燈
MP3	綠燈

耳機孔

電源鍵

模式鍵
點讀
錄音
MP3

MIC

STANDBY
READING
RECORDING

音量鍵

錄音孔

光學筆頭

一點就讀、一點就聽,學語言超 *Easy!*

TLC 互動英語 珊曼沙教你用英語暢遊歐洲《點讀版》讀者回函卡

謝謝您購買 LiveABC 互動英語系列產品

如果您願意，請您詳細填寫下列資料，免貼郵票寄回 LiveABC 即可獲贈
《CNN 互動英語》、《Live 互動英語》、《每日一句通報》電子學習報 3
個月期（價值：900 元）及 LiveABC 不定期提供的最新出版資訊。

姓名		性別 □ 男 □ 女
出生日期	年 月 日	
住址	□□□ 聯絡電話	
E-mail		
學歷	□ 國中以下 □ 國中 □ 高中 □ 大專及大學 □ 研究所	
職業	□ 學生 □ 資訊業 □ 工 □ 商 □ 服務業 □ 軍警公教 □ 自由業及專業 □ 其他＿＿＿＿	

您從何處得知本書？
- □ 書店
- □ 電子型錄
- □ 雜誌
- □ 其他＿＿＿＿
- □ 網站
- □ 他人推薦

您以何種方式購得此書？
- □ 一般書店
- □ 網路
- □ 其他＿＿＿＿
- □ 連鎖書店
- □ 郵局劃撥

您覺得本書的價格？
□ 偏低　　□ 合理　　□ 偏高

您對本書的評價

	很滿意	還不錯	普通	不滿意	很後悔
書名	□	□	□	□	□
封面	□	□	□	□	□
內容	□	□	□	□	□
編排	□	□	□	□	□
紙張	□	□	□	□	□

您希望我們製作哪些學習主題？

您對我們的建議：

縣市

市區

鄉鎮

村里

路街

段

巷

鄰

弄

號

樓

室

1 0 5

台北市松山區八德路三段32號12樓

希伯崙股份有限公司客戶服務部 收

英語數位學習第一品牌